Night of Flames

Extent of the German Occupation of Europe in 1942 – – –

Night of Flames

A NOVEL OF WORLD WAR II

Douglas W. Jacobson

McBooks Press, Inc.
www.mcbooks.com
ITHACA, NY

Published by McBooks Press, Inc. 2007
Copyright © 2007 Douglas W. Jacobson

Dust jacket and book design by Panda Musgrove.
Cover Photo: Night view of part of Santa Fe R.R. yard, Kansas City, Kansas, 1943, by
Jack Delano, courtesy of American Memory, The Library of Congress.

The hardcover edition of this book was cataloged by the Library of Congress as:

Library of Congress Cataloging-in-Publication Data
Jacobson, Douglas W., 1945-
  Night of flames : a novel of World War II / by Douglas W. Jacobson.
    p. cm.
  ISBN 978-1-59013-136-7 (hardcover : alk. paper)
    1. World War, 1939-1945—Fiction. 2. Poland—History—Occupation, 1939-1945—
Fiction. I. Title.
PS3610.A35675N54 2007
813'.6—dc22

                          2007014386

Printed in the United States of America
9 8 7 6 5 4 3 2

For Margot, Allison, Christine,
Ainsley, Ella, Cully and Jessica

The most powerful weapon on earth
is the human soul on fire.

Field Marshal Ferdinand Foch

The Invasion of Poland

September, 1939

➤ German Invasion—September 1, 1939

▷ Russian Invasion—September 17, 1939

PART ONE

Poland

1939

Central Poland
September, 1939

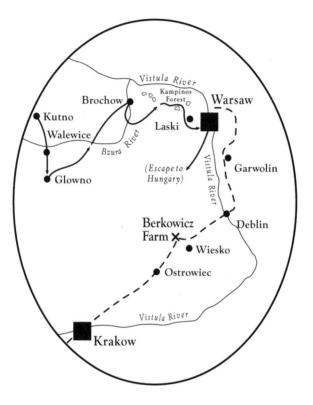

- → Route of Wielkopolska Cavalry Brigade, Battle of Bzura
- – – Route of Anna, Irene, Justyn

Chapter 1

ANNA KOPERNIK SLEPT on this hot, muggy night, but it was a restless sleep troubled by strange dreams. The sheets were clammy and her thin cotton nightgown clung to her back. A paltry breeze drifted in through the open window with little effect. The still, humid air on this September morning hung over Warsaw like a massive wet blanket.

It was five o'clock and Anna drifted back and forth between consciousness and sleep, the dream flitting in and out of her mind like an annoying gnat. The telephone rang. Then it stopped. She wanted to answer it but couldn't find it. It rang again, but it wasn't a telephone; it was something else . . . a bell, perhaps, or a horn. Anna kicked at the sticky, twisted sheet and rolled onto her back. She was almost awake but still just below the surface. The noise returned, louder now, a harsh clanging boring into her head. She kicked the sheet completely off, struggling to understand. What was it? A horn . . . or . . . a siren.

Anna's eyes snapped open and she sat bolt upright. The shrill sound blasted into her brain, penetrating through the fog of sleep like an icy wind. She blinked and looked around the dark room, trying to focus on shadowy images as the sound wailed on and on.

She ran to the window. It was still dark but the night sky held a hint of gray. An early morning mist shrouded the streetlamps, casting a gloomy, almost spooky glow along the deserted sidewalk below. The grating noise of the air-raid siren raised the hair on the back of her neck and suddenly she was shivering. Anna crossed her arms over her chest and stared into the dull, charcoal sky. Then she heard another sound.

It came from the west: a deep angry drone like a swarm of giant bees, growing louder by the second. Anna tried to move but her feet didn't respond. Immobilized, riveted in place, she stared out the open window as the pounding vibration of a hundred propellers enveloped her. The thunderous roar of the bombers drowned out the air-raid sirens, and the entire building seemed to sway in rhythm with the oscillations.

Anna snapped out of the spell and instinctively reached out to pull the window closed. A flash of light blinded her, and an eardrum-shattering blast threw her backward amid a shower of glass and falling plaster. She fell heavily against a small wooden night table and collapsed on the floor.

Another blast rocked the building. Frantic and disoriented, a searing pain in her head and a million lights dancing in her eyes, Anna tried to crawl under the bed, oblivious to the shards of glass that sliced through her hands and knees. Jarring detonations punctuated the deafening thunder of the airplanes.

Then, as abruptly as it started, it was over, the pulsating thump of propellers receding into the distance. Anna lay still, her head under the bed. Seconds passed, then a minute, and the only sound she heard through the ringing in her ears was the continued wailing of the air-raid sirens. She crawled backward and tried to stand, but her legs gave out. She fell against the bed and back onto the floor, this time wincing in pain from the glass and chunks of plaster that littered the floor. Holding the edge of the bed, she struggled to her feet and staggered across the room.

Through the ringing and the sirens Anna heard another sound: someone screaming in the hall. She lurched through the doorway and tripped over Irene, who was crawling on her hands and knees, covered with plaster dust. Anna reached down and helped her friend to her feet.

Irene stared at her with blank eyes then pushed past her. "Justyn!" she screamed. "Oh my God, Justyn!"

They stumbled down the dark hallway to the bedroom at the top of the stairs. The door was split down the middle, hanging from the top hinge. Anna pushed it open, and they stepped into the dust-filled room.

As her eyes began to clear, Anna squinted, trying to see through the haze. The small room was completely shattered with a gaping hole in the outside wall. On the left, where the bed had been, she spotted the ten-year-old boy lying still, face down under a pile of wood and plaster.

Irene shrieked and rushed to her son, clawing away at the rubble.

Anna knelt down beside her, and they turned the limp boy onto his back. His eyes were closed and his breathing was shallow; blood oozed from a ragged gash on his forehead. Anna spotted a pillow amid the rubble. She pulled off the pillowcase, shook out the dust and ripped it in half. As Irene held her son's head, Anna wrapped the makeshift bandage around the wound, tying it tightly to stop the bleeding.

Justyn's voice croaked, "Mama? What . . . ?" The boy flinched in pain, tears welling up in his eyes, and Irene cradled him in her arms, rocking him back and forth.

Anna stood up and rubbed her eyes, which were burning and irritated from the thick dust.

She smelled something.

It was more than dust.

Smoke.

She reached down and grabbed Irene by the arm, yelling over the wailing siren, "We've got to get out of here!"

Irene looked up at her, clutching her son, not comprehending.

"The building's on fire!" Anna screamed, pulling her friend to her feet. She hoisted the boy into Irene's arms and pushed her out of the room.

The hallway was quickly filling with smoke as they scrambled down the stairs. By the time they reached the ground floor Anna's eyes were burning, and she could barely find her way through the foyer to the front door. She grabbed Irene's arm, pulled open the heavy wooden door and they burst out, coughing and gagging into the humid predawn air.

In the street it was chaos. Dense, black smoke filled the air. People clad in nightclothes screamed and ran in every direction. The howling sound of the sirens echoed between the buildings, broken by deep, booming thumps from anti-aircraft batteries.

Anna rubbed her temples, trying to collect her thoughts, when she was jolted by a piercing, high-pitched screeching noise that shot through her like an electric shock. She spun around and stared, dumbstruck, at an airplane swooping in above the rooftops. Before she could react, the plane's machine guns erupted in a hammering clatter, and a crowd of frantic people swarmed over her, crushing and jarring her, knocking her backward as a lightning trail of bullets ripped through the street in a shower of concrete and dirt. An instant later the clattering stopped, the screeching noise fading into the distance. Anna tried to move, but a woman had collapsed on top of her. Struggling to her feet, Anna grasped the woman's arm to help her up then recoiled in horror. The arm swung from her hand, severed from the woman's limp, bloody body.

Anna went rigid as her brain struggled to comprehend the nightmare scene. She heard a scream and staggered backward, dropping the severed arm. A man crawled across the ground in front of her. Another man shoved Anna aside and dropped to his knees in front of the fallen woman.

Anna blinked and shook her head. Irene? Justyn? She spun around, searching the faces of the panic-stricken crowd. "Irene!"

Nothing.

Her heart was in her throat. "Irene!"

"Anna." The voice was muffled.

Anna shoved her way through the throng of people and spotted Irene huddled against the building with Justyn in her arms. She knelt down beside them and looked her friend in the eye. "Irene, we've got to get off the street. Is there anywhere we can go?"

A blank stare.

Anna gripped her shoulders. "Irene, think! Do you know anyone?"

Nothing.

Anna stood up and looked around, fighting panic. Three men lifted the body of the fallen woman and started down the street, pushing others out of their way. One of them carried the arm. Anna looked back at Irene. "Irene, think! Do you know anyone in the neighborhood?"

No response.

"Irene!" she screamed at her friend.

"Mrs. Kopernik?"

The soft, tentative voice startled her. Anna turned to see a short, thin man with a black beard and wire-rimmed spectacles pushing through the crowd. He wore a skullcap and a blue suit coat over his pajamas.

"Come quickly," he said, motioning with his hand.

Anna stared at him. He looked familiar.

"I'm Bernard . . . Bernard Simowitz," the man said. "I was at the funeral. Come quickly. Get Irene and the boy and follow me. We've got to get off the street."

Anna reached down and pulled Irene to her feet. She picked up Justyn and followed the man through the rubble to an undamaged building on the other side of the street.

Bernard Simowitz held the door open for them, then squeezed past and led the way to a staircase, beckoning them to follow. "Down here, in the cellar. Follow me."

When they reached the bottom of the stairs, Anna set Justyn down and looked around in the dim light. They were in a damp earthen-floor room about ten meters square. The walls were made of stone, and a single bare light bulb hung from the rough, wooden ceiling. Across the room, a group of people sat on blankets.

One of them, a plump, blond woman, got to her feet and rushed across the dank room. "Irene! Mrs. Kopernik! Thank God, you're safe."

Anna stared at her, confused. Who was she?

The woman knelt in front of Justyn. "Come with me, sweetheart," she said. "We'll get you cleaned up."

Then Anna remembered. It was Bernard Simowitz's wife, Cynthia. Irene had introduced them at the funeral.

Cynthia took charge, leading Justyn by the hand and calling over her shoulder, "Bernard, get some water from the cistern and bring it over here—quickly now. Mrs. Kopernik, please come. Bring Irene over here and sit down."

Three other women and two men who had been sitting on the floor moved over to make room. Another blanket appeared, and one of the men spread it on the floor. Bernard arrived with a clay pitcher filled with water, and Cynthia began undoing the crude bandage on Justyn's head. "I spotted you from our window as we were running down to the cellar," she said, glancing at Anna. "It's a good thing you stand out in a crowd."

Anna was used to hearing comments like that. She was an attractive woman, taller than most, and her long red hair did indeed make her stand out in a crowd. This morning it had saved their lives. "I'm very grateful," she said. "I was frantic not knowing where to go."

Cynthia smiled at her then motioned with her head toward Irene, who sat clutching her knees, staring straight ahead, her eyes wide and vacant. Anna nodded and leaned back against the cold stone wall, putting her arm around her friend.

· · ·

An hour passed, perhaps more. It was difficult for Anna to tell. The sirens stopped and the anti-aircraft guns fell silent. The cellar was quiet. The building's tenants huddled in corners, staring at each other, some of them glancing at the wooden ceiling as though it might collapse at any moment. Anna absently fingered the cuts on her knees, struggling to control her fear, the visions still vivid and raw: Justyn lying in a pile of rubble, the diving airplane, the severed arm. She glanced at Irene and Justyn. They were both asleep on the blanket.

Anna heard a shuffling sound and looked up to see Cynthia standing over her, holding a bundle of clothing and some shoes. "You must be getting cold," Cynthia said. "It's very damp down here." The heavyset woman set the bundle on the blanket.

While Anna put on a dress, socks and a pair of brown leather shoes that fit reasonably well, Cynthia set the rest of the clothing and shoes next to Irene and Justyn. She covered them with a long woolen coat and looked back at Anna, shaking her head. "All this happening on the day after her mother's funeral—it's no wonder she's in shock."

Anna looked curiously at the woman. Her blond hair was neatly combed and she wore an elegant silk robe over her nightgown. Incredibly, she was also wearing a string of pearls. Had she worn them to bed? Anna pushed the foolish thought out of her mind and took Cynthia's hand. "Thank you . . . for everything. I don't know what we would've done if Bernard hadn't appeared when he did."

They sat down on the blanket. "We just thank the Lord that you're safe," Cynthia said. "Irene's mother, dear Izabella, worried about her all the time, living so far away."

"Did you know her a long time?" Anna asked.

"Ever since Bernard and I moved into this building, ten years ago. Her husband, Issac, ran the tailor shop in the back of their home across the street. Everyone in the neighborhood knew them. After he died, it was hard for Izabella with Irene living in Krakow and no other children. Usually, she would celebrate the Sabbath with us, but mostly she kept to herself."

"I met her just once," Anna said. "It was two years ago, when she came to Krakow for a visit."

Cynthia smiled. "I remember. Izabella spoke very fondly of you: Irene's friend, the college professor. She was pleased that Irene had such a good friend—even if you weren't Jewish. I believe you just got married, yes?"

Anna nodded.

"And your husband? He's an officer in the military?"

Anna took a deep breath. For months she had tried to convince herself that this day would never come. That Hitler was bluffing. That Germany would never be foolish enough to attack Poland now that Britain and France had pledged their support. Wasn't that what all the politicians had said? Then, when the officers were mobilized, they said it was just a precaution. She took another breath and wiped the tears from her eyes with the sleeve of her dress. "Jan is a major in the cavalry. It's his career."

"And Irene's husband—Stefan?"

"Stefan was a reserve officer in the cavalry for years. When all the tension started with Germany the brigade called their reserve officers back to active duty. He's been assigned to Jan's regiment."

Cynthia patted Anna's hand. "May God protect them . . . and all of us."

They sat in silence for a while. In the quiet, the horror of the early morning came back. Anna shivered. Maybe she and Irene had been foolish to travel to Warsaw two days ago. But this wasn't supposed to happen, not now, not so soon. Irene's mother died unexpectedly. What else could they do?

Anna closed her eyes. Talking about Jan left her feeling empty. It had taken her a long time to find love, a long time alone, focused on her career, looking after her father in the aftermath of her mother's death. But from the moment she and Jan met, she knew. He was the one. She could see him now, just as plainly as if he were standing before her: tall, blond, broad-shouldered, his face more rugged than handsome, he looked younger than his thirty-eight years. A tear rolled down her cheek. She left it there. It felt better to cry.

She heard Bernard's voice and opened her eyes. He knelt in front of her, next to Cynthia. "You can stay here with us," he said, "until this all blows over. It will be too dangerous to travel by train until this is settled."

"We came by auto," Anna said, "my father's car. His driver brought us here."

"By auto? But your driver . . . the car?"

"Henryk has relatives in Praga. He dropped us off the day before yesterday and went to stay with them. He's supposed to pick us up tomorrow."

The three of them just looked at one another.

Chapter 2

MAJOR JAN KOPERNIK tightened his grip on the reins and patted the chestnut mare's neck. The horse snorted and pawed the ground, nervous from the thundering noise of the bombers flying overhead. Jan stared at the sky, mesmerized by the awesome sight. There were hundreds of them, black droning machines, blanking out the morning sky like a giant storm cloud. That's exactly what this is, he thought, a storm . . . an ugly, dark storm. The planes were heading west at high altitude, back to Germany. Of one thing he was certain: somewhere to the east, in Radom or Warsaw, people had already died in this storm.

He turned in the saddle and glanced at Kapitan Stefan Pavelka. His friend glared back at him, acknowledging the grim reality. It was starting.

Jan looked up again at the massive bomber formation, and his thoughts went back to the night he got the call, canceling his leave and ordering him to report for duty. Anna had been standing next to him when he hung up the telephone. "So, this is it?" she had asked, gripping his hand. He had wanted to tell her it was just a precaution. He had wanted to tell her that everything would work out and he would probably be home in a week, maybe two. But he hadn't. She knew.

Something darted out from the cloud of heavy bombers. Jan reached back and pulled the binoculars from the leather pack. Settling deep into the saddle to calm the jittery horse, he dropped the reins and held the binoculars with both hands, focusing on the tiny objects that had separated from the bomber formation. There were four of them, small single engine airplanes. They banked to the north and began a steep dive toward the ground. A moment later he heard a sound, barely discernable through the roar of the bombers. It was a high-pitched, screeching noise.

"Stefan, over there," Jan said, pointing toward the diving planes.

Stefan took the binoculars and looked up at the four airplanes. "What the hell?"

Jan looked down over the valley to the north and wondered where they were going. The brigade's camp was more than five kilometers away, in the other direction. There was nothing down in the valley, no railroads or bridges, nothing that he could see except a small farming village. He scanned the sky and spotted the four planes again. They were rapidly approaching the ground.

"Jan, take a look." Stefan handed the binoculars back to him and pointed toward the village.

Jan took the binoculars and zeroed in on the tiny collection of ramshackle buildings. He panned slowly to the east, his line of sight following a thin, dusty ribbon of road. Three horse-drawn wagons filled with hay plodded toward the village. Then, incredibly, one of the wagons burst apart, wood splinters and hay exploding in every direction. An instant later the next two wagons disintegrated in a cloud of fiery smoke. Jan was dumbfounded. He struggled to keep his hands from shaking and raised the binoculars, locating the four black airplanes with white swastikas on their tails. They swooped in a long arc and began climbing.

Jan watched in disbelief as the planes banked again and dove toward the village. A sudden, boiling rage swept over him as he fought off a futile urge to pull out his pistol and shoot at the bastards. He jerked on the reins, and the mare clopped backward, snorting loudly, shaking her head in protest. His rage faded into anguish when the first shabby building exploded in a ball of fire, the thumping sound of the explosion rolling across the valley, then another, and another. In seconds, the peaceful, bucolic village erupted into a roiling inferno.

Jan stared at the inconceivable scene. His mind went blank, and he slumped in the saddle, his eyes dropping to the hard, rocky ground beneath the horse. He was grateful they were too far away to hear the screams of people burning to death in the village.

They sat there for awhile. Jan looked up once or twice at the plume of smoke rising from the serene valley. The planes were gone now, swallowed up by the haze of the western sky as though they had never existed.

Jan gathered up the reins, and the mare moved to the left, still shaking her head and snorting. He glanced at Stefan. "We'd better get back. The briefing will be starting soon."

They rode down the embankment to the dirt road that led back to the camp.
"What do you know about those planes?" Stefan asked.
"They're called Stukas. We had a briefing on them last month. They're dive-bombers. The Luftwaffe first used them in Spain to attack infantry troops—and cavalry."
"Cavalry? That's just great. First we hear they've got a thousand tanks and now they've got dive-bombers. We won't know whether to look up or down." Stefan removed his flat-topped *capszka,* ran a hand through his curly black hair and wiped the sweat from his forehead with his sleeve. "I guess the bastards have also decided to use them to attack hay wagons and farm villages."
"You heard the sound they made?" Jan asked.
"Yeah, that high screeching noise? Pretty strange."
"The intel' officer at our briefing said the Krauts actually created that noise intentionally, as a terror tactic."
Stefan looked at him and shook his head.
They reached the dirt road and kicked their horses into a canter. Jan had known all along that it would come to this, but now that it had, he was surprised by his emotions. Wasn't this precisely the moment he had been training for, preparing for, his entire adult life? Shouldn't he be relishing this moment, this opportunity to lead his men into battle? Was it fear? He had been in combat before and he hadn't been afraid. He didn't fear the Germans. His men were well trained and morale was high. He knew he could count on them in a fight.
They crossed an old wooden bridge and slowed to a trot. The creek below them was dry, the ground hard and cracked. The camp was just a kilometer ahead. Moving easily with the rhythm of the horse, Jan closed his eyes. Anna was there. She was standing on the platform, smiling at him as the train pulled out of the station in Krakow. It was windy, and she brushed her long red hair out of her eyes. She waved. Then she was gone. It *was* fear.

The field headquarters of the Wielkopolska Cavalry Brigade was set up in the railroad yards near the town of Srem, in the Poznan region of western Poland. They were less than a hundred kilometers from the German border.
The rail yard was teeming with activity when Jan and Stefan returned. As they trotted across the vast compound, Jan was relieved to see that several trains had pulled in while they were gone. Hundreds of soldiers and horses

were arriving. Uniformed men piled out of passenger cars, tossing their duffel bags on the dusty ground, and groomers led snorting, prancing horses down wooden ramps from boxcars. A long line of two-wheeled howitzers, heavy machine guns and Bofors anti-tank guns had materialized.

It's about time, Jan thought. The officers had been mobilized in secret a week ago, but the fools in the government had delayed the general mobilization. Hoping for negotiations to begin, they kept saying. It was all bullshit—and now the Germans were bombing his country.

They dismounted near one of the makeshift stables, handed off their horses to a groomer and set off on foot, joining the line of officers heading to the headquarters tent. Anna's image flashed through Jan's mind again: her soft red hair and liquid brown eyes. Just two years, that's all the time they'd had together. He forced the thought from his mind and stepped into the tent.

It smelled of a mixture of canvas and kerosene from lanterns that had been burning all night. A large map of Poland hung from support poles along the far wall. A soldier stood in front of the map, attaching red arrows at locations along the German border, and the deputy brigade commander, Colonel Adam Romanofski, sat at the center of a long wooden table, his head down, studying a smaller map. Two staff officers stood behind him, one of them pointing emphatically at the map. Behind the table sat a wireless operator, busily transcribing a message.

Positioned at equal intervals across the center of the tent were five flagpoles displaying the brigade's regimental banners. Jan took up his position at the head of the officers standing behind the banner of the Twenty-ninth Uhlans. He glanced at his watch. It was 0700.

Colonel Romanofski stood up, and the room instantly fell quiet save for the muted tapping of the wireless. The staff officers took their seats, and Romanofski stepped around to the front of the table. The colonel paused for a moment, looking over the group of officers, then spoke in a calm, steady voice. "Gentlemen, about two hours ago the German Luftwaffe initiated bombing raids over Warsaw. We are now at war with Germany."

Jan's stomach tightened. He stared at Romanofski as the squat, balding colonel addressed the assembled cavalry officers, his bearing confident and determined. He was a good man, Jan thought. They had known each other for a long time—since 1920, when Jan and Stefan had run away to join the cavalry and fight the Russians. Romanofski had been their squadron leader. It seemed like another lifetime.

The colonel picked up a pointer and thumped the map. "We've been getting reports of Wehrmacht troops crossing the border since 0500 this morning." He pointed at two of the red arrows near the top of the map. "In the north, at least two panzer divisions have crossed the border near Chojnice, and infantry units are crossing over from East Prussia." He slid the pointer to the arrows at the bottom of the map. "In the south, we've gotten reports of another panzer division and as many as three infantry divisions crossing over from Gleiwitz down to the Jablunka Pass."

Romanofski turned to face the silent group. The news got worse. "Two waves of bombers have already attacked Warsaw, and more are on their way. We've also gotten reports of bombing raids in the areas around Krakow, Lodz and Radom where the Luftwaffe are going after our airfields."

Jan stared at the arrows on the map. His skin crawled and his hands felt clammy. Beads of sweat trickled down his forehead. He had expected a fight but this . . . this was so sudden . . . so big. It was an all-out assault on a scale that was difficult to comprehend.

Romanofski tapped the map again. Jan blinked and moved his feet, shifting his weight. The colonel pointed to the middle of the long border between Poland and Germany. "We expect that the Germans will also launch an offensive aimed at the center of our defense perimeter here in the Poznan region." He set the pointer on the table and stepped forward, his beefy hands on his hips. "As you know, the mission of the Wielkopolska Cavalry Brigade is to provide mobile firepower, support and reconnaissance for the Poznan Army. Our recon units have already been deployed. General Abraham will be arriving this morning to assume command of the brigade. It is expected that we will engage the German Eighth Army within the next twenty-four hours."

Jan heard the shuffling of feet behind him. He wanted to look around, to make eye contact with Stefan and his fellow officers. But he stood transfixed, staring at Romanofski.

Slowly and deliberately, the colonel looked at each of his five regimental commanders.

Jan felt the man's steely eyes boring into his soul.

When Romanofski spoke again his tone was crisp and resolute. "You have your individual orders. You are well trained, highly skilled professional soldiers. Your troops, horses and equipment are arriving as we speak. By this time tomorrow the brigade will be at full strength: six thousand of the finest cavalrymen in the world." He paused, his eyes scanning the entire assemblage of officers. Abruptly, he stiffened.

Jan and the other officers snapped to attention.

"Gentlemen, we are going to throw the Huns back where they came from!"

Chapter 3

IN THE SIMOWITZ'S CELLAR another hour had passed, and it remained quiet. Anna was daydreaming, random images of Jan, her father and her students at the university flitting through her mind. She heard a sound from outside and looked across the room to where Bernard sat with Cynthia. The sound became louder. Truck engines and clanging bells, squealing brakes, men shouting. "Fire trucks," Bernard said, as he got to his feet. Anna followed him along with another man, up the stairs, through the hallway to the front door. Bernard pushed the door open, and they stepped outside into bright sunlight.

It took a moment for Anna's eyes to adjust, but the sight before her made her gasp. Plumes of gray smoke billowed from the charred windows of the shattered building where Irene's mother had lived. The roof had collapsed leaving behind just a few blackened timbers. The building next to it was reduced to rubble, nothing more than a massive pile of bricks, shattered glass and broken wood. A crater in the street gushed with water from a broken main.

Anna looked to her left where the fire truck stood in front of a building in flames. She doubted that it could be saved. To her right, past the crater and up the block, the street, which earlier had been swarming with terrified people, was now deserted—except for a solitary man. Anna took a few steps closer and held her hand up to shield her eyes from the sun. The man was stocky and broad-shouldered with a thick black mustache. He stood next to an automobile. The auto . . . it couldn't be. She blinked and looked again. "Henryk!" she yelled, waving her arms. "Henryk!"

Bernard came alongside of her, an incredulous look on his face. "Anna, is it—?"

"Yes!" She yelled again. "Henryk!"

The man looked across the street and spotted her. He waved a thick hand and began stepping carefully over the debris and around the crater. Anna's eyes clouded as she watched him approach. A bit of her fear melted away.

They stayed in the cellar the rest of the day, listening to the sporadic thumping sounds of bombs falling in the distance. As darkness approached, Henryk sat down next to Anna. Quietly, he said, "I think we should set out for Krakow."

Anna looked at him uncertainly. At this moment, Krakow seemed very far away.

He gave her a reassuring smile. "Traveling at night will be safer, especially if we keep to the back roads."

"But what if Krakow has been bombed or if we get attacked along the way?" For one of the few times in her life, Anna felt unsure of what to do.

Henryk's eyes narrowed, and he glanced around the room. He leaned closer and whispered. "It's possible that Krakow has also been bombed, perhaps other cities as well. But, I think we both know that no place in Poland is a bigger target than Warsaw."

Anna nodded. Of course he was right. She looked over at Bernard and Cynthia, and the others, sitting quietly, lost in their thoughts. What would happen to them? She glanced at Irene. Her friend's black hair was speckled with dust and chips of plaster, her thin face white, her eyes hollow, ghost-like. Justyn was asleep on her lap. Anna rubbed her temples, trying to push the fear out of her mind, grateful beyond words for Henryk's presence, the man who had been her father's driver, gardener and handyman for as long as she could remember. Right now he was a rock.

As Henryk drove through the dark, chaotic streets of Warsaw, Anna stared vacantly out of the car window. Fire trucks roared past with sirens blaring. Thick, acrid smoke billowed from burning buildings, but it barely registered. She was so tired, she could hardly keep her eyes open, but she was terrified to close them and have the visions return.

She tried to focus, to help Henryk find the way out of the city, but she couldn't concentrate, overwhelmed by the enormity of what had happened: the destruction, the injured people, the blood. How could this be happening so soon? Was her father safe? Was Jan? *Oh, God, Jan!*

She felt Henryk's hand on her arm and turned to look at him. The stocky man seemed to sense her thoughts. The look in his eyes said, "He's a good soldier . . . he'll survive."

Chapter 4

HENRYK STOPPED THE CAR and jumped out to flag down a mounted policeman. "We're heading to Krakow," Henryk shouted as a fire truck roared past, siren blaring and bells clanging. "Do you know if they've attacked anywhere else?"

The policeman struggled to keep the nervous horse under control. He shouted back, "I don't know about Krakow, but we heard reports that both Lodz and Radom were bombed. I'd stay away from there and stay off the main roads." He waved and trotted off.

"What now?" Anna asked when Henryk got back in the car. "Don't we have to go through one or the other to get to Krakow?"

Henryk reached over and pulled a map and a flashlight from the glove box. He studied the map for a few minutes then held it out for Anna to see. "If we cross over to the east side of the river and head south out of the city it looks like there's a back road that goes through Garwolin to Deblin. From there we can cross back over the river and then head southwest toward Krakow. I've never gone that way and I doubt if the roads are very good, but at least we'd be off the main highways."

"Well, we're sure not staying here," Anna said. Having a plan, as vague as it was, rejuvenated her a bit. She looked into the backseat at Irene. "Is that OK with you?"

Irene stared at her with a blank expression and shrugged her shoulders.

Anna turned back to Henryk. "Let's go."

They made their way out of the confusion of the city and headed south, but it was slow going. Hundreds of people trudged along the side of the asphalt road, some lugging suitcases, pulling carts or leading children by the hand. A line of cars, trucks and creaking, horse-drawn wagons crawled along, all heading in the same direction, out of Warsaw.

Henryk's thick, stubby fingers drummed the steering wheel and his black, walrus-like mustache twitched impatiently as he leaned out the window, looking for a chance to pass. Anna leaned back in the seat and closed her eyes, wondering what she would have done if he hadn't found them.

An hour later, the car bounced and Anna's head banged against the window. She opened her eyes, realizing she had fallen asleep.

"Sorry. Pothole," Henryk said.

Anna sat up and stretched, trying to get the kink out of her neck. They were on a narrow, gravel road and had just passed a family walking along the side. The man was pushing a cart covered with a canvas tarp. She didn't see anyone else. "Looks like you found the back road," Anna said. "Where are we?"

"Hopefully, on the road to Garwolin."

"Are you all right?"

He nodded. "Yes, I'm fine."

Anna glanced into the rear of the car. Irene and Justyn were curled up on the seat, sound asleep. She turned back to the front. It was a clear, moonlit night, and on both sides of the road, the vast expanse of farmland extended as far as she could see. Other than a pale orange glow in the dark sky behind them, the countryside appeared completely normal, as if nothing had happened.

Another hour passed, and they descended a hill, entering a small village that wasn't on the map. It was dark and quiet. They passed a blacksmith shop, a butcher shop, and a store with pots and pans hanging in the window and burlap bags filled with potatoes piled on the wooden porch. In the central square stood a water-well and a brick church with a red tile roof. Neat stucco homes with wood shutters lined the narrow, cobblestone street, some with lace curtains in the windows and flower boxes filled with geraniums. There were no lights and no signs of activity except the sound of a barking dog as they drove past.

Anna glanced at Henryk and shook her head. The tiny, peaceful town was asleep, untouched by the violence of Warsaw. She wondered if they even knew their country was at war.

As they drove on, Anna stared out the window, mesmerized by the steady rumble of the engine and the hum of the tires on the uneven road. *Jan is out there . . . somewhere,* she thought, closing her eyes, imagining that he was next to her, holding her hand. She smiled. They always held hands when they walked. They had been married only two years yet she could barely remember what her life had been like before they met. At thirty-four years old, she had finally found love and happiness. But now, in the space of one unimaginable day, it could all be gone. Was this really happening? Or had she descended into some bizarre dream? Perhaps when she opened her eyes—

Henryk cursed and hit the brakes, throwing Anna against the dashboard. Irene and Justyn tumbled off the backseat onto the floor as the car screeched to a halt. Anna sat up, gingerly fingering a welt on her forehead.

A mule pulling a rickety cart, laden with tools and household goods, had lurched across the road right in their path. The man leading the mule stared wide-eyed at the car and waved apologetically as he struggled to pull the animal out of the way. A woman, holding the hands of two small boys, scrambled across the road. The man yelled something that Anna couldn't make out, and she rolled down the window.

"Stay out of Garwolin! It's a mess!" the man shouted, jerking on the reins of the stubborn animal. "There are fires everywhere . . . the main road is blocked."

He finally got the mule under control and off to the side of the road. "Where are you going?" he asked, breathlessly.

"Krakow," Anna said.

The man was silent for a moment, then turned to the woman, who just shrugged. She seemed impatient to keep moving. The man looked back at Anna and said, "There's a dirt road just ahead that goes off to the west. It will take you along the river, all the way to Deblin."

"Thank you," Anna said and waved at the man as Henryk put the car in gear.

They found the turnoff and headed down the dirt road, which soon degenerated into little more than wagon ruts as it meandered through farm fields and orchards. Eventually, they came to a crossroads, and Henryk pulled out the flashlight, aiming it at a battered wooden sign nailed to a tree. It said *Deblin*, with a faded arrow pointing south. The road improved to a relatively flat, gravel path, but the moon had disappeared behind the clouds. It was pitch black and eerily quiet, as though they had been swallowed up by the night.

When they arrived in Deblin, the town was just coming awake. They followed an ancient truck as it rumbled slowly along the main street, passing shopkeepers sweeping the walks in front of their stores. Two old men in work clothes sat on a bench in front of the post office. They returned Justyn's wave as the car drove by.

"They just seem to be going about their business like nothing is happening," Anna said.

Henryk glanced at her and shrugged. "What else would they do? It hasn't affected them yet."

"They could be next," Irene said from the backseat.

Henryk nodded. "That's true, but my guess is that until it happens most of them will just go on doing what they've always done."

Just past the center of the town they spotted a faded metal sign with the word *Bensyna* in peeling yellow paint. Henryk pulled the car up to a single fuel pump in front of a shabby brick building. A thin, middle-aged man wearing grease-stained coveralls pulled open a creaking, wooden door revealing an old tractor up on blocks inside the building. He kicked a couple of bricks in front of the door to keep it open and shuffled over to their car.

"Could you fill the tank for us?" Henryk asked, getting out of the car.

The man grunted and shuffled over to the pump, spun the crank and removed the hose. As he pumped the gas he looked over the car and bent down, peering inside. "Nice car," he muttered. "Where you goin'?"

"We're heading to Krakow," Henryk said.

"Krakow? What for?"

"We live there. We're heading home."

"Shouldn't be headin' west." The man spat tobacco juice on the ground and wiped his chin with his hand. "The fuckin' Germans are comin'. Probably get to Krakow before you do."

"Well, that's where we're going," Henryk said. "Is there a café nearby where we could get some breakfast?"

Anna had rolled down her window and was listening to the exchange. The man put the cap back on the car's gas tank and hung the hose on the pump. "If I had a nice car like that I wouldn't let the Krauts get it. I'd be headin' east." He leaned against the pump and spat on the ground again.

Anna could tell that Henryk was getting annoyed. He opened his wallet and pulled out a few zlotys. "Well, you may be right, but we're heading to Krakow all the same. How much do I owe you?"

The man reached out, took the money and started back toward the shed, shoving the money in his pocket. Without looking back, he waved his hand to the left. "The next street over, there's a café. Don't know if they're open, though."

The small café was empty except for a heavyset woman of about sixty wiping off the top of one of the round wooden tables. A bell jingled as they walked through the door, and the woman looked up at them with a smile, wiping her hands on her apron. "Come in," she said, rushing to one of the tables and pulling out the chairs. "Please, come in and sit. I'll bring some coffee."

They sat at the table, and the woman produced a pot of steaming hot coffee and three well-used mugs. She disappeared behind a swinging door and returned with a pitcher of milk and a glass, which she set in front of Justyn. Without asking what they wanted, she disappeared again. From behind the swinging door came the sounds of clanging pots and the woman's husky voice barking orders at another person.

Anna took a sip of the strong coffee and looked across the table at Henryk and Irene. "I don't care what she brings. At this point, I'll eat anything."

"I'm starving," Justyn said, finishing off the glass of milk and pouring another.

The woman reappeared, set the table with simple white plates and mismatched silverware and disappeared again.

Henryk took a sip of the coffee and set the cup down, rubbing his eyes. "This came along just in time," he said.

"You've got to be very tired," Irene said. "Perhaps we should find a place to get some rest."

He looked at her and smiled, taking another sip of coffee. "The coffee helps. I'll be fine after some food. We need to keep moving."

When the woman emerged from the kitchen again she was trailed by a slender gray-haired man in coveralls carrying a large tray. The woman removed two platters from the tray and set them in the center of the table. One was heaped with sliced ham and boiled sausages, the other with thick slices of coarse, dark bread, a bowl of jam and a plate of sliced cucumbers. "Please, eat," she said. "I can bring more if you're still hungry." Pushing the man ahead of her, she disappeared again behind the door.

The food tasted marvelous, at this moment as wonderful as in any restaurant in Krakow, Anna thought. She helped herself to a second boiled sausage and slice of bread, glancing at the others. Their heads were down, concentrating on the food, too hungry for conversation.

When they were finished the woman set about clearing the table, and the gray-haired man reappeared with a cup of coffee in his hand. He pulled over a chair from one of the other tables. "Where you folks from?" he asked, striking a match to a pipe.

"We've just come from Warsaw," Henryk said. "We're heading to Krakow."

"Warsaw?" exclaimed the woman, removing the last of the empty plates. She backed into a chair and sat down heavily, holding the plates in her hands. "God in heaven, what will become of us? We heard more of those awful airplanes again this morning. I don't know what to do."

The man got up and went into the kitchen. He returned a moment later with a map, which he spread out on the table. "I've been around here all my life. I know the back roads. I'll show you how to keep off the main highways."

They stayed at the café awhile before continuing on. The couple had a telephone, and they made several attempts to call Anna's father in Krakow, all unsuccessful. They listened to news broadcasts on the radio, but the information was confusing and contradictory. Some reports said the Germans were advancing rapidly while others said the Polish army was mounting fierce resistance. But one thing seemed clear: Luftwaffe bombers were striking all over Poland with little or no resistance from the Polish Air Force.

They left Deblin a little before eight, and by midday it was hot. The roads were abominable, and the jarring motion of the car gave Anna a headache. Their progress had been agonizingly slow all morning and now slowed to a crawl as they bumped along, choking on dust from two farm wagons ahead of them. The horse-drawn wagons, heavily laden with potatoes, creaked and lurched over every bump and rut.

With her hand over her mouth to keep out the dust, Anna stared out the open window at the neatly planted fields, broken occasionally by small groves of trees. Farmers plodded behind mule-carts, finishing off the last of the late summer harvest. Cows grazed on the hillsides, and hogs wallowed in their pens. She thought that rural Poland had probably looked exactly like this for centuries.

Henryk's gravelly voice jerked her out of her lethargy. "Listen, can you hear it?"

Anna glanced at him.

He was leaning over, trying to look up at the sky through the windshield. He stopped the car to let the wagons gain a little distance in front of them and allow the dust to settle.

Anna peered out the window, squinting in the bright sunlight, searching the sky.

"What is it?" Irene asked, gripping the back of the seat.

"Airplanes," Anna said. She had just spotted them, a dozen or so, high and off to the right. She held her breath, watching the sky as the planes passed overhead.

Justyn stuck his head out the back window as Henryk put the car in gear and started moving forward again.

"Oh God, look!" Anna yelled, pointing out the window on Henryk's side.

Two of the planes dropped out of the formation and banked sharply to the right, circling back.

Henryk cursed and honked the horn, trying to get the attention of the farmers driving the wagons.

The planes circled around until they were directly in front of them then plunged toward the road, growing frightfully large. The high-pitched screeching noise sent a wave of fear washing over Anna as visions of the horrific attack in Warsaw came flashing back.

Henryk bellowed, "Get down!" He jerked the steering wheel to the right and stomped on the accelerator.

The shrill clattering noise of machine-gun fire drummed in Anna's head as the car plunged into the field, bouncing wildly over the rough ground. She braced herself against the dashboard as Henryk struggled to steer the vehicle, aiming for the safety of a grove of trees. Suddenly the windshield exploded, and the car careened out of control.

The last thing Anna heard was the jarring crunch of metal as the car plowed into a large birch tree.

Chapter 5

FOR THE FIRST TIME in his life, Thaddeus Piekarski felt helpless. His world had spun out of control, and he had absolutely no idea what to do next. He sat at the table in the white-tiled kitchen and stared into a cup of tea, stirring it listlessly. He was exhausted from lack of sleep but dared not close his eyes because every time he did he saw Anna's face smiling at him. "For the love of Christ," he said out loud, "what has become of my daughter?"

There was no one around to hear him. It was Sunday morning, and his housekeeper, Janina, had gone to church. Perhaps her prayers will persuade God to intervene on the side of the Poles, he thought. He got up from the table and wandered through the quiet house, his mind detached, passing from room to room like a visitor in a museum. He shuffled through the formal dining room and the stiffly elegant parlor, pausing at the doorway of his study. It was a comfortable room, with oak-paneled walls and a soft, brown leather chair in front of the fireplace. The mail and legal journals he had been reading Thursday night were still on the desk next to the empty brandy snifter. Janina never touched anything on his desk.

He entered the study, stepped over to the fireplace and picked up a picture of Anna from the mantel. It was one of his favorites, taken in Antwerp, Belgium, at the home of his friend Rene Leffard. Anna had lived with the Leffards during her university years. In the picture, she was laughing and waving her diploma in her hand. If only her mother had lived to see it, he thought every time he looked at it. He set it down and glanced into the mirror above the mantel.

The reflection was unfamiliar. It was the same thin face, the same white hair and wire-rimmed glasses. But behind the glasses, the eyes were strange and alien, the eyes of someone who didn't know what to do, the eyes of someone who was helpless.

As he stared at the strange image in the mirror, the events of the last two days thundered through Thaddeus's mind: the air-raid sirens, jarring him awake early Friday morning, Janina screaming from downstairs, the thundering roar of airplane engines and muted thumps off in the distance. He remembered how confused he had been, struggling to clear his mind of the fog of sleep, thinking it was a drill or an exercise of the Polish Air Force.

The explosions got louder; Janina had screamed again. Thaddeus had grabbed a shirt and pulled on a pair of trousers. The stout, gray-haired housekeeper stood barefoot at the bottom of the staircase, clad only in her nightgown, clutching the banister, her eyes wide with fear. Thaddeus ran down the stairs, out to the front yard and stared up at the sky. Airplanes! Dozens of enormous airplanes were passing overhead, black-and-white crosses on their fuselages and swastikas on their tails.

The rest of the day had been a blur of madness. Explosions around the city continued for several hours and then stopped. Nothing was damaged in their neighborhood, but the streets were soon filled with confused, terrified people. Thaddeus had tried to telephone Irene's mother in Warsaw, but the lines were already down. He could still make calls within Krakow and, with some effort, reached the main office at the university. They couldn't get through to Warsaw either. Then, in the late afternoon, the air-raid sirens started again, and he and Janina went down to the cellar to wait it out until dark.

On Saturday, there had been sporadic bombing raids over the city, and radio bulletins reported intense fighting as Poland's Krakow Army clashed with the Germans southwest of the city. Statements from officials in the government encouraged Poland's citizens to be brave and not panic. "Our armed forces are holding off the German onslaught. England and France will be at our side in just a few days."

Thaddeus had listened to all this, struggling to remain calm. But the German invasion had taken him completely by surprise. Negotiations between Germany and Poland had just begun. How could they have broken down already? Why had these idiots in the government continued to tell everyone that things were under control—and how could he have been foolish enough to believe them?

What was happening to Anna, Irene and Justyn? He knew Henryk would do anything to protect them, but what can anyone do against airplanes and bombs? Were they still in Warsaw? Had they tried to make a run for it? He had considered taking a train to Warsaw but that was sheer folly. Even if he could get on a train, it might take days to get to Warsaw, if he got there at all. No, he had finally decided, the only sensible thing to do was to stay put and wait to hear from them.

The image in the mirror was pathetic, and Thaddeus turned away. He plodded back to the kitchen and switched on the radio to listen to the latest news bulletin. He picked up the cup of cold tea as a crackling voice began reading an announcement.

His hand stopped in midair.

He stared at the radio, not sure if he had heard correctly.

The voice repeated the announcement. "Krakow has been declared an open city. The Polish High Command has determined the city cannot be defended. The Krakow Army is retreating to the east."

Thaddeus dropped the cup, oblivious to the shattering china and the liquid splashing over his arm. He stood up and gripped the edge of the table. His chair toppled over. Krakow an open city, left undefended? The royal city—the Mecca of Poland for a thousand years—occupied by the Germans? Was this possible in just two days?

He stared out the window overlooking the terrace. If Krakow couldn't be defended after only two days, what did it mean for the rest of Poland?

He stepped outside and sat down in one of the wooden chairs positioned in a neat semicircle on the brick terrace. Hunched over with his elbows on his knees, and staring at the potted geraniums, a cloud of fear descended over him. He squeezed his intertwined fingers so hard that his hands shook, trying to resist the urge to smash every one of the goddamn pots.

Janina burst through the kitchen door and onto the terrace. "Dr. Piekarski, have you heard? The Germans are coming!"

Thaddeus turned toward her. Strangely, the frightened look in her eyes had a calming effect on him. "Yes, Janina, I've just heard."

"Everyone is leaving! We have to get out of town! Where will we go, Dr. Piekarski?"

"What do you mean, 'everyone is leaving'? Who's leaving?"

"It's the talk all over. At the church. In the tram. Everyone is saying we'll have to leave or the Germans will round us up and put us in work camps!"

Thaddeus took the plump woman by the arm and led her to one of the wooden chairs. She sat down heavily, clutching her white silk purse with both hands. "Janina, listen to me," he said. "There's nowhere to go. It'll be more dangerous out in the country than here in the city. Our troops are retreating to the east of the city, and that's where the fighting will be. German airplanes will be bombing the roads and the railroad tracks. Leaving the city now would be foolhardy."

"But what will we do if the Germans come into Krakow?"

Thaddeus took a deep breath. "They *will* come into Krakow—and they'll occupy the city, probably within the next few days. Nothing can stop that now." He took another breath. The thought was abhorrent. He put his hand on Janina's shoulder. "There are hundreds of thousands of people in Krakow," he said, "with businesses to run and factories to operate. The Germans need those factories. They aren't going to round us up or haul us off to work camps. They'll take over our local government for awhile, until the British and the French jump into this thing. We'll just have to sit tight and be patient."

She looked at him for a long time, and the fear slowly drained from her face. She dabbed her eyes with a handkerchief and stood up. "Thank you. I feel a little better now. Of course, you're right." She started back toward the house then abruptly turned toward him again. "But, Dr. Piekarski, what about Anna and the others? How will they get home now?"

He looked at her but did not answer.

Janina nodded and stepped into the house.

The next three days were beyond anything Thaddeus could have imagined. Hundreds of panic-stricken people fled the city in cars, horse-carriages, wagons, or simply on foot, carrying bundles on their backs. The railway stations were mobbed, and through all the confusion, convoys of army trucks filled with dejected-looking Polish soldiers rumbled through the city, heading east.

But most of Krakow's citizens decided to stay. In quiet desolation they stood along the streets or leaned out the windows of their homes and apartments, watching the exodus of soldiers and would-be refugees. Thaddeus stood among them, his heart breaking. They were being abandoned.

Finally, an eerie quiet descended on the city. The artillery fire ceased. The bombing stopped. Now, nothing stood between the people of Krakow and the German Wehrmacht.

When the first convoy of German troops entered the city, Thaddeus was having lunch with his friend and fellow law professor, Jozef Bujak, in a café on the Rynek Glowny. Led by motorcycles, with black and red flags snapping crisply in the wind, the motorcade descended upon the historic square—long black cars, gray canvas-covered trucks and clanking tanks, with leather-capped crewmen standing in the open turrets. Announcements in German and Polish blared from megaphones on the tops of the cars. "The fighting is over! Go about your business! There is no need to be concerned!"

The motorcade proceeded to the center of the square and halted in front of the town hall. Several hundred people, who had been walking through the square or, like Thaddeus and Bujak, sitting in cafés around its perimeter, stopped what they were doing and watched the incredible scene unfold in complete silence.

Two dozen Wehrmacht soldiers, armed with rifles and submachine guns, jumped from the trucks and quickly encircled the massive, gothic structure. The doors of the lead car opened, and two black-uniformed SS officers emerged, followed by a soldier carrying a large bundle. They entered the building.

The silence of the anxious crowd was broken by muted gasps as an enormous red banner unfurled from the top of the town hall. Centered in a stark white circle in the middle of the banner was a large black swastika.

Chapter 6

JAN SHIFTED AGAIN and leaned back against the rough wooden walls of the old barn. The smell of dung and urine was overpowering, but at least they were out of the weather. A drizzling rain had started just after dark and was such a welcome relief after the sweltering heat of the last week that most of the men had just collapsed in the fields to cool off.

But, over the next several hours, more than a hundred tired and wet soldiers had sought refuge inside the barn. Others pitched their small two-man tents in the fields or just curled up under the few trees in the area. Jan could hear a few men snoring, but for him, and for most of the troopers of the Wielkopolska Cavalry Brigade, sleep would not come tonight. In the morning they would launch the counterattack.

The expected confrontation with the German Eighth Army at the outbreak of the war had not materialized. Instead of a frontal attack near the city of Poznan, the Eighth Army had crossed the border in a narrow strike well to the south and made a dash for Warsaw. For the last week, the Wielkopolska Brigade, along with the entire Poznan Army, had been slogging eastward, trying to keep up with the enemy's rapid advance.

Jan had read the reports coming in from the other sectors, which grew more ominous every day. A large part of the Polish Air Force had been destroyed in the first two days. With no further threat of air attacks, and concentrating their forces along tight, narrow fronts, the panzer divisions of the German Wehrmacht had ripped through Polish defenses and were advancing on the ground with alarming speed. In the north, they swept through Danzig and were closing in on Warsaw. In the south, they marched into Krakow then veered north, also driving toward Warsaw.

Jan stood up and stretched. His back ached and his knees were sore from seven days in the saddle. He looked at his watch in the thin moonbeam drifting through a crack in the wall. It was 0130. He stepped carefully around the resting troopers and made his way to the door. In one hour the Wielkopolska Brigade would ride out ahead of the main force of the Poznan Army and strike the first blows of the counterattack.

The rain had stopped and the clouds lifted, revealing a bright starlit sky. Off in the distance, Jan could see a glow from some smoldering town left behind by the German war machine. Now, seven days into the war, he realized what they were up against. The Luftwaffe were not only bombing railroad bridges, factories and water towers, they were randomly dropping incendiary bombs on rural hamlets and farm villages. Dive-bombing Stukas machine-gunned fleeing peasants with as much ferocity as they did Polish troops. The German *blitzkrieg* was not just a military strategy—it was an all-out campaign of terror intent on the total destruction of his homeland.

Jan pulled a crumpled pack of cigarettes from his shirt pocket and shook one out, trying to push the frustration out of his mind. The irony of their situation was tragic. Like a piercing dagger, the German Eighth Army had driven a hundred kilometers into the heart of Poland, leaving the brigade—and the entire Poznan Army—in its dust. Poland was being overrun, and they hadn't fired a shot.

As he struck a match to the cigarette, Jan reflected on another grim irony . . . the rain last evening. It had hardly rained all summer. If the antiquated and outgunned Polish army couldn't slow down the enemy, Poland's notoriously greasy, muddy roads and wide rivers might have. But it was not to be. The roads were rutted, but they were dry and hard. The riverbeds were wide but shallow and easily forded. The flat, open terrain provided few obstacles for the mechanized, ever-advancing Wehrmacht.

He leaned against a tree and took in the sight before him. Six thousand cavalrymen and another thousand support troops camped out over the high, flat plain north of the Bzura River. Their artillery was arrayed in a neat row along the dirt road, ready to be hitched to horse teams to follow the frontline cavalry troops into the Bzura valley.

The men were starting to move around now. They gathered up their gear and saddles, and dug out their ration packs. In the fields beyond the rutted road Jan could make out the silhouettes of hundreds of horses wandering about, grazing in the wet grass. The groomers moved among them for a last check of horseshoes and harnesses. For all of them, man and beast alike, it was likely the last peaceful moment they would have.

"You have any of those left?" Stefan's voice startled him. He hadn't noticed him walking down the road.

Jan pulled the pack from his pocket and handed it to him. "Keep 'em. They're not very good."

Stefan nodded and lit one of the limp, hand-rolled cigarettes.

"Couldn't sleep?" Jan asked.

Stefan blew a cloud of smoke in the air and shook his head. "I haven't slept much at all since we heard about Krakow."

Jan looked down at his scruffy boots. They'd gotten the word about Krakow two days earlier. "Well, at least there won't be any fighting there. We can be thankful they're not getting bombarded like the poor devils in Warsaw or Lodz."

"Yeah, that's true. But they're sitting in a city controlled by fuckin' Nazis. Irene must be—"

Jan took a step closer to his friend. "Look, don't dwell on that. There's nothing we can do about it except to try and get out of this mess alive and get home."

"You know what they think of Jews, Jan."

Stefan had reason for worry. They had all heard about Jews in Germany losing their jobs, Jewish children being expelled from the schools, and synagogues being vandalized in Munich and Nuremberg. But Jan needed Stefan to stay focused on the mission. "The Allies will be jumping into this any day, Stefan. They'll force some kind of settlement. We've just got to hang on."

Stefan took a breath to speak then looked over Jan's shoulder and stopped.

Jan turned and stubbed out his cigarette as Colonel Romanofski approached along with two other officers. Jan and Stefan joined them and headed for the brigade officers' briefing.

"Any news from Warsaw?" Jan asked.

"Latest news from the runners is that it's bad," Romanofski said. "Water towers are all blown to hell, and the rail yards are gone. Communications are down, and there are fires everywhere—hundreds of casualties. And that's as of yesterday afternoon. It's probably a lot worse by now."

Jan glanced at Stefan and shook his head. That last comment said as much about their situation as anything. The Polish army still relied almost entirely on messengers or civilian telephones for communications, and one of the first objectives of the Luftwaffe had been the destruction of the telephone lines. Now, with tens of thousands of terrified civilians fleeing their towns and choking the roads in every direction, communications were in chaos.

As Jan and the other officers filed into the headquarters tent, the brigade commander, General Roman Abraham, stood behind a table at the front. He was a tall, severe-looking man with thin gray hair and icy blue eyes. His field officer's uniform was immaculate: crisply pressed khaki coat with leather belt descending across his chest, and brown leather knee-height boots.

When they were assembled, the general began speaking. His voice was quiet, his tone somber. "Gentlemen, we have received our final orders to launch the counterattack. All other Polish forces have been ordered to fall back to the Vistula River for the defense of Warsaw." He paused and looked over the silent group, his countenance stark and forbidding in the flickering light of the kerosene lanterns. "The situation is serious. The northern and southern army groups are under constant artillery bombardment and are being harassed by air strikes. They are in danger of being surrounded. To make matters worse, the roads are clogged with refugees. It's doubtful they'll get to Warsaw in time." He paused again, staring straight ahead. "Our counterattack from the rear represents the only chance of slowing down the enemy's drive toward Warsaw."

He glanced at one of the staff officers, who rolled out a map. The officers closed in around the table. The general pointed to a spot on the map and continued. "The Poznan Army has halted here, just outside the railroad junction at Kutno. At dawn, their infantry divisions will strike along the Bzura River valley and attack the northern flank of the German Eighth Army."

The general stepped aside, and Colonel Romanofski moved forward as the staff officer unrolled a second, more detailed map of the area. "Glowno is critical to the success of our counterattack," the stocky colonel said, jabbing at a spot on the map twenty kilometers south of the Bzura River. "It is being held by the enemy's 210th infantry division. At all costs, the 210th division has to be contained and prevented from coming to the aid of the rest of the German Eighth Army. The job of crossing the Bzura and taking them out of action has been assigned to us."

Romanofski glared at each of the officers then bent over the map again. Jan edged in closer, studying the map, as the colonel continued. "The road from the Bzura River to Glowno passes through this village, Walewice." The colonel looked up, locking eyes with Jan. "Major Kopernik will lead the Twenty-ninth Uhlans into Walewice and secure it to block any escape of the Germans from Glowno." Romanofski turned to a reconnaissance officer who was standing off to the side. "Kruzak, what do we know about Walewice?"

Kruzak coughed and produced a tattered notebook. "Our scouts have spotted a small contingent of German troops in the town. They've also gotten information from a few of the local farmers. No machine guns or artillery have been reported. We estimate it's just a small unit—two or three rifle platoons, probably not even on alert."

"How old is this information?" Jan asked.

"Most of it is from late yesterday morning, twelve to fifteen hours ago," Kruzak said.

"OK, that's the situation," Romanofski declared. "Jan, it sounds like these guys in Walewice are just sittin' on their asses. Take the Twenty-ninth in there and secure it before they can radio any alarms. You'll have surprise and darkness on your side so go in hard and fast. When you've got it secured, leave one squadron behind and head down the road to Glowno to cut off any Krauts trying to head north."

Romanofski turned to the other four regimental officers. "The rest of the brigade will launch the main assault on Glowno."

Jan only half listened. He wondered about twelve-hour-old scouting reports. Then put them out of his mind. They were all the information he was going to get.

When the briefing ended, Jan headed for the Twenty-ninth Uhlans' staging area. Kapitan Lech Peracki, one of his squadron commanders, came up alongside him. "Shit, Jan, it sounds like we're going to miss all the action."

Jan glanced at the younger man. He was a good officer, perhaps a bit eager, but fearless in battle and completely dependable. "There're plenty of Germans out there, Lech. We'll get our chance."

"I hope so," Peracki said, with a grin. "We've chased the bastards halfway across the country."

Jan watched as Peracki moved on, and thought about the exchange. He understood Peracki's disappointment at not being part of the main assault on Glowno. Yet, his own reaction had been concern over the scouting reports on Walewice. The cavalry meant everything to him, it always had. This was their big moment. What the hell was wrong with him?

• • •

At 0215 the buglers gave the call to saddle the horses and, fifteen minutes later, the call to mount and form up. Sitting astride his horse, Jan looked left and right across the lines. It was, indeed, an impressive force: six thousand horsemen grouped in tight regimental formations, sabers at the ready and standards rippling in the night breeze. His mare pawed the ground, and he turned in the saddle, glancing at Stefan, Peracki and his third squadron commander, Karol Bartkowicz. Stefan and Bartkowicz stared straight ahead. Peracki gave him a "thumbs-up."

At the front of the brigade Colonel Romanofski raised his saber. The buglers sounded the call to move out, and twenty-four thousand hooves pounded toward the Bzura valley. Jan leaned forward in the saddle, settling into the rhythm of the powerful horse. Invigorated by the rush of crisp night air, his anxiety about Anna faded, his fears of what lay ahead displaced by the sheer exhilaration of the moment.

The ground shook beneath the galloping horses as the brigade entered the flat plains of the valley and separated into attack formations. The night was clear, the ground dry and hard having easily absorbed the short evening rain, and they made good time. The Twenty-ninth Uhlans arrived at their final attack point just before 0300.

When Jan sighted the Bzura River, he brought the regiment to a halt. The map of the area and the tactical plan were etched in his mind. The Bzura River ran east–west at this point. On the other side, less than two kilometers farther south, was the village of Walewice. The terrain between the Bzura and Walewice was flat and open. Another river, the Mroga, flowed north into the Bzura and would be on their left as they headed into the village. The Mroga River formed the eastern boundary of Walewice, and the road from Glowno passed over a bridge at the edge of the village.

With his horse prancing nervously, Jan turned and shouted to the squadron commanders. "The village is about two kilometers south of the river. We'll split up here and ford the river. On my signal, we go in at full gallop right to the edge of the town before dismounting. Stefan, First Squadron will go in on the left flank, along the Mroga and directly to the bridge. Bartkowicz, you're leading Second Squadron with me up the middle, straight into the town. Peracki, Third Squadron will cover flank on the right. We'll be going in fast so be alert. We'll have surprise on our side but stay sharp. If it's wearing a uniform . . . kill it!

Chapter 7

UNTEROFFIZIER KONRAD SCHMIDT was miserable. It had been another long day in the sweltering heat, choking on dust from the rutted dirt roads. He had thought that riding in the back of the truck with the machine guns and ammo boxes was better than walking, but now he wasn't so sure. The ride was bone-jarring, and the damn machine guns took up so much space that none of them had any room to stretch their legs. He was squeezed into a narrow space between the side of the truck and a stack of ammo boxes, and he began to wonder if he'd ever be able to stand up straight again.

He felt someone kick his foot and looked over at Willy who pointed toward the sky. Schmidt gripped the metal railing and squinted in the bright sunlight as a vast formation of Luftwaffe bombers roared overhead. They were heading east, toward Warsaw. At least that's what they were told, though it seemed to him there were plenty of other targets. During the last seven days, the battalion had passed through dozens of small towns that were practically leveled. Dead animals and human corpses were strewn about like so much litter among smashed and burning buildings.

To Schmidt, it seemed completely random. Many of the communities the battalion rumbled through were undamaged and, except for the lack of people on the streets, looked similar to the rural villages he was used to back home in Germany. They passed farmers working in their fields, then, farther down the road, wrecked wagons and dead bodies would be lying in a ditch.

Schmidt had been terrified the day they crossed the border into Poland. It was his nineteenth birthday, and he was convinced he'd never see his twentieth. He had tried to imagine what it would be like to be in a battle, what it would sound like and how he would respond. He imagined all sorts of things, but nothing had prepared him for what he witnessed in some of these shattered villages. At first he could hardly look at the dead bodies, and when the wind was coming from the wrong direction, the stench of rotting flesh was overpowering. But with each day his senses had dulled, and now he barely noticed.

One thing Schmidt had not seen during these last seven days was action. The officers had told them they would meet Poland's Poznan Army on the first day, but that didn't happen, nor had it happened on any day since then. At the beginning, they had been on high alert. Everyone was anxious, and the officers barked a steady stream of orders. But, day after day, they continued to move east, and the enemy was nowhere in sight. It seemed like nothing was going to happen until they got to Warsaw.

Early that morning, a rumor filtered through the battalion that they had received new orders. They were heading to a place called Glowno to join the 210th Infantry Division garrisoned there. Schmidt had no idea where Glowno was or, for that matter, where any of these damn places were. Shit, no one he knew could even pronounce the names.

It was growing dark when they stopped in yet another shabby village with an unpronounceable name. This time the stop was longer. Schmidt leaned over the side of the truck, watching a group of officers engaged in an animated conversation with two old men who had been sitting on a bench in the village square when the battalion thundered in.

The conversation dragged on, and gradually soldiers began climbing out of the trucks and off the wagons. With considerable effort, Schmidt extricated himself from the corner of the truck and jumped down. Moving his head from side to side to work the kink out of his neck, he walked over to the small grassy area in the village square to take a piss.

He had just finished when Oberleutnant Kluge shouted at him, "Schmidt! *Komm!* Round up your gun crew and get your asses back on the truck. We're heading out. *Mach schnell!*"

Schmidt started to complain but caught himself in time. Kluge was not someone who took any shit from the troops. He motioned to Willy, his ammo tender, and trudged back to the truck.

"Where the hell are we going now?" Willy griped. "We just got here for Christ's sake."

"Damned if I know," Schmidt said. "I didn't ask any questions."

Buchwald, the truck driver, had stubbed out his cigarette and was climbing into the cab.

"What the hell's going on?" Schmidt asked.

Buchwald shrugged. "I think these dumb bastards are lost. Get on the truck."

An hour later, the convoy entered a town situated along a river. The truck hit a pothole and bounced heavily. One of the ammo boxes toppled off the stack and landed on Schmidt's foot.

"*Verdammt!*" he howled and grabbed the metal railing, struggling to his feet. All he wanted was to get out of this damn thing and get some sleep. He leaned over the side of the truck and looked up ahead as the headlights illuminated a small wooden sign on the side of the road. It read, *Walewice.*

It was raining when they finally stopped at the north end of the town. The homes and shops all appeared intact, but the town was dark and quiet. Just as in most of the other towns they had entered, the locals seemed to melt into the background. Schmidt was about to jump off the truck when he spotted a group of German soldiers emerge from between two houses and approach the truck at the head of the convoy. A second group appeared as Kluge and two other officers jumped out of the lead truck.

Schmidt watched as a heated conversation erupted, the officers and the soldiers from the town all looking at a map in the headlights of the lead truck. Kluge was jabbing his finger at the map, yelling something that Schmidt couldn't make out. Buchwald and a few other drivers got out of their trucks and wandered over to the group, standing back, listening.

A few minutes later, Buchwald came back to the truck, and shouted, "*Raus! Raus!* Looks like they finally figured out where we are. It's another twenty kilometers to Glowno, so we're spending the night here and headin' there in the morning."

Willy jumped down first, shaking his head. "Maybe in the next war we should bring along somebody who can read Polish."

"Who the hell are these other guys?" Schmidt asked, as he climbed off the truck.

"Sounds like they're part of the 210th," Buchwald said. "Supposedly, they've been here a couple of days, guarding the town. Kluge was pretty pissed at them; looks like they were all sleepin' or just fuckin' off."

After seven hot and dusty days, the drizzling rain felt so good that Schmidt just dropped to the ground next to the truck. He lay flat on his back and let the cool rain wash over his face. He had just closed his eye when he heard a shout from Kluge to deploy the machine guns. He couldn't believe it. Hell, it was the middle of the night and they were leaving first thing in the morning.

Kluge stomped over shouting at them, "*Fertig machen!* Get off your asses! *Sofort!*" and pointed out a spot overlooking a meadow. Grumbling under his breath, Schmidt helped Willy haul one of the MG-34s into position. Buchwald drove the truck farther down the road, where the other gun crews set up positions closer to a bridge at the east end of the town.

"Make sure you set up that tripod, Schmidt," Kluge yelled over his shoulder as he walked off down the road.

What a pain in the ass, Schmidt thought. They did this every time they stopped. Kluge's orders, by the book, no questions. By now, Schmidt knew it all by heart: "All the artillery's up ahead with the panzers. These 34s are the only thing we've got to stop an attack." Attack? Shit, all the Polish troops were supposedly up ahead, hauling ass to Warsaw. But Kluge was Kluge, and he knew better than to argue.

It was almost midnight when they finished the setup. Schmidt and Willy had some cold rice and tinned sausage, and settled down under a tree to get some rest until they had to take over the second watch at 0300.

It seemed to Schmidt as if he had just fallen asleep when he felt someone shaking his shoulder. "Schmidt, get up you lazy bastard, it's your watch." It was the gunner from the first crew.

Schmidt sat up and tried to clear the cobwebs from his brain. "Anything out there?"

"*Nein.* Same old shit. They're all in Warsaw. Fuckin' Kluge's just a fanatic."

Schmidt got to his feet, rousted Willy and walked over to the machine gun. He sat down on top of one of the ammo boxes and rubbed his eyes, still groggy from the deep sleep he had fallen into. He noticed that the rain had stopped and the moonlit sky overhead was bright with stars. Out in front of them, the wide, flat meadow sloped gently toward the river on their right. Schmidt looked around. On the other side of the road was a row of simple stucco homes. He wondered about the people who lived in them, guessing they were probably all hiding in the cellars. He decided he didn't really care.

Willy tapped him on the shoulder. "I'm going to take a piss. Don't shoot me," the ammo tender said as he took a few paces into the meadow. When he was finished, Willy buttoned up his pants and started to head back. He stopped and turned back, staring into the darkness. "Schmidt! *Komm!* Something's out there!"

"What is it?" Schmidt asked, getting to his feet and stretching.

"I don't know, I thought I saw some movement out there—or heard something, I'm not sure."

"Ah, you're imagining things," Schmidt said as he came alongside.

Schmidt felt it before he saw it—a slight tremble that rippled up from the ground and through his boots. He glanced at the ground then back into the meadow. He squinted. Then he saw it. It was just barely visible, a thin line of moving shapes spread out across the entire width of the meadow. He blinked. The shapes were still there, now larger, moving toward them.

"*Meine Gute!* Horses!" he sputtered. "It's cavalry, holy shit!" He stumbled backward and tripped over Willy, who was staring into the meadow, his mouth hanging open. "Get to the gun!" Schmidt yelled. He grabbed Willy by the arm and shoved him back toward the machine gun. "Get up! Get up!" he yelled to the other gun crew who were just settling in for some sleep. "It's cavalry! Get Kluge! *Schnell! Mach schnell!*"

Schmidt scrambled behind the machine gun and grabbed the handle. He looked down the long barrel of the big gun trying to sight in on the shadowy images. They appeared to be just out of range.

Schmidt heard Kluge's voice shouting from behind, "Hold! Hold!"

He could just make out the riders.

Schmidt's hands trembled. The horses were getting bigger. He knew he had to wait but, goddamn it, they were getting really close. His eyes blurred and he blinked to clear them.

Kluge yelled, "Fire! Now, Fire!"

Schmidt squeezed the trigger and the big gun exploded into an eardrum-shattering, hammering noise that shut out everything around him. He stared down the fire-belching barrel, struggling to keep it aimed at the charging horses.

Nothing happened. The horses kept coming. Schmidt could see the riders—and something glinting in the moonlight.

"Christ, they've got sabers!" Willy yelled.

The gun blazed away, the smoke burning Schmidt's eyes, the noise banging his mind into numbness.

The horses began to scatter.

Schmidt was frozen to the handle of the wild, clattering machine, terror building in his heart. He was certain he'd missed them. Then they started to fall. First one, then another and another, the horses crashed to the ground, their legs flying wildly, their riders propelled into the air like dolls.

He was no longer in control of the killing machine blazing away at the end of his arms. It had taken on a life of its own. He was just hanging on, no longer hearing or feeling, completely transfixed by the terrible scene unfolding before him. Horses, now by the dozens, charged into each other and tumbled to the ground. Riders, tossed in every direction, staggered to their feet only to be trampled by another stampeding animal. Schmidt's heart screamed for them to get out of the way. He closed his eyes unable to continue to witness the carnage.

Willy's shouting jarred him back into the moment. "*Stoppen Sie! Stoppen Sie!* Barrel change! Barrel change!"

Without thinking, Schmidt instinctively released the trigger, set the safety lever and rotated the barrel jacket counterclockwise. His glazed eyes fell upon Willy, and he watched the ammo tender slide out the smoking barrel and slide in the spare. But he did not comprehend. It was like watching a slow-motion dream of something he had never seen before. A strange person was doing a strange task that had nothing to do with him.

Willy reached over him and rotated the barrel jacket back into position.

Schmidt did not understand how it happened, but the big gun was firing again and horses were falling. He prayed for it to be over.

It seemed like it would never end . . . and then it did. He felt someone's hands on his shoulders, pulling him back.

"*Stoppen Sie!* Hold fire! Hold fire!" Willy yelled.

Schmidt collapsed backward and almost toppled to the ground before catching himself and getting to his knees. His ears were ringing and his hands were numb.

"Kluge called a cease-fire," Willy yelled. "They've retreated out of range."

Schmidt turned toward the meadow. The remaining cavalrymen were galloping to the north, disappearing into the darkness. He looked around. The battalion's riflemen had scrambled into positions between the machine guns, and officers were shouting orders. Engines fired up and vehicles began moving.

Above the din, he heard Kluge's voice. "Machine gunners stay at your posts! Ammo tenders get reloaded! Stay alert! Stay alert!"

As Willy pried open an ammo box, Schmidt looked again into the meadow. The sight was appalling. Horses stumbled about aimlessly, shadowy images in the night, heads bobbing and tails twitching. Dark heaps lay on the ground. He couldn't see them very well, but he could imagine them: not moving, or kicking their feet and raising and lowering their heads.

Among the stricken animals, he knew there were men. He couldn't make them out but he knew they were out there, crawling away or, like the horses they had been riding, lying in their own blood on the hard ground. They were too far away for Schmidt to hear their cries.

Chapter 8

JUSTYN SAT UNDER A TREE in the small orchard, staring down at the brown burlap bag of apples he had been collecting. Of the various chores he had been given, this was his favorite. The orchard was cool and shady, and the branches hung low, within his reach if he stood on his tiptoes. It didn't take long to collect enough to fill the bag.

He picked one of the apples out of the bag and turned it over in his hand, trying to decide exactly where to take the first bite. Justyn liked being here. He felt safe. He bit into the apple with a crunch, and the juice ran down his chin. That was his favorite part, the first bite. He wiped his chin and leaned back against the tree.

A week had passed since his grandmother's funeral, but it seemed longer. That was before . . . before the bombing, and the long drive, and . . . the airplanes. He stared at the apple, watching a drop of juice trickle down the slick red skin. Visions of the funeral flitted through his mind: old men with black beards and dark coats, women with powdery faces who smelled like flowers, patting him on the head or putting their hands on his shoulder, telling him what a brave lad he was. It was the first funeral he had ever been to, and he wondered why he hadn't cried. He cried when they buried Henryk and he wasn't even a relative. That wasn't really a funeral. They didn't even have a rabbi, although his mother told him that Henryk wasn't Jewish, so they wouldn't have had a rabbi anyway.

Thinking about Henryk made him remember the attack. He shivered and gripped the apple in both hands. He didn't want to think about it, but he couldn't help it. It was just there, in his mind. He remembered Anna spotting the airplanes, then Henryk honking the horn at the wagons in front of them.

Then it was all a blur, the car bouncing through the fields and the noise—the noise was the worst, the loud screeching noise. He had covered his ears, and then he saw the tree.

How could Henryk have been killed? He was so strong. He remembered opening his eyes and seeing Henryk slumped over the steering wheel. He remembered the blood. Anna was next to Henryk in the front seat, lying on her side, her long red hair soaked with blood.

"Justyn!"

He blinked and looked around.

"Justyn!"

His mother was calling. He stood up, took another bite of the apple and slung the heavy sack over his shoulder. He trudged across the farmyard, past the brick, tin-roofed barn, and headed for the house.

His mother stood on the porch and when she saw him she yelled, "Run and get Mr. Berkowicz! Anna is awake!"

Justyn dropped the apple and the bag in the dust and sprinted toward the toolshed, shouting, "Mr. Berkowicz! Mr. Berkowicz!"

Standing at the door of the toolshed, shuffling his feet in the dust, Justyn watched Mr. Berkowicz wipe his tough, gnarled hands on a dirty rag, toss it into a bucket in the corner and pluck a black felt hat from a nail on the wall. As they walked to the house, Justyn felt the reassuring grip of the old man's hand on his shoulder.

They stood in the doorway peering into the tiny bedroom. Anna was lying on a wrought iron bed underneath the only window, which was propped open to let in some air. It didn't help much. The room was hot and sticky. Anna's face was white, like chalk, and her red hair was plastered to her forehead. Justyn's mother sat on the edge of the bed, wiping Anna's face with a wet cloth. Mrs. Berkowicz stood next to the bed holding a pan of water. She was a short, round woman and took up most of the extra space in the small room.

Justyn wiped a tear from his eye as he looked at Anna. He had tried not to think about it, but he realized now that he had been terrified she would die, too. The doctor Mr. Berkowicz had fetched from the town that first day had said something about a concussion, that there was nothing he could do and they would just have to be patient. Justyn held his breath as Anna lifted her head and looked around the room. Her eyes seemed glazed and distant. She started to say something then fell back on the pillow.

"Anna?" Justyn's mother leaned over and stroked Anna's forehead with the cloth. "Anna, it's Irene."

"Irene?" The word formed slowly. Anna looked up at her. "Where . . ."

"Here, take a drink of water," his mother said. She put her hand behind Anna's head and brought a small glass of water to her lips.

Anna took a sip of the water and looked around the room again. "What . . . Where are we?" Her voice was raspy. She coughed.

Justyn's mother held the glass as Anna took another sip. "We're in the home of Leizer and Beata Berkowicz. They found us after the attack by the airplanes."

Anna's eyes widened. "The airplanes . . . Justyn?"

Justyn took a step forward. "I'm here, Anna." He squeezed into the room and stood at the foot of the bed. Mrs. Berkowicz set the pan on the floor and put her arm around him.

Anna's lips curled upward into a thin smile. Then she looked around again. "Henryk? Where's . . . Henryk?"

Justyn's mother took Anna's hand. "Henryk is dead, Anna."

"Henryk . . . dead?"

Justyn clenched his fists, but the tears he had tried to hold back spilled over, running down his cheeks.

Anna stared at his mother. Her lips moved but no sound came out. Then she closed her eyes and laid her head back on the pillow.

The next afternoon, Anna sat on a wooden rocker on the porch of the farmhouse looking out at the fields of dark, rich soil that had been recently harvested. The trees in the orchard were heavily laden with ripe fruit, and a gentle warm breeze carried the pungent scent of farm country. It was as though she were in a dream, far away from the horrors of Warsaw and the desperate trip in the night.

It was barely possible to believe Henryk was gone. He had been with her father for as long as she could remember, and he always seemed so capable, so indestructible. Her father must be beside himself with worry, she thought. He'd be crushed when he heard about Henryk.

The door creaked, and Irene came out of the house carrying two glasses filled with dark brown liquid. "How are you feeling?" she asked, sitting down on a bench next to the rocker. She handed one of the glasses to Anna.

Anna managed a smile. "Still groggy, like being in a dense fog." She took a sip of the drink. It was cool and sweet. "Apple cider?"

Irene nodded. "They make it themselves and store it in the cellar." She took a sip from the other glass. "There's something I have to tell you," she said.

Anna turned slowly, trying not to move her head any more than necessary. "What is it?"

Irene glanced down at the rough wooden planks of the porch floor then looked back at Anna. "The Germans have taken Krakow."

"What?" Anna jerked her head, and a searing pain shot through her skull like a knife. She spilled part of the drink trying to set the glass on the floor.

Irene reached out and took the glass. She put a hand on Anna's arm. "The doctor from town told us when he came out to check on you—four days ago. He heard it on a news bulletin."

Anna pressed her hands against the side of her head. "Germans in Krakow?"

Irene nodded. Her thin face was pale, her dark eyes fearful.

Anna leaned back in the rocker and looked out at the serene farmland. Cows grazed on a distant hillside. A fantasy crept into her mind that she and Jan were together, right here in this place. They would stay here and pretend the war was happening on some other continent. He would take her hand, and they would walk through the lush fields and sit together under a tree . . .

She heard Irene say something. "What?"

"There was very little damage," Irene said. "In Krakow. It happened so fast; the news bulletin said there was very little damage."

Anna rubbed her temples and thought about her father. German troops were in Krakow. He must be devastated. But, if it happened that fast, at least he was probably out of harm's way. He wouldn't have left, she was certain of that. Although her father had been born in England, the only son of a Polish nobleman and his class-conscious wife—who'd insisted on Anglicizing her son's name—Anna knew he was a true Polish patriot. He would never let the Germans drive him out of his beloved city. "Have you heard any other news?" she asked.

"It doesn't sound good," Irene said. "There's heavy fighting east of Krakow and up in the north. They're bombing all of the big cities, especially Warsaw . . ." Her voice trailed off.

Anna leaned back in the rocker and closed her eyes. She felt very tired.

He was there, standing in front of her, smiling. His uniform was crisp, neatly pressed, and his boots were shiny. Then it was raining, just a light rain, falling gently, pattering on the roof, dripping off the leaves. It felt good . . . cool and soothing. He was fading away. *No!* She reached out to him. *Stay! Please stay!* But he was gone . . . and she was alone.

Anna opened her eyes. She was still sitting in the rocker. Beata Berkowicz smiled at her and dipped the wet cloth back in the pan. The woman's face was round, her skin tanned and heavily creased by years in the sun and wind. "Thank you, that feels good," Anna said.

Beata wrung the dripping cloth, folded it and gently stroked Anna's cheeks, then her arms. The fog in Anna's mind began to lift. She leaned forward in the rocker and thought about standing up but sat back when the throbbing in her temples returned. "What time is it?" she asked.

Beata put the cloth back in the pan and sat down on the bench. "Almost five thirty. Irene and Justyn went into town with Leizer. They should be back soon, and then we'll have supper."

Anna turned toward her, holding a hand against her head. "Thank you . . . for everything."

Beata smiled and patted her hand. "Where did you learn to speak French?"

Anna looked at her, confused. "French?"

"A few nights ago, I went into your room to check on you. You must have been dreaming. You were saying something in French."

Anna smiled at her. "I attended university in Belgium. Antwerp. I lived with a friend of my father's, and they all spoke French. Rene and Mimi Leffard—he's a law professor, like my father."

"We don't hear other languages very often out here," Beata said. "There are some Jews in town who speak Yiddish with each other. Maybe we'll be hearing German soon." She looked at Anna and raised her bushy eyebrows.

"My husband speaks German," Anna said. "He grew up in the west, near Poznan. All the schools were German."

Beata nodded.

"He also speaks French, though not as well as German. His mother was French. He helps me with German and I help him with French. We both—" Anna realized she was rambling. She looked at the plain, down-to-earth woman and smiled. "You've been very kind."

"You'll stay here with us," Beata said. It was more than an invitation. It was a declaration. Before Anna could respond, Beata stood up and placed a hand on her shoulder. "I'll get supper ready."

Chapter 9

AT FIRST IT WAS JUST a shadowy form in the moonlight, swishing back and forth across his field of vision. Jan blinked and tried to focus as the shapeless form swished again. Then he heard a sound—a snort—and abruptly rolled over, scrambling away from the hobbling horse.

The sudden movement sent a sharp pain slicing through his head and down his neck. He turned his head slowly from side to side and flexed his arms and legs. Nothing seemed broken. With some effort, he got to his knees, trying to get his bearings. Horses were all around, lying on the ground, struggling to get up or, like the one he just escaped, stumbling about, dazed and confused.

Jan looked toward the town but couldn't see anything from this distance except the outline of houses and low buildings. He crawled away, in the other direction, and then his hand came down on something soft and wet. He jerked it back, staring down at the body of a cavalry trooper lying face up in the grass, his chest covered in blood. He took a deep breath and crawled on, moving cautiously to avoid the thrashing hooves of desperate horses in their last moments of life.

Above the dull cacophony of whinnies and nickers, human groans and sobbing, Jan heard a sharp cry for help. He followed the sound to a young trooper struggling to free his foot from under a horse. Jan crawled up to him and shoved his arms under the massive, bloody animal, gripping the boy's ankle. Suddenly the wounded horse snorted and tossed its head. The trooper screamed in pain. Jan pulled on the boy's leg, but the horse thrashed again, threatening to roll over the panic-stricken trooper. Jan leaned his forehead against the horse's sweat-soaked back, gagging on the stench of blood and urine. He closed his eyes, waiting a moment for the animal to settle down.

Then he slowly withdrew his arms from the boy's ankle, stood up and removed his revolver from the holster. He took a long breath then placed the barrel of the gun against the horse's head and pulled the trigger. The horse jerked then quivered before a long sigh of exhaling breath. Jan reached under the animal and again gripped the wide-eyed trooper's ankle. "Now, pull," he said. The trooper grunted and jerked his foot free.

Jan held the boy's bare foot and ankle, moving it slowly back and forth. "I don't think it's broken," he said to the lad who was sweating profusely and biting his lower lip. "Follow me and stay low."

They crawled off and found another trooper lying face down, dead, then another, groaning and clutching his head. The blood oozed through the boy's fingers, and he rolled his eyes toward Jan, silently pleading for help. Jan swallowed hard and patted the boy's leg. Half his skull was gone. He would be dead in a few minutes.

Up ahead there was movement, shadows of horses and riders gathering, beyond the range of the machine guns. Other shadows rose from the meadow, men running and hobbling toward the group.

Jan stood up and looked at the young trooper. "Can you stand? We've got to get out of here."

The boy struggled to his feet and limped forward. "I'll make it."

Jan put his arm around him and they trudged through the tall grass toward the assembling group. As they got closer, Jan spotted Kapitan Peracki dismounting, and shouted, "Lech! Send a rider to get the artillery squadron!"

Peracki turned toward him, startled. "Jan, thank God. Yes, right away."

"And tell them we'll need wagons for the wounded."

Peracki nodded and hustled off.

Jan moved into the midst of the assembled troopers, pressing his hands to his head, rubbing his temples. The pain was easing. He glanced around the group, spotted Bartkowicz, then looked for Stefan but didn't see him or anyone else from First Squadron. He stepped over to a medic pulling supplies out of a cart and said, "Pick out ten men to help you. Spread out and stay low. They'll have snipers so just try to help anyone you can find within about a hundred meters but don't go in any closer. We can't afford to lose anyone else now."

Peracki returned as the medic selected men and handed out supplies. "Have you seen anyone from First Squadron?" Jan asked.

Peracki shook his head. "We veered off to the right when the shooting started, and I saw them heading toward the river. I doubt they made it to the bridge."

Jan nodded and glanced back toward the town. They were at least a kilometer away. "For now, organize the rest of these men in a defense perimeter with rifles and bayonets. As soon as the artillery gets here we're going in on foot." Peracki turned away, shouting orders.

Jan looked over the meadow. In the moonlight he could make out the shapes of horses but it was too dark to see the men he knew were out there. He glanced at his watch. It was a little before 0400. Less than an hour ago the regiment had stood on the other side of the Bzura River, poised for a surprise attack on a weakly defended enemy position. Less than an hour—and now more than a hundred of his men lay dead or badly wounded.

He shook his head and glanced around at the flurry of activity. Troopers carrying medical supplies advanced into the meadow, staying low, keeping their heads down. The rest of the regiment were gathering their rifles, fixing bayonets and taking up defensive positions. The horses that survived were moved back, out of harm's way. Peracki and Bartkowicz had things under control. There was nothing to do now but wait for the artillery.

Jan made his way to the top of a small hill, trying to get a better view of the Mroga River. He could catch only a glimpse, a thin silver ribbon shimmering in the moonlight. He hoped Stefan was out there with his squadron, hunkered down, safe for the moment. Stefan was a good officer. He would know what to do. He would know they were bringing in artillery, and he would wait.

Jan looked at his watch again—0430. The artillery squadron would be here soon. The sky was brightening in the east as he headed back to join his men, dreading the sunrise when he would actually be able to see the extent of the carnage.

Unteroffizier Schmidt sat on the ground near his silent machine gun. It had been almost two hours since the Polish cavalry troops had retreated, and his hands had finally stopped trembling. The sky was beginning to lighten and he could see a little more clearly, but out in the meadow nothing was moving. Willy sat on the other side of the gun, neither of them having said a word for a long time.

Schmidt heard Kluge's voice behind him and turned. The oberleutnant stood a few meters away, talking into a field radio. *"Nein! Nein!* I don't know where they came from," Kluge said. "They just appeared, charging through the meadow right at us."

Kluge was silent for a few seconds then spoke again, his voice louder. "They retreated back to the north. I don't know what else is out there, but there were several hundred cavalry troops."

Schmidt kept watching as the oberleutnant shook his head and looked up at the sky. "We're still on alert!" Now Kluge was yelling. "I told Muller the same thing an hour ago! *Verdammt!* The machine guns are already deployed! That's how we stopped them, but if they bring in artillery we won't be able to hold them! We're going to need reinforcements!"

Kluge ripped off the headset and threw it at the radioman. *"Schweinhund,"* he mumbled. "How would I know where they came from? He's the genius who keeps saying they're all heading for Warsaw."

Schmidt turned away, but it was too late: Kluge had spotted him. "Hey, Schmidt, you whining little turd, now you know why we set up those guns every night. If you had your way you'd have one of those sabers stuck up your ass!"

Schmidt looked back, but the oberleutnant had already stormed off, yelling at someone else.

"What a prick," Willy whispered from the other side of the machine gun.

Schmidt glanced at the ammo tender then turned back to the meadow. It was quiet, spooky, the shadowy heaps lying on the ground barely visible.

He blinked at a sudden flash of light.

The concussion from the blast hammered Schmidt onto his back, pelting him with rocks and clumps of dirt. He rolled over and managed to get to his knees when he was flattened by another blast. With his mouth full of dirt and his ears pounding, he tried to stand but collided with another soldier and tumbled back to the ground. Then a hand was under his arm and he was on his feet, stumbling across the road. He flopped to the ground between two houses and crawled against a wall, glancing back toward the meadow as a thundering explosion ripped his machine gun into a thousand pieces. He couldn't see Willy.

Schmidt cowered against the brick wall of the house, choking on smoke and dust, a million pinpricks of light dancing in his eyes. A truck exploded in a searing blast and disappeared into a smoking crater, littering the road with smoking bits of steel and charred body parts. Schmidt went rigid. His stomach heaved, trying to vomit but nothing came out. Thundering detonations and bursting flashes of light closed in around him, pounding him down. A shower of broken glass cascaded over him, and he wrapped his arms over his head, whimpering, waiting for the blast that would bury him.

Schmidt didn't know when the shelling stopped, the constant drumbeat in his head indistinguishable from the bombardment. But gradually, new sounds drifted in: crackling fire, men shouting, gunshots. He lifted his head and peeked around. Black smoke billowed from the burning truck. A motorcycle roared past then spun off into the ditch. He tried to get up, but he was frozen, his legs turned to lead. Three riflemen sprinted down the road and ducked between the houses. One of them stopped and looked down at him. Schmidt recognized him, an unteroffizier from his battalion. He had bummed a cigarette from him the day before.

"*Raus! Raus!* Get the hell out of here!" the rifleman shouted. "They're coming through the meadow!" Then he was gone.

Schmidt tried again to get to his feet, but fell back against the brick wall. He couldn't breathe. On his butt, he squirmed backward along the base of the house and pulled his knees tight against his chest. When he saw them he pissed in his pants.

Like spirits emerging from hell, the Polish troopers charged out of the meadow, screaming and shouting, bayonets and sabers glinting in the firelight. Gunfire erupted from every direction.

In an instant, they were on top of him, like madmen, stomping over him. A heavy boot kicked him in the back, and Schmidt rolled over, trying to get away. Out of the corner of his eye, the last thing he saw was the flashing blade of a saber.

Jan stood in the middle of the road leading out of Walewice, watching the last of the retreating German soldiers disappear over a hill. He turned to Peracki who leaned against the frame of a wrecked truck, looking exhausted. "Lech, what have you heard about the bridge?"

"It's secure, Jan. A runner came over just a few minutes ago with a message from Stefan."

Jan sighed and put a hand on Peracki's shoulder. He guessed the young officer wouldn't be complaining any longer about missing the action. "Get a detail to go through all these houses and shops," he said. "Squadron commanders will meet on the bridge at 0800."

Peracki nodded and walked away.

Jan wandered back through the now-quiet town. Dead bodies were everywhere. Just boys, he thought. Polish and German boys, distinguishable only by the color of their soiled uniforms.

Smashed and burning vehicles littered the streets, along with some that were completely intact, abandoned by the German troops in their frantic retreat. His men were already attending to the wounded and setting up a makeshift field hospital. A few of the townspeople had emerged from their homes, looking frightened and tentative, but joining in to help. The artillery squadron rumbled in from the meadow, the big horse-drawn howitzers maneuvering around the craters and debris.

Jan leaned against the side of a building and removed his helmet, rubbing his eyes. Three wagons rolled past, bringing in more wounded from the meadow. The dead ones were still out there. How many of his men had he lost? He didn't want to know.

The pain in his head had returned and his back was sore. He closed his eyes, allowing himself the indulgence of a moment thinking about Anna. The Germans were occupying Krakow, but at least the fighting there had ended and he found some comfort in the fact that she was probably safe for the time being. For how long? That was another question. One for which he had no answer.

A horse-drawn cart creaked past. Three wounded soldiers were sitting in the back, one of them holding a bloody cloth to his head with his left hand. When he noticed Jan, the injured boy saluted. Jan straightened up, put on his helmet and returned the salute.

Chapter 10

THADDEUS PIEKARSKI was only half listening to the conversation going on around him at the back table in the White Eagle Pub. He took a sip from the glass of beer that had been sitting untouched in front of him and, once again, his thoughts drifted to the frustrating, endless quandary about Anna. It had been ten days without any word of her whereabouts and now that Krakow was under German occupation the prospects of getting any information were nil.

A fist banged the table, and Thaddeus swallowed hard, almost choking on the beer. His friend, Jozef Bujak leaned across the table and pointed a thick finger at Fryderyk Wawrzyn, a legal counsel for the city of Krakow. "The French and British *will* attack Germany, anyone can see that," Bujak declared. He shot a quick glance at the others sitting around the table then lowered his voice, drawing them in. Thaddeus had seen his burly colleague in action many times. His theatrics were surpassed only by his passion. Bujak pressed on. "Hitler has made a gross miscalculation. Germany is finished. Our allies will not let him grab Poland without a fight."

"I think you're dead wrong," Wawrzyn said. "The French are sitting comfortably behind their Maginot Line, and they're not going to stick their necks out for Poland. If they wouldn't help the Czechs why would they help us?"

"Christ, Fryderyk, England and France have declared *war* on Germany," Bujak hissed. "Of course, they'll attack."

"Oh hell, the French were coerced into that by the Brits, Jozef. You're beginning to sound like those jackasses running our government. The Brits can't do anything without France and the French aren't going to attack Germany. That declaration of war was just an attempt to throw Hitler off balance. It's hollow."

Bujak glared at him, took a gulp of beer and called out to the waiter to bring another round. He set the empty glass down with a thump and turned toward Thaddeus. "Thaddeus, help me out here. That friend of yours in Belgium, the one Anna lived with for awhile, what the hell's his name?"

"Do you mean Rene Leffard?" Thaddeus asked, looking at his friend with concern. Bujak's fleshy cheeks had reddened as they always did when he got worked up, a result of his excessive weight and high blood pressure.

"Yes, that's it. If I recall, he's pretty well connected in France and Belgium and you correspond with him. What's his view on this?"

Thaddeus pushed his beer glass to the side and placed both hands on the table in front of him. "Well, it certainly won't be possible to correspond with him any longer, not until this is all over. But in his last few letters he sounded increasingly doubtful that the French would attack Germany to help out Poland."

"But damn it all, Thaddeus, what about—"

Thaddeus held up his hand. "Let me finish, Jozef. Leffard thinks the political situation in France is too unstable, and I have to agree with him. The French will talk tough but, in the end, I think they'll just sit tight and see what happens."

Bujak slumped back in his chair with a scowl and turned back toward Wawrzyn. "Well, Fryderyk, if we're in this alone, what's the city government going to do to protect its citizens now that we're under occupation?"

"What city government are you talking about?" Wawrzyn shot back. "It's all under German control now. Our advice to the city officials who are still in place is to take a low profile and try and cooperate. You heard about what happened in Poznan, didn't you?"

Bujak shook his head.

"The SS moved in right behind the Wehrmacht and dragged the mayor and his wife out of their home and shot them, right in their own backyard."

"Good God," Thaddeus gasped.

Bujak glanced at him and took a swig from his fresh glass of beer.

Wawrzyn continued. "And, in Bielsko, over two thousand Jews were rounded up and hauled into a school yard. They beat them with clubs and poured boiling water over them. Some they tortured by putting hoses in their mouths and pumping water into them. Christ, this was just two days after the invasion!"

Wawrzyn leaned forward and lowered his voice to a whisper. "There's a lot more. The stories are coming into our office every day. These are not people you can bargain with. The best thing any of us can do is to try and keep out of their way, and if you get stopped or challenged, be as cooperative as you can."

"So, you're telling us to act like house pets in our own city," Bujak growled. "That's bullshit! We need to do whatever we can to help root these bastards out."

"Watch yourself," Wawrzyn said, glancing around the room. "That's the kind of talk that'll get you in big trouble. This is not something to take lightly. They're in charge in Krakow now, and they mean business."

They were interrupted by a thin, balding man who entered the pub and rushed to their table. Thaddeus recognized him: Felek Slomak, a legal assistant to Wawrzyn. "Have you heard the news?" Slomak asked breathlessly. "A major counterattack is under way!"

Wawrzyn shook his head and glanced at the others. "No, we haven't heard a thing."

"Where is it happening?" Thaddeus asked.

"The report on the radio said that it was near Kutno, along the Bzura River. It started sometime yesterday, and they've got the Germans on the run."

Bujak slammed his fist to the table again, this time rattling the glasses. "That's more like it! Now, France and the Brits will get into it for sure."

Late the next afternoon Thaddeus stood by the window in his second floor office at Jagiellonian University's Collegium Maius and looked out at the stone courtyard below. A young man and woman were sitting on the edge of the well in the center of the courtyard. Only a few students were on the campus since the start of the fall term was still three weeks away, and Thaddeus wondered if classes would go on as usual. He hadn't heard otherwise, but no one knew anything for sure.

He stepped over to his desk and stared down at the jumble of papers and books. He had work to do. He had to prepare for the seminar he would be teaching on contract law, and he hadn't made much progress on the paper he was to present at the symposium in Amsterdam. Amsterdam in October—he shook his head at the foolish notion. It had been planned in another lifetime.

"Are you about to leave, Thaddeus?"

He looked up. Jozef Bujak stood in the doorway. Thaddeus glanced down at the cluttered desk again, but it was useless to pretend. He couldn't concentrate on any of it. "Yes, I am," he said.

"I'll walk with you. Perhaps we can get a drink."

They left the ancient building and headed toward the Rynek Glowny. "Did you hear about what happened earlier today, right here in Krakow?" Bujak asked.

"You mean the family that was shot . . . because they wouldn't hand over their car? Yes, I heard about it a few hours ago."

"They were not Jews, Thaddeus! This could have been any of us. And in Mielec—"

Thaddeus heard the clacking sound of iron-shod hooves on cobblestone and glanced toward the street as two German soldiers astride enormous black horses rode past. They wore green uniforms with wide black belts around their waists and the eagle and swastika insignia on their sleeves. Hanging from a chain around each man's neck was a half-moon-shaped metal badge that Thaddeus recognized from pictures he had seen.

Bujak nudged him with his elbow. "Feldgendarmes."

Thaddeus nodded. The German military police. He recalled articles he had read about their actions in Czechoslovakia when they followed the Wehrmacht into occupied cities and towns to maintain order. The articles referred to them as *kettenhund*—chained dogs.

They arrived at an outdoor café and sat at a small table off in a corner away from the few other patrons, each ordering a glass of beer. When the waiter left, Bujak leaned across the table. "This won't stop with the Jews. You know that."

The waiter returned with their beers and left again. Thaddeus took a sip and set the glass down. "The war's not over. I still have hope. You should too."

"Yes, I hope . . . and I pray," Jozef said. "But what if we lose, what then?"

"Jozef, I don't understand. Yesterday you were certain that the French and British were coming to our rescue."

"Ah, you know how I get when I'm around Wawrzyn. Maybe they will, maybe they won't—who can tell? If they don't, I think we're in big trouble." Bujak took a gulp of beer and looked around at the other tables. He leaned forward and whispered, "I've heard talk of a Resistance developing."

"Heard talk? Or, started talk, Jozef?"

"What's the difference? There's talk. It's starting."

Thaddeus stared at him for a long moment then picked up his glass and took a drink.

"It's very quiet," Bujak continued. "But it's starting."

Thaddeus set his glass on the table. "Why are you telling me this?"

"Because you need to know."

Thaddeus wrapped both hands around the beer glass and stared down at the table. "This is very dangerous."

"Can we count on you—when the time comes?"

Thaddeus's head jerked up. He glared at Bujak. "This is very premature, Jozef. We haven't lost the war yet. You said it yourself. The Allies could still come in and—"

Bujak reached across the table and gripped his arm. "When the time comes, Thaddeus. Can we count on you?"

Thaddeus leaned back in his chair and closed his eyes. Good God, he thought, where was this heading? He hadn't seen Anna in almost two weeks and he had no idea if she was even alive. Jan was out there somewhere fighting the Germans. And now this. He knew what it meant. Once he started down this track, there would be no getting off. He finished his beer and stood up, looking into his friend's eyes. "Yes, Jozef—when the time comes."

Chapter 11

THE TWENTY-NINTH UHLANS had been moving fast. For two days following the debacle at Walewice Jan led the regiment in relentless pursuit of the
retreating Wehrmacht infantry, outflanking them at every turn and inflicting
heavy casualties. When the enemy sought refuge in the marshes, the cavalry
troopers drove them out. When they hid in barns, they kicked in the doors.
They had the enemy on the run.

But it didn't last. The German commanders recovered from the surprise of
the counterattack and regrouped. They brought in reinforcements and moved
their artillery units to the outskirts of Glowno.

Early on the third day, the Twenty-ninth Uhlans joined the rest of the
Wielkopolska Brigade trying to force their way into the city. But the reinforced
German 210th repelled every thrust. For twenty-four hours it was a standoff.

Then the panzer units moved in.

Lying in the grass at the top of a small hill, Jan adjusted the binoculars, focusing on the line of German tanks that seemed to stretch all the way to the
horizon. He scanned slowly, left to right, trying to get a count, difficult because
of all the dust they were kicking up. They were spreading out into attack formation. He shoved the binoculars back into the leather case and slid down the
hill. It wouldn't be long now.

He paced along the perimeter of the regiment for a last-minute check. The
Bofors anti-tank guns were set, the horses had been moved to the rear and the
riflemen were in position. They were as ready as they could be—if the Bofors
guns had the range to actually do some good.

Jan crawled back to the top of the knoll, pulled out the binoculars and swept
the horizon again. The tanks were closing in, engines growling, steel tracks

clanking and squeaking. Through the cloud of dust he spotted German infantry troops plodding along between the rows of tanks.

A flash of light caught his eye, and he squeezed the binoculars. Another flash, then a dozen more burst from the line of advancing tanks. Thunderclaps of cannon fire echoed across the flat plain, and a mountain of dirt flew across his field of vision. They were out of time.

He turned and shouted at Peracki, "Commence firing!"

The Bofors guns erupted with a deafening noise, and Jan struggled to hold the binoculars steady, following the tracer smoke. The shells were falling short. The gunners fired a second salvo, and a tank burst into flames, black smoke spewing out of the open hatch. A second tank was hit and shuddered to a halt.

But the line of clanking machines continued to advance, maneuvering around the wrecks, strafing the regiment's lines with cannon fire and machine guns.

There were too many of them. They were moving too fast.

Jan scrambled down the hill, shouting at the squadron commanders and gun crews, "Fall back! Fall back!"

It didn't help. The tanks closed in before they could set up, and the fusillade of incoming fire escalated into a torrent of paralyzing noise and blinding flashes. Polish troopers bolted for cover.

Jan crouched behind one of the gun crews, screaming at them to hold their position, when a messenger on horseback charged up from the rear, dismounted and ran over to him, shouting in his ear, "Fall back! To the Stanislawow Woods! The brigade is regrouping—"

A thunderous BOOM!

A shower of dirt and rocks!

Darkness.

Nothing.

Then . . . deep in his brain . . . a ringing noise . . . and a smell . . . acrid, foul.

Jan blinked and rolled over, his head pounding. He staggered to his feet and stared at the crater. Barely visible under the rocks and smoking pieces of twisted metal were the remains of the gun crew. He stepped back and stumbled over the messenger crawling on his hands and knees. Grabbing the terrified boy under the arm, he jerked him to his feet and shoved him after the horse that had bolted away.

Jan wiped the dirt from his face and ground his boots into the sandy soil, struggling to keep his balance. Through the smoke and haze, he spotted Stefan running toward him and waved him off. "Forget the Bofors!" Jan shouted. "Get the men back to the horses!"

In the Stanislawow Woods, halfway between Glowno and Walewice, Jan and the rest of the brigade's remaining officers crowded around a wagon in the middle of a stand of scraggly pine trees. General Abraham stood in front of the wagon, his uniform rumpled and soiled, his face streaked with dirt. When he spoke his tone was clipped and short. "Gentlemen, we're calling off the assault on Glowno. The situation farther north is deteriorating. Within the last hour we've learned that the German Fourth Panzer Division is moving toward Brochow."

A staff officer unrolled a map on the bed of the wagon and pointed to Brochow, forty kilometers to the northeast.

The general continued. "If the Germans take the bridge over the Bzura River at Brochow, the Poznan Army's entire northern flank will be exposed and the counterattack is finished." He stepped back and nodded at Colonel Romanofski.

"The brigade has been ordered to pull out of here and get up to Brochow," Romanofski said. "Our mission is to secure that bridge before the Fourth Panzer Division gets there. Get your units together and brief them. Bugle call to saddle up is in thirty minutes. Dismissed."

The Wielkopolska Brigade's remaining cavalrymen charged out of the Stanislawow Woods, heading northeast through the rural countryside toward Brochow. The main road followed the path of the Bzura River in an east–west direction to Lowicz then north to Brochow. But there was no time for the easy route. With red and white banners flying, the brigade galloped in a straight line over flat, open fields and farms. They charged through tiny hamlets, sending villagers scurrying to get out of the way.

Darkness was falling as the brigade approached Brochow from the west side of the river. The Twenty-ninth Uhlans were the first to arrive, and Jan led the regiment thundering across the bridge. The town was set back half a kilometer from the river with flat, open terrain in between. In the gathering gloom, he could just barely see the outline of houses and buildings.

He didn't spot the tanks until they opened fire.

Jan jerked his horse's reins and led the galloping regiment in a wide arc to the north hoping to outflank the tanks.

A second panzer unit emerged from the town, cutting them off.

From two directions the tanks closed in, driving the Uhlans toward the river. In another few minutes they'd be trapped. Cursing their bad luck, Jan shouted at the bugler, "Sound the retreat!" and turned his horse toward the bridge.

The Uhlans charged back across the bridge, dismounted and raced along the riverbank lugging machine guns and handheld anti-tank guns. As the brigade's other regiments arrived they dismounted, spreading out to back up the Uhlans.

When the first panzer unit reached the middle of the bridge, Jan gave the order to commence firing, and the two lead tanks erupted in flames. Their hatches flew open and frantic German crewmen scrambled to escape the fiery deathtraps, but a second line of tanks lumbered up from behind, shoving the burning wrecks over the side of the bridge.

The next hour was chaos.

The German tanks that managed to cross the bridge bulldozed through the ranks of Polish troopers, turrets swiveling, machine guns rattling, crushing the Uhlans and their anti-tank guns. German infantry units followed the tanks over the bridge, and the battle quickly degenerated into a hand-to-hand bloodbath.

Shouting over the clamor, his eyes watering from the smoke, his head pounding from the deafening noise, Jan desperately tried to bring some order to the regiment's battle lines, but it was hopeless. The only thing possible was to pick out a target and kill it before it killed you.

The tide of battle turned steadily against the Uhlans as a continuing stream of German tanks, armored cars and infantry units rumbled across the bridge. A bugle sounded the inevitable retreat and Jan, aching with fatigue, hobbled along the riverbank searching for his squadron commanders. He found Peracki, then Stefan. "Where's Bartkowicz?" Jan shouted.

Stefan looked around and shouted back. "I don't know. I think they went in closer to the bridge."

"Get your men out of here. I'll be right behind you." Jan jogged toward the bridge then stopped when he realized Stefan was right behind him. "I told you to get your men out of here."

"Brody has them, they're heading out. Let's go."

Running toward the bridge, they stopped dead in their tracks at the top of a rise. Fifty meters ahead, in the middle of a flat open area, dozens of bodies lay scattered among gaping craters and piles of smoking rubble. The silhouettes of three tanks moved off in the opposite direction. A group of Polish troopers stumbling up the slope emerged through the smoke. "Where's Kapitan Bartkowicz?" Jan yelled as the first trooper made it to the top of the rise.

The dazed boy looked at him with a blank expression and shook his head.

"Goddamn it, where's Bartkowicz?"

A second trooper pointed to the bodies in the open field. "He's dead, sir. Over there, the tanks . . . Oh, shit he's . . . they're all . . ." The exhausted trooper fell to his knees.

Stefan grabbed the boy under the arms, helped him up and shouted at Jan, "Come on, let's get out of here."

Jan stood motionless, staring into the open field at the smoking debris and dead bodies.

Stefan gripped his shoulder. "Jan, they're gone, let's go."

Jan turned and looked at Stefan. His friend had lost his helmet. His black curly hair was matted with sweat and his face streaked with dirt and blood. Jan wondered if he was hurt. Then he blinked and shook his head. "Yeah, let's go."

Chapter 12

ANNA DROPPED THE GARDEN RAKE and held her hand over her eyes, squinting at the massive bomber formation flying overhead. A few moments earlier she had been perspiring in the heat of the sun, but now she was cold. The rivulets of warm, soothing sweat running down her back turned to icy fingers of fear. She wrapped her arms around her chest and watched the droning airplanes disappear over the northern horizon. It was the sound, the thumping vibration, that brought back the memory of that horrific early morning in Warsaw.

In the peace of the Berkowicz farm it had almost been possible to believe the war wasn't happening. She was regaining her strength, the headaches had all but disappeared and the work in the gardens had lifted her spirits. But the bombers brought it all back. The thundering formations, heading north in the morning and south in the afternoon, brought with them the memories of death and destruction.

As she reached down to pick up the rake she heard someone shout, "Anna!" and looked up to see Leizer on a horse-drawn wagon entering the farmyard. The elderly farmer called out again and waved her over as he climbed off the wooden seat. She waved back and stepped carefully through the garden to the stable.

"I have some news," Leizer said as he unhitched the mellow, dappled gray gelding. "I heard a report on the radio at the post office. A counterattack is underway."

"A counterattack? Where?" Anna asked, following the old man as he led the horse to the stable.

"North of here, along the Bzura River, near Kutno and Brochow." He opened the door to the stall and gave the horse a pat on his massive hindquarter. The animal trudged into the stall, and Leizer turned to Anna, looking her in the eye. "The report said the Poznan Army and the Wielkopolska Cavalry Brigade are involved."

Anna stared at him. The icy fingers returned.

"They're brave lads," he said, "heroes. Don't you worry."

Anna heard a shuffling behind her and turned to see Irene and Justyn. "You heard?" Anna asked.

Irene nodded. She put her arm around Justyn and they walked away.

The next day Anna rode into town with Leizer. Sitting on a bench at the post office, gripping the arm with white knuckles, she listened to the announcer read a disjointed flurry of reports from the battlefield. ". . . Wielkopolska Brigade . . . battling the Fourth Panzer Division . . . Brochow . . ." Her stomach heaved.

She stood up and started for the door just as a man in the corner of the room muttered, "Poor bastards. Guys on horses aren't going to have much of a chance against those tanks."

Anna whirled around and glared at the man, who was standing with two companions near the spittoon. "One of those 'poor bastards' is my husband," she hissed. "Don't you dare say they don't have a chance! Don't you dare lose hope! Don't ever . . ." Tears streamed down her face as she turned away from the startled man and ran to the door.

She stopped outside the post office, bending over and taking deep breaths, praying she wouldn't get sick.

Leizer followed her out and stood next to her, shuffling his feet in the dirt. "I'm sorry, Anna. The man's a boor. He has no idea what he's talking about."

She straightened up. "I understand. It's all right."

"I'll take you home," Leizer said.

Anna glanced around at the activity in the town's central square. It was Saturday morning—market day. "No, let's stay awhile. You've got things to do. I'll be fine."

"Are you sure?"

"Yes, I'm sure. I'll look around the market."

The town was a dusty little village called Wiesko, which Anna had never heard of and which didn't appear on the map of Poland tacked to the door of Leizer's toolshed. One morning when she had asked about it, the old man had scratched an X on the map indicating a spot between Ostrowiec and the Vistula River.

Across the square from the post office was a tiny, whitewashed church with a tile roof. A faded inscription in Latin, *Domus Salvatoris Nostri*, painted above the stout oak door proclaimed it as The House of our Savior. A ramshackle stucco building with a rickety wooden porch occupied the left side of the square. It was the village's only store, and its odd assortment of merchandise ranged from animal feed and fertilizer to women's clothing and cookware. From a counter in the back of the building the Jewish proprietor also dispensed beer, vodka and a very potent fermented apple cider, which Anna had tried once, on her only other visit to the town. On the right side of the square was the market—a dozen wooden stalls where farmers sold vegetables, fruit, dairy products, sausages and a variety of ciders every Wednesday and Saturday morning.

Following the pungent aroma of cheese and spicy sausage, Anna wandered among the stalls, surprised at the number of local people who smiled at her, nodded and bid her good morning.

A voice behind her said, "You're something of a celebrity, you know."

She turned around to see a pudgy man of about sixty wearing a black felt hat and a rumpled woolen suit coat.

"We don't get many visitors out here," the man said. "I'm Dr. Simanski. It's good to see you up and around."

It took her a moment to make the connection. "Oh, Dr. Simanski . . . yes, of course. Forgive me but I'm afraid I don't remember much about your visit."

The doctor laughed and tipped his hat. "No, I'm sure you don't. You had a pretty nasty blow to the head." He looked around and indicated a stall where a farmer sold a mixture of apple cider and blackberry wine. "It's really quite good. Shall we have some while we talk?"

They sat in front of the church, on a bench shaded by a large oak tree, sipping the sweet beverage and watching the bustle of country people on market day. "It's hard to imagine there's a war going on," Anna said.

Dr. Simanski shrugged. "War comes and goes, but the people who work the land continue on, one generation after another."

Anna regarded the doctor. His face was creased with age, but his gray eyes were sharp and penetrating. "Are you from around here?" she asked.

He nodded. "My family had an estate a few kilometers to the east, near the Vistula. I did my medical training in Warsaw, spent some time in Radom, but this is home." He took a sip from the clay mug. "I understand you're from Krakow. You're a university professor?"

"Associate professor, actually—European history."

"Ah, history. Then you can appreciate my comment."

"That war is an inevitable part of life? That we just set aside our routine tasks to kill each other then pick them up again when it's over?"

He sighed. "Well, history teacher, when has it not been so?"

Anna shook her head and sipped the wine. "I keep hoping that one day we will rise above that."

The doctor touched her arm. "You're young and you have hope, two very good things. Do you have any plans?"

"No," Anna said, staring into the distance. "I want to get home but, to be honest, I haven't thought very far ahead."

The doctor glanced up at the huge tree towering above them. He set his empty mug on the grass and turned toward Anna. "I'm the only doctor for quite a distance so I travel between a dozen or so towns. I also go to the hospital in Ostrowiec every week. I see and hear a lot of things."

Anna didn't respond.

"The German army marched in from the west and swept through Ostrowiec in a day," he said. "The hospital administrator told me that he was relieved it was over so quickly." The doctor shook his head. "Out here, in the country-side, the people know that it's not over. Poland has always had more than one enemy. They remember—and they watch the east."

Anna turned and locked eyes with the old doctor. "The Russians are coming, aren't they?"

"They always do, Anna."

Chapter 13

JAN HANDED THE BINOCULARS to Stefan and backed away from the perimeter. He'd seen enough. Scattered among the dead horses, smashed wagons, and burned-out trucks and tanks lay the bodies of a thousand young men rotting in the midday sun. The brigade had fallen back, out of range of the German guns, their casualties staggering and the chance to take the bridge over the Bzura River lost. As he headed for the HQ tent, Jan knew it was only a matter of time before the Luftwaffe discovered their location and finished them off.

He stopped at the field hospital where a few haggard doctors were doing what they could. As Jan moved among the injured soldiers, talking quietly with them and squeezing their hands, he was amazed at how they smiled at him. Some could barely lift their heads, but when he took their hand they smiled and asked how it was going. He thought they were all so young.

When Jan arrived at the HQ tent Colonel Romanofski was standing outside conferring with one of the brigade's reconnaissance officers. "Any news about reinforcements?" Jan asked.

"Forget it," Romanofski snapped. "Lowicz has just fallen. Lodz fell last night. And we just got word from a messenger that the Germans are moving part of their Tenth Army toward Kutno." Romanofski glanced at the reconnaissance officer. "I need to talk with Jan for minute."

The officer nodded and walked away.

Romanofski looked tired and when he spoke his voice was raspy. "The counterattack is collapsing. There's a real danger that the Poznan Army will be trapped between Lowicz and Brochow within the next forty-eight hours."

Jan stared at the colonel, not knowing what to say.

Romanofski pulled a pack of cigarettes from his shirt pocket and offered one to Jan. "I just came from a meeting with General Abraham," the colonel said, striking a match. "He's received orders to move the brigade out of here."

"We're abandoning the Poznan Army?"

The colonel took a long drag on his cigarette and rubbed his bloodshot eyes. "Yes, we are. The truth is the infantry is stuck here and will eventually have to surrender. But the High Command wants to get the cavalry out."

"To where?"

"Warsaw, if we can make it . . . through the Kampinos Forest."

"The Kampinos? Jesus Christ."

"Yeah, I know," Romanofski said. "It's rugged country, and the Germans have held the whole area for over a week. But at least we might have some cover from the fuckin' Luftwaffe. Every other route is completely closed off. Abraham says the city is almost surrounded. It's the only possible way in."

"So, when do we leave?"

"Tonight. They want us out of here now, before the air attacks get any worse and we all get blown to hell."

The brigade moved out that night, circling well to the south of Brochow. As they forded the Bzura River and headed east for the Kampinos Forest, Jan felt empty. In a little over two weeks the Germans had all but crushed the bulk of Poland's armed forces. Just a few days ago the Wielkopolska Brigade charged into the Bzura valley at full gallop, bugles blowing and banners streaming, one of Poland's proudest and most formidable military organizations. Now they were escaping under the cover of darkness, leaving behind a hundred thousand of their fellow soldiers.

Jan knew it was unfair to think about it that harshly. They had no choice, the military doctrine was clear. The cavalry could save itself from the graveyard along the Bzura and the infantry couldn't—it was that simple. He was a career officer and he knew all that. Still, he felt empty.

The Kampinos Forest covered an area of more than three hundred square kilometers from the Bzura River to the outskirts of Warsaw. The Twenty-ninth Uhlans were at the head of the brigade as they entered the forest under bright moonlight. Jan had never been here before, and it was not what he expected. Large stands of birch and oak trees dotted the landscape, but they were widely spaced with virtually no underbrush. Dense tracts of pine trees were interspersed with marshes and sand dunes. Frequently they had to dismount and lead the horses through valleys of rocky, uneven terrain. The narrow, winding trails were difficult to follow, and some of them would abruptly spill out onto open, flat expanses where the cavalry had no protection at all.

It was grueling work, and by the time the sun came up the brigade was spread out over a wide area. With the daylight came Luftwaffe bombers, wave after wave of giant Heinkels that sent the cavalry troopers scattering through the trees like frightened rabbits. When the bombers drove them into the open, they were strafed by dive-bombing Stukas. From all directions Jan heard staccato bursts of artillery and machine-gun fire as other regiments ran into pockets of German forces.

By midmorning they had to stop, and Jan led the Uhlans into a low-lying area densely populated with tall conifers that offered a measure of protection from the air attacks. The regiment was down to less than half of its men, and they were desperately in need of rest. Many of the horses were lame, and those that weren't were weak with fatigue. They were so low on basic supplies that the groomers were forced to wrench the shoes off the dead horses to re-shoe those that could still walk. The worn-out troopers slid off their mounts, and as soon as they unsaddled the weary beasts and found some water, they collapsed on the ground, keeping close together in the middle of the hollow where the big trees provided the best cover.

Jan snapped awake, feeling a hand on his shoulder. He looked up to see a messenger kneeling next to him holding a small brown envelope.

"It's a message from Colonel Romanofski," the messenger said.

Jan ripped the envelope open and read the handwritten note. He glanced at the messenger then read the note a second time.

"The colonel is expecting an acknowledgement," the messenger said.

Jan studied the note and nodded. "Tell the colonel, I acknowledge."

As the messenger rode off, Jan got to his feet, rousted Stefan and Peracki and led them to a small hill where they were out of earshot of the troopers. "I just received a message from Colonel Romanofski," he said. "The Russians attacked early this morning."

The two squadron commanders stared at him.

"I don't have any details," Jan continued, "but the message says they're spread out over the entire length of the border and heading toward Warsaw."

"Don't suppose they're here to help us beat the fuckin' Germans, are they?" Peracki quipped, pulling a cigarette out of a crumpled pack.

Jan and Stefan looked at Peracki for a second then broke out in spontaneous laughter at the absurd notion. Patting Peracki on the back, Jan stood up and looked over the regiment's fatigued troopers sprawled all over the hollow. "We'll spend the rest of the morning here," he said, glancing up at the lofty pine trees. "At least we have some cover. The men and the horses need the rest. Our objective is Laski. That's the last major hurdle before we get to Warsaw. We move out at 1200."

Oberleutnant Kurt Meier felt confident as he piloted the Stuka over the treetops of the Kampinos Forest. He had flown several sorties over this area in the past three days and was now quite familiar with the terrain. This had turned out to be easier duty than the missions he had flown over Warsaw. There were no anti-aircraft batteries to worry about out here, only Polish cavalry troops trudging through the forest, and whenever they caught them in the open they were easy targets.

Meier recalled his first sortie over the area and that first attack on the cavalry troops. They had spotted them galloping across a sandy field, heading for a stand of trees. Approaching from behind, the Stukas had swooped in and caught them by surprise, mowing them down like gophers. It had been exhilarating. But every sortie after that had been the same, and now the exhilaration was gone. It was becoming routine, almost boring. He kept expecting that the Polish troopers would give up, but each time out, there they were, trotting through the trees then darting at a gallop through the open fields. A few would escape, but they would kill most of them.

The plane jolted as they passed through some low clouds, and Meier cleared his mind for the task ahead. Each day their sorties had taken them farther east as they tracked down the tenacious cavalrymen. This morning they were flying over the easternmost end of the forest, near Laski.

As he banked the plane into a turn, Meier listened to the scratchy sound of the voice coming through his earphones. Cavalry troops had been spotted at the edge of the forest. He knew the drill. Dive in at low altitude, just over the treetops. The cavalry troopers wouldn't hear them until it was too late.

• • •

As he led his squadron eastward, Stefan felt the pain returning to the small of his back. The rest stop had helped, but now his back ached and his feet were cramping again. Plodding along the uneven, rocky ground his game little mare stumbled more than she had the day before. She was nearing the limit of her strength.

They reached the edge of the forest, and Stefan held up his hand bringing the squadron to a halt. A broad, open plain spread out before them. On the other side was Laski. He looked to his right and saw Peracki, a hundred meters away, bringing the other squadron to a halt. Jan rode alongside Peracki.

The two squadrons waited inside the tree line, searching the sky, their horses standing motionless, breathing heavily, heads hanging. Stefan reached down and rubbed the tired mare's neck. "One more time," he whispered. He tightened his grip on the reins, going over the plan again. The squadrons would charge across the field simultaneously. Peracki would lead his squadron to the south, and Stefan would lead his to the north. He wished now that they had done this last night, in the dark.

Stefan leaned forward in the saddle, scanning the sky. Nothing. He looked over at Jan and saw his hand go down, signaling the charge. Stefan jabbed the heels of his boots into the mare's ribs, and the fatigued animal obediently bolted into the open.

The Stuka approached the open field, and Meier saw the scene unfolding before him. Two cavalry squadrons, appearing no larger than toy soldiers from this altitude, charged across the field toward Laski, one to the south and one to the north. The group heading south had the shorter distance and would make the tree line before the Stukas got there. But the group heading north was in trouble.

When his plane cleared the trees Meier shoved the stick down, dropping low over the field, and the doomed cavalrymen came into clear view. No banners streaming, no regimental flags snapping in the breeze, just steel-helmeted Polish Uhlans hunched low in their saddles, some wielding sabers, their horses struggling to maintain the gallop.

The lead planes opened fire, and the cavalry troopers instantly scattered in a mad panic to escape. But Meier knew it was hopeless. They were caught in the open. He sighed as he squeezed the trigger, and the Stuka's machine guns erupted in a clatter, dropping horses and riders by the dozens.

He pulled up on the stick and gained altitude, following the leaders around in a tight circle then dropped in for a second pass. This time only a few cavalry troopers were still moving, and the lead planes took care of them. Meier glanced down at the carnage and shook his head. What a shame, he thought. He had always loved horses.

Chapter 14

THE TRAIN STATION in Ostrowiec was a mess. The clamor of a hundred conversations, crying babies and raucous children resonated off the brick walls of the ancient building. Hordes of families lugging battered suitcases and farmers toting wicker baskets laden with food, clothing and household utensils overflowed onto the street amid cackling chickens and bleating goats. German soldiers leading large muzzled shepherds patrolled the platform, shouting orders and swatting with their nightsticks anyone who happened to wander too close.

Anna sat on the wooden seat of the wagon next to Leizer watching the chaotic scene, wondering what they were getting into. "Where are they all going?"

Leizer shook his head. "Some are running from the Germans, some from the Russians. Most of 'em are just scared and don't know who they're running from."

Anna turned around and glanced at Irene who sat on a hay bale in the back of the wagon, her arms wrapped protectively around Justyn. Irene had kept Justyn close ever since Warsaw, perhaps as much for her own comfort as Justyn's. Anna reached back and touched her friend's arm. "I'll go and find out about tickets. You and Justyn stay here with Leizer."

For over an hour, pushed and jostled from all directions, Anna stood in the queue at the ticket window, hoping they were doing the right thing. Leaving the comfortable womb of the Berkowicz farm had been the most difficult decision she had ever made. But with the news of the Russian invasion, something inside her screamed that they had to leave now or they might never have another chance. Irene had been terrified at the prospect of leaving, and Beata

Berkowicz begged them to stay. In the end, it was Dr. Simanski who convinced Anna they had to leave.

She recalled the somber look on the old doctor's face the day before when he had ridden out to the Berkowicz farm to deliver the news. They sat around the kitchen table for an hour, drinking coffee from tin cups, Irene sullen and quiet, Beata struggling to hold in her tears and Justyn glancing around at all of them, his eyes wide with anticipation.

"I've just come from Ostrowiec," Dr. Simanski said. "The fighting has moved off to the north. There's some talk of rail service to Krakow starting up again."

"Perhaps we should just stay here," Irene mumbled, staring at the floor.

The doctor reached over and put his hand on Irene's arm but he spoke directly to Anna. She remembered every word. "Anna, you've studied history. Poland has been occupied for much of its history, by both Germans and Russians. Life under German rule in a city like Krakow may be difficult. But the Russians ruled this part of Poland with an iron fist for over a hundred years—and they will never forget the humiliation of defeat in 1920."

Anna nodded slowly. "*Saving Civilization from the Bolsheviks.* I was fifteen, I remember the banners. Both of our husbands fought in that war. Now they're cavalry officers. If they're captured by the Russians . . ." Her voice trailed off.

"Or if their wives are captured," the doctor whispered.

"We could protect them," Leizer said, "or hide them."

Anna took the old man's gnarled hand and smiled. "No, Leizer, you couldn't. Everyone in the area knows who we are. They'd find us, and you'd all be killed—or worse."

Dr. Simanski gripped his coffee mug with both hands and closed his eyes. For a long moment he was quiet, his head moving slowly from side to side. Then he took a deep breath and looked at her.

At that moment her decision was made. Anna knew she would never forget the sadness in the old doctor's eyes when she whispered, "We cannot be here when the Russians come."

When Anna finally reached the ticket window the haggard railway agent informed her that he had no idea when, or if, there would be a train to Krakow. "Civilian rail service was suspended at the outbreak of the war," he said in a weary, bureaucratic monotone. "A few trains have formed up within the last several days, but we never know when. You'll just have to take your chances."

Anna shoved some zlotys through the window, took three tickets and pushed her way out of the station.

Leizer would not leave them. He rigged a cover over the back of the wagon with an old canvas tarp, and they sat on hay bales, nibbling on the boiled potatoes and brown bread that Beata had sent along. That night, Anna lay awake for a long time, listening to the voices of peasants singing Polish folk tunes around a campfire, thinking about Jan. Perhaps he was sitting near a similar campfire, surrounded by his men and their horses, out of harm's way. Perhaps. It was a nice thought . . . a thought she would try to keep.

Late the next afternoon an ancient, steam-hissing locomotive chugged into the station pulling four passenger cars, and hundreds of pilgrims charged the platform, overwhelming the German soldiers whose curses of "Polish swine" were drowned out in the stampede. Anna and Irene followed closely behind Leizer, who gripped Justyn's hand and forced his way onto the platform, pushing to the front of the pack. When the train halted and the door opened, the old man shoved the three of them into the car. Struggling against the crush of the throng, Anna reached out for Leizer's hand. The old man looked at her with tears in his eyes and said something in a hoarse voice that she couldn't make out. Then the crowd swept them into the car, and he was gone.

The trip took a day and a half. The train stopped so often that Anna gave up trying to keep track of where they were. They stopped in the middle of the countryside and sat for hours with the hot sun beating down on the suffocating, overcrowded cars. They were diverted onto sidings while other trains loaded with armaments and German troops roared past in the opposite direction. At one point, Anna watched with some amusement as a conductor tried to push his way through the crowd, collecting tickets. Halfway down the car, the beleaguered man retreated and never returned.

It was almost midnight when they finally arrived in Krakow. As the train rolled slowly into the station, passing stoic German soldiers standing on the platform with rifles and submachine guns, a blur of emotion and anxiety raced through Anna's mind. Would her father be at home? Was he safe? What if the house had . . .

The train jerked to a halt, and the throng of frustrated, weary travelers erupted in a mad rush to get out of the hot, smelly car. Anna gripped Irene's and Justyn's hands, struggling to stay together as the crowd pushed them toward the door and belched them onto the platform.

The scene out on the street was chaotic. Hundreds of people hurried about, some leaving the station and some trying to get in. There were no taxis and only a few buses, all of which were crammed with people and bound for towns outside the city. Anna spotted two armored cars parked directly across from the station. A group of German soldiers stood in front of the massive vehicles, smoking cigarettes and joking with each other, seemingly oblivious to the teeming mass of people around them.

When they had extricated themselves from the confusion at the station, Anna led the way along familiar streets toward Ulica Basztowa where they caught a tram at the stop across from the gates of the old city. As the tram clacked along the rails, Anna looked out the grimy window, thinking that the city appeared pretty much the same as it always had—except for the German soldiers and army trucks they passed every few blocks. She was certain that she would never get used to that.

Half an hour later they stood in the doorway of her father's home. The door opened, and Anna stared into her father's astonished face. She felt a weakness in her knees, then his strong arms around her waist as darkness closed in.

A week later, Thaddeus sat alone in his study, staring blankly into a cup of cold tea as Poland's last glimmer of hope was extinguished. It was the twenty-seventh of September, and Radio Warsaw played Chopin's "Death March" as the besieged capital capitulated. The government fled to exile in Romania, and Poland was once again partitioned by Germany and Russia.

That evening Anna came to dinner, as she had every night since her return. Thaddeus invited his friend Jozef Bujak and his wife, Elaina, to join them. Food supplies were already limited, but Janina had gone to the butcher shop early in the morning and managed to purchase some sausages, which she prepared with beets and boiled cabbage.

The nights were getting cooler. After dinner Thaddeus lit a fire in his study and poured glasses of cognac from a half-full bottle that was his last. Bujak took a sip of the smooth liquor and asked Anna about her ordeal in Warsaw.

A knot formed in Thaddeus's stomach. He had broken into tears when Anna told him the story the morning after her return. Now he listened once again to the grim tale of the bombing, the harrowing auto ride and Henryk's violent death. When Anna told about the peasants singing Polish folk songs around the campfire at the train station, Bujak slapped his hand on his knee. "That's what they'll never take from us," he snapped, "that spirit, that will to survive. They don't understand—the goose-stepping Nazi fascists or the slovenly Bolshevik mongrels—neither of them, they don't understand that we'll never just lie down and die."

Bujak got up from the leather chair and looked down at Anna. "Have you heard anything from Jan?"

Anna shook her head.

"Our prayers are with him," Bujak said.

Anna managed a smile. "Thank you."

Bujak lit a cigar while Thaddeus refilled their glasses. He blew a cloud of smoke in the air and glanced around the room. "Have any of you heard about the order issued by Field Marshal Smigly-Rydz?"

Thaddeus looked at Anna and shrugged.

"I had lunch with Fryderyk Wawrzyn today," Bujak said. "Anna, do you know . . . ?"

"Yes, I think I know who he is. A legal counsel for the city?"

Bujak nodded and continued. "According to Wawrzyn, the Field Marshal sent an order to all Polish troops still in the field to seek sanctuary in neutral countries. He has ordered them to make their way to France where the Polish army will re-form and fight on."

Thaddeus watched Anna as she stared at Bujak for a moment then stood and took a few unsteady steps toward the fireplace. He jumped up to help her.

"No, Papa, it's all right. I'll be fine." She placed a hand on the mantel and turned toward Bujak. "I know that Jan will . . ." She stopped and wiped her eyes, leaning against the brick fireplace. Thaddeus took her hand. "I know that Jan will do whatever he's ordered to do," she said. "Nothing will prevent him from doing that if . . . he's . . ."

The room fell silent except for the crackling of the fire. After a moment, Elaina asked, "Anna, how is your friend Irene?"

Anna squeezed her father's hand and wiped her eyes again. "Not very well, I'm afraid. I see her every day. She's terrified."

"Has she gone back to work?"

"Yes. She's working at the pharmacy that Stefan managed. The owners have been very kind to her, but they're concerned about their business. They keep hearing rumors about the Germans closing Jewish businesses. Just this morning, when they opened the shop they found *Jude* painted on the front window."

"Have you heard what's happening in Lublin?" Bujak asked.

"No," Anna said.

"Wawrzyn told me this as well. The Germans have been rounding up Jews in Prague and Vienna and are transporting them in railroad boxcars to Lublin."

Thaddeus was stunned. "My God, what are you talking about, Jozef?"

"Wawrzyn is part of a city delegation that was called before the Gestapo. They were told that the German Reich has begun to transport Jews from the occupied countries to Lublin."

"That's crazy," Anna said. "What are they going to do with them in Lublin?"

"Wawrzyn said they're setting up some type of camps for Jews. Probably work camps."

"Why Lublin?"

"Who knows? Probably because it's far enough east that it'll be years before anyone else in Europe ever finds out."

Thaddeus glanced at Anna. He knew she was thinking about Irene and Justyn. "Does he think this will happen in Krakow?" he asked Bujak.

"Your guess is as good as mine," Bujak said. "You know what Hitler is like."

Thaddeus pulled another log from the wood box and placed it on the glowing embers. "Does Wawrzyn know anything about the Krakow police?"

Bujak waved his hand dismissively, "They're under the control of the SS and the Feldgendarmes. They can't be trusted. We've all got to be careful dealing with the police now, especially Jews." He looked at Anna. "Your friend has to be very careful."

Anna stood facing the flickering fire, shaking her head. When she turned around her eyes were wet with tears. "I watched a woman get machine-gunned on the streets of Warsaw," she said, her voice quaking. "Henryk was killed trying to keep us alive, and God only knows what's become of my husband. Our country has been gobbled up by Germans and Russians and now Jews are being sent to work camps. We can't just sit here and do nothing, can we?"

Thaddeus felt Bujak staring at him. Bujak had not brought up the Resistance movement again, but Thaddeus was certain that it had gotten started and that his friend was involved. He knew it was only a matter of time before he would be brought into it himself. He also knew Bujak's passion—he would recruit Anna in a heartbeat. Thaddeus met Bujak's gaze and imperceptibly shook his head.

Bujak sighed, glancing at his watch. He motioned to his wife. "Well, it's late. We'd better be going." At the door, he kissed Anna's cheek and said, "What all of us can do is keep up our spirits. Your husband and others like him will get to France and join our allies. Our enemies will be defeated, one way or another. I'm certain of it."

Chapter 15

HE WATCHED AS THE PLANES CIRCLED around and dove in again, mowing down the last of the troopers caught in the open. Horses and riders fell . . . screams, shouts . . . blood. He pulled out his carbine and started shooting, shooting at the planes, the ugly, stub-winged black planes. He sighted in on one plane and fired, again and again, aiming at the glass canopy, at the god-damn pilot. He could see the pilot's face. The face looked back at him. It was Stefan. He tried to run into the field, but something held him back. He struggled. He had to get to the field. He heard a voice behind him, yelling. He struggled harder. The voice yelled.

"Jan, wake up!"

Jan snapped awake. Peracki was leaning over him, shaking his shoulder.

"You were dreaming again," Peracki grumbled and returned to his bunk.

Jan sat up and swung his legs over the side of the narrow bunk. He was drenched in sweat. He sat for a few minutes listening to the sounds of the other men sleeping then fumbled around for his pack of cigarettes, pulled on his boots and walked to the door.

The chill breeze blasted his wet body like a thousand icy daggers, and his hands trembled as he struck the match. He knew it was no use trying to go back to sleep after the dream. He'd had the same one half a dozen times since Stefan was killed in the field outside Laski.

Jan followed a dirt pathway between crude wooden barracks to the perimeter of the camp. He walked alongside a flimsy barbed wire fence and took a drag on the cigarette, recalling the Hungarian border guards who had welcomed them when what was left of his regiment trudged out of the forest the day before. He smiled as he remembered the conversation with the young officer who had explained that it was his duty to take their weapons and confine them to the camp. "I can assure you, Major, your men will be well fed and any sick or wounded attended to," the officer had said in a confusing mixture of Polish and Hungarian.

"Where is your commanding officer?" Jan demanded.

The young officer became flustered and said something about his commander being away on an inspection trip of the border.

Jan had remained on his horse, one of the few still able to carry a rider, looking down on the officer and the group of nervous border guards in their snappy, clean uniforms. His regiment was down to less than a hundred men and, though they were battle-weary and hungry, he knew they could have overwhelmed the Hungarians in a few minutes had he given the order.

Now, walking along the fence line in the moonlight, Jan looked around at the poorly constructed, haphazardly guarded internment camp, still feeling confident that they could break out if they had to. He approached the main gate and spotted two guards sitting on a wooden bench, their rifles propped against the fence. He stubbed out his cigarette, walked a few steps closer and coughed to get their attention. The guards scrambled to their feet and stared at him. Jan joined them and said in Polish, "Couldn't sleep."

The guards looked at each other and shook their heads.

"*Sprechen Sie Deutsch?*" Jan asked.

The taller of the two nodded, and Jan repeated what he had said in German.

The guard laughed and explained to his partner in Hungarian. He turned back to Jan and, speaking passable German, asked, "Have you been to Warsaw?"

Jan nodded.

"Was it bad?"

"We arrived just before the end," Jan said. "The city was in ruins, thousands of civilians dead."

The German-speaking guard translated for his partner. The partner said something in Hungarian and they both nodded.

"What did he say?" Jan asked.

"He wonders who'll kill us first, the Germans or the Russians."

The next day Jan was summoned to the camp commander's office. When he entered the small cabin, a lanky officer with slick black hair and a pencil-thin mustache stepped around from behind a desk and extended his hand. Speaking

Polish, the officer said, "Welcome, Major Kopernik. I am Colonel Sebastian Tolnai, commanding officer of the Second Hungarian Hussars."

Jan shook his hand.

The Hungarian colonel smiled. "Please, Major Kopernik, have a seat. I have heard about your brigade. You fought in the battle of the Bzura River, if I recall correctly, and then you went on to Warsaw?"

"That's right," Jan replied.

Colonel Tolnai offered him a cigarette and lit it for him. "Please, tell me what happened."

Jan leaned forward, looking down at the floor. The vision of Stefan caught in the open field flashed through his mind. He wouldn't talk about that. "The last few days around Warsaw were completely chaotic," he said. "The bombardments were nonstop, and it was impossible to keep the brigade together. We were practically out of ammunition, and completely out of food and water." He leaned back in the chair, wiping perspiration from his forehead. "The city was a mess, fires everywhere, no running water, thousands of corpses . . . women . . . children . . ."

Jan stopped and ground out the cigarette in the ashtray. He stood up and walked to the window, looking out at the rows of wooden barracks. "Just before the city capitulated, we received orders to get our units out of the area. We were ordered to head for Hungary or Romania and then to France."

Colonel Tolnai picked up a document and glanced at it. "Have you heard that the Polish government-in-exile has moved on to Paris? General Sikorski is now in charge."

Jan shook his head. "I didn't know. But Sikorski's a good man."

The colonel motioned to the chair, and Jan sat down again. "So, Major, as you headed south how did you manage to avoid capture by the Russians?"

"I guess we were lucky," Jan said. "We traveled mostly at night, tried to keep off the main roads. We'd lay low during the day and send out a few men at a time to scrounge for food. The cold and the rain in the mountains were the worst part."

"You are the senior officer?"

"Yes. Our brigade commander, General Abraham was wounded and taken to a hospital. The deputy commander, Colonel Romanofski, was killed by a sniper."

Colonel Tolnai leaned forward, his hands folded on the desk. "As a fellow officer, you have my admiration, Major Kopernik." He hesitated a moment, then cleared his throat and continued. "You understand, of course, that my government's official position in this conflict is one of neutrality. I am under orders to hold you and your men in confinement. Your men will be well taken care of. They will be in no danger."

Jan looked into the colonel's eyes. "And I'm sure you understand, Colonel Tolnai, that I, too, have orders. Those orders are to get my men to France."

Colonel Tolnai stood up and walked around the desk. "This is a temporary border camp. Polish troops have been arriving for the past week. We have sent most of them on to the permanent camp at Putnok." He extended his hand. "Perhaps, Major Kopernik, you and your men could remain here for a while. I can make no promises but, for the time being, accept our hospitality, such as it is."

Jan stood and took the colonel's hand. "My men are tired. They need food and rest. For the time being, Colonel, we accept your hospitality. But I have my orders."

Chapter 16

THADDEUS WASN'T SURPRISED when it was announced that the beginning of the fall term at Jagiellonian University was being postponed. The heel of the conqueror had come down hard as the German Wehrmacht pulled out and the SS moved in. Bombardments gave way to executions. Villages were burned to the ground. The borders were sealed. Newspapers and radio stations were shut down. Hitler's destruction of Polish society had begun, and Thaddeus could only imagine what must be happening in the Russian-controlled regions.

He was in his office, going through the morning's mail, when a brown envelope caught his eye. Leaping out from the upper left-hand corner was the eagle and swastika. The envelope was addressed to *Dr. Thaddeus T. Piekarski, Professor of Law, Jagiellonian University.* He held it in his hand for several minutes, turning it over, considering the possibilities of its contents. Finally, he slit it open and inside found a card from the *Office of the Governor.* He read the card in astonishment. It was an invitation. He was asked to attend a seminar on *The Philosophy of the German Reich toward the Sciences.* He reread the incredible document. The seminar was being held next week, right here at the university—the university the Nazis were threatening to close.

Baffled by the implausible piece of mail, Thaddeus walked down the hall to Bujak's office. His colleague was on the telephone so Thaddeus stood in the doorway impatiently until Bujak finally hung up. Thaddeus held out the invitation. "Did you receive one of these?"

"Yes, incredible isn't it?" Bujak replied.

"What do you suppose it's all about?"

"I haven't a clue. Perhaps they want to convince us that they're not complete barbarians."

"Like hell," Thaddeus snapped. "They'll probably bring in some phony Nazi scientists and try to 'educate' us about the superiority of the Teutonic race. Are you going?"

"Our attendance is mandatory."

"Oh, really?"

"From the Rector himself. He told me about an hour ago. Anyone who gets this is required to be there. I'm sure you'll hear from him yourself."

"Do you know who got these?" Thaddeus was thinking about Anna.

"According to the Rector, only full professors, department heads, and 'others of special standing' received them."

"'Others of special standing'? What does that mean?"

Bujak shrugged.

"Well," Thaddeus said, with some relief, "they probably didn't invite Anna. She'll be spared the problem of refusing to attend."

Thaddeus spent the rest of the day trying to keep busy with paperwork, but the bizarre invitation continually crept back into his mind. A little after three o'clock in the afternoon he looked up to see Anna standing in the doorway of his office. Her eyes conveyed a need to talk. He finished filling out a requisition form for new textbooks—as if he would actually need them—and they left the building together. It was a damp, chilly October afternoon, and the sun was already low in the western sky as they walked in the direction of Anna's apartment.

"Irene called me about an hour ago," Anna said when they were alone on the sidewalk. "She's beside herself."

"What happened?"

"Two Krakow policemen and a German SS officer came into the Ginsberg's pharmacy today and shut it down."

"What?"

"That's only the beginning."

Thaddeus stopped and looked at her.

"They demanded to see Irene's ID card," Anna said, "Mr. Ginsberg's also. He was the only other one in the store at the time. She said they stamped a large black J on the front of each card and threw them on the counter. She . . ." Anna stopped and took a deep breath. "She said the SS officer told her to carry the card with her at all times. If she was ever caught without it or if she tried to alter it she would be shot."

"For the love of God," Thaddeus said, running a hand through his white hair.

"Irene said they were ordered out—couldn't even get their coats. They told Mr. Ginsberg that if he tried to come back he'd be shot."

They started walking in silence. After several minutes Thaddeus said, "I think Irene and Justyn should move into the house with me."

"What?"

"I'm serious. Things will be very difficult for her now. For one thing, she's just lost her livelihood. She probably won't be able to keep her apartment. But, more important, if they're shutting down Jewish businesses there's no telling what may happen next. They'll be safer staying with me."

"Papa, are you sure?"

"Yes, absolutely. I've got plenty of room, and Janina would love to have them around. Irene can be a big help."

"You know that's not what I mean," Anna said, looking around. She lowered her voice. "It could be dangerous for you."

"If anyone asks, I'll tell them they work for me; they're housekeepers."

She looked at him, skeptically.

"There's no other choice. Let's go get them."

"Now?"

"Yes, right now."

That evening Janina prepared a simple meal of beef stew for the new extended family. Afterward, Thaddeus sat at the table, drinking coffee with Anna. Justyn had gone upstairs to do his schoolwork, and Irene was in the kitchen helping Janina with the dishes. Thaddeus handed the seminar invitation to Anna. She read it then looked up, frowning. "A seminar? What's this all about?"

"Amazing, isn't it?"

Irene came in from the kitchen. "What is it?" she asked. Anna handed her the card. Irene read it and shook her head. "I don't understand . . . the philosophy of the German Reich toward the sciences? Are they serious?"

Anna pushed her coffee cup aside. "I don't understand either. Papa, who else got this?"

Thaddeus shrugged. "Apparently all professors and department heads at the university. Other than that, I don't know."

Irene pulled out a chair and sat down. "Certainly you're not thinking of going, are you?"

Thaddeus glanced at her. "Word came down from the Rector that attendance is mandatory."

Anna and Irene stared at each other.

"I'm sure he wasn't given a choice," Thaddeus said.

Anna gripped her father's arm. "Papa, I have a bad feeling about this. I really don't think you should go."

"Oh, I don't think there's anything to worry about. My guess is they want a captive audience so they can strut around and impress us with how advanced they are and tell us how lucky *we* are to have them taking over. What else could it possibly be?"

Anna shook her head. "God only knows. I don't trust them. Just sitting in the same room with the vile creatures would make my skin crawl."

"That's probably why they didn't invite you."

"Don't joke about it," she exclaimed. "They're up to something."

Thaddeus took his daughter's hand. "No, it's not a joke. It's tragic. It's tragic that we have to go and listen to them lecture us about their magnificent new society while they're murdering our countrymen." He glanced at Irene. "It's tragic that they're here at all. But that's what's happened."

Irene leaned across the table, her eyes wide. "Thaddeus, Anna's right. You can't—"

"I have no choice," he interrupted. "The Rector made that quite clear. I'm certain that the SS or the Gestapo, or whoever the hell is organizing this told him that they expect a full turnout. And I'm not going to put him in jeopardy."

Thaddeus could see the frustration in his daughter's eyes as Anna got up and carried her empty cup to the kitchen. He glanced at Irene who slumped back in the chair, shaking her head.

Anna returned to the dining room and kissed him on the cheek. "You're right, Papa . . . the whole thing is an absolute tragedy. I'm going home to bed."

At 7:45 on the night of the seminar, Thaddeus, Bujak and Fryderyk Wawrzyn walked up the tree-lined pathway leading to the Collegium Novum, the main building of Jagiellonian University. At each of the five archways framing the entrance of the neo-Gothic structure, black-uniformed SS troopers stood at attention. Thaddeus followed his colleagues up the steps and into the building. They proceeded across the atrium and entered the Lectures Hall. He was not surprised to see the large red flag, with the now all too familiar white circle and black swastika, hanging from the stage.

As they made their way down the left aisle, Thaddeus looked around the auditorium, recognizing many of his colleagues from the university as well as a number of professors from other colleges in the area. He spotted the headmasters from some of the local vocational schools and several bankers, doctors, businessowners and lawyers. He guessed there were close to two hundred in all, most of them looking around the room nodding and smiling but not saying much.

As they took their seats, Wawrzyn leaned over and whispered, "Rather a subdued group, wouldn't you say?"

Thaddeus nodded. "That goddamn flag will do it."

"Perhaps they should have provided champagne," Bujak said, a little louder than necessary. The comment drew some smiles and nods from the men seated in front of them.

At exactly eight o'clock, the house lights dimmed and a spotlight shown on the podium in the center of the stage. An SS officer stepped briskly across the stage to the podium.

"Hun efficiency, right on time," Bujak whispered.

The officer looked over the crowd and began speaking in German. "*Guten Abend, ich bin* SS-Sturmbannfuhrer Mueller. I represent the German Reich, which has rescued the Polish people by overthrowing their corrupt and warmongering government."

A murmur rippled through the crowd. Dozens of men translated for those who didn't speak German.

Sturmbannfuhrer Mueller continued, "Under the enlightened guidance of the Reich, the New Poland will be transformed into a model society of workers freed from this yoke of oppression."

Bujak nudged Thaddeus with his elbow. "What the hell is this garbage?"

Mueller paused and looked over the audience, his bearing erect and deliberate. Then he thumped his hand on the podium. "For many years, this university and other institutions within the city of Krakow have been guilty of subversion and anti-German activity. This treasonous behavior will no longer be tolerated."

The murmuring grew louder. A knot formed in Thaddeus's stomach.

At the podium, Mueller looked up and glanced at the back of the room. He nodded.

Thaddeus jumped in his seat as the doors at the back of the room banged open. The house lights brightened, and two columns of SS troopers carrying submachine guns stomped into the auditorium. The black-clad troopers marched up the aisles, did an abrupt turn and stood facing the stunned audience.

Mueller declared, "You are all under arrest!"

The audience erupted. Dozens of men leaped from their seats shouting at the SS officer.

"You can't do that!"

"We've done nothing wrong!"

"It's against the law!"

A man sitting behind Thaddeus leaned forward and grabbed his shoulder. "What did he say? I can't understand."

Thaddeus was about to translate for him when Mueller screamed from the podium, "*Ruhe jetzt!* Silence!"

The room instantly fell silent.

"*Setzen Sie!*" he shouted. The SS troopers leaned into the rows, pointing submachine guns at a few shaken men still standing. They slumped into their seats.

"You are prisoners of the German Reich," Mueller said, his tone of voice lower but cold and menacing. "Do exactly as you are told and no harm will come to you. Anyone who tries to escape will be shot!"

Murmurs and groans rippled through the audience, excited voices translating. The man behind Thaddeus tugged at his shoulder.

"*Ruhe!*" Mueller commanded. "From this point on, none of you are allowed to speak!" Anyone who disobeys my orders will be shot! Beginning with the front row, you will stand and file out the back of the auditorium. There are trucks waiting outside. Do not speak to anyone, and do not attempt to escape or you will be shot."

Thaddeus's stomach heaved. He swallowed hard and clenched his hands together, praying he wouldn't get sick. He glanced at Bujak. His burly friend's face was red with rage, sweat dripping from his forehead. When it came time for their row to file out, Bujak hoisted his bulky body out of the seat then rocked back on his heels, bumping into Thaddeus. Thaddeus put a hand on his back to steady him, but an SS trooper reached over and grabbed Bujak by the collar.

"*Raus! Raus!* Move it, fat ass!" the trooper snarled, pulling him into the aisle.

Bujak jerked away, mumbling something under his breath.

The trooper instantly jabbed him in the back with the butt of the submachine gun. Bujak grunted and staggered forward, grabbing the shoulder of the man in front of him.

Thaddeus quickly stepped into the aisle in front of the SS trooper and gripped Bujak under the arm to steady him as they proceeded toward the door.

Outside the building a line of green-uniformed Feldgendarmes barked orders and swung nightsticks, herding the bewildered crowd toward a convoy of canvas-covered trucks. Thaddeus kept a grip on Bujak's arm, praying his profusely sweating friend wouldn't stumble. When Bujak attempted to climb into the truck, his foot slipped off the bumper and he fell heavily on the cobblestones. Thaddeus reached for him, but a Feldgendarme charged in and shoved him aside. The German policeman swung his nightstick and brought it down in a crushing blow on Bujak's shoulder. Without thinking, Thaddeus jumped in front of the Feldgendarme and gripped Bujak under the arms. Another man grabbed Bujak around the waist and they hoisted him into the truck.

Thaddeus scrambled into the truck after his friend, expecting the crunch of a nightstick to come any second. Holding Bujak up, he stumbled forward in the dark canvas enclosure, pushed along by the bodies being shoved in behind them. The Feldgendarme jumped up on the bed of the truck and ordered everyone to sit on the floor. He swatted two men standing near him who didn't react soon enough. Thaddeus was shoved against a metal railing at the front of the truck and had to kick the man in front of him to avoid getting crushed. Bujak collapsed heavily at his side. The Feldgendarme jumped to the ground and pulled a curtain across the back of the truck.

Chapter 17

ANNA AWOKE EARLY. The telephone rang just as she climbed out of bed. Glancing at the brass clock on her bed table, she hurried to the hallway and picked up the phone. It was a few minutes past six.

The voice on the other end was frantic. "Anna, something has happened . . . I don't know . . . he didn't . . ."

Anna could barely understand. "Irene? Slow down. What is it?"

A deep breath, then, "Anna, your father . . . I don't know what . . ."

"Irene! What are you talking about?"

"Last night, the seminar . . . he never came home."

The fog of sleep lifted quickly as Anna remembered the seminar. "He didn't come home?"

"No. But it wasn't very late and we went to bed. But this morning—"

"Irene, stop! Stop and take a breath and tell me slowly exactly what happened."

A pause. Then Irene's voice, quieter. "He hadn't come home by the time we went to bed, but it wasn't very late, so I didn't think much about it. But, when we didn't see him this morning I . . . Oh, God, Anna, I'm sorry." A deep breath. "His hat and coat weren't hanging on the hook in the hallway. I knocked on his door, but he wasn't there. They've done something, Anna!"

Anna stepped backward, leaning against the wall, staring at the beige and gold floral print of the wallpaper, trying to think. "Irene, listen to me. Perhaps he got into an accident. Maybe he was injured on the tram. He might have been taken to a hospital. I'll make some calls and—"

"Anna, Dr. Bujak is missing too."

"He is? How do you know?"

"Just as I was going to call you, the telephone rang. It was Mrs. Bujak. She wanted to know if your father was home."

Anna slumped to the oak parquet floor. It wasn't making sense.

"Anna? Are you there?"

"Yes, I'm here." Anna heard her own voice as if from a distance. "I don't know what's going on . . . I've got to think . . . I've . . . got to make some calls. I'll be over as soon as I can."

"What could have happened? What—"

"I don't know what happened!" Anna snapped, interrupting her friend. She paused and closed her eyes. "Irene, I don't know what happened. I'll make some calls. Look after Janina, I'm sure she's pretty upset. I'll be over as soon as I can."

Anna's knees were weak as she got to her feet and hung up the phone. She put a hand on the wall and breathed slowly, in and out, her eyes resting on the walnut shelf above the phone table. She reached out and slid a finger gently over the smooth surface of the cut-glass model of a hand that rested on the shelf along with her Hummel collection. It was the symbol of Antwerp, a gift from the Leffards when she graduated from university. Her father had been so proud.

She shook her head, wiping away a tear, and stepped unsteadily into the small, tiled kitchen, opened the cupboard and took out a glass. She tried filling it with water, but her hands were shaking so badly that the glass slipped and shattered in the sink among last night's dirty dishes.

She slumped into one of the arrow-back chairs and propped her elbows on the walnut pedestal table her father had given her and Jan as a wedding present. Who could she call? No one would be at the university at this hour. *Think! Think!* A name came to mind: Wawrzyn, a friend of her father's. What was his first name? Fryderyk, that was it! Fryderyk Wawrzyn. He was some type of lawyer for the city. Would he have been at the meeting?

She ran to the hall table, grabbed the telephone book and ripped through the pages.

A woman answered on the first ring. "Hello?" Her voice was tentative, nervous.

"Is this Mrs. Wawrzyn?" Anna asked, forcing herself to speak calmly.

"Yes. Who is this?"

"Mrs. Wawrzyn, my name is Anna Kopernik. I'm Thaddeus Piekarski's daughter."

"Oh yes, Thaddeus," she said excitedly. "Is Fryderyk there with Thaddeus?"

Anna's heart sank. She started to speak but nothing came out. She put her hand over the mouthpiece, breathing rapidly. She tried again. "No, Mrs. Wawrzyn, your husband's not here. My father didn't come home last night. I was hoping you might know something."

Silence.

"Mrs. Wawrzyn?" Anna picked up the small cut-glass hand from the shelf and turned it over, rubbing the smooth surfaces with her fingers. It was heavy and solid, its feel familiar and reassuring.

"I knew this would happen," the woman sobbed. "When I heard you mention your father's name, I hoped that . . ." Her voice trailed off.

"Mrs. Wawrzyn, have you called anyone else?"

"Yes, I did. I . . . excuse me, I'm sorry. Yes, I called Felek, Fryderyk's assistant. But he had no idea. He wasn't invited to the meeting. He suggested I call the Rector at his home and I did, but there was no answer. I just don't know. Should we call the police?"

"The police? No! I mean, no, not yet. Don't call them yet. Let me check into this. I'll call you back . . . all right?"

"Oh, yes . . . thank you. I'll wait to hear from you."

"Mrs. Wawrzyn, this assistant of your husband, what's his last name?"

"Felek? Oh, it's . . . excuse me . . . I've been up all night and I can't . . . just a minute, dear. Here it is. It's Slomak, Felek Slomak. Do you want his number?"

"Yes, thank you."

Felek Slomak agreed to meet Anna inside the Mariacki Church at ten o'clock that morning. When Anna entered the cavernous basilica, it took a moment for her eyes to adjust. The muted sunlight filtering through stained-glass windows at either end only partially illuminated the baroque interior, which smelled faintly of incense. She walked slowly down the Gothic nave, under the arched stone vaulting, glancing at the familiar blue and gold walls decorated with Matejko friezes. Her heels clicked on the ancient stone floor as she passed a group of worshippers kneeling in front of the Chapel of Our Lady of Czestochowa with its image of the Black Madonna. Halfway up the nave she stopped and glanced around, spotting a thin, balding man with steel-rimmed spectacles sitting alone in a pew. She made a quick sign of the cross and slipped into the pew. "Mr. Slomak?" she whispered.

"Yes, Felek Slomak," the man said, his eyes darting around. Several groups of people knelt in the pews at the front of the church, near the altar.

"Thank you for agreeing to meet me," Anna said. "Have you found out anything?"

Slomak nodded then leaned close to her. Anna noticed beads of perspiration on his forehead. He spoke in a whisper. "I have a few contacts in the city government that I can trust. The few still left. I spoke with one of them right after you called." He paused, glancing around a second time. "Your father . . . along with everyone else who attended the seminar, was arrested by the SS."

It took a moment to sink in. "Arrested . . . ?"

"I'm sorry, Mrs. Kopernik."

"Why?"

Slomak hesitated. "According to my contact, it may be the beginning of—" He shook his head. "I'm sorry, Anna, I really don't know."

"What are you saying? . . . the beginning . . . I don't understand . . ."

"The Nazis may have considered them a threat."

"A threat? How could they feel threatened by some college professors?"

Slomak took out a handkerchief and wiped his brow. "Mrs. Kopernik, I really don't know. Let me check into it some more. I'll—"

"Where have they been taken? What's going to happen?"

He folded the handkerchief and put it back in his pocket. "I don't know. Neither did my contact. Give me a few days. I'll contact you."

"What can I do in the meantime? Who can I call? There's got to be someone."

Slomak touched her arm. "I know how you must feel, Mrs. Kopernik. But please try and understand. There's nothing you can do. There's no one you can call. The SS and the Gestapo have spies everywhere."

Anna bit her lower lip. She felt like she would explode.

Slomak gathered his hat and coat. "I'll contact you. You have my word. Give me a few days."

Anna sat in the church for a while after Slomak left, gazing at the majestic high altar at the east end. The immense three-paneled wood carving crafted by the Nuremberg master Veit Stoss was perhaps the finest example of Gothic art in all of Europe. Anna had known it her whole life, but she stared at it as though seeing it for the first time. She studied the gilded figures of the Holy Family on the outer panels of the folded triptych then closed her eyes, recalling the scene on the center panel, her favorite, visible only on Sundays when the altarpiece was opened. The exquisite life-size figures of the Dormition of the Virgin depicted the graceful figure of Mary reclining into her final sleep in the arms of the Apostles. It had always reminded her of her mother, a graceful soul ascending into heaven. Her father had sat with her on those Sundays . . .

She left the church and walked across the Rynek Glowny, glaring in contempt at the red swastika banner hanging from the town hall. She crossed the Planty and waited while a tram rumbled past. A large sign in the window of each car proclaimed, *Juden Verboten*. She thought about Irene and Justyn, and her anxiety deepened. Just a few days ago, the boy had been sent home from school in tears. Jews were now forbidden to go to school. She felt like she was suffocating, as if she were caught in the jaws of a giant vise squeezing the life out of her. Get control, she told herself. Get control and think.

She spotted a small café, went inside and ordered a cup of tea. Sitting quietly in a corner, she forced herself to concentrate. Going back to the university was unthinkable. The Germans would very likely shut it down soon anyway. She stared into the cup and saw only darkness. She felt dizzy, nauseated. She closed her eyes and swallowed. Breathe . . . breathe. She took a sip of the tea. One day at a time, she thought. Take it one day at a time and wait to hear from Slomak.

Chapter 18

ON HIS WAY BACK to the barracks of the internment camp after the regiment's morning calisthenics, Jan stopped in his tracks and stared into the late October sky, awestruck by the hundreds of enormous white and black birds thundering overhead. In a cacophony of whooping and flapping, the flock of majestic Common Cranes headed south over the woodlands of eastern Hungary on the way to winter resting grounds in Africa.

"Spectacular isn't it?" came a voice from behind him. It was Peracki.

Jan glanced at him and nodded, then looked back at the sky. "I remember reading about this when I was a boy. Never imagined I'd see it in the middle of a war."

"Anything new from Tolnai about getting us out of here?" Peracki asked, wiping his face with a towel.

Jan shook his head. "No, nothing yet."

"You must be getting to know him pretty well by now. What've you had, five or six meetings?"

Jan smiled at his only remaining squadron commander. "Yeah, something like that. I'm getting tired of that apricot brandy he keeps in the desk drawer, but he sure loves to talk. He's quite well educated, traveled all over Europe, loves music, literature, beyond me most of the time. But he's been guarded about everything else."

"Any chance of sending a message back home?"

"None. On that he's been very clear. The borders are sealed, telephones and telegraphs are down. Poland's cut off."

They walked on in silence. Peracki jerked his thumb toward the rickety chicken-wire fence strung between thin wooden posts with a single roll of barbed wire strung along the top. "Say the word, Jan. You know the men will jump at the chance."

Jan looked his friend in the eye. "I know they would, but what then? We're foreigners in a neutral country under German influence—no horses, no passports, a thousand kilometers from France." He glanced around, making sure they were alone. "It may come to that, Lech, but we're not there yet. Tolnai has gone out of his way to keep us here, and he's chosen to spend a lot of time with me. I don't know what it all means, but for some reason I trust him."

Peracki nodded and threw the towel over his shoulder. "Or, maybe he just wants someone to talk to."

That night the tall German-speaking guard found Jan and said that Colonel Tolnai wanted to see him. This time, however, Tolnai was waiting for him outside. When the guard departed, the colonel motioned for Jan to follow, and they walked in silence to the main gate where the guard on duty unlocked it and pushed it open.

They walked out of the camp and about a hundred meters down a narrow dirt road cut through a dense stand of conifers. It was a clear night, under a full moon, the crisp autumn air pungent with the scent of pine. Tolnai stopped and turned toward Jan. "Fifty meters farther down the road you'll come to a bridge. On the other side of the bridge, there'll be an auto with a man inside who would like to talk to you."

Jan glared at the colonel, wary.

Tolnai smiled. "Trust me, there's no danger. Go. When you're finished, walk back to the gate and the guard will let you in. Then come and see me."

Before Jan could respond the colonel turned and started back to the camp.

Jan stood motionless, watching the colonel disappear up the road. Except for the night breeze rustling the pine trees, it was completely quiet. His hands were clammy, and he wiped them on his pants before continuing down the road. He crossed the one-lane plank bridge and spotted a black sedan parked off to the side. He approached the vehicle slowly, and when he got to the driver's side window, he bent down and peered inside. A man with thick black hair looked up at him. Speaking Polish, the man said, "Good evening, Major. Please come around to the other side and get in the car."

Jan stood where he was. "Who are you?"

"If you get in the car, you'll find out. Please, Major, I'm straining my neck looking up at you."

Jan stepped around to the passenger side of the sedan and got in. The man behind the wheel smiled and extended his hand. "Major Kopernik, my name is 'Ludwik.' I am an officer with the Polish Free Forces under the command of General Sikorski."

Jan didn't respond. The man appeared to be about fifty years old. He was slightly paunchy and was wearing corduroy trousers and a dark pullover sweater.

The man's smile disappeared, and he folded his hands in his lap. "Major, I understand that this probably seems very strange to you, but—"

"That's an understatement," Jan snapped.

The man exhaled slowly. "Allow me to explain, if you would, please."

"Go ahead."

"Thank you. Now, Major, you have orders to get your men to France and join the Polish Free Forces. I'm here to help you do that."

Jan's eyes narrowed.

"It's true. I have the means at my disposal to get you and your men into France."

"When?"

"When you have completed a task for General Sikorski and the Polish Resistance."

"The Resistance? What the hell would I know about that? I'm a soldier."

"I'm well aware of the fact that you're a soldier. So am I, and I'm here under the authority of General Sikorski. We've got a job that we need you to do."

Ludwik started to reach into the back of the car, but Jan grabbed his arm, pinning it against the seat.

"Whoa, hold on, Major. I just want to get a briefcase."

Still gripping the smaller man's arm, Jan glanced into the rear of the car. A brown leather case was lying on the backseat. He released his arm. "Sorry, go ahead."

"Perfectly understandable, Major. No problem." Ludwik grabbed the leather case, placed it on his lap and looked at Jan. "Major, a little over a week ago, the SS conducted a *special action* in Krakow. They arrested over two hundred university professors and other prominent citizens and sent them to a concentration camp in Germany."

Jan stared at him.

"Among those arrested were two key Resistance operatives. A vital link in our communication network has been severed, and it is extremely important that it be re-established."

Jan tried to concentrate on what Ludwik was saying but his thoughts drifted: "university professors . . . prominent citizens of Krakow." Anna's father? . . . Anna? . . . *No, don't do that. Don't* . . . He blinked and tried to focus on the man sitting next to him.

"Major? Are you all right?"

"Yes . . . I'm . . . Please, go on."

"Well, as I said, it is vital that we re-establish the communication link in Krakow. You have been identified as someone who can help us do that."

"Me? How?"

"You speak fluent German, as I understand."

"Yes, that's right."

"And you've lived in Krakow; you know the city."

"Just a couple of years—and I was away a lot . . . the military . . ."

"All the better. Less chance you'll be recognized."

"Recognized?"

"We want you to go to Krakow, Major. And deliver a package for us."

Chapter 19

ANNA WALKED INTO THE MARIACKI CHURCH and slid into the pew next to Felek Slomak. This time the church was practically empty. She spotted only two other people, a young couple kneeling at an altar in one of the side chapels. As soon as she saw Slomak's face she knew the news was bad.

"I'm sorry I haven't gotten back to you before now," he whispered, "but I wanted to be absolutely certain about your father."

Anna realized she was holding her breath.

"They've been taken to a place called Sachsenhausen," Slomak said. "It's a prison camp in Germany."

"Germany?" The word caught in her throat. Anna gripped the back of the pew. "What's going to . . . ?" She couldn't find the words.

It took Slomak a long time to respond. "Anna, there's something you need to know. Your father's friend, Jozef Bujak, and the man I work for, Fryderyk Wawrzyn, were involved in the Polish Resistance."

"What?"

"The AK, Armia Krajowa, it's a Resistance movement, just getting started—Bujak and Wawrzyn were involved."

Anna's mind was a blur. What was he talking about?

"I don't know about your father, but it probably wouldn't matter. If the Gestapo knew about Bujak and Wawrzyn, his association with them would be enough to—"

"Good God, is that why they were arrested?"

Slomak shook his head. "No, I don't think so. According to my sources the arrest was what the Germans call a *sonderaktion*—a special action—to eliminate intellectuals and people of influence. It's happening all over the country."

"Then what's all this about the Resistance?"

"From what I've been able to find out, the Gestapo knew about Bujak and Wawrzyn. They would have been arrested soon anyway."

Anna's eyes drifted to the front of the church and the magnificent high altar. She had heard that the Germans planned to remove it and take it to Germany. Tears filled her eyes, blurring the image. She could feel her father's presence, sitting next to her as he had on so many Sunday mornings, gentle and kind, always there, always. "He's not coming back, is he?"

Slomak shook his head, wordlessly.

They left the church and walked across the Rynek Glowny. There was a November chill in the air, and the sky was heavy with steel-gray clouds. It was a little after four o'clock in the afternoon, and the vast square was bustling with people hurrying to buy whatever meager supplies they could find before the shops closed.

Slomak knew a pub just off the other side of the square and they slipped inside. They were the only patrons. He ordered a glass of wine for each of them, and they sat in silence until the elderly proprietor brought the glasses and disappeared into the back room.

Anna took a sip. She could hardly swallow it.

Slomak set his glass on the table and leaned forward. "Anna, you should get out of Poland."

She blinked and sat back in her chair. "What are you talking about?"

"I think you should get out of Poland."

"Felek, that's crazy." She looked to see if the proprietor had come back in the room. He hadn't. She lowered her voice. "It's not like any of us can just get on a train and leave, you know."

"I know." He held the stem of his wineglass between his thumb and forefinger, staring at the red liquid inside. "But . . . there are ways."

"Felek, you're scaring me. Am I in danger?"

Slomak hesitated then looked up. "Yes, it's possible you are."

"What?"

"Anna, no one knows what these people might do. But we're finding out every day that they're capable of atrocities no one dreamed were possible." He locked eyes with her. "Right now, they may not know you're Dr. Piekarski's daughter—"

"Oh, God!"

He reached over and touched her hand. "Anna, I don't think they know, but I certainly haven't asked anyone. I wouldn't use your name." He glanced at the door to the back room. They were still alone. "My sources have told me that the Gestapo are tracking down the families of anyone even remotely connected with the Resistance. They're very thorough. I think they'll eventually put it together."

"But why would they bother with me? I'm nobody."

"Anna, they've shot people for walking on the wrong side of the street, you know that. You're the daughter of a prominent law professor, a well-known Polish patriot who has close ties to people active in the Resistance—and you're the wife of a Polish cavalry officer. Think about it."

For two days Anna wandered through the apartment, mired in the muck of what could only be a bad dream. She shuffled back and forth, from the tiled kitchen through the hallway into the parlor, slumped onto the brown velvet sofa and stood in front of the leaded-glass window, staring at the street below, pondering the situation. Irene and Justyn had moved in with her. Janina had gone home to her mother. Would it make a difference? Were they safe from Gestapo thugs tracking down families? She lay awake at night, waiting for a pounding on the door. She thought about her father and cried. She thought about Jan and cried. She thought about Slomak—about getting out of Poland—and it overwhelmed her. Could she trust him? What did she really know about him?

Then, in the evening of the second day, the dream ended and reality smacked her in the face. She walked into the kitchen and found Irene sitting at the table, staring ashen-faced at the newspaper. Irene stood up and handed her the paper. The announcement was printed in red ink.

EFFECTIVE IMMEDIATELY

ALL JEWS OVER THE AGE OF NINE ARE ORDERED TO WEAR A WHITE ARMBAND MARKED WITH A YELLOW STAR OF ZION ON THE RIGHT SLEEVE OF THEIR INNER AND OUTER GARMENTS. ANY JEW NOT WEARING A STAR WILL BE EXECUTED ON THE SPOT.

HANS FRANK, GOVERNOR
GENERAL GOVERNMENT OF POLAND

Anna sat heavily, rereading the announcement. She glanced up at her friend. "Irene, I don't know what to say."

Irene leaned against the tiled wall, staring at the floor. Her voice was barely audible. "There's something else."

Anna waited.

"I haven't told you . . . but I think . . ." Irene folded her arms across her chest. There were tears in her eyes. "I think I'm pregnant."

Anna exhaled slowly, dropping the paper on the table.

Irene sobbed. The tears streamed down her face.

"How far along are you?"

"Three months, maybe. I'm not sure."

Anna stood up and stepped over to her friend, taking her hands.

"Anna . . . this baby . . . what will happen?"

"You're going to be just fine, dear. Don't worry. Justyn and I are right here with you. We'll—"

Irene jerked her hands away and backed toward the doorway. "Don't worry? Anna! For God's sake!" Her face was red. She began to tremble, spitting out the words. "I'm a *Jew!* They'll probably . . . they'll . . . Oh God!" She slumped to the floor, burying her face in her hands.

Anna got down on her knees and held her friend in her arms. Tomorrow she would call Slomak.

Chapter 20

SLOMAK WAS WAITING for her outside the church. "Let's walk," he said. "It's safer." It was noon and the Rynek Glowny was busy. They melted into the crowd.

"Where are we going?" Anna asked.

"Just keep walking," Slomak said. "The Gestapo arrested Mrs. Bujak and Mrs. Wawrzyn last night."

Anna stopped and stared at him.

Slomak took her arm. "Please, keep walking, Anna." They walked across the vast square toward the massive Renaissance Cloth Hall. Slomak continued, "Bujak's son and his family were staying with Mrs. Bujak. They were also arrested."

Anna could hardly breathe. Arrested? Last night? She thought about Irene and Justyn back at her apartment and stopped again. "Felek . . . do they know about me?"

He turned and stepped close to her, whispering. "I don't know, but it's only a matter of time. You've got to get out."

"Get out? Get out of where? Krakow? Poland? What the hell are you talking about?"

Slomak glanced around. Anna saw fear in the eyes behind his thick glasses. He took her arm again. "Keep walking—and keep your voice down."

They walked around the Cloth Hall and crossed the tree-lined Planty. Slomak handed her a slip of paper. "Go to this address and see a man named Di Stefano; he's expecting you."

Anna stopped and grabbed the sleeve of Slomak's coat. "Felek, this is crazy!

You're scaring the hell out of me. Who is this Di Stefano? What's this all about?"

Slomak took a deep breath. "His name is Mario Di Stefano. He can help you. That's all I can say."

"Help me? Help me with what?"

Slomak took her hand. His eyes were intense. For the first time she realized she was actually taller than he was. "Anna, listen to me. You're in danger. You've got to get out. Di Stefano can help you. Go and see him."

"When?"

"Now."

"Now? Felek . . . Good God . . . I . . ."

"Right now, Anna. Don't waste any time."

Anna was still shaking when she got off the tram on Ulica Rakowicka. She turned the corner onto Grochowska and looked for the address Slomak had given her. It was at the end of the block, a gray three-story apartment building. The row of buttons had names below them. She pushed the one marked *Di Stefano*. The buzzer sounded, and she pushed open the heavy wrought-iron door. As she stepped into the foyer, a door opened across the way and a handsome, dark-haired man wearing an expensive-looking gray suit stepped out. "Good afternoon, Mrs. Kopernik. Please come in." He spoke Polish with an Italian accent.

He ushered her into a small but well-appointed room. In the center stood a round mahogany table and four chairs on a red oriental rug. Two upholstered chairs stood on either side of the only window. On her left was a sideboard with a silver tea service.

The man took Anna's coat, laid it over one of the upholstered chairs and offered her a seat at the table, which was covered with thick folders. "Allow me to introduce myself, Mrs. Kopernik. My name is Mario Di Stefano. I am in charge of a special diplomatic mission to Poland on behalf of the government of Italy."

Anna glanced around the small room.

"Our office is actually in Warsaw," Di Stefano added, "but since I come to Krakow every week, I have found it convenient to keep a second, smaller office here. May I offer you some tea, or coffee, perhaps?"

Anna shook her head. "No, thank you."

Di Stefano smiled and sat down across from her. "Mrs. Kopernik, the government of Italy is trying to maintain relations with Poland under what we all realize are extremely difficult circumstances."

Anna remained silent.

Di Stefano leaned back in his chair and folded his hands in his lap. "Regardless of any opinions you may have about Italy, Mrs. Kopernik, let me assure you that, at the present time, our official policy toward the conflict between Germany and Poland is one of neutrality. The people of Italy are sympathetic with the plight of the people of Poland, and in certain cases we can offer our assistance."

"Assistance? Certain cases? I'm afraid I'm not following you Mr. Di Stefano."

"I know your father, Mrs. Kopernik."

It took her breath away. "My . . . father?"

Di Stefano leaned forward, smiling. "Yes. I met your father, Dr. Piekarski, two years ago, at the European Law Symposium in Rome."

Anna had a flicker of recognition. She remembered her father talking about the trip.

Di Stefano continued. "We served on a committee together, and we have corresponded occasionally since then." His expression darkened. "I was deeply disturbed when I heard the news of his arrest from Mr. Slomak."

"He told you about that?"

"Yes. He knows about our diplomatic mission here and has made other referrals. When he brought up your name and told me about the arrests at the university, I became curious. Eventually your father's name came up, and of course, I told him I would meet with you immediately."

"I'm afraid I still don't understand, Mr. Di Stefano. Referrals for what?"

He smiled. "Mr. Slomak is even more discreet than I imagined. He didn't tell you?"

Anna shook her head.

"Mrs. Kopernik, I can arrange a travel visa for you to Italy."

Anna stared at the Italian diplomat, not sure that she understood what he had just said.

Di Stefano waited for a moment then elaborated. "The government of Italy is offering a limited number of travel visas to certain citizens of Poland. The purpose of our diplomatic mission here is to facilitate the process. Obviously, we cannot accommodate everyone who might want to come, so we are operating on a very confidential, referral basis."

"Italy? I'm sorry, I don't . . ." She didn't know what to say. Nothing made sense.

"From Italy you could go anywhere in Europe," Di Stefano said.

Anna sat back in the chair, rubbing her temples. Could they do it? Just . . . leave? She thought about Irene and Justyn and looked at the man across the table. "Mr. Di Stefano, this is . . . overwhelming . . . but . . ."

"But?" He raised his eyebrows.

"I have a very close friend. She just lost her mother and has no other family. Our husbands are serving together in the cavalry. My friend has a ten-year-old son. I couldn't leave them."

He looked at her for a long moment then nodded. "Of course, Mrs. Kopernik. I will also accommodate your friend and her son."

"They're Jewish, Mr. Di Stefano."

Di Stefano was silent for a moment. "I see. Well I'm sure we can still—"

"My friend's passport and identification papers have been stamped with a J. I can't risk any surprises when we get to Italy."

"Our government is not anti-Semitic, Mrs. Kopernik. They will be welcome."

"Will the Germans let them out of Poland?"

He leaned forward, clasped his hands on the table and exhaled slowly. "That, of course, is the question, isn't it?" He paused, glancing at the folders on the table. "They will be traveling with legal visas issued by the government of Italy. We have issued these to other Jews who have successfully entered our country."

"All of them?"

"I don't know, Mrs. Kopernik. But I will be honest with you—I doubt that they all made it."

Anna closed her eyes. Visions of the German soldiers and muzzled dogs at the train station in Ostrowiec flashed through her mind.

Di Stefano waited until she looked at him. "I am confident that your friends will have no problem with the Italian immigration authorities. I'm also quite sure that they will not have a problem with the Polish police. Even the German Wehrmacht will probably not bother them. The unknown, of course, is the SS. One never knows where they will show up or what they will do. There's no guarantee, Mrs. Kopernik. I will issue their visas. Beyond that, unfortunately, I have no control."

Anna stood and stepped to the window. A solitary woman clutching a paper sack, her head covered with a gray shawl entered a building across the street.

Was it possible? Had a door suddenly opened? From Italy they could get to France—or Belgium. They could get to Rene and Mimi Leffard.

Di Stefano's voice interrupted her thoughts. "However, you must understand the highly confidential nature of our mission here. No one must know where you and your friends are going or we will be overwhelmed. You will have to promise me that you will just quietly slip away."

"When could this be done?" Anna asked, her voice barely a whisper.

"Come back tomorrow at this same time, and I will have the visas for you." Anna's eyes widened. "Tomorrow?"

Di Stefano stood up and stepped over to the upholstered chair. He picked up Anna's coat. "Mrs. Kopernik, I urge you to move quickly. Quite frankly, the German Reich is putting pressure on our government to close this mission. I have no idea how much longer this opportunity will be available." He held her coat while she slipped it on. "Given what's happened to your father, Mrs. Kopernik, you should leave immediately."

Chapter 21

THE TRAIN GATHERED SPEED as it pulled away from the last stop in Hungary and crossed the border into Poland. The only remaining passengers in Jan's car were German soldiers and a few civilian men. The civilians were dressed much the same way he was: dark suits, conservative ties, topcoats folded neatly on the overhead racks. He wondered if they were *real* Gestapo agents.

He slid a hand under his suit coat and touched the leather pouch in the breast pocket for perhaps the hundredth time. He had been rehearsing for two days but was still unnerved by the diplomatic passport, emblazoned with the swastika, identifying him as Heinrich Brunkhorst, agent of the Gestapo.

He heard a *hiss* as the door of the car opened and a Polish conductor stepped into the car followed by two SS officers. Jan looked down at his newspaper, pretending to read. The car became quiet.

Shortly after they'd left Budapest, a sloppily dressed Hungarian conductor had given his papers a cursory glance and moved on. But this was a different crew and a different drill. The presence of the SS was clearly having an effect on the Polish conductor. He spoke heavily accented German, demanding "tickets and papers" as they stopped at each row of seats. The passengers gave their papers to the conductor and the conductor handed them to the SS officers who scrutinized them and barked questions. Jan struggled to control his breathing as the conductor and SS officers continued down the aisle, approaching his row. He remembered what Ludwik had said about his papers. "Good, but not perfect . . . should hold up as long as you,"—what were the words?—"looked and acted convincing."

He felt a jab in his ribs. The German soldier sitting next to him, in the seat by the window, was moving around. Earlier in the trip, the soldier had been drinking out of a bottle wrapped in paper and had eventually fallen asleep. Now he was awake and mumbling about needing to take a piss.

The soldier leaned over and rolled his head toward Jan. His eyes were bloodshot and his head bobbed around like it was mounted on a swivel. He sputtered, "*Aus,* let me out—or I'll piss all over you."

Jan tried to ignore him.

The conductor and the two SS officers stopped at the row in front of them. The conductor had just handed a set of papers to the SS officers when the drunken soldier tried to stand up, stumbled and fell on top of Jan. "*Verdammt!* Move!" the soldier slurred, flailing his arms in the air.

Jan's reaction was instantaneous. He leaped from his seat into the aisle and shouted at the soldier, "*Schweinhund!* What the hell do you think you're doing?" He whirled toward the conductor and shoved a finger into his face. "You! Get this drunken bastard out of here!"

The conductor froze.

Jan screamed at him, "*Jetzt!* Now, asshole! Get this scumbag out of here or I'll have these officers throw your ass out the window!"

The wide-eyed conductor dropped his notebook on the floor and reached past Jan. He grabbed the drunken soldier under the arms and started maneuvering him down the aisle toward the end of the car.

Jan stood in the aisle. He could feel everyone in the car looking at him. The two SS officers, caught off-guard by his sudden outburst, had regrouped and were glaring at him. Jan smiled at them and slapped the one closest to him on the arm. "Ah, don't worry about it," he said. "I don't really care how drunk he gets. God knows they deserve their fun. I just didn't want him puking all over my new suit."

The black-uniformed officers stared at him for a moment then broke out laughing. The one he had slapped on the shoulder said, "*Ja,* and I just polished these boots. He better not puke on them."

The two officers moved down the aisle without asking for his papers.

Chapter 22

THE VISAS WERE LYING on the kitchen table. Irene stared at them then looked up at Anna. Her face was pale, and she clasped her hands together to keep them from shaking. "What would we do in Italy?" she asked, her voice raspy.

Anna smiled, forcing herself to stay calm. "It's a way out of Poland, Irene. Once we're in Italy, we can make our way to Belgium—to the Leffards' home in Antwerp."

Irene reached out and brushed her fingers over one of the visas. It was the one pasted to her passport—the passport stamped with a black J. "The Leffards?"

"You remember, Rene and Mimi Leffard, my father's friends in Antwerp. I lived with them when I was attending university."

Irene nodded. "But Stefan and Jan? What if they come back here?"

Anna reached across the table and took her friend's hand. "You know they won't be coming back, Irene. They're on their way to France."

"Or, they're prisoners in some camp."

Anna stood up. "No. They're not prisoners." She leaned on the table and looked Irene in the eye. "If they were prisoners—and they're not—but if they were, they'd never be allowed to return home. You know that. They're officers, the Germans would—" She took a deep breath and glanced at the ceiling. "They're on their way to France."

Justyn's voice came from the doorway. "How long will it take?"

Irene held out her hand and the thin, pale-faced boy stepped over to his mother. Anna was worried about him. Her father had adored Justyn and always spent time with him when Jan and Stefan were away. Since the arrest, the boy had been sullen and quiet, spending most of his time sitting on his bed with a book. Irene put her arm around her son and smiled. "Not long, dear, a day or two, perhaps." She wiped a tear from her eye and looked at Anna. "Isn't that right?"

Anna nodded. "Yes, not long."

They packed lightly and left that evening, tiptoeing down the two flights of stairs. Leaving without saying good-bye to anyone was the hardest part. Anna kept telling herself it was only temporary; they would return when the war was over.

On the ground floor they stepped lightly across the foyer, past the door to the Grucas' apartment. Anna prayed that the elderly couple wouldn't hear them and open their door. Yet another part of her hoped that they would.

Out on the street, they walked down Ulica Marka, turned the corner on Slawkowska and headed toward the train station. It was three hours before curfew, and though it was dark, there were other pedestrians on the streets. Irene and Justyn wore their white armbands with the bright yellow stars. Anna knew it was a risk; the Germans had begun randomly pulling Jews off the street. But they had legal travel visas and a reason to be walking to the train station. Would it matter? Anna walked faster. Thinking about it made her sick to her stomach.

The street outside the station was busy, and they headed for the entrance, mingling with the crowd. Out of the corner of her eye, Anna spotted three Feldgendarmes leaning against the building. "Look straight ahead and keep walking," she whispered to Irene and Justyn.

As they passed the green-uniformed German policemen, one of them called out to Justyn in heavily accented Polish, "Hey, Jew-boy, catch," and flipped a cigarette butt at him. It bounced off the boy's shoulder. Anna and Irene grabbed Justyn's hands and hustled him into the terminal.

They waited in the queue at the ticket counter for over a half hour while the only agent on duty, a thickset man of about fifty with a shock of unruly white hair and thick glasses, methodically collected money and issued tickets. When they finally got to the window, Anna said, "Three one-way tickets to Milan, please."

The ticket agent peered at her, then at Irene and Justyn, his eyes moving down to their armbands. "Milan? You have visas?"

Anna shoved the passports and visas under the window.

The agent took his time, studying each document, comparing the photographs. Finally, he shrugged and shoved the documents back under the window. "There's a train leaving for Berlin at ten o'clock. You can make a connection there for Milan."

Anna felt a tingling on the back of her neck. She shot a quick glance at Irene, who looked as if she was going to faint, and turned back to the agent. "Is there another way? Another connection we can make?"

The agent hesitated for a moment then nodded. "There's a train to Prague that has a connection with Vienna. From there you can get a train to Milan. Takes longer, though, and doesn't leave until tomorrow morning."

"That will be fine; we'll wait," Anna said. "Give us three tickets."

Chapter 23

THE TRIP OVER THE CARPATHIANS from the Hungarian border to Krakow seemed interminable as the plodding train switched tracks countless times, avoiding the Russian-held region of eastern Poland. Jan had finally fallen into a restless sleep after several depressing hours staring through dirt-streaked windows at the grim reminders of defeat. Shattered apartment buildings, churches and hospitals. Burned-out market towns littered with wrecked trucks, wagons and other debris of war. And everywhere, in every train station in every town and village, the heavy footprint of the invader—German soldiers, trucks and tanks, swastika banners and large signs with the heading, *Achtung!*

It was mid-afternoon when the train finally pulled into the station in Krakow. It was overcast and gloomy with a drizzling rain. Jan shook off the cobwebs of sleep and followed the other passengers along the platform, up the steps and out of the station.

He walked along Ulica Pawia and glanced around at the familiar street. It was bizarre. He felt like a stranger, as if he was trespassing on someone's property. Through the horrors of the last two months, the one thing that had sustained him was the hope of coming back . . . to his home . . . to Anna. Now he was here and he felt like a stranger.

He pulled his hat down to fend off the rain and thought about his plan. He would make his contact and deliver the documents in his briefcase. Then he would find Anna. The fear crept back, the gripping fear that she might be . . . *No! Stop it!* He would find her and take her with him . . . back to Hungary. How he would manage it, he wasn't sure. But somehow he—

The growl of a powerful engine startled him. He glanced over his shoulder and jumped out of the way just in time to avoid being drenched as the accelerating car splashed through a puddle and sped past him. Jan caught a glimpse of men in black uniforms sitting in the rear. He put his head down and hurried toward the hotel.

The tired-looking, dark-haired man behind the reception desk at the Hotel Polonia snapped to attention when Jan handed him his diplomatic passport. "*Guten Tag* . . . Herr Brunkhorst," the man stammered in very poor German. "It is pleasure to have you stay with us. I get bell boy to assist with bags?"

"*Nein*, that won't be necessary," Jan snapped. "Is there a telephone in the room? Do they work in this decrepit city?"

"*Ja, natürlich*, Herr Brunkhorst." The man was nervous. A bead of perspiration slid down his forehead. "Is anything else I can do?"

"*Nein*, nothing else." Jan grabbed the key and walked to the elevators. He would never get used to this.

Inside the small, stuffy room, Jan threw the briefcase on the bed and picked up the phone. The same nervous man at the front desk connected him to an outside line, and Jan gave the operator the number he had memorized. On the second ring a man answered and, speaking Polish, Jan initiated the conversation he had rehearsed a dozen times. "Is Mr. Slomak in?"

"This is Slomak."

"I bring greetings from Ludwik," Jan said.

There was a long pause. When the voice on the other end responded the tone was cautious. "Is Ludwik well?"

"Yes, he is fine. I'd like to tell you about his new project."

Another pause, this time shorter. "Yes, of course. We could meet at the Café Zarwas, just off the Rynek Glowny. Do you know it?"

A picture flashed through Jan's mind: red and green walls and bright yellow tablecloths. He and Anna had been there the week before he left. "Yes, I know it. I'll meet you there in an hour."

Jan left the hotel and walked across the busy street, through the gates of the old city and into the Stare Miasto district. It was getting colder, and the rain had turned to sleet. The cobblestone streets were wet and slick. He did not head for the Rynek Glowny. He knew they were not meeting at the Café Zarwas.

Jan shook his head in disgust at the covert activity. He felt ridiculous. His military training had prepared him to meet the enemy head-on, not slink around in the shadows. Get this over with, he thought. Get rid of the documents in the briefcase and get on with finding Anna.

He walked quickly, trying to avoid eye contact with other pedestrians, thinking about Ludwik's warnings—orders, actually. "Get in and get out as quickly as you can. Avoid people as much as possible and—above all—do not reveal your real name to Slomak. It will put both of you in grave danger if he knows who you are."

Jan stopped at an intersection and pretended to look into a shop window as a German army truck rumbled down the street. He looked at his reflection, wondering what he was getting into.

He turned away from the shop, continued on to Ulica Sienna and located the address he had memorized. He stepped into the foyer and pushed the buzzer marked *101*. A moment later, a thin, balding man wearing steel-rimmed eyeglasses opened the door.

"Mr. Slomak?" Jan asked.

The man nodded and glanced up and down the street. "Please, come in."

Slomak led him into a sparsely furnished apartment, took his dripping hat and coat, and hung them on a hook near the door. He motioned for Jan to take a seat at the table. "Would you like a drink?"

"Yes, thank you," Jan said, realizing how cold he was.

Slomak opened a wooden cabinet and extracted a bottle of vodka and two small glasses. He filled both glasses and sat down at the table. "Have you brought the 'architectural drawings'?"

Jan swallowed the vodka, nodded and opened the briefcase. He removed the thick brown envelope and laid it on the table.

Slomak picked up the envelope, got up from the table and stepped over to a bureau. He opened the top drawer, placed the envelope inside and closed it. Then he opened the second drawer and withdrew a different envelope. He sat down and laid the envelope on the table. "Give this to Ludwik," he said.

"I wasn't expecting to take anything back."

"This just came in. It's very important. Ludwik will know what to do with it."

Jan looked at the envelope but didn't pick it up. He realized that he had not thought about anything beyond delivering the documents and finding Anna.

"Is there a problem?" Slomak asked. "You *are* going back, aren't you?"

Jan picked up the envelope and put it in the briefcase. "Yes, of course," he said. "There's no problem. It will get to Ludwik."

Slomak stared at him. His eyes narrowed and he leaned forward. "You understand it's vital that Ludwik gets this information. The Germans have closed all the schools and universities. They've shut down the newspapers and the publishing houses. Thousands of people have already been arrested and either executed or thrown into work camps." He paused and adjusted his eyeglasses, then took a deep breath. "When you leave here I will no longer exist. The information in that envelope is a critical link in our connection with the outside world."

Jan regarded the thin, intense man. When they parted, Jan would be going to France to carry on the fight. But it would be with an army—thousands of well-trained, well-equipped soldiers, in the company of allies. This man was staying here in Poland, going underground in the midst of the enemy. He stood up and gripped Slomak's hand. "I'll get it to Ludwik," Jan said. "You have my word. Good luck to you."

Slomak shrugged. "We make our own luck."

Chapter 24

ANNA SNAPPED AWAKE and glanced at her watch as the train came to a halt with a burst of venting steam inside the central station in Prague. It was almost midnight. She stretched and looked across the aisle at Irene who was pale and perspiring. Justyn was curled up in the seat next to her. Anna reached over and touched her friend's arm. "Are you all right?" she asked.

Irene nodded. Her voice was a whisper. "Just a little nauseated. I'll be glad to get some fresh air." She leaned over and whispered to Justyn, shaking his shoulder gently.

Anna reached into the luggage rack above her seat and retrieved their coats and the two small bags, handing one to Justyn, who yawned and rubbed his eyes. She helped Irene with her coat, and they followed the other passengers off the train.

Anna glanced around at the grand Art Nouveau terminal building. She had been to Prague once before, with her father, the summer she graduated from university. Tears welled up in her eyes, and she pushed the memory out of her mind. It was an eternity ago.

They were making their way through the terminal when Irene suddenly stopped and gripped Anna's arm, her face dripping with perspiration and her black hair matted against her forehead. "I've got to use the toilet," she whispered. "I'll be right back."

Anna's first impulse was to go with her and make sure she was all right. Then she thought about Justyn, a ten-year-old with a star on his sleeve, alone in the middle of a train station in a German-occupied city. "I should stay with Justyn," Anna said. "Will you be all right?"

Irene bent down and said to Justyn, "Stay with Anna. I'll only be a minute."

"We'll wait right over there," Anna said, pointing to a section of benches in the center of the station.

Irene glanced over her shoulder, nodded and hurried away.

Ten minutes passed. Then another ten minutes. Anna stood up, took Justyn by the hand and led him toward the toilets. They were a few meters from the door when a woman burst out yelling in Czech. Anna couldn't understand but broke into a run. When they reached the door, she dropped her bag on the floor and knelt down in front of Justyn, pushing him gently against the wall. "Stay right here. I'll be out in a minute."

The boy stared at her with wide eyes and nodded.

Anna rushed into the toilet and found Irene lying on the floor, her legs and shoes covered in blood. The female bathroom attendant stood in the corner, wide-eyed, clutching some neatly folded towels in her trembling hands. Anna knelt down beside her unconscious friend and checked to make sure she was breathing. "Please, wet one of those towels and hand it to me," Anna said to the attendant.

The woman flinched and mumbled some words in Czech.

Anna stood up, grabbed a towel from the startled woman's hand and stepped over to the sink. Then the door burst open and two policemen charged in. They shouted a few coarse words in Czech and pushed her aside. Out of the corner of her eye Anna saw Justyn peeking through the open door.

"Mama!" the boy shrieked and ran into the room. Before Anna could grab him he was on the floor, his arms around his mother's neck, crying out, "Mama! Mama!"

The policeman shouted again and pulled a long black nightstick from the holster on his belt.

"No!" Anna yelled, pushing past the burly policeman. She knelt down beside the boy. "Justyn, it's all right. It's—"

Anna suddenly felt a sharp jab on her shoulder from the policeman's nightstick. Wincing in pain, she looked up at him. "It's all right. I'll take care of her."

The policeman's face reddened. He reached down and grabbed Anna under the arm, jerking her to her feet. The second policeman grasped Justyn by the wrist, but the boy screamed and swung his free arm, striking the man in the face. The policeman pushed the boy away and started reaching for his nightstick when a voice bellowed out in German, *"Ruhe, jetzt!* Silence! What the hell's going on?"

The policeman holding Anna released his grip and backed up as an SS officer stepped into the room. Anna immediately took Justyn's hand and pulled him close to her, dragging his feet through the blood.

The terrified boy tried to squirm away and cried again, "Mama!"

The SS officer glared at Anna and the attendant. *"Raus!"* he snapped, and waved his hand toward the door. *"Raus jetzt!"* The attendant immediately started backing out of the room, leaving bloody footprints on the dirty tile floor. She motioned for Anna to follow.

Anna clenched her arms tightly around Justyn and managed a few words in German. *"Bitte, Offizier,* this is my friend. I'm trying to help her."

The SS officer took a step closer. *"Raus! Jetzt!"*

With her arms around Justyn, Anna tried to pull him from the room. The boy kicked his feet and hollered, "No! I'm not going!" Anna leaned over and whispered sharply in his ear, "Justyn! Stop it! Settle down."

When she got him out of the room Anna knelt down, gripped Justyn by the shoulders and looked into his frantic eyes. "Justyn, please listen to me."

"Mama's dead!" the boy wailed.

"No! She's not dead, Justyn. She just fainted. She's not dead. We'll get a doctor."

Anna realized that a crowd had gathered and called out, "Does anyone speak Polish?"

A tall man wearing a white shirt and tie pushed his way through the crowd and extended his hand to help her up. "I am Karel Zajic, the assistant station manager," the man said in Polish. He helped Anna to her feet, reached down and scooped Justyn into his arms and pushed through the crowd. He led Anna to one of the benches and set Justyn down. The boy was quiet now, but tears were streaming down his face. "I've called for the ambulance. They should be here any moment. What happened?" Zajic asked.

"My friend collapsed. She's pregnant and—" Anna stopped and took a breath. She looked down at Justyn and put her hand on the boy's shoulder. He leaned against her. Anna took another breath and looked back at the man named Zajic. "My name is Anna Kopernik. This is Justyn. My friend is his mother."

Zajic nodded. "I assume you just arrived on the train from Krakow. Are you staying in Prague? Do you have relatives here?"

"No, we're on our way to Milan," Anna replied.

"Milan? You have visas?"

"Yes."

The sound of sirens pierced through the station, and Zajic motioned for Anna to sit down. "Listen carefully, please. With the SS present, the police won't give out any information to foreigners. You'll have to stay out of the way. Have a seat here, and I'll find out where they'll be taking your friend."

Anna stood silently, her heart pounding.

Two medics carrying a stretcher entered the station and Zajic waved at them, pointing toward the toilet. "Stay here," he said. "I'll be right back."

Anna felt Justyn tugging at her sleeve and sat down next to him. "Is Mama going to be all right?" he asked. His eyes were red and his face streaked with tears.

Anna wiped his face with her fingers, put her arm around him and sat back on the bench. "The doctors are here now. They'll take care of her, let's just wait and see."

It was less than fifteen minutes, but it seemed like an hour, when the medics came through the door carrying Irene on the stretcher and hustled through the station toward the main entrance. The SS officer was right behind them. Anna got to her feet, took Justyn's hand and started to follow them when Justyn jerked away.

"I can walk by myself," the boy grumbled.

"Justyn, I'm sorry, but—"

Anna saw Zajic walking toward her, motioning for her to stay where she was. The two policemen stood by the door of the toilet. "It's OK Justyn, just stay here, next to me."

Zajic stepped up to her. "They're taking your friend to a hospital not far from here. The policemen want her passport."

"I'll bring it with me to the hospital," Anna said. "Can I get a taxi?"

Zajic shook his head. "No, they want it now. I told them you don't speak Czech and that I was helping out."

"I'm not just going to hand her passport to the police," Anna snapped. She glanced past Zajic. The two policemen were watching them.

"Mrs. Kopernik, please understand," Zajic said. "You don't have a choice. They must have her passport to admit her to the hospital. Trust me, this isn't something you want to make an issue of."

Anna looked into the tall man's dark eyes then glanced at the policemen again. One stood fidgeting with his nightstick. She reached into her handbag, extracted Irene's passport and handed it to Zajic.

"I want to go with Mama," Justyn said.

Anna knelt down and took the boy's hands. "Justyn, please, listen to me. Do you remember what your mother and I said about the Germans, about how we have to act around them?"

The boy nodded, tears trickling down his cheeks.

"This is one of those times," she said. "We'll go see your mother, but we have to be patient."

Justyn nodded again and turned away.

After a minute or two of conversation with the policemen, Zajic returned. He smiled at Anna and patted Justyn on the shoulder. "Please, come with me to my office. I'll make some tea."

Anna shook her head. "Thank you, but I'd rather just go to the hospital and see about my friend."

Zajic sighed. "Mrs. Kopernik, it's almost one o'clock in the morning. Visiting hours ended long ago. You've just come from Poland, so I'm sure you understand how things are. Czechoslovakia has been occupied for over a year; one must be very careful about rules and regulations." He placed a hand on her shoulder and extended his other hand, pointing down the hallway. "You won't be able to see your friend until tomorrow afternoon. Please, come with me and have a cup of tea."

"Tomorrow?" Justyn wailed. "I want to see my mother!"

"I know you do, Justyn," Zajic said, patiently. "But that won't be possible right now. The doctors are with her. Will you trust me?"

"Can I see her tomorrow?" he asked.

"Yes, perhaps . . . if she's feeling better."

Zajic's office was on the second floor of the station, overlooking the red-tiled roofs and church spires of the Stare Mesto, Prague's medieval old town. He poured the tea and managed to find some cookies for Justyn, but the boy ignored them and curled up in a brown leather chair. Anna joined Zajic at a small table in the corner and took a sip of the warm, sweet tea. The image of Irene lying on the filthy floor in a pool of blood burned in her mind.

"Do you have anywhere to stay tonight?" Zajic asked.

Anna blinked. "No, not really," she said, realizing she hadn't thought about that until just this minute. "I guess we'll get a hotel nearby."

Zajic leaned forward putting both hands around his cup of tea. "Mrs. Kopernik—"

"Anna. Please, call me Anna."

He smiled at her. "All right, Anna it is." He spoke quietly. "Staying at a hotel would not be wise."

Anna felt the tingling on the back of her neck again. Icy fingers.

Zajic continued. "The hotels are obligated to report all Jewish guests to the authorities. I realize your friends have travel visas for Italy, and had you just passed on through, chances are they'd have had no problems. But now that you have to stay, there's no telling what may happen."

Anna swallowed hard. Tears trickled down her face.

Zajic paused while she set down the teacup and rummaged through her handbag for a handkerchief.

"I'm all right," she said, wiping away the tears. "Go ahead." She glanced at Justyn. He was still sitting in the same position, curled up and staring at the floor, clutching his woolen cap against his face.

"Perhaps your friend will be feeling better by tomorrow, and you'll be on your way before anyone bothers you," Zajic said. "On the other hand, it's a risk. The Germans started deporting Jews from Czechoslovakia to Poland over a month ago."

Anna felt a dull throb in her temples. "Yes, I know. But, what choice do we have? If we can't see Irene until tomorrow we'll just have to chance it."

"Let me suggest another alternative," Zajic said. "A woman I know runs a small rooming house in the Stare Mesto district. It's not a hotel so she doesn't have to file any reports—and it's small enough that no one ever bothers her."

"I don't know . . ."

Zajic looked her in the eye. "I've sent Jewish travelers to her before, Anna. Everyone calls her 'Mama Zdena.' She speaks German and she's very discreet. You'd be quite safe." He got up and stepped over to his desk. "With your permission, I'll give her a call."

Anna looked up at him, warily. This was crazy—who was this man? Why would he care?

As if he were reading her mind, Zajic said, "I have relatives in Poland, Anna. We haven't heard from them in months. I'd like to help."

Chapter 25

It was late afternoon, and Jan stood in a freezing drizzle in the tiny triangular-shaped park at the corner of Marka and Reformaka, his stomach in knots. Across the street was their apartment building. He glanced around. The area was deserted save for two nuns huddled together under an umbrella just disappearing through the front archway of the convent down the street. He looked back at the gray stone building and stared at the two second floor windows nearest the corner, hoping for a sign of activity. Ludwik's final order flashed through his mind: *Do not make any attempt to contact your family or anyone you know.* Jan tightened his grip on the briefcase, thinking about the envelope inside he had promised to deliver. His entire career had been built on obeying orders.

He crossed the street, entered the building and took the key ring out of his pocket to unlock the foyer door. Then he saw it: the heavy, wrought iron door was open and the glass was missing, jagged around the edges as though it had been smashed. He ran down the hallway, raced up two flights of steps, punching the button that turned on the stairwell lights, and stopped in front of the door to their apartment. He listened for some sound of movement.

Nothing.

He found the second key on the ring and reached for the lock. But this door was ajar, too. He looked closer, examining the casing. It was cracked, as though someone had forced the door. He pushed it open, stepped inside and froze.

The parlor was a mess: furniture turned over, lamps broken, papers and books scattered on the floor. Jan stepped into the room, calling out, "Anna!"

He crossed the parlor, stumbling over the litter and stopped in the hallway, staring in disbelief at the broken pictures and fragments of Anna's Hummel collection lying on the parquet floor. He turned toward the bedroom door. It was closed. He stared at it, terrified, his hand trembling as he reached for the knob. When the door creaked open it was all he could do not to close his eyes. He started breathing again when he saw the room. The covers had been ripped off the bed and the bureau drawers dumped out—but Anna wasn't there.

He was dizzy and his heart pounded as he lurched back through the hallway and into the kitchen, crunching through broken glass. He yelled again, "Anna!"

Jan had no idea how long he had been sitting on the kitchen floor, but he suddenly realized it was almost dark. He got to his feet, picked up the briefcase and shuffled back through the ransacked apartment. He stood in the middle of the parlor, looking around at the chaos, when his eyes fell on a familiar object reflecting a thin beam of light from the streetlamp outside. It was a small cut-glass model of a hand, sitting on the mantel above the fireplace. It was Anna's favorite, the symbol of Antwerp, where she attended university.

He stepped over to the mantel and picked it up, rubbing his fingers over the smooth surface, the precisely cut fingers and thumb. Memories flooded back. It was a gift from Rene and Mimi Leffard, the Belgian friends Anna had lived with in Antwerp. He turned the miniature object over in his hand several times looking at it, remembering. He and Anna always held hands when they walked together. He slipped it into his coat pocket.

Jan glanced around the room again, rubbing his forehead, trying to think. The other tenants . . . they had to have heard the commotion. *Do not make contact.* His wife was missing. It was a chance he would have to take.

He left the apartment closing the door behind him and walked down the stairs to the first floor, stopping in front of Mrs. Koslofski's apartment. The door was ajar. He pushed it open and stepped into the parlor. Chairs were overturned and lamps were lying on the floor amid broken knickknacks and shattered pictures. He looked into the bedroom and the small kitchen. Mrs. Koslofski was gone.

Jan took several deep breaths and continued down to the ground floor. He tried the door to the Grucas' apartment. It was the same . . . ransacked . . . they were gone.

• • •

The rain had stopped but an icy wind was blowing out of the north. Jan turned up the collar of his coat and headed down Ulica Reformaka. An elderly woman stood at the door of the next building, removing a key from her purse.

Jan hesitated.

The woman put the key in the lock and pulled the door open.

"Pardon me, Madame," Jan said, stepping forward.

The woman glanced at him then moved quickly into the building.

Jan held the door. "Please, Madame, I won't hurt you." The woman's eyes were wide with fear as she backed away.

Jan didn't recognize her. He'd never been home long enough to meet the people in the neighborhood. He held the door open but stayed outside the building. "I'm a relative of the Grucas in the next building. Do you know them?"

The woman shook her head, her back pressed against the inner door.

"Please, Madame, I'm looking for the Grucas . . . do you know what happened?"

The woman stared at him, her hand reaching around behind for the knob of the inner door. "It was the Germans," she whispered. "They came last night very late."

"Did they arrest . . . ?" Jan's voice caught. "Did they arrest everyone?"

The woman shook her head. "I don't know. I saw the Germans . . . in the black uniforms . . . then I went to the cellar. I don't know what happened." She opened the inner door and disappeared inside.

A half hour later Jan stood in the shadow of a large tree on the other side of Ulica Prusa looking at Thaddeus's stately home. Fond memories of their traditional Wednesday night dinners came back, and he could almost hear the banter between Anna and her father.

The lights were on but the curtains were drawn. He watched, looking for shadows, not really knowing why he had come. Were Janina and Henryk still here? How could that be possible? And even if they were, how could they help him?

He stepped off the curb to cross the street when the front door of the house opened. Slowly, Jan backed up, straining to see. A man stood on the porch and appeared to be fumbling in his pocket for something.

Jan watched.

The man turned back to the door, opened it and yelled to someone inside—in German. A moment later a woman appeared and handed him something. The man gave her a kiss on the cheek and stepped off the porch. Jan heard the woman yell after him. She wanted him to hurry back.

Jan took another step back, into the shadows, watching as the German backed a Mercedes-Benz out of the driveway and headed down the street. The car stopped at the corner, waiting for a truck to pass. Jan glared at it, breathing rapidly, fighting the urge to dash into the street and drag the bastard out of the car. He closed his eyes and squeezed the handle of the briefcase. When he opened them the car was gone.

Chapter 26

ANNA LOOKED AT HER WATCH and glanced around the nearly empty hospital waiting room. She was getting nervous. When she arrived she had taken a pen and paper out of her handbag, written Irene's name on it and handed it to the severe-looking woman at the reception desk. The woman stared at it for a moment then said something in Czech, motioning for Anna to have a seat. The woman made a telephone call and returned to her paperwork. That was twenty minutes ago.

Anna stood up and stepped back to the desk, asking again, in German. "Irene Pavelka? *Verstehen Sie?* Irene Pavelka?"

The woman looked over the top of her glasses then back down at her papers.

"Irene Pavelka? *Verstehen Sie?*"

The woman ignored her.

Anna backed away from the desk, trying to control her anger, when she spotted a nurse in a crisp white uniform walking toward the elevators. She hurried over and caught her before the doors opened. "Excuse me. *Sprechen Sie Deutsch?*" she asked the young woman.

The nurse nodded. "*Ja.* Can I help you?" Her German was heavily accented.

Anna sighed. "I'm here to visit a friend, but I don't speak Czech and I'm having trouble communicating with the woman at the reception desk."

"What is your friend's name?"

Anna handed her the slip of paper. "Irene Pavelka."

The nurse walked to the reception desk while Anna stood back, listening but not understanding. The woman behind the desk repeated the same phrase over and over, shaking her head. She mentioned someone's name several times.

Finally, the nurse turned away and returned to Anna looking perplexed. "She said she's been given instructions not to release any information about your friend."

"My friend and I are from Krakow," Anna said. "We were on our way to Italy when—" She stopped. The nurse's eyes were darting around the room. Anna reached out and touched her arm. "*Bitte!* Could you find out about her condition? If I can't see her, could you just check and let me know how she is?"

The elevator door opened, and a dapper man wearing an elegantly tailored blue suit stepped out, marched across the waiting room and paused at the reception desk. He spoke quietly to the woman behind the desk, who pointed toward Anna then looked back down at her paperwork.

The man approached and shot a glance at the nurse. The young woman backed away and disappeared into the elevator. He looked at Anna through steel-rimmed spectacles, his eyes moving up and down the length of her body. He had thin gray hair plastered straight back on his head. "*Setzen Sie,*" he said in crisp German and pointed to a chair.

Anna didn't think he was Czech.

When they sat down the man smiled thinly. "So, I understand you are here to see a patient—Irene Pavelka, is it?"

"*Ja,* that's right," Anna replied. "I've been waiting a long time."

"Are you a relative of this person?"

"*Nein,* I'm her friend. We're on our way to Italy, and she became ill at the train station. May I see her?"

The prim man glanced at his fingernails. "And you are . . . ?"

"My name is Anna Kopernik."

"I see. Well, our regulations permit only family members to visit patients."

Anna glared at the man. "But she has no family here. As I said, we're traveling together to Italy. I'm the only person she knows in Prague. Please, I'm very concerned about her. May I see her?"

"*Nein.* I'm afraid I can't help you. Our regulations are very explicit: family members only." He paused as though he was expecting her to say something. Then he leaned forward and whispered, "I understand her son is traveling with her. Perhaps if he were here . . ."

Anna's heart pounded. The man stared at her with the same thin smile. She struggled to control her breathing. "I'm afraid he's not feeling well," she managed to say. "He's come down with the flu. I don't think it would be wise to bring him here."

The man shrugged and stood up.

Anna pressed on. "If I could just see my friend for a minute, I'm sure it would—"

He leaned over and peered at her, his black eyes magnified by the spectacles. "Perhaps when her son is feeling better you can bring him here and he can see his mother. *Auf Wiedersehen.*" He turned away and headed for the elevator.

"Can you at least tell me how she is?" Anna called after him.

Without answering the man stepped into the elevator and the doors closed behind him.

Anna stood on the front steps of the hospital, wanting to scream. It was cold, and a strong wind blew as she stood quietly for several minutes, staring at the ground until she started to shiver. She buttoned her coat, wrapped a scarf around her neck and walked down the steps, heading back toward the Stare Mesto and Mama Zdena's house.

After a five-minute walk she found herself standing on the corner of a busy intersection, waiting for the light to change. A familiar voice from behind said, "*Guten tag, Fräulein.*" Startled, Anna spun around. The nurse from the hospital stood behind her, wearing a brown overcoat with a blue shawl over her head.

"Follow me," the nurse said.

The lights changed and they crossed the intersection, walking in silence for several minutes. They came to a narrow, cobblestone side street, and Anna followed the nurse around the corner. In front of a four-story brick apartment building, the nurse stopped and looked at Anna. Her face was pale. "Your friend isn't in the hospital," she said.

Anna felt the tingling, the icy fingers. "Where is she?"

The nurse slumped against the building. She spoke softly, and Anna had to strain to hear her. "She's dead."

Anna staggered back, grabbing the iron railing on the steps. She stared at the young woman and tried to speak but nothing came out. She took a deep breath, then another, gripping the railing. "What . . . what happened?"

The nurse looked down at her shoes. "I was on duty in the emergency room when they brought your friend in from the train station. She was unconscious and had lost a lot of blood."

Anna closed her eyes and the image came back . . . Irene on the floor . . . Justyn's shoes in the blood . . .

The nurse continued, her voice just a whisper. "The doctor on duty was examining her when a policeman and an SS officer came in and went into the examining room. The doctor told them to wait outside, that the woman, your friend, was in very serious condition. The SS officer . . ." The nurse fell silent.

Anna opened her eyes and looked at her. The nurse glanced around. She looked frightened. "Please, go on. Tell me what happened."

The young woman wrapped her arms around her chest. "The SS officer closed the door. I heard more yelling, but I couldn't make out what they were saying. Then the door opened and the doctor stormed out. His face was red. He stripped off his gloves and walked out of the emergency room."

Anna's stomach churned. She sat down on the front steps of the building.

The nurse sat next to her. Tears streamed down her face. "They wouldn't let us help her. They said . . . they . . . *Ach Gott!* . . . I'm sorry."

They sat on the steps for a while in silence. It had started to snow, but Anna was numb, oblivious to the cold. "What is your name?" she asked.

"Kristina," the nurse said.

"I'm sure it was dangerous for you to tell me all this. *Danke schön,* I'm very grateful."

Kristina nodded. "I should be going."

They stood up and Anna suddenly realized how cold she was. She embraced the young woman and kissed her on the cheek. "*Danke,* Kristina."

"What will you do?" the young woman asked.

"I've got to tell a ten-year-old boy that his mother has died," Anna said, surprised that she could even get it out. "Then I'm going to get him out of harm's way."

Kristina nodded and turned away.

Anna watched the nurse as she rounded the corner and disappeared into the crowd. A moment later the snow covered her footprints.

Belgium
during World War Two

North Sea

NETHERLANDS

Maas
River

Ostend

Antwerp

BELGIUM

GERMANY

River
Schelde

Brussels

Liege

Meuse
River

Charleroi

A R D E N N E S

FRANCE

LaRoche

LUXEMBOURG

Anna's Chalet

PART TWO

Belgium
1943

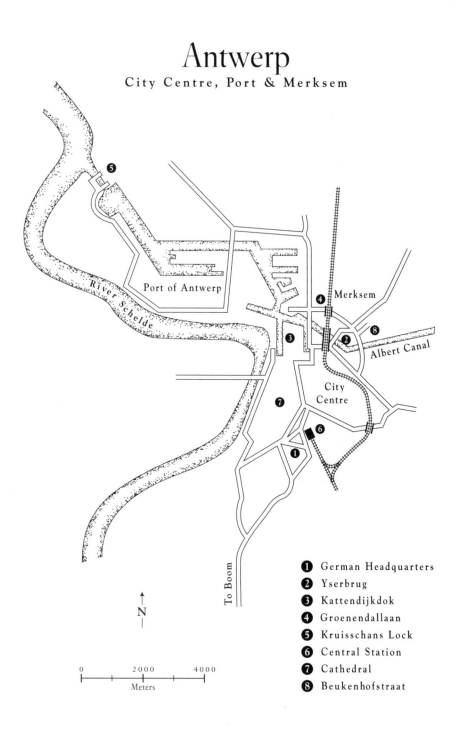

Antwerp
City Centre, Port & Merksem

River Schelde

Port of Antwerp

❺ Kruisschans Lock

❹ Groenendallaan · Merksem

❽ Beukenhofstraat

❸ Kattendijkdok

❷ Yserbrug

Albert Canal

City Centre

❼ Cathedral

❻ Central Station

❶ German Headquarters

To Boom

N

0   2000   4000
Meters

❶ German Headquarters
❷ Yserbrug
❸ Kattendijkdok
❹ Groenendallaan
❺ Kruisschans Lock
❻ Central Station
❼ Cathedral
❽ Beukenhofstraat

Chapter 27

THE DIRT ROAD FOLLOWED a high flat ridge for more than a kilometer, bisecting a field of freshly planted potatoes and a pasture before it disappeared down a gentle slope into a thick pine forest. The valley below extended far to the south and on a clear day it was possible to see all the way to Luxembourg.

Justyn had trekked along this road so often in the last two years, making the trip to and from the tiny village of Warempage, that he long ago stopped paying attention to the view. He concentrated on the wagon he pulled carefully over ruts in the road, trying to avoid tipping it over and spilling its precious cargo of fresh milk, eggs, butter and a smoked ham. It had taken a week of sweat, mending fences on Monsieur Marchal's farm in the late August heat, to earn the food. Losing any of it along the way was unthinkable.

Justyn pulled the cart down a slope toward the pine forest, where their chalet was nestled in a secluded clearing, when he heard the sound of an airplane from the east. He looked up as an enormous four-engine bomber soared overhead, engines sputtering, trailing a thick plume of black smoke. Justyn stared transfixed as the mortally wounded American B-17 carved a long, smoky arc in the sky and disappeared in a thunderous explosion deep in the valley.

An instant later an immense fireball ballooned into the sky, and Justyn dropped to his knees, covering his eyes. When he looked up again, the fireball had dissipated, and a cloud of thick, black smoke drifted off to the south. Then he noticed the parachute.

The small white umbrella, with a figure dangling below, floated across his field of vision and dropped out of sight at the far end of the south field. Justyn sprang to his feet, leaving the wagon in the middle of the dusty road, and sprinted across the field. When he got to the south fence line he searched the valley below and spotted the white material flapping back and forth in the middle of a wheat field belonging to M. Marchal's neighbor. The burning wreck of the airplane flared in the distance. He hurtled the fence and raced down the hillside.

Justyn slowed to a walk as he approached the downed aviator, watching as the man struggled to sit up, his right foot bent backward at a severe angle. Justyn stepped up to the man, grabbed the parachute lines and gathered up the billowing cloth, securing it with rocks. Then he bent down and unfastened the harness from the aviator's chest.

The man tried to sit up again but Justyn put a hand on his shoulder and said, "*Laissez moi vous aider.* Let me help you."

The man looked confused, apparently not understanding French. He mumbled something that Justyn vaguely recognized as English but couldn't understand.

"*Laissez moi,*" Justyn coaxed.

The aviator nodded and laid back, closing his eyes and clenching his fists.

Justyn heard someone shout his name and turned to see M. Marchal and Anna standing at the fence.

The trip by bicycle from Warempage to La Roche normally took Anna a little over an hour. Justyn could make it in less than forty-five minutes, but he was fourteen and had grown tall and muscular. Anna was anxious to get there and find out what van Acker intended to do about the aviator, but it was a warm day and she stopped along the side of the hilly, winding road to rest.

She knelt on a rock alongside a narrow stream flowing from the hillside and bent over to scoop some water when she paused, taking in her reflection. Her red hair, now cropped short, was beginning to show a few streaks of gray and her face was thinner than it had been. Had been when? When she last had a normal life? When she had last seen Jan?

Anna cupped her hands, dipped them into the cool water and took a drink. She splashed some water on the back of her neck then stood up and stared into the stream, recalling his image. It was always the same . . . he was in uniform, blond hair tousled from the wind. He was waving . . . waving good-bye.

It was almost noon when Anna arrived in La Roche. She pedaled along the narrow cobblestone street running through the center of the ancient resort town, turned a corner and parked her bicycle behind van Acker's butcher shop. It was a simple, single-story structure constructed of the ubiquitous brown and gray shale of the Ardennes region of southern Belgium. Without knocking she let herself in the back door and nodded to van Acker's assistant who was busy carving a fat hog from one of the local farms. Anna knew that the meat, if it could be hidden from German field agents, would bring at least 3000 francs on the black market.

She proceeded through the cool, damp cutting room, stepping around the pools of blood, to a small office. She knocked twice and opened the door. A rotund, bald man sat behind a cluttered desk, his bloody white apron lying in a heap on the floor. He glanced up and waved for her to come in.

Anna stepped into the cramped office, closed the door behind her and removed a pile of dusty newspapers from a chair in front of the desk.

Jules van Acker took off the small, rimless glasses that were perched on the end of his bulbous nose and leaned forward with a smile, exposing a row of yellow, uneven teeth. *"Bonjour, Anna."* His voice was a gravelly rumble. "A couple of buffoons from the local Gestapo stopped in here earlier this morning. They were asking questions about the crash of the American bomber—wanted to know if there were any survivors. I thought you might find that interesting."

Anna's pulse quickened at his mention of the Gestapo. She shifted in the chair and said, "You've heard about my new 'house-guest,' *sans doute.*"

"Oui, bien sûr. Marchal told me about it; very gracious of you to take him in. How's he doing?"

"His ankle was fractured and he has several cracked ribs, but his color is good and he's eating like a horse."

Van Acker leaned back in the swivel chair. It creaked under his weight. "Well, if it's any consolation to you, I think the incident is quite well contained. No one here in town seems to know anything about survivors, and Marchal tells me that none of your other neighbors out there noticed the parachute."

"What about the doctor?" Anna asked.

"Perfectly fine, Peeters is one of us. He's seen a lot more than this. Don't worry." Van Acker shifted his bulk in the rickety chair.

"What's next?" Anna asked, wondering what she would be getting into now that she was harboring an enemy of the German Reich.

Van Acker leaned forward across the small, wooden desk. "In a few days I'll stop by and have a discussion with your aviator friend. If he is who he says he is, we'll wait until he can get around, then we'll link him up with the . . . ah . . . Comet Line."

Anna stared at him for a moment then smiled. "I was wondering if it was still in operation."

"*Oui, oui.* They're still in operation," van Acker said. "Very covert, but quite efficient—transported several hundred Allied airmen back to Britain during the last couple years."

Anna nodded, her mind wandering, remembering a young, intense woman back in Antwerp.

"You knew her, didn't you?" van Acker asked.

Anna blinked. "Andree de Jongh? I met her a few months after Justyn and I arrived in Antwerp, February or March of '40, I think. She was trying to get it started."

Van Acker leaned back and smiled, the chair continuing its creaking protest. "Leffard mentioned it to me once right after you moved out here. I got the impression he didn't approve of your involvement."

"Oh, I wasn't really involved," Anna said, "not as an escort, certainly. I did small things, delivered some 'packages' around the city, nothing big. Rene wouldn't hear of it. Besides, I had to think of Justyn."

Van Acker's eyes brightened at the mention of the boy's name. "He's a good lad, gotten quite tall and his French is excellent. You'd never know . . ." He caught himself and stopped. "Marchal says he works like hell, puts his own boys to shame."

Anna smiled. She knew how fond he was of Justyn. "I guess country life agrees with him." She looked into van Acker's eyes. "We're very grateful, Jules; you know that."

Van Acker pushed the creaking chair back and got to his feet, waving a meaty hand dismissively. "Of course. Go take care of the fly-boy. *À bientôt.*"

It was after nine o'clock that evening before Anna got a chance to rest. The aviator, who had identified himself as First Lieutenant Andrew Hamilton of the US Army Air Corps, had dropped into a deep sleep after taking the pain medication. Justyn had left shortly after dinner for the Marchals's house.

Anna poured a cup of the malt and chicory concoction that substituted for coffee and went out onto the porch. The sun was setting, and the sky was an array of pink and purple cast against a darkening blue background. She sipped the hot, bitter drink and pondered her situation.

She had felt relatively safe living in this out-of-the-way rural area the past two years. Certainly it was safer for Justyn, compared with what was happening in Antwerp and Brussels, where tens of thousands of Jews were being deported to "the east." She gazed at the rippling colors in the sky and thought about her conversation with van Acker, the Comet Line, Andree de Jongh and Rene Leffard. She sighed, thinking about Rene and Mimi Leffard and how much she missed them. They had been their saviors, taking them in when they arrived in Antwerp four years ago, accepting Justyn as one of their own, the grandson they never had. And when it became too dangerous for Justyn in Antwerp, Rene had brought them here, to Jules van Acker and Leon Marchal, who protected their secret.

She took another sip of the hot drink, trying to remember what real coffee tasted like, and looked around at the tall pines and birch trees. Jan would like it here, she thought. He would like these people—van Acker, Marchal and the other men in the area—tough, solid men, anti-Nazi partisans of the *maquis* carrying on the fight. Though they didn't discuss it with her, she knew about their affiliation with the White Brigade, about their connection with Leffard and the money he raised to finance acts of sabotage against the Germans.

Anna was so engrossed in her thoughts, she didn't hear Justyn return until he clomped up the wooden steps. The tall, wiry youth flopped down on a bench and pulled off his boots, which were caked with mud.

"Where did you get into all that mud?" she asked.

"Checking out the drop site," Justyn answered.

"The drop site?"

"Yeah, it's just off the road to Ortho, on the other side of the Delacroix place."

"Justyn, what are you talking about? A drop site for what?"

"For supplies. Jean-Claude says we've got to scope out some sites . . . for the Allied planes to drop supplies."

Jean-Claude was the Marchal's seventeen-year-old son. Now Anna understood. She set her cup on the railing. "Justyn, I thought we had an agreement. *C'est dangereux.* You promised me you weren't getting involved."

He looked up at her and shook his head. "*Non, non.* This is just, you know, scouting around. Luk and I are helping Jean-Claude—it's nothing."

The boy looked more like his father every day, she thought. He even sounded like him, though she had never known Stefan to speak French. But his voice, his mannerisms, the mop of unruly black hair, it was all Stefan. "So, when is this 'drop' supposed to take place?" she asked.

"I don't know. That's a secret. Only M. Marchal knows. He won't even tell Jean-Claude. We're just supposed to check out possible sites. Hey, did you hear there's another American!"

"What? Where?"

"I don't know. Jean-Claude said he heard that another one had bailed out. Must be holed up somewhere close by. How's Andrew?"

"He's . . . he's fine . . . sleeping," Anna muttered, shaking her head. A second American?

"*Très bien,*" Justyn said. "I'm going in to read for a while." He got to his feet, dropped his muddy boots next to the door and disappeared inside.

Anna winced as the screen door slammed. The rapid-fire conversation reminded her of discussions with her students at the university back in Krakow and how the most incredible information would be dispensed with casual indifference. Drop sites. A second aviator.

She picked up the cup and looked out over the small patch of land adjacent to the chalet that had been cleared from the dense pine forest. In the gathering dusk she saw a doe standing just inside the tree line. She watched as the animal glanced around, then lowered its head and nibbled at the underbrush. Peaceful. Unafraid. It reminded her of her life during these past two years—a quiet, peaceful respite from the madness of the war.

The night was getting cool and Anna wrapped her hands around the cup, feeling the last of its warmth. She glanced at Justyn's muddy boots and took a deep breath. He'd been off checking out "drop sites." And an American aviator was sleeping in her house. She felt the respite coming to an end.

Chapter 28

RENE LEFFARD WAS IN A BAD MOOD. He stood on the platform at Antwerp's Berchem station and ran a hand through his thick, black hair. He looked down the railroad tracks then glanced at his watch. Thirty minutes late. Scowling, he turned and retraced his steps along the platform grumbling in silence at how fouled up the country had become.

He glanced at a man standing at the newsstand buying the evening paper and shook his head. What a fool, he thought. Who would pay money for a newspaper filled with nothing but German propaganda? He knew that some people actually believed the garbage they read in the paper, but there were others who didn't believe it but didn't care anymore. It was just something to read. Those were the people he really worried about.

A whistle blew, and a few minutes later he heard the chugging steam engine approach from the south. He glanced at his watch again. Thirty-five minutes late.

Leffard spotted Willy Boeynants stepping off the train and waved to him. The tall, silver-haired man, wearing a navy-blue three-piece suit with the point of a white handkerchief protruding from the breast pocket, waved back and walked briskly across the platform. Leffard embraced his friend, and they headed down the stairs toward the street. "*Bonjour,* Willy. *Heureux de te voir,* good to see you. How was the train today?"

Boeynants grimaced. "*Insupportable.* Late and dirty, as usual. I was lucky to even get on because the air-raid sirens went off just as we were boarding. The train pulled out immediately and left a couple hundred people standing on the platform. As usual, it was nothing. Then we stopped in Mechelen and sat for half an hour. And all the while a crowd of drunken Wehrmacht soldiers hung around in the back of the car singing those disgusting German songs." He patted the thick briefcase he was carrying. "But, I did manage to bring some wine."

The Leffards' home on the Cogels-Osylei was a short walk from the Berchem station, in Antwerp's exclusive Zurenborg district. The three-story house was of the Art Nouveau style of architecture that had been popular in Antwerp around the turn of the century, and Rene Leffard loved every brick and every pane of stained glass. It was old and comfortable and charming, and coming home every night made him forget, if only for a few brief minutes, the drudgery of life in an occupied country.

Mimi Leffard met them at the door, and Boeynants embraced her. "You look wonderful, my dear," he said.

She blushed and pushed him away. "*Oui, oui, merci.* Such a liar you are."

Leffard gave his wife a kiss and closed the door. Her dark brown hair, showing more streaks of gray every day, was pinned back in a bun. She looked tired, he thought. He knew that she had probably spent several hours standing in ration lines trying to get something decent for tonight's dinner. "Willy has brought some wine," he said.

Mimi smiled. "*Merveilleux!* I'm certain it will be the best part of the dinner."

The dinner was a meager affair—a vegetable soup made with carrots and leeks, some crusty white bread from the black market and a small portion of tinned mackerel. But the wine, a Chateauneuf du Pape '38 that Willy uncorked with a flourish, helped immensely, and Mimi surprised the two men by producing a bread pudding for dessert.

"*Délicieux!*" Boeynants said as he scooped some of the gooey concoction into his mouth. "How did you manage it?"

Mimi dabbed her fork into it and tasted a small bite. "I had a few eggs left, and I managed to get a little sugar on the black market." She tried another bite and shrugged. "Well, it's one way to use up that awful ration bread."

After dinner, Leffard and Boeynants helped Mimi clear the table and do the dishes. It had been almost a year since the Leffards' housekeeper left to take care of her parents, and they had not replaced her. Mimi was not a strong woman, and Leffard had become accustomed to helping out.

When they were finished Leffard led Boeynants to his study, and Boeynants lowered his long, lanky frame into one of the leather chairs in front of the fireplace. Leffard opened a cabinet and withdrew a bottle of cognac and two snifters, glancing at his refection in the gilded framed mirror hanging on the wall. He was a stocky, solidly built man, but he looked thinner, his neatly trimmed black mustache also flecked with gray. The war was aging all of them, he thought. He held up the bottle and swirled it around, looking at Boeynants. Just a few centimeters remained. "*Enfin*, this is the last of it, my friend. God knows when I'll be able to find more." He poured some into each of the glasses and handed one to Boeynants. "*À la vôtre!* To friendship—and to the day we kick these bastards out of our country."

"I'll drink to that," Boeynants said as they clinked glasses.

Leffard sat in the other chair, took a sip and looked at his friend. "You've heard about what happened in Warempage?" he asked.

Boeynants nodded. "I understand Anna has a 'visitor' staying with her now. How is she doing?"

"Van Acker says she's handling it quite well, but she's a little nervous. The local Gestapo's been snooping around. Have you heard anything?" Boeynants was an official with the Department of the Interior, and Leffard knew he was in a position to hear things.

"Not much," Boeynants said. "The Gestapo knows the plane came down, of course, but they seem to be leaving it up to their local boys in La Roche to track down the survivors. I'll stay on it."

Leffard took another sip of cognac. "It's damned unfortunate that they brought that aviator to the chalet. Anna's been pretty good about staying out of things since she's been down there."

Boeynants smiled. "*Oui, je sais.* And for Anna that's an accomplishment."

Mimi came in carrying a tray with a carafe of coffee, two cups and a plate of small biscuits. "I will apologize in advance for the awful coffee," she said.

Boeynants smiled at her. "I've actually grown quite used to our so-called coffee after all this time. I wonder how I'll adapt if we're ever able to get the real thing again."

"Rene will adapt instantly," she said. "The only time he thinks it's palatable is if he can mix in a little cognac."

Leffard laughed. "But we can't get that either."

When Mimi left the room, Boeynants poured a cup of coffee and asked Leffard, "Have you heard anything about another drop?"

Leffard nodded. "*Voici,* here are the coordinates." He pulled a folded piece of paper from his shirt pocket and handed it to his friend. "Let me know if you hear of any extra Gestapo activity in that area. It will be sometime next week."

Boeynants took the paper and nodded.

Leffard said, "The code is *wild boars are foraging in the valley*. French broadcast on the BBC, as usual."

Boeynants repeated the words and took another look at the slip of paper before tearing it up.

Chapter 29

Twenty-four hours after the code was broadcast on the BBC, Leon Marchal and his older son, Jean-Claude, left their two-story farmhouse and headed for the barn to hitch up the horses.

Marchal felt good. He was forty-five years old, a short, lean man, weathered and physically fit from a lifetime of hard work. He was a veteran of the Chasseurs Ardennais, Belgium's most elite military organization, and tonight, as he did on every mission, Marchal donned the Chasseurs' customary green beret.

The door banged open behind them, and fourteen-year-old Luk Marchal called out from the porch, "*Attends!* I want to get Justyn and come along."

Marchal motioned for Jean-Claude to continue on, then headed back toward the house, meeting Luk at the bottom of the steps. He put his arm around his younger son's shoulder. "We've been through this before, Luk. You can't come with us. Not until you're sixteen. And I know that Justyn is not allowed to come along either."

"But it's not fair," the boy protested. "Justyn and I helped find the site and dig the holes."

"I know you did, and that's your contribution. But you cannot go along on the night drops. *C'est dangereux!* No one can until they're sixteen. You know the rules."

"But the war will be over by then, and I'll miss all the action."

Marchal sighed. "I pray to God every day that's true." He gave his son a hug.

• • •

By eleven o'clock everything was ready. Marchal walked around the field for a last-minute check. The field was about two hectares of clear, flat grass surrounded on three sides by dense pine trees. The fourth side, also well populated with pine trees, sloped down to the Ourthe River. At each corner of the field was a hole, approximately a meter across and a meter and a half deep. Jean-Claude, Luk and Justyn had dug them last week then carefully concealed them with tarps and pine branches.

Now the tarps were removed and lanterns placed at the bottom of each hole. As soon as they heard the airplane they would light the lanterns, which would be easily spotted from the air but invisible to anyone at ground level.

Marchal walked to the side of the field nearest the river and joined the rest of the crew standing inside the tree line with the horses and wagons. There were seven of them: four men and three teenage boys. They all knew their tasks. They had done this before.

A little after one o'clock in the morning, Marchal heard an approaching airplane. He looked at his friend Paul Delacroix and nodded. The sound was the low, reverberating rumble of a heavy transport and not a Luftwaffe fighter. Marchal shouted, "Go," and the three boys ran out to light the lanterns.

The plane passed overhead, circled around and headed back toward the field. Marchal sat in his wagon and watched the plane approach, just above the treetops. One by one, five parachutes emerged from underneath the wide fuselage and descended to the field. Large, wooden crates swinging from the bottom of each parachute dropped with a dull thud onto the field as the plane gained altitude and disappeared.

Jean-Claude and the other two boys ran into the middle of the field as soon as the last crate hit the ground and began pulling in the parachutes. Marchal flicked the reins, and his horse trotted into the field, pulling the wagon. Paul Delacroix did the same in the second wagon.

In less than ten minutes all five crates were loaded onto the wagons, the lanterns extinguished and the four men were gone. The three boys stayed behind to fill in the holes and remove all traces of the operation.

By two-thirty in the morning the crates were unloaded and the materials stored in the cellar below Delacroix's barn. The husky, gray-haired man wiped his hands on his coveralls and produced a dusty bottle of *pequet* from a shelf above the tool bench. He handed it to Marchal who took a swig of the potent, locally produced liquor and passed it around. It was vaguely similar to vodka but a long way from the cognac they would normally have had during better times.

Delacroix read aloud from the checklist that had come with the drop. "Fifty kilos of plastique, sixty-five detonators and timing pencils, twenty Colt 45s, ten Sten guns, one Bren gun, two thousand rounds of ammunition, thirty hand grenades and ten thousand francs in small bills."

"*Pas mal,*" Marchal said, "not bad. I guess that'll take care of a few more freight trains and supply dumps."

He glanced at Jean-Claude as his seventeen-year-old son, tall and blond, big-boned but still youthfully slender, took a swig of the *pequet.*

The boy grimaced, caught his father's eye and smiled.

After two weeks of surveillance Jean-Claude knew the schedule. The heavily laden trains hauling coke from the plants in Liege to the German-controlled steel mills in Luxembourg crossed the Ourthe River every night between eleven o'clock and midnight. Once over the bridge, the trains labored to climb the grade and slowed to less than 10 km/hr as they headed south. The terrain was hilly, heavily wooded and very remote. It was perfect.

Standing on the tracks, Jean-Claude looked back toward the lean-to he and Henri Delacroix had constructed. It was well concealed in a hollow about fifty meters downhill and west of the raised rail bed. It had served as their home for most of the last two weeks. He glanced at Henri then looked at his watch. It was a little after three o'clock in the afternoon, and the two teenagers set off along the tracks toward the bridge.

They crossed the bridge and continued along the tracks for another kilometer until they came to a crossing with a narrow dirt road. They left the tracks and found a spot hidden among the trees to wait.

An hour later Jean-Claude heard the creaking sound of wagon wheels. The two boys waited until the wagon was almost on top of them and they were certain who it was, before emerging from the cover of the trees.

Jules van Acker drove the wagon, and Jean-Claude's father sat next to him. Paul Delacroix sat on a bench in the back of the wagon along with another man from La Roche, a quiet, thin man of about fifty, whom Jean-Claude knew only as "Gaston." Jean-Claude guessed from the man's cultured, more refined accent, that Gaston might originally be from Brussels.

When the wagon groaned to a halt, the two boys hurried to the back and be-gan lifting out the heavy canvas packs, which had been concealed under a load of freshly harvested beans. Without exchanging a word, the two boys, their fathers and Gaston each strapped on one of the canvas packs and set off down the railroad tracks. Van Acker turned the wagon around and headed back.

Back at the lean-to, Jean-Claude watched as his father and Gaston re-moved the materials from the backpacks and spread them neatly on the canvas tarp that served as the floor. There were twenty kilos of putty-like plastique, which Gaston carefully divided into four, 5-kilo packs, wrapping each one in a piece of heavy cloth. His father removed four reels of wire from the packs and handed two each to Jean-Claude and Henri.

Then the five saboteurs climbed up the hill to the railroad tracks and headed south to a point where the rail bed began banking and curving to the east. Gaston held up his hand, and the group stopped. The thin man looked care-fully north and south along the tracks.

Jean-Claude knew he was calculating the curvature of the tracks and the angle of the bed.

"A little farther," he said and the group walked another thirty meters down the tracks.

Gaston stopped and nodded. He knelt on the wooden ties and pointed to a spot alongside each of the rails. Paul and Henri Delacroix set to work attaching the packs of plastique to the rails. Jean-Claude and his father followed Gaston another forty meters down the tracks and did the same.

When all four charges had been secured to the rails, Jean-Claude stood off to the side and watched Gaston meticulously insert the detonators and make each connection to the reels of wire. He must be an engineer of some type, the boy thought, perhaps an army officer, a demolitions man. Had he been in the *Chasseurs Ardennais* like his father?

Finally Gaston stood and wiped his hands on his trousers. Marchal and Delacroix began to unwind the reels, backing off the rail bed and down the hill.

It was dark by the time the group returned to the lean-to and settled in to wait for the train.

Jean-Claude looked at his watch when he heard the first unmistakable chug-ging of a steam locomotive. It was 11:15. His father doused the lantern, and the dark moonless night enveloped the saboteurs.

The sound grew louder.

They were all on their knees. Marchal gripped the handle of the plunger.

The venting steam and scraping wheels of the massive freight train grew louder and louder.

"Should be crossing the bridge now," Jean-Claude said, his voice cracking. He and Henri had been listening to these trains for fourteen days, and he had become intimately familiar with the sounds and vibrations that ran through the ground. He was excited. Ever since the war broke out he had longed to be a part of the action, to be a fighting man like his father, and now he was getting his chance. He was proud of the surveillance work he and Henri had done. He hoped his father would be as well.

The clamor of the straining locomotive became deafening, then abruptly dropped in pitch as it passed their position, heading south.

Gaston put a hand on Marchal's shoulder and counted, *"Un, deux, trois, quatre—"*

He squeezed Marchal's shoulder.

A flash of brilliant white light . . . Then a thunderous explosion knocked Jean-Claude to the ground. Three more flashes and eardrum-shattering concussions followed in split-second intervals.

Jean-Claude covered his ears and crawled to the far corner of the lean-to as the shrill sound of screeching metal penetrated every fiber of his body.

Massive trees snapped like matchsticks as the heavily loaded railcars careened off the tracks and plunged into the forest with deep, booming *thuds*.

It continued for several long minutes: screeching metal, snapping trees, and *thud* after *thud* as the railcars and thousands of tons of cargo piled up in the valley on the other side of the tracks.

Then it was over and the forest was quiet.

Chapter 30

RENE LEFFARD SAT at one of the small round tables in front of the Den Engle café on the Grote Markt, in the center of Antwerp. He took a sip from his glass of weak, wartime beer. Of all the finer things about life in prewar Belgium that Leffard missed, the normally excellent beer ranked right at the top. Fine wines, real coffee, good food—all just distant memories.

But, as he glanced around, Leffard smiled. It was a warm September afternoon, and the cafés around the Grote Markt were practically full. Most people in Antwerp had difficulty just finding enough food but here, on a pleasant autumn afternoon, they joined their friends at the cafés, as they had for generations. In his heart, Rene Leffard knew they would survive.

"*Bonjour*, Rene," Willy Boeynants said as he slipped into the metal chair across from Leffard.

Leffard nodded and signaled to the waiter to bring another beer. The two friends exchanged small talk about the weather until the waiter delivered their beers and departed.

Boeynants took a sip of beer and grimaced. He set the glass down and glanced around at the other patrons. "The last train wreck has caused quite a stir," he said quietly. "The head of our department is beside himself, and the Gestapo boys are running around like crazy covering their asses."

"Anything we need to be worried about?" Leffard asked.

"*Non*, not any more than usual, I suppose. But it may be a good idea to tell van Acker to lay low for a while. There's a lot of pressure coming from Berlin, and the Gestapo's going to pull out all the stops trying to find out who's doing this. We've hit them pretty hard the last few months, you know."

Leffard stared into his beer glass contemplating the situation. Boeynants was right of course. Van Acker's White Brigade cell had indeed hit the Germans pretty hard. Since late spring they had pulled off three train wrecks, blown up two refueling stations and set fire to a munitions plant. Was it time to lay low?

Leffard lifted the glass and took a sip. That may be the prudent thing to do, he thought. But, they were at war. Risks had to be taken. He finished the beer and tossed some coins on the table. *"Je comprends.* Just let me know if you hear anything more."

Chapter 31

IT WAS UNCHARACTERISTICALLY HOT for early October in London. Colonel Stanley Whitehall sat in his steamy office at the headquarters of the Special Operations Executive on Baker Street, staring at the latest decoded dispatch from Poland. He loosened his tie, stained with gravy from this noon's lunch, and read it over a second time, wiping sweat from his brow with a handkerchief. This was the third report forwarded to him from MI-6 on the same subject and, from the tone of the note attached to it, the intelligence boys were getting nervous. They wanted verification, and that meant only one thing: someone would have to go over there. Where in the hell is Blizna? he thought to himself as he got up and lumbered across the office to get a map of Poland from the filing cabinet.

A few minutes later, Captain Roger Morgan walked into Whitehall's office, carrying the file he had been reviewing, and sat down in the single wooden chair, sliding it a few feet to the left to catch some of the paltry breeze from the fan whirring away on the top of the filing cabinet.

Whitehall looked up from the map that was spread out across the cluttered metal desk and squinted at him over the top of his wire-rimmed reading glasses. "Christ, it's way down south, east of Krakow."

"What is?" Morgan asked, in confusion.

"Blizna," Whitehall said removing his glasses and rubbing his eyes. "The bombed-out little village where all this crazy activity is supposedly taking place. God, these Polish names will drive me up the wall. Is that the file?"

"Yes," Morgan said, tossing the thin folder on top of the map.

"Give me a summary," Whitehall said, leaning back precariously in his chair.

Morgan took the file and opened it, flipping through the first few pages. "Well, the chap's name is Jan Kopernik. He's a cavalry officer, career man, a major with some demolition training to boot. He was a regimental commander with the Wielkopolska Brigade in '39. Fought in the Battle of the Bzura—"

"God, bloody affair that was," Whitehall interrupted. "Sorry, old man, go on."

"Well, let's see, after Warsaw fell he led what was left of his regiment out of Poland and made it to Hungary where they were interned. He was, as you know, sent off on that mission to Krakow then returned to Hungary. He eventually got his men to France though they didn't arrive until just before the invasion in May of '40. He fought at Montbard where he was pretty severely wounded, evacuated from Marseille in a hospital ship and spent a year recuperating in London. In '42, he was transferred up to Scotland and assigned to the Polish First Armored Division."

"So, that's where he is now?" Whitehall asked, wiping sweat from his brow again.

"Looks that way," Morgan said, scanning the file. "According to this he's put in for intelligence work in Poland, but nothing's come up."

"Until now," Whitehall interjected.

"Yes, until now."

"Languages?"

"Polish, of course. The file says he's also fluent in German, decent in French and coming along pretty well in English since he got over here."

"I'd guess his German would be pretty good if he got away with impersonating a Gestapo agent in Krakow," Whitehall remarked with a yawn as he hoisted himself from the chair, tucking a shirttail back under his sagging beltline. "God, this bloody heat's enough to put you to sleep in the middle of the day. So, how's this chap's health?"

"According to this, he's recovered. Seems like it was shrapnel wounds and a badly fractured leg."

"Anything else?" Whitehall asked, anxious to get out of this suffocating office and over to the Lion's Head for a drink.

"Yes, this may be important," Morgan said, looking back at the file. "When he went on that mission to Krakow, he apparently found out that his wife had been arrested by the SS and imprisoned."

"Really? How do we know that?" Whitehall asked.

"It's a note written in by one of the doctors at the hospital. Probably something Kopernik told him—or a nurse; you know how it is with wounded soldiers."

"Hmmm, yes . . . quite right. Well, that obviously explains why he's offered to go back. Has it affected his work at all?"

"There's nothing in the file about depression or anything of that sort," Morgan replied. "His fitness reports are all first class. He appears to be a top-notch officer."

"Who's itching for a reason to go back to Poland and look for his wife. Certainly would solve the problem of retrieving whomever we drop in there."

"You mean . . ."

"Why not? We drop him in, he verifies the identity of the contact in Poland and the accuracy of these reports, then he'd be free to go off looking for his wife."

Morgan squirmed in his chair. "But . . . the army is going to want him back."

Whitehall waved his hand dismissively. "I'll take care of that with MI-6. If they want this done, they'll have to square it with the army chaps. Besides, by the time they sort it all out, the invasion will be on. There are a million troops in England at the moment, and thousands more arriving every week. One officer more or less, and a Polish officer at that, who the hell's going to notice. Get him down here for a chat. I've got to get moving on this. MI-6 is getting their knickers in a tizzy about verifying the contact in Poland, and Kopernik here is the only one we know of that's ever met this bloke . . . this . . . what's his name again?"

"Slomak."

"Yes, Slomak. Well, that *was* his name, anyway."

Jan had not been back in London since he was transferred up to Scotland over a year ago. He remembered how it had been then, during the blitz. The constant blackouts, air-raid sirens blaring in the night, the fires he could see in all directions from the windows of the hospital. But now the city was bustling with activity as he stood in front of King's Cross station trying to hail a taxi.

Finally, one of the venerable black vehicles pulled up, and a middle-aged man wearing a bowler hat stuck his grizzled face out the window. "Hop in, laddy. Where to?"

"The Northumberland Hotel," Jan remarked as he climbed into the backseat of the spacious automobile, throwing his bag on the seat.

"Right-O," the man said as he whipped the car into the traffic, right in front of a red double-decker bus. "Don't recognize that uniform, laddy—where you from?"

"Poland," Jan replied.

"You don't say. You're the first I've met from Poland. Pretty tough, I guess, wasn't it?"

"Yes, it was," Jan said. He stared out the window, not knowing what else he could add that would matter now.

The room on the fifth floor of the hotel was completely bare except for a battered metal desk and two wooden chairs. The windows were open to let in what breeze there was, and a fan had been set on the floor doing little good. Jan removed his coat, following the invitation of the portly man sitting behind the desk who introduced himself as Colonel Whitehall of the SOE.

Whitehall looked up from the file he was studying, took off his reading glasses and folded his pudgy hands on the desk. "So, Major, how are you getting on in Scotland?"

"Very well," Jan said, "but we're all getting a little restless to get back into action somewhere."

"Yes, yes, I can imagine," Whitehall said. "Lot of fighting ahead of us yet before Jerry throws in the towel, I should think."

Jan nodded but didn't respond.

Whitehall cleared his throat, looked at the file and then back at Jan. "Major, according to the notes in this file, you apparently believe that your wife was arrested by the SS back in '39. Is that correct?"

Jan sat back in the chair, stunned by the unexpected reference to Anna's disappearance. He stared at Whitehall. Did this man have some information about her? No, he knew better than that. The army wouldn't go through this elaborate setup just to tell him they'd located his wife. Besides, thousands of soldiers were worried about their families, and it wasn't the army's concern. This was something else. "Yes, Colonel, that's correct," he said.

"And how did you happen to come by this information?"

Jan hesitated. Where was this going? He leaned forward and locked eyes with Whitehall. "I'm sure that file you have there, Colonel, makes reference to the undercover mission I was sent on to Krakow in 1939. While I was there I tried to find my wife. Our apartment had been ransacked by the SS and . . ." Jan paused and took a breath. He hadn't talked about this in a long time. "What's this all about?"

Whitehall closed the file folder. "Well, Major, we may be able to help each other out. We'd like to send you on another mission—a very important one—back in Poland."

Jan remained silent and continued to stare at Whitehall.

The colonel stood up and walked to the window. He turned around and lowered his bulk onto the windowsill. "I think it goes without saying that anything we discuss here is strictly between us. Nothing leaves the room. Understood?"

Jan nodded.

Whitehall looked at him for a moment then continued. "A little over a month ago the RAF carried out a massive bombing raid on an enemy facility near a small village named Peenemunde located on an island in the Baltic just off the coast of Germany. The raid was prompted by reports that British intelligence had received concerning German *wunderwaffen*. Do you know what I mean, Major?"

"Wonder weapons?"

"Yes, quite. Wonder weapons. In this case, rockets, unmanned rockets carrying warheads. The Germans were building them in secret at Peenemunde."

Jan ran a hand through his hair. Unmanned rockets?

Whitehall continued. "Well, we now have some new information that suggests the raid was only partially successful. Information, you will be interested to know, supplied by agents of the *Armia Krajowa*. You're familiar with them, Major?

Jan nodded. "Armia Krajowa, the AK. It means 'the home army,' the Polish Resistance."

"Yes, quite correct," Whitehall said, "a courageous group."

"They were just getting started when we were ordered to escape," Jan said.

"Well, according to these reports from the AK, the Germans have shifted much of the work on the *wunderwaffen* to a new facility located in Poland near a village by the name of Blizna. Do you know where that is?"

Jan had to think a moment. "Blizna . . . yes, I think so. It's in the south, east of Krakow, I believe."

Whitehall pushed himself off the windowsill and plodded around the small room. "Major Kopernik, when you were sent from Hungary on the mission to Krakow, you made contact with a man named Slomak. Is that right?"

Jan leaned forward, now very curious. "Yes, that's right."

"Well, this Slomak now goes by a different name. But he is supposedly the one sending the messages about the rocket facility at Blizna. Needless to say, the British government is very concerned about this but, quite frankly, we have no way of knowing if these reports are real or just a ruse to throw us off. The Germans sealed off Poland like a drum after driving out the Russians, and it's almost impossible to get anything out of there except for these messages from the AK. Bottom line is someone has to go over to Poland, verify the identity of this chap and find out what the hell is going on." Whitehall paused and managed a thin smile. "And I'm afraid that you, old fellow, are the only one we know who would recognize him."

They looked at each other in silence. Finally Jan stood and walked over to the window watching the traffic on the street below. The building across the way was boarded up, apparently a casualty of the blitz. "It's a one-way trip, isn't it," he said, turning back to Whitehall.

Whitehall shrugged. "Well, retrieval does pose some difficulties at the moment, as I'm sure you can understand. We'll be in communication, of course, through the chaps in the AK . . . and conditions may change in the next few months. If our boys make some progress in Italy it may open up some airstrips and perhaps . . ."

"Yes, I think I understand, Colonel."

Tadeusz Kaliski perched on a rock at the top of a hill overlooking a small grassy field near Blizna, Poland. On the other side of the field lay a dense forest and beyond that the SS training grounds. It was from this forest, three weeks ago, that he had first seen the extraordinary airplane without wings streaking toward the heavens.

Today, Tadeusz had a radio transmitter and a compass, taking his three-hour shift watching the launch site. If a launch occurred he would send a coded message indicating its direction and alerting the AK cell in that area to begin a search for the crash site.

He was nervous. When the wind was right, he could hear the barking of the German guard dogs that roamed through the woods with the sentries. Off to his left, less than a half kilometer away was the newly constructed railroad spur that ran from Blizna, through the forest and into the training grounds. An hour ago a freight train had rumbled along the tracks toward the training grounds. Tadeusz had counted twenty-seven freight cars draped with canvas tarps, moving slowly as though heavily loaded. Armed sentries guarded every car. If he were caught out here he would be executed on the spot. Of that, he was certain.

A thunderous roar suddenly jolted Tadeusz out of his reverie. He lost his grasp on the compass and reached down to grab it before it rolled down the hill. He looked up just in time to see an enormous cylinder emerge from the trees, trailing a blazing white fire. With his ears ringing and his hands shaking, Tadeusz scrambled to his feet and checked the compass.

In a few seconds it was over. The rocket had vanished from sight as quickly as it had emerged. The rumbling noise trailed off leaving behind an uneasy silence in the forest.

Chapter 32

ANNA SAT IN A WICKER CHAIR on the porch of the chalet and watched Andrew swing the axe, cleanly splitting another log. Justyn picked up the two pieces and stacked them on the pile.

The late October air was crisp, and the leaves had begun to turn. They would need the firewood for the winter, and she was grateful for the help of the American aviator. Andrew's ankle had healed nicely, and judging by the way he was swinging the axe, his cracked ribs had mended as well. Anna watched as he pulled a rag from his back pocket and wiped his forehead, then picked up another log and set it on its end. He seemed pleased at the opportunity for some exercise after being confined to crutches for so long.

Andrew had been with them for almost two months. He was no longer reticent and enjoyed talking about his family and his life back in America, where his father worked as a welder at a factory in Milwaukee that produced bomb casings, and his mother was as an administrator in a hospital. He described their home and the neighborhood where he grew up. Anna found herself enthralled with his tales of America and excited by the opportunity to practice her English, which she had studied during her university years.

She was surprised to learn that this city in the heartland of the United States was home to thousands of German and Polish immigrants. She found the irony of Germans and Poles living and working together in an American city while they slaughtered each other in Europe distressing but, in another way, hopeful. It sounded like a nice place to visit with Jan when all of this was over.

Her thoughts turned to Jan, as they inevitably did, wondering where he was and if he was safe. She never allowed herself to dwell on her fear for his safety—but it was always there, right beneath the surface.

Anna stood up to go inside and prepare lunch when she heard the snort of a horse and the creak of wagon wheels. She stepped around the corner of the chalet and saw Leon Marchal climbing down from the wagon.

Marchal waved at her then glanced toward the cleared area where Andrew and Justyn were still at work. He motioned her over to the wagon. "Van Acker needs to see you today. There's been a development."

"What's going on? What development?" Anna asked.

"He didn't say. He just asked me to drive out here and tell you he needed to see you."

Anna let herself in the back door of van Acker's butcher shop. His assistant was not there, but she could hear van Acker's gravelly voice in the front of the shop. She slipped into his small, cluttered office and waited. A few minutes later the bell jingled on the front door of the shop as the customer left, and van Acker lumbered into the office, sliding his large frame around her and sitting down at the desk.

"We have a problem," the big man said, wiping perspiration from his fore-head with a questionable-looking rag. "Andree de Jongh and her father have been arrested by the Gestapo."

Anna stared at him in disbelief. *"Mon dieu!* What happened?"

"Apparently an informer turned them in. They were both in Brussels and were picked up the night before last. But that's not the worst of it."

Anna was silent.

Van Acker wiped his brow again and continued. "Two other Comet Line operatives were also arrested. One of them was the escort designated to take the American aviators to Paris."

Anna felt queasy. "What are we going to do? They can't stay, can they?"

"*Non,* they can't stay," van Acker said. "And we're running out of time. A couple of Gestapo goons were in here this morning."

"In here? This morning? What did they want?"

"They said they knew someone in the area was harboring enemy fugitives. They wanted me to know how serious it would be for whomever it was. I'm not sure what they really know, but we can't risk it any longer. They have to go now."

"But how? Who's going to escort them?"

Van Acker looked at her.

"Me? Jules, you can't be serious? *Non*, I can't do it!"

"Anna, I wouldn't ask you if the situation weren't so serious. I can't do it; the Gestapo's watching me now. Marchal and Delacroix have to stay here because there's a drop scheduled for next week. The second American is staying with some people in Warempage, but they're elderly, and only barely speak English or Flemish. They would have no idea what to do."

"Jules . . . it's . . . it's out of the question. What about Justyn?"

"Couldn't he stay with the Marchals?"

"Well . . . I suppose he could but . . . *Non! C'est impossible* . . . it's too . . . I can't leave Justyn. There must be another way."

Van Acker was silent. He stared at the desk, the veins in his nose more pronounced than ever.

Anna's heart pounded. She knew there was no alternative. They could certainly provide the Americans with train tickets and false passports—but to send them off on their own would be a death sentence. They didn't speak the language. They couldn't read signs or menus. They'd never get past the border guards or railway conductors. And she knew van Acker would never take the risk of their capture and interrogation by the Gestapo. She knew what he would have to do to them. A knot in her stomach tightened. Andrew had become like a brother. "When would we have to leave?" she said softly.

Van Acker looked up at her. His eyes were moist.

"I have all of their documents right here," he said. His voice cracked. "I know your English is decent. How is your Flemish?"

Anna felt like she was being sucked into a whirlpool. "My Flemish? It's been a couple of years, Jules. Not since Antwerp, and then only passable. Most everyone in the Leffards' circle spoke French. How good will it have to be?"

Van Acker shrugged. "I'm sure you'll be fine. Don't worry about it. Marchal has a couple of suitcases with appropriate clothing for them. Word will be sent to the contact in Paris to expect you. You should leave tonight. Marchal will use my car and drive the three of you to the station in Bastogne. If everything goes according to plan you should be back home in four or five days."

The second American was a twenty-year-old Californian from San Diego named Brian Chesterman. He had thick blond hair and a muscular frame and looked to Anna like someone who had spent a lot of time doing push-ups on a beach.

Both of the aviators had false passports and identification papers that identified them as residing in Merksem, a working-class suburb of Antwerp. They were to appear as Flemish-speaking Belgians who understood neither French nor German. Over the past few weeks they had been taught to speak some superficial phrases in Flemish, which would hopefully be convincing enough in the event of a brief encounter.

Anna knew the concept had been used successfully by the Comet Line in the past since it was uncommon for either French or German soldiers to understand Flemish. Anna also had a set of false documents with an address in Antwerp. She wondered when van Acker had obtained them.

The train stopped in Lille, just across the French border, and a French conductor entered their car, accompanied by a German Feldgendarme. They began checking documents. Anna tried to remain calm as the two officials proceeded down the aisle, resisting the temptation to look at either Andrew or Brian. The conductor stopped at their seat and took the ticket and passport that Andrew handed to him. He checked them over carefully then addressed Andrew. "*Bonjour, monsieur.* What is the reason for your trip to Paris?"

Anna's heart skipped a beat. She was about to intercede and explain that Andrew didn't understand French when the aviator responded in Flemish. "*Ik begrijp het niet.* I don't understand."

The conductor glanced over his shoulder at the Feldgendarme who just shook his head. He turned back to Andrew but Anna tapped him on the arm. "*Excusez-moi, monsieur,* they're both traveling with me," she said. "I'm afraid neither one of them speak French or German. Perhaps I can help." She held out her ticket and passport.

The conductor glared at her for a second then snatched her papers. "Very well, madame," he said. His tone was official, condescending. "What is the reason the three of you are traveling to Paris?"

Anna stole a quick glance across the aisle at Andrew and Brian. Andrew appeared surprisingly relaxed, but Brian fidgeted and looked at the ground, beads of perspiration on his forehead. Anna smiled at the conductor and touched his arm again, lightly. She spoke quickly to keep his attention. "I'm sorry to cause this confusion for you, *monsieur,* but our company has contracted for some welding equipment with a small firm in Paris. These men are being sent there to inspect the equipment before it is shipped. I am their interpreter."

The conductor held Anna's eyes for a moment then returned her documents. Abruptly, he turned and barked at Brian for his papers.

Brian frowned and shook his head.

Anna held up her ticket and passport. *"Kaartje en paspoort,* show him your ticket and passport," she said in Flemish.

Brian nodded and produced the documents.

Anna tried to keep her breathing under control while the conductor examined Brian's papers. No need to worry, she told herself. Everything should be in order. The clothing that had been provided for the two aviators had been well selected and their hair had grown out to the point where their outward appearance seemed fairly typical of young Belgian men.

Suddenly the conductor spoke to Brian in English. "So, you are an engineer?" he asked.

Anna stiffened.

Brian looked up. He stared at the conductor and stammered, *"Pardon? Ik begrijp het niet."*

The conductor glared at him, then tossed back the ticket and passport, grunted something unintelligible and moved on to the next row.

It was a little after seven o'clock in the evening when they disembarked at Paris's Gare du Nord. Anna led the way through the busy station. As they had worked out in advance, Andrew and Brian went into the toilet while Anna walked over to the newsstand and purchased a Parisian magazine. She sat down on one of the nearby benches and pretended to leaf through the magazine while glancing about the cavernous station at the hundreds of people moving about in all directions. She felt foolish and frightened, not knowing exactly what she was supposed to be looking for.

In the car earlier, on the way to Bastogne, Marchal had told her to appear as nonchalant as possible but to watch the crowd; if she spotted the same person more that once, it might indicate that she was being followed. It sounded pretty vague and haphazard to her, but Marchal had said that it was the best they could do in the way of training on short notice.

As Anna watched the ebb and flow of people moving about she noticed something. Standing out from the throng of Parisians in their worn, drab clothing were groups of well-dressed Germans, chatting and laughing, clutching bags from some of Paris's finest shops. Most likely they were officers and their wives on a shopping holiday in the jewel city of their conquered lands, she thought.

Anna watched the Germans parade through the station, haughty and arrogant, her contempt building. Her fear began to dissipate and a myriad of suppressed emotions flooded back. She thought about her father . . . about Jan . . . and about Irene, lying on the floor of the toilet in Prague.

Her resolve stiffened. She knew exactly what she had to do. Get these young aviators on their way back to England and back into the war, and send these despicable creatures back where they came from.

She blinked, looked across the station and spotted Andrew and Brian emerge from the toilet. Andrew lit up a cigarette, as he had been instructed to do, and the two of them looked over in her direction. As a signal that she believed they were not being followed, Anna stood up, placed the magazine into her bag and walked toward the exit. Andrew and Brian followed a minute later. It was dark outside and the night air was cool. The pedestrian traffic on the sidewalks was heavy with people commuting home from work. The three of them had all studied maps of this section of Paris, and they split up, each heading in a different direction.

Twenty minutes later they reunited at the intersection of rue La Fayette and rue de Chateaudin, and set out on foot for the address Anna had memorized. It took over a half hour to reach the neighborhood on the Left Bank of the Seine, but Marchal had warned Anna to avoid the subways and the police checkpoints that were randomly set up at the stations.

The building on rue Lobineau was a nondescript three-story structure with a black tile roof, not unlike thousands of others in Paris. They stepped inside the small entryway and located the doorbell labeled *Martel*. The buzzer sounded and they passed through the second door and climbed the stairs.

Monsieur Martel was a pale, boney man with a neatly clipped goatee and gray hair. He wore rimless glasses and looked to Anna like an accountant or banker. In fact, she learned that M. Martel was both. He was an accountant for one of Paris's larger banks and had his office in a building just a few streets away.

Over a glass of wine and some brie spread on thin slices of bread, Martel

informed them that he had assisted more than thirty British and American aviators and a handful of French Jews during the last two years. Most of them had
spent the night in his apartment.

"I am devastated when learned of Andree de Jongh's arrest," he said. His
English was broken but understandable. "She recruited me personally, such
sincere, dedicated person." He glanced at the cracked ceiling and sighed. "I
was frightened. Had decided to quit. Then got word of two Americans being
escorted by attractive redheaded woman." He glanced at Anna with a smile
and shrugged. "What can I say? Was intrigued." He raised his glass. "À la
votre! The report correct."

Anna smiled back. "What is the next step, M. Martel?"

Martel set his glass on the small coffee table and glanced at the three of
them. "You all spend night here. Anna, you leave after breakfast, return to
Belgium. Andrew and Brian will be picked up here later in day and taken out
of city. God willing, back in London in few weeks."

A look of disappointment came over the faces of the two young aviators at
the words "a few weeks."

Martel leaned forward, tapping Andrew's knee. "Trust me," he said, "we
get you back to England, back in airplane so you can bomb hell out of maniac
Huns."

The next morning was cold, the sky slate gray. Anna turned up the collar of
her thin, woolen coat as she left the apartment building. She felt empty. Saying
good-bye to Andrew had been harder than she imagined. In just a few short
months she had become very attached to him. And now he was gone. Like so
many others in her life. She had forced herself not to cry when he embraced her
and said that he would never forget her. But she cried now, crossing a bridge
over the gray, swirling waters of the Seine. She knew that the image of the two
American boys standing in the doorway, looking lost and alone, would stay
with her for a long time.

Chapter 33

JAN SNAPPED AWAKE as the plane hit a pocket of turbulence above the Baltic Sea. He glanced at his watch but couldn't see it in the dark interior of the Halifax. Up front, in the green glow of the instruments, he could make out the silhouettes of the pilot and copilot, their heads slowly turning as they scanned the dark skies.

The other two crew members with him in the back were sound asleep, oblivious to the droning oscillations of the four-engine bomber. Jan stretched his legs and readjusted the duffel bags he was leaning against to provide some protection from the cold, metal skin of the fuselage. He realized he should try to get back to sleep, but his mind was once again alive in anticipation of what lay ahead.

It was November and almost four weeks had passed since his meeting with Colonel Whitehall in London. Between the crash courses in radio operation and ciphers, basic rocket design, parachute jumping and meetings with a seemingly endless stream of intelligence analysts, he'd had very little time to himself. In retrospect, that was probably a good thing, he thought.

During the past year, Jan realized his mental attitude was darkening with the growing number of stories he'd heard about atrocities being committed by the Nazis in Poland. In his sessions with MI-6 he'd pressed for information but hadn't gotten much. Either they didn't know or they weren't talking. He knew it was probably naive to think that just because he was being sent to Poland he'd be able to find out something about Anna, but it was better than sitting on his ass in Scotland. Maybe when he got there he could—

Jan felt a hand on his shoulder. It was the copilot. "We've reached the coast,

Major. We're about twenty minutes from the drop site. You'd better get your gear on."

Jan nodded at the British officer and got to his feet. His left leg ached from the cramped position he'd been in, and he rubbed it vigorously to stimulate the circulation. Once again he felt a surge of gratitude for the skill of the British doctor on board the hospital ship.

The pitch of the propellers changed as the big plane banked to the left and began descending to parachute altitude. Pushed to the maximum extent of its range, the stripped-down Halifax would be dropping Jan just a hundred kilometers beyond the Baltic coast in a remote area of northern Poland. It was a long way from Blizna, but Whitehall had assured him that everything had been arranged and he would be met at the drop zone by agents of the AK. He wondered briefly how Whitehall would feel about such "assurances" if he were the one jumping alone into an occupied country, but he put it out of his mind. He just wanted to get it over with without breaking his leg again.

The copilot shouted something unintelligible. Apparently the other crew members understood, however, because they both gave him a "thumbs-up." One of them pulled the door open, and the noise level jumped several orders of magnitude. An icy rush of air blasted Jan, and his mind went blank as he watched the two airmen slide heavy wooden crates across the floor and shove them out into the black abyss.

Jan snapped onto the static line. He felt a pat on his back, closed his eyes and stepped into the void. In an instant, the noise vanished and the parachute exploded above his head, jerking him upward.

When he looked down, Jan spotted a flickering light off to his right. With surprising speed, the ground rose up to meet him and he thumped down hard, tumbling over on his left side.

It was over.

He lay there for a second, flexing both legs, then jumped up and began hauling in the parachute.

He pulled in the last of the billowing white cloth and stuffed it into the pack just as several shadowy figures emerged from the trees. He dropped to his knees and pulled out his pistol, glancing over his shoulder, to the left and right. He couldn't see anyone else, so he trained the gun on the three advancing figures and waited.

The figures stopped twenty meters away, their rifles now visible. One yelled out in Polish, "Have you seen the night hawk?"

Jan felt a surge of relief at the expected phrase and started to reply when his voice caught. He cleared his throat and yelled back, "Yes, it's flown off to the north!"

The three figures exchanged glances. They lowered their rifles and ran to him. The one who had yelled out, looked beyond Jan to the tree line on the other side of the field. He pulled out a small flashlight and switched it on and off three times. Without a word he touched Jan's shoulder and motioned for him to follow as the three men turned and trotted back the way they had come.

Just before they reached the trees, Jan looked back over his shoulder and saw another group of men run into the field from the opposite tree line. They headed toward the crates.

Jan turned back and followed the three men into the woods and along a narrow path to a small creek. Still without saying a word, they sloshed through the shallow water and up a small rise to a clearing where they finally stopped. The one who had spoken earlier wiped his hand on his rough, woolen trousers and extended it to Jan. In a coarse voice he asked, "You are Albin?"

"Yes," Jan replied with considerable relief. The forged papers in his jacket pocket identified him as Albin Tominski, a Polish citizen from a town near Poznan in western Poland. He gripped the short, stout man's hand and repeated, "Albin Tominski."

The man smiled and said, "I am Tadeusz. This is Pavel and Zenek."

The other two men stepped forward and shook Jan's hand.

"We'd better keep moving," Tadeusz said. "It's another twenty minutes to the cabin. Then we can have something to eat."

It was a small wooden cabin with a thatched roof, nestled among a clump of birch trees at the edge of a wheat field. Beyond the field, Tadeusz explained, was a dirt road that led to a town where they would be able to catch the train.

They kicked the dirt off their boots and entered the simple cabin, warmed by glowing embers in a stone fireplace. A gray-haired woman dressed in a rough woolen skirt and a threadbare sweater placed a large bowl of steaming stew on the table, which was set with four places. She set out a bottle of vodka and four glasses then retired to one of the other rooms without being introduced or saying a word.

The man called Zenek poured a small amount of vodka into each of the four glasses and passed them around. He raised his glass to Jan and said, "When you return to England, tell our British friends the AK appreciates the supplies. We will make good use of them when the time comes."

Jan tilted his glass toward each of the three hard, weathered faces in the dimly lit room. He could tell from their accents they were rural men, most likely farmers or woodsmen. He wondered what these partisan fighters had seen and done during the past four years of Nazi occupation. He was sure he would find out soon enough.

Zenek motioned toward the table. "Now, how about some food?"

It was almost nine o'clock in the evening, two days later, when the train pulled into the railway station at Tarnow, still scarred from bombings during the invasion. A fat Polish policeman, his uniform unkempt, his breath smelling of alcohol, examined Jan's papers. At the end of the platform two green-uniformed Feldgendarmes leaned against the wall of the station, drinking coffee and smoking cigarettes. One of them held a muzzled German shepherd on a chain.

The policeman handed back his papers, and Jan followed Tadeusz down the platform, silently grateful for the skill of the British forgers. His papers looked exactly like those that Tadeusz carried, dirty and wrinkled, as though he had been carrying them around for years.

As they passed the two Feldgendarmes the dog approached Tadeusz and sniffed at his pant leg. The one holding the chain jerked it and pulled the dog away. "*Nein*, Freda. You'll catch fleas from these vermin."

The other Feldgendarme burst out laughing, spitting his coffee down his chin.

Jan pretended he didn't understand and kept walking, knowing that most Polish peasants spoke no German. His knowledge of the language might be useful in the right situation . . . but he had to be careful.

When they got outside they stood for a few minutes breathing in the cold air of the November night. After two days of foul railcars and stinking, war-torn rail stations, the fresh air was a welcome relief. Tadeusz put a hand on Jan's shoulder and motioned with his head. "We'd better move along. It's not a good idea to be on the streets at night. The fuckin' policemen have been sitting on their asses most of the day drinking, and at night they try to find a little sport. Most of them are harmless, but there're some crazy ones out there. The

Feldgendarmes are the worst. It's easy to get shot if you get in their way."

Jan nodded. "Where are we going?"

Tadeusz glanced around. "There's a safe house on the outskirts of the city. They're expecting us."

A half hour later Jan and Tadeusz turned onto a narrow gravel road that crossed a field and led to a gray stucco house. Three other houses were nearby, and at the far end of the field stood the remains of a bombed-out factory.

The door opened as they approached the house, and a large man with deep-set dark eyes and a heavily pock-marked face stepped out on the porch. Without a greeting, he motioned for them to enter, followed them in, and closed and bolted the door behind them.

Jan glanced around. A woman in a red flowered dress sat on a faded brown sofa on the other side of the small parlor. The other furniture in the room consisted of two upholstered chairs and a small round table with an incongruous oriental lamp.

"We were expecting you yesterday," the tall man said to Tadeusz. "I was getting worried. Is this our visitor from the West?"

Tadeusz nodded and turned toward the woman who got up and hurried across the room. She embraced Tadeusz, kissing him on the cheek. "Thank God you're here," she said. "I always imagine the worst."

The evening passed with several rounds of bitter potato vodka along with some cheese, dark bread and boiled potatoes. Jan ate with relish. It was the first thing resembling real food he had had since the stew back in Zenek's cabin.

The conversation with Fryderyk and Helena was friendly and spirited. Though Jan doubted those were their real names, he could tell they were city people, educated, teachers perhaps. They wanted to know everything he could tell them about what was happening in the West. Were they starving in France and Belgium? Was Churchill well? What about the Americans? Could they be counted on to help? When would the Allies launch the invasion?

"The BBC broadcasts in Polish every night," Fryderyk said. "We try to listen as often as we can, but we have to be careful. The Gestapo have spies everywhere. If they catch you with a radio, it's trouble. The first time they usually just take it away. The second time . . . it's 'ziiit.'" He made a slitting gesture with his finger across his throat.

Jan was quiet for a few minutes, reflecting on the last two days, traveling through the bleak, war-scarred country. The dusty roads in the countryside were largely deserted except for battered peasant wagons and farmers leading mules and oxen. In the towns, shabbily dressed people queued up in front of shops that had little for sale. As he observed the street scenes and watched people come and go on the train, Jan realized something. Practically all the people he saw were women, small children and old men. There were few young men—and there were no Jews.

Fryderyk leaned across the table and touched his arm as though he were reading his thoughts. "The young men that weren't killed or captured have all been sent to Germany," he said. "Forced laborers. A few come back in the winter, when the harvests are over, but they're sent back to Germany in the spring."

"Those who are able to slip through the net hide in the forests, working with the AK," Tadeusz added. "You'll meet some of them."

Jan nodded. He hesitated for a moment, thinking about Irene and Justyn. "Tell me about the Jews," he said.

The three people around the table all looked at each other. They were silent for several long moments.

Fryderyk took a breath and spoke quietly. "During '41 and '42 Jews from all over Poland were rounded up, forced out of their homes and brought into the cities. The SS herded them into areas called ghettos, sealed off with barbed wire and brick walls. All the big cities had ghettos—Warsaw, Krakow, Lodz, even here in Tarnow. Hundreds of thousand of Jews crammed into areas where only five or ten thousand had lived, sometimes fifty people to a house, all starving."

Jan looked at the somber faces around the table. He had heard stories. Now it was real. "You said the cities *had* ghettos." He wasn't sure he wanted to hear the rest.

Fryderyk gulped the last of his vodka and set the glass down, staring at the table. His voice was barely audible. "Earlier this year most of the ghettos were cleared out. SS troops and Feldgendarmes stormed in, usually in the middle of the night, and rousted out the Jews who were still alive. They herded them into trucks and railcars and sent them away—to the camps."

Jan's stomach heaved, thinking about Irene and Justyn . . . and Anna. He knew Anna would never leave them. He stood up, gripping the back of the chair for support. The vodka, the food and the days with little sleep had finally caught up with him. Helena took his arm and showed him to a small bedroom on the second floor. He was asleep, fully clothed, within minutes.

The next morning it turned colder and a sleeting rain fell. Jan and Tadeusz climbed into Fryderyk's battered, ten-year-old truck and set out for Tadeusz's farm near Blizna.

"I am allowed to keep the truck only because twice a week I deliver supplies for the Germans," Fryderyk said, "to a work camp, twenty kilometers north. A hundred or so Polish boys are working there, clearing land for one of those camps."

Jan swallowed hard. "What you told me last night . . . in Britain we've only heard stories, rumors."

Fryderyk glanced at him. "It's all true, whatever you heard." He shook his head and stared straight ahead, gripping the steering wheel with both hands.

The trip took almost four hours over deeply rutted, muddy roads, passing through war-torn towns and villages. They were forced to make several long detours just to find bridges that were passable.

When they finally arrived at Tadeusz's farm, the sun had come out, and a stout woman was hanging wash on a clothesline strung between a tree and the single-story brick house. The woman waved to them and hurried over, sloshing through puddles. She embraced Tadeusz, and kissed Fryderyk on the cheek, then turned to Jan, introducing herself as Lidia. She had a surprisingly strong grip as she shook Jan's hand. "Krupa is inside," she said abruptly to Tadeusz. "He arrived this morning."

When they entered the house a thin, practically bald man wearing steel-rimmed eyeglasses rose from a wooden chair at the kitchen table and stepped forward. Jan found himself looking into the eyes of the man he had met on his mission to Krakow four years earlier. The man he had known as Slomak.

Chapter 34

LEON MARCHAL LEANED ACROSS his kitchen table for a closer look at the plans, adjusting the wick on the kerosene lamp. They had been over this at least a dozen times but he was still uneasy about the distance from the north fence line to the repair building. He measured it again, referring to the scale in the lower right-hand corner, and came up with the same answer he had each time before. "*Mon dieu*, it's almost a hundred meters," he mumbled and sat down, rubbing his eyes.

Paul Delacroix sat on the other side of the oak-plank table and nodded.

Jules van Acker stood at the cast-iron woodstove and poured himself another cup of coffee, filling the chipped pottery mug to the brim. The farmhouse kitchen was small with a rough pine floor and stucco walls but Marchal's wife, Antoinette, had brightened it up with frilly lace curtains and a glass cupboard filled with blue and yellow hand-painted china. The men used the pottery cups. Van Acker took a sip of the bitter coffee and said, "*Je comprends*, Leon. We've been through it over and over. There's no other way in. The main gate on the south side is always guarded. The west side is blocked by the coal pile and the conveyor system, and the east side is all swamp. You've got to go in from the north."

"But it's wide open, no cover at all," Marchal said.

Delacroix looked at his friend. "It'll be a moonless night, Leon. Everyone will be wearing dark clothing. We'll just have to move quickly."

Marchal studied the large sheet of paper another time and rubbed his forehead. Acquiring the plans of the German's new railroad refueling and repair depot had been a major coup that Willy Boeynants had somehow pulled off.

Marchal knew how important this was. Van Acker had been informed in a message from Leffard that it was an opportunity the leaders of the White Brigade and the SOE in London did not want to miss.

Van Acker stepped over to the table and put a beefy hand on Marchal's shoulder. "How are your supplies?" he asked.

Marchal didn't look up. "We have plenty for this. There were fifty kilos of plastique in the last drop—the new material, PE-2. That's not the problem."

Van Acker was silent for a moment. "You know how critical this is, Leon."

Marchal stood up and walked over to the stove. "*Oui, oui, bien sûr.* And the location is ideal, remote, away from everything. The Germans never learn. They always try and hide these things." He grabbed the coffeepot and filled his cup. "Everything's fine except for that first hundred meters." He took a sip and looked at van Acker. "Don't worry, Jules, we'll get it done. Tell Leffard and Boeynants that we'll handle it."

The next evening was windy and cold, not uncommon for early December in the Ardennes region of Belgium, although they had not as yet had any snow. The men who gathered in Marchal's barnyard shuffled and stamped their feet to keep warm. They passed around a bottle of *pequet* to take the chill away.

Marchal looked over the group as he pulled open the heavy wooden barn door and they stepped inside to get out of the wind. There were seven of them: he and Paul Delacroix, their sons Jean-Claude and Henri, as well as Gaston, and two men from Bastogne known only by their first names, Richard and Franc. Richard was a big, loud man with a thick, black beard who cleared away a corner of the workbench, challenging the two boys to an arm-wrestling match. Franc was more like Gaston, quiet and serious.

Marchal had served with elite, professional soldiers in his years with the Chasseurs Ardennais, but he had no reservations about this band of tough, solid men. Though their "uniforms" consisted of a hodgepodge of heavy woollen coats, leather work boots, felt hats and berets, they were determined anti-Nazi partisans. Brought together by Leffard and van Acker, Marchal had led the group on four previous missions and would trust his life to any of them. Jean-Claude and Henri, already toughened by the train derailment in September, would learn much from these men.

Van Acker and his assistant from the butcher shop arrived a few minutes later with a car and a truck. The men loaded their supplies and piled in.

The two vehicles traveled by different routes, arriving an hour later at a deserted farm near the small village of Beho. The refueling station was less than five kilometers away, but, trekking overland through dense forests and over hills, Marchal had calculated it would be close to midnight before they arrived.

Marchal and Delacroix took the lead, carrying the packages of PE-2 in their backpacks. They each carried a Colt 45 and three hand grenades. Marchal also carried a Walther P-38 he had taken from a Wehrmacht officer in 1940, then fitted with a silencer. Jean-Claude and Henri followed, carrying a heavy-duty bolt cutter, a sledgehammer, folding shovels, flashlights and extra ammunition in their packs. Gaston, Richard and Franc brought up the rear. Franc and Gaston each carried Sten guns and hand grenades, detonator cords and timing pencils, food and water. Richard lugged the larger Bren gun and the folding bipod.

A half hour before midnight, they came to the crest of a hill. Below them, on a flat plain, a half-kilometer to the south, lay the refueling depot. Marchal leaned against a tree and stared down at the vast fenced-in yard. It was larger than he had imagined.

Four sets of railroad tracks entered the depot from the south, through the main gates. A water tower stood in the middle of the yard with two sets of tracks passing on either side. At the north end of the yard, closest to their position, loomed the massive repair building. Along the entire west side sprawled an enormous coal pile and conveyor system. A dirt road ran north and south the length of the yard in front of the conveyor system. The east side of the yard was flat and grassy with a few small buildings, then gradually fell off into a marsh.

A four-meter-high chain-link fence with rolled barbed wire along the top surrounded the entire facility. Just as Marchal had seen on the plans, the fence along the north side was set back from the repair building about a hundred meters.

Marchal slipped the pack off his back and set it on the ground. He turned to the group. "We'll stop here and rest."

Franc opened his pack and passed out thick slices of bread and cheese.

Delacroix took a pair of binoculars out of his pack, stood up and looked toward the depot. There were spotlights shining down into the yard, mounted on the top of the water tower and on the roof of the repair building. He spent several minutes slowly scanning back and forth, muttering *Mon dieu* under his breath. He turned toward Marchal. "There's a guardhouse at the main gate with at least three or four guards hanging around. I also spotted a pair of guards patrolling the west side, on the road in front of the conveyors. There appears to be a railcar parked near the water tower, but most of the view is blocked by the repair building."

He turned back toward the depot, this time scanning carefully the long back wall of the repair building and the open ground between it and the fence. After a few minutes he handed the binoculars to Marchal.

As Marchal studied the terrain, another set of guards came into view, patrolling the north fence line. They carried submachine guns, and one of them led a large black Doberman on a chain leash. The importance of this facility to the German war effort became evident when Marchal saw their uniforms. These weren't Feldgendarmes; they were Wehrmacht soldiers.

Marchal continued to study the area for another few minutes then set the glasses down. He looked at Delacroix and nodded. Marchal turned toward the rest of the group and pointed toward the northeast corner of the yard. "There's a narrow area from the northeast corner of the repair building extending all the way to the fence that's shaded from the lights. That's the spot where we'll have to cross the field. There's a set of double doors in the center of the north wall of the repair building. We'll have to get across the field to the building and over to the doors, open the lock and get inside during the time that the guards are out of sight."

Marchal picked up the binoculars and handed them to Jean-Claude, pointing to a flat area between two pine trees halfway down the hill. "Make your way down to that spot and monitor the movement of the guards. We need to know how much time we've got to get across the field and into the building."

Marchal looked at Richard. "Go with him and set up the Bren gun. From that spot you should be able to cover the whole north end of the yard and the east side of the building. It's as good a field of fire as we're going to get." He glanced around at the others. "The rest of us will make our way along the ridge and down to the fence in the shaded area." Marchal turned back to Jean-Claude and looked his son in the eye. "As soon as you know the time interval, come down and join us at the fence."

• • •

An hour later Marchal's group was ready to go. The two guards, walking slowly and smoking cigarettes, had just disappeared around the northeast corner of the repair building. They took the enormous black dog with them. By Jean-Claude's calculations they had twenty minutes before the guards would reappear at the northwest corner.

Delacroix and his son, Henri, began snipping the chain-link fence with the heavy bolt cutter. It took three minutes to cut a slit large enough, and then the six men slithered through, one-by-one on their stomachs, and sprinted across the field.

Staying against the side of the building, out of the light, the group moved down to the large sheet steel doors. The handles were chained and padlocked.

Gaston pulled a small pouch out of his pack, removed a set of picks from it and gripped the padlock.

Marchal fidgeted as he watched the man insert one pick after another, searching for the right one as calmly as though he were fixing a watch in the comfort of his home. Marchal glanced at his own watch—seven minutes had passed.

Another three minutes passed, and Gaston was still selecting picks and trying the lock. Marchal reached into his knapsack, removed the Walther P-38 and attached the silencer. Another two minutes and he would make his way to the northwest corner of the building, wait for the guards and shoot them as they rounded the corner.

The lock clicked open.

Marchal took a deep breath and stuck the Walther under his belt.

Delacroix grabbed one of the large handles and pulled the door open just far enough for all of them to slip inside.

The cavernous room was dimly lit by a few bare bulbs high in the ceiling. It smelled of machine oil and sulfur. Delacroix pushed the door closed, leaving a slight gap.

Marchal removed the Walther from his belt and handed it to his son. He gave Jean-Claude a hard look. "*Soyez courageux*. If those guards stop to investigate, you know what to do."

Marchal led the group away from the door and spread the plans on the dirt floor near a giant steam locomotive parked on a turntable. He pulled a flashlight from his pack. Alternately looking at the plans and shining the light around the room, Marchal spotted several huge lathes and drill presses. Along one wall was a welding booth almost ten meters wide with a bank of acetylene tanks chained to the wall.

Marchal turned to Gaston, who had removed several packages of PE-2 from his pack and was selecting detonator cords and timing pencils. "You and Henri set the charges inside the building," he said.

Gaston nodded and began preparing the charges.

Marchal, Delacroix and Franc gathered their packs and sprinted toward the other end of the building. They found a small service door, which led out to the main yard. It was unlocked.

Marchal pushed the door open. They were in luck. On the track closest to the building was another locomotive attached to a coal car. He scanned the area then ran to the locomotive followed by Delacroix and Franc.

Marchal peeked around the side of the locomotive toward the coal pile on the west side of the yard. The main framework of the conveyor system was about thirty meters to the west, across the narrow dirt road, but it was bathed in light from the spotlight at the top of the water tower. The area was wide open and in plain view from the main guard shack.

He cursed to himself. They would have to forget the conveyor. But the locomotive and its coal car extended all the way from the repair garage to the water tower. One of the four steel legs supporting the tower was in the dark, shaded by the coal car. The three men squatted next to the locomotive, and Marchal broke out the remaining packets of explosives, handing three of them to Franc who crawled off toward the tower.

Marchal and Delacroix began fixing the explosive charges to the locomotive. When they were finished, Marchal waved at Franc over by the water tower. Franc activated the timing pencil on the charges he had fixed to the leg of the tower, then crawled back to the locomotive, joining Marchal and Delacroix.

Marchal checked his watch. He waited two minutes then crushed the glass ampoules at the top of the timing pencils. It would take twenty minutes for the sulfuric acid released inside the tube to corrode the steel wires holding back the plungers. Then the detonators would explode the charges. They would have to be well out of the yard and back up the hill by that time.

The three men slipped back into the repair building and headed for the double doors. Marchal waved at Gaston who activated the fifteen-minute timing pencils on the charges he had set and then joined them.

When he got to the double doors, Marchal found Jean-Claude sweating profusely and studying his watch. "What's the situation?" he asked his son.

"The guards walked by five minutes ago," Jean-Claude said, his voice cracking with tension. "They should be around the corner of the building by now."

Marchal nodded and pulled the door open.

At his post on the hill, Richard was worried. The guards and the dog had again rounded the northeast corner of the building without noticing either the missing lock or the slit in the fence.

But instead of continuing on to the south, they stopped and one guard unbuttoned his long, gray coat, handing the dog's leash to his partner. Richard cursed under his breath as he watched the man undo the fly of his trousers.

He looked back to the building and saw the door slide open. Marchal's group started filed out and moved along the side of the building. He wanted to scream at them but couldn't without alerting the guards. He grabbed the handle of the Bren gun and swung it around, aiming at the two Germans. He released the safety and waited, holding his breath.

Out of the corner of his eye he saw his comrades, one-by-one, sprinting across the open field toward the fence. His heart pounded, but he forced himself to wait.

The guard finished relieving himself and buttoned up his trousers. The second guard turned toward him, then went rigid and pointed at the fence. He dropped the dog's leash and raised his submachine gun.

Richard squeezed the trigger, and the Bren gun erupted in a staccato burst echoing off the hillside.

Both guards fell to the ground. The dog bolted away, but the guard with the submachine gun started to get up. Richard fired another burst, and he went down again.

Richard shot a quick glance toward the yard in time to see Henri slither through the slit in the fence. Jean-Claude, a few meters behind, crawled after him on his stomach. Franc and Gaston dove to the ground behind him.

Jean-Claude made it through the slit, then Franc. Gaston started wriggling through.

Richard looked back to the dead guards and froze in horror. From the corner of the building charged the huge black Doberman, barking and snarling, the chain leash flapping behind. Richard looked back to the field. Paul Delacroix was almost to the fence, but Marchal was still thirty meters away, running hard.

An instant later the massive dog leaped onto Marchal's back and knocked him to the ground. Marchal rolled over, struggling to get away, but the dog lunged for his throat. Marchal raised an arm, and the frenzied animal's jaw clamped on the sleeve of his jacket, shaking it back and forth.

Richard swung the Bren gun around, trying to aim but it was no use. From this distance he could just as easily hit Marchal as the dog. Delacroix whirled and ran back to Marchal, clubbing the dog with the butt of his Sten gun. Marchal rolled on the ground and broke free.

In that instant, the dog hesitated, unsure which man to attack. It was enough. Richard sighted down the barrel of the Bren and squeezed the trigger. The dog collapsed on the ground.

Marchal tried to get up but stumbled. Delacroix grabbed his arm and helped him toward the fence.

Richard spotted four guards sprinting along the east side of the yard toward the repair building. *"Vite! Vite!* Hurry! Hurry!" he screamed at the group then swung the Bren gun to the east and inserted a fresh magazine.

Delacroix and Marchal made it through the opening and the group scrambled up the hill.

The guards shouted. Shots rang out.

Richard squeezed the trigger and fired a burst. When he stopped and looked over the smoking barrel, two of the guards were sprawled on the ground but the other two had apparently made it to the corner of the building. He scanned the area, trying to spot them, but they were hidden in the shadows.

A siren wailed, and Richard looked back toward the guard shack at the main gate. Another group of guards ran along the conveyor toward the repair building. Then Marchal and the others were at his side.

"How many do you see?" Marchal asked, his breathing labored.

"Two are down, but two others made it to the north wall of the building," Richard said. "There's at least four more running in this direction."

Marchal glanced at his watch. "Two minutes before the charges inside the building go off. *Restez vigilant!* Keep those guards pinned down." He turned to the others. "Start making your way back to the top of the hill."

Richard swung the Bren gun back and forth, sighting down the barrel, looking for movement. He heard Marchal say, "One minute."

Suddenly, Richard saw two guards break for the fence. He pulled the trigger, and the burst from the big gun sent both of them diving to the ground. Richard sprayed the area as the guards clawed back toward the building. He released the trigger, and the gun fell silent . . . just as the first explosion went off.

In a jarring detonation the northeast corner of the building blew open, and tons of iron and steel rocketed through the air, crashing in the field. Three seconds later another blast erupted, and the metal roof shredded into a thousand shards of scrap iron.

Richard was knocked to the ground by the blasts and, wiping dirt from his eyes, gathered up the Bren gun and started climbing the hill, following Marchal and Delacroix. He turned to look back at the building just as the third charge went off. It was the one strapped to the acetylene tanks.

A thundering concussion echoed over the hillside, followed an instant later by a monstrous fireball belching through the gaping hole in the roof.

Richard staggered backward, the heat so intense that he was certain his eyes and hair had been scorched. He saw Marchal yell something and wave at him, but his ears rang so badly that he couldn't hear him. Richard scrambled to the top of the hill as the next set of charges went off.

The explosives strapped to the leg of the water tower went first, and the top of the tower dipped a meter or two and then stopped.

"Goddamn it!" Franc cursed. "It's not going to fall!"

Time seemed to stand still. Then another blast erupted, from the charges strapped to the locomotive. The immense machine lifted off the ground, enormous sections of steel flying in all directions. The attached coal car rocked wildly then rolled on its side, toward the water tower. Richard watched in fascination as the heavily laden car toppled into the base of the now three-legged tower. The tower shuddered then, in agonizingly slow motion, began to collapse. It tipped about thirty degrees when its roof split open and, with an enormous *whoosh*, a half million liters of water cascaded over the yard.

The torrent of water slammed into the yard like an avalanche, swamped the conveyor system and smashed it into kindling.

· · ·

Marchal stood silently at the top of the hill, mesmerized by the awesome sight. He knew the raging inferno in the repair building would continue for several days. Two locomotives and a coal car had been destroyed, along with the water tower and the conveyor system. The facility would be out of commission for a long time. Managing a smile, he glanced around at the rest of the group who stared transfixed at the wreckage, their faces illuminated by the blazing flames in the night.

Chapter 35

JAN FOLLOWED TADEUSZ and Slomak into a wooden shed hidden among a stand of colossal oak trees at the end of a rutted dirt road. Inside, another man, thin and hard, perhaps in his early twenties, struck a match to a lantern. The man blew out the match and hung the lantern from a hook, illuminating a workbench covered with a gray canvas tarp. Jan moved in closer as the man rolled back the tarp revealing dozens of rocket fragments.

Jan sifted through the parts, examining the strange devices with care. Some had wires protruding at odd angles, others were nothing more than blackened metal shards and twisted sheet steel. He looked up from the workbench and turned toward the young man who was lighting a hand-rolled cigarette. "Where did you find these?" he asked.

The man took a drag on the cigarette and picked a speck of tobacco from his lower lip. "In a field about two kilometers from here. A rocket crashed in the middle of the night. This was all we could get before the SS showed up."

Jan sifted through the jumble of debris a second time, examining each piece, trying to understand what he was looking at. It was always the same—the rockets crashed with such incredible explosions that little remained. "I don't know what these are," he said. "Some of them look like a type of timing device . . . but I don't understand the significance. I don't know how it all fits together."

Jan rubbed his eyes and looked at Slomak. "We've been at this for almost a month, sifting through these shattered fragments. And I don't know any more than when we started. If we could find something that was more intact . . ." His voice trailed off. Frustrated, he pulled out his notebook and made some sketches and notations while Tadeusz took some photos. Slomak and the young man stepped outside. Jan had not been introduced to the man, which he had now come to realize was the way things were done in the AK. Everything was on a strict "need-to-know" basis.

When they were finished, Tadeusz extinguished the lantern and fastened the padlock on the door. Slomak waited for them, sitting in the cab of the ancient Russian-built truck provided by operatives of the AK. The young man was gone.

Tadeusz hid the notebook and the photos in the compartment under the floorboards then climbed in, behind the wheel. Jan settled in next to Slomak, and they drove off without a word.

Jan stared out the window at the bleak countryside and recalled the first time he had witnessed a rocket launch from the forests near the training grounds. At that instant he knew this weapon was infinitely more lethal than the British had imagined. During his training sessions at MI-6 headquarters, British agents had shown him aerial photographs of German rocket launch sites discovered in northern France. The fuzzy pictures revealed what looked like inclined ramps hidden in fields and forests. The British speculated that the ramps were a type of catapult for launching moderate speed, unmanned rockets. They called them V-1s for "vengeance weapons."

But what Jan had seen blasting into the sky near Blizna was entirely different. This was a missile, launched vertically at unbelievable velocity, that disappeared from sight in seconds. The destructive potential scared him to death.

They drove on in silence, keeping to the back roads, avoiding villages and towns. The truck bed was full of rusty wheels and an old engine block that took up half the space—part of their cover as scrap metal dealers. Jan wondered how that would hold up if they were stopped but pushed the thought from his mind. There wasn't much he could do about it.

It was almost six o'clock in the evening and completely dark when they drove into a farmyard on the outskirts of a small village Jan had never heard of. The temperature had been dropping all afternoon, and flakes of snow danced in the headlights of the lumbering truck. Tadeusz stopped the truck in front of a barn. A minute later a man emerged from the darkness, carrying a lantern and bent over against the wind. The man slid the barn door back, and Tadeusz pulled the truck into the ancient timber and fieldstone structure.

As they climbed out of the truck, the man lit two other lanterns, hung them from wooden beams and left the barn without a word, pushing the door closed behind him.

"Let's get the radio out," Slomak said. He lifted a ladder off two wooden pegs and set it up in a corner opposite the door. Carrying one of the lanterns, Slomak climbed the ladder, pushed open a well-concealed trapdoor and waved for Jan to follow as he disappeared through the hole.

Jan glanced at Tadeusz, who indicated that he would wait by the truck, then followed Slomak up the ladder.

When he got to the top, Jan pulled the ladder up behind him and closed the trapdoor. They were in a loft about ten meters square and four or five meters high with a small window at each end. Under one of the windows stood a crude workbench and a small, three-legged stool. Slomak reached under the workbench and dragged out a wooden crate. Jan stepped over to help, and they lifted the crate onto the bench. Slomak opened the crate, revealing a long-range wireless set.

"Nice piece of equipment," Jan said, examining the precision instrument with its English dial markings.

"We have several of these at various locations, compliments of our British friends," Slomak replied as he connected wires to a 12-volt battery. "You brought one with you on the plane." He glanced at Jan with a rare smile.

The remark took Jan by surprise. It was the first reference anyone had made to the crates that had been shoved out of the airplane before he jumped. He leaned against a beam in the center of the room and lit a cigarette, letting Slomak tend to the task of tuning in the radio signal. As he watched him twist the dials and adjust the headset, he pondered again what an enigma the man was.

It was frustrating. Jan was certain that Slomak, who went by the name "Krupa," had recognized him when they met at Tadeusz's farm. But the taciturn AK operative had not acknowledged it—not then or at any time since. Whenever Slomak was with them he was all business, never any conversation beyond what was necessary. He would spend a day or two with them then disappear. They might not see him again for several days, often as long as a week. There was never an explanation, and Jan had realized he shouldn't ask.

"I've made contact. You can send your message." Slomak said, getting up from the stool and removing the headset.

Jan crushed out his cigarette and stepped over to the radio, pulling a piece of paper out of his shirt pocket. The paper contained a message he had encoded as they were driving that afternoon. He had sent a message to SOE in London shortly after his arrival in Poland advising them he had made contact with the AK, but this would be his first scheduled status report. He sat on the stool, smoothed the scrap of paper on the bench and tapped out the message which, decoded on the other end, would read,

MAN IN QUESTION GENUINE. EXAMINING COMPONENTS WITH DIFFICULTY. DEVICE DIFFERENT FROM EXPECTED. EXTREMELY LETHAL.

Chapter 36

THE GESTAPO'S BELGIAN HEADQUARTERS were housed in a twelve-story building at the intersection of Avenues Louise and DeMot in Brussels. The building towered above the private homes in the area and had served as a suitable symbol of power and dominance.

It had, that is, until a Belgian pilot named Baron de Longchamps, returning to England from a mission over Germany, flew his Typhoon through the city at treetop level and strafed the top floors of the building with machine-gun fire. Six Gestapo officials died in the exploit and now, almost a year later, the top four floors of the building remained boarded-up and vacant.

Oberstleutnant Rolf Reinhardt was one of the lucky ones. He had been out of the building that day. But his spacious office on the twelfth floor had been destroyed, including several valuable paintings confiscated from the home of a prominent Jew. For months after the incident, Reinhardt fumed over the loss, imagining how the paintings, especially the Rubens, would have looked in the parlor of his home in Munich.

But Reinhardt had a larger problem on his hands. He had just hung up the telephone after a blistering one-sided conversation with Berlin over the destruction of the newly constructed refueling depot near La Roche.

He was in charge of Gestapo activities in that part of Belgium and, as his superior had reminded him in no uncertain terms, this was *his* problem. The incidents of sabotage had been escalating dramatically in the last few months, but this was the coup de grâce.

Reinhardt was on the spot. The highest levels in Berlin now knew about the destruction of the depot. If he didn't find the bastards who did it and get them in front of a firing squad, he'd soon be slogging through the snow on the Russian front.

Reinhardt closed his eyes and took a few moments to collect himself, then reached for the buzzer on his desk. "Send him in," he commanded.

The door opened and Hans Wolter stepped into the cramped office.

"*Setzen Sie*," Reinhardt grumbled and Wolter slumped into the chair closest to the door.

Reinhardt looked at him with contempt. Wolter was his lead investigator, in the area around LaRoche and, in Reinhardt's opinion, was only slightly less incompetent than the rest of the Gestapo crew down there.

Reinhardt was a resourceful man, a determined and thorough investigator, but this group of Resistance operatives in La Roche had him frustrated. He knew the saboteurs had to be locals—farmers or merchants—operating right under the noses of Wolter and his agents in the area. Reinhardt was certain the group was attached to the White Brigade and financed through a connection in Brussels or Antwerp. He had some names . . . but he couldn't put it together.

Reinhardt glared at Wolter. "Berlin is going to have my ass over this refueling depot. But before they do, by God, I'll have yours!"

Wolter squirmed in the chair.

"Do you know anything?" Reinhardt shouted. "Anything at all? Or are you and your worthless crew just sitting down in La Roche with your thumbs up your asses!"

Wolter cleared his throat and the effort caused him to cough. His eyes began to water.

Reinhardt sat back and waited while Wolter regained his composure. "Now then, do you have any suspects at all?"

Wolter straightened up. His voice was shaky. "We still suspect that fat butcher in La Roche, but we don't know where his orders come from. We know he owns a small chalet near the village of Warempage that he rents to some woman and her son, and he has a connection in Antwerp, but we haven't been able to—"

Reinhardt leaned across the desk, cutting him off. "Christ, they've been blowing up rail yards and trains for months. *Jetzt das!* What do you intend to do about it?"

Wolter squirmed again. He wiped perspiration from his forehead. "Let's haul the butcher in and break his knees. We'll get him to talk."

Reinhardt looked at him with disgust. Breaking bones seemed to be the extent of the man's intellectual capabilities. "Yes, of course. A wonderful idea," he snarled. "Brilliant. In a small town like that, the instant you arrest him everyone will know, and they'll burrow so deeply underground you'll never find them, even if the man talks, which he probably won't."

Wolter slumped back in the chair.

Reinhardt rubbed his eyes and stood up. He walked around the desk and glared down at the defeated agent. "Here's what I want you to do. Leave the butcher alone. I don't want him to know that we suspect him of anything. But we need to send a message to these bastards. Pick out three people in La Roche, any three, it doesn't matter. But not the butcher or any of his known friends. *Verstehen Sie?*"

Wolter nodded.

"Arrest them in broad daylight. Then drag them into the street and shoot them. Three people, today. Got it?"

"*Ja,* three people . . . today. *Verstehen.*"

Reinhardt motioned toward the door. "Now get the hell out of here and let me think."

After Wolter left, Reinhardt sat at his desk and rubbed his temples. He was running out of time. Wolter and his crew were useless thugs. They'd never figure this out. He needed to take another tack, but he didn't know in which direction. He had to find the linkage between this group of saboteurs and whoever was financing them and running the organization . . . but how? It was maddening.

For the first time in his career he was stumped. He sat in the drafty little office and looked out the lone window at the bleak December sky, forcing himself to go over the whole thing again and look at it from another angle. There had to be a way.

Chapter 37

IT WAS CHRISTMAS EVE and the snow, which had been falling all day, accumulated into drifts more than a half meter high. The windows of the Marchals' house were frosted over and a fire crackled in the fieldstone fireplace. A small fir tree decorated with ribbons and candles stood in the corner. The parlor was small and simple save for the bright red Persian rug that covered most of the rough planked floor and Antoinette's hand-painted flowers and birds that circled the kerosene sconces on the stucco walls. The rug had belonged to Antoinette's grandmother, the only thing left after the Great War.

Justyn had gone upstairs with the Marchal boys, and Antoinette gathered up the last of the gift wrap paper, folding it neatly to be used another time. Anna sat on the worn upholstered sofa, holding a half-full wineglass, watching the fire. The mood in the small farmhouse, if not festive, was one of warmth and camaraderie. Feeling festive, even on Christmas, was close to impossible for anyone in this small rural community still reeling from the horror of the Gestapo murdering three innocent people.

Anna sipped the wine and stared at the flickering flames, silently fighting the rage and despair that crept into her heart at moments like this. The Nazis had arrested her father because he was an intellectual. And left her best friend to die because she was a Jew. Now three people had been gunned down in the street like dogs. Where would it end?

She wondered where Jan was on this Christmas Eve, hoping and praying that he was safe, perhaps at some army base in England or Scotland preparing for the invasion. She clutched the thin stem of the wineglass. There were other possibilities, possibilities she would not allow herself to contemplate, not tonight. Not on Christmas. Jan was safe. She believed that.

When she finished folding the paper, Antoinette sat next to Anna and placed a warm hand on her arm. "I'll bet Jan is sitting in some pub in Scotland right now thinking about you," she said.

Anna sighed. "Sometimes he seems so real, so close, as though he's about to walk into the room—and other times I can barely remember what he looks like."

Antoinette picked up her own wineglass from the rough-hewn coffee table and took a sip. "When Leon was fighting during the invasion, and whenever he's off on his missions, I always try to think of some place where he and I would go, *privé*, just the two of us. A place I can always recall."

Anna smiled mischievously. "And where would *that* be?"

Antoinette laughed. "*Ah bien*, besides *that* . . . the place I was thinking about was a sunny little spot along the Ourthe River near Mormont. We went there for picnics in the summer, every Sunday, the first year we were married." She shook her head. "*Mon dieu*, we haven't been there in years."

Anna was silent for a moment, remembering. "Jan and I would sit at the same little café on the Rynek Glowny in Krakow every Sunday evening. We'd have a glass of wine then take a walk." She glanced at Antoinette. "We always held hands when we walked."

Antoinette laughed again. "So did we back then. But now it seems like there's no time for anything."

The kitchen door swung open, and Leon stomped in with a load of firewood in his arms, kicking snow off his boots. Anna got up to help, but Antoinette stopped her. "Just sit and enjoy the fire," she said. "I'll get some more wine."

Anna sat back, soothed by the fire—and the friendship. During the last two years she had grown as close to Antoinette as she had to any other woman in her life. But their friendship was different than her friendship had been with Irene. Irene had leaned on her and depended on her. And the guilt would always be there, that she had failed to protect Irene in her most vulnerable hour. But Antoinette was a woman of considerable strength, a woman who understood the danger her family lived with because of Leon's involvement with the *maquis*, but didn't dwell on it. She did what needed to be done and went on with life. When Antoinette had learned that Anna would be leading American aviators to Paris, her only reaction had been to give her a hug and assure her that she would look after Justyn. To Antoinette, Anna was only doing what needed to be done. Just like the rest of them.

Leon dumped an armful of split logs in the wood box and brushed the dust off his sleeve. "Well, I'm ready for a glass of wine," he said. *"C'est Noël."*

A party of twelve had gathered for the Christmas Eve celebration at Rene and Mimi Leffard's home on the Cogels-Osylei in Antwerp. The guests included several of Leffard's business associates; a few neighbors; and his two closest friends: Rik Trooz and his wife, Audrey, and Willy Boeynants, accompanied by a lady friend.

Boeynants was a lifelong bachelor with an active social life, and the Leffards were always interested to see who was accompanying him. Tonight it was actually someone they had met before, a blond Dutch woman named Hendrika.

The group had pooled their resources and managed to secure a veritable feast, given the times in which they were living. The menu included an Ardennes ham, which Leffard provided from the source in La Roche known only to him and Boeynants. The other guests brought additional varieties of black market delights, including crusty white bread, sardines and mackerel in oil, real butter and, most spectacular of all, a tiny box of chocolates which Boeynants ceremoniously produced after dinner. "One for each of us," he said. *"Joyeux Noël!"*

Antwerp had suffered mightily during the past year, and it was impossible to prevent the conversation around the table from dwelling on it. Hundreds of prominent citizens had been arrested by the Gestapo and thrown into prison. Jews by the thousands were being deported to the "east." The curfew had been shortened, and food and clothing were increasingly hard to come by.

And it wasn't only the Germans who caused the suffering. Allied bombing had destroyed bridges and factories all over the country.

Eventually Leffard prevailed upon his guests to set aside their troubles and enjoy the spirit of the season. He was, as always, a persuasive man, and the rest of the evening passed in festive banter.

It was almost ten thirty before the party broke up and the Leffards' guests began to leave. Rik Trooz and his wife, along with Boeynants and Hendrika, lingered after the others had left. It was obvious that Trooz had something on his mind. Mimi poured the women another cup of coffee, while Leffard led his two friends to his study.

They settled down with a final glass of cognac. "I have a business acquaintance I think you should meet," Trooz said to Leffard. "His name is Paul de Smet. Do you know of him?"

"Paul de Smet?" Leffard repeated. He thought for a minute, trying to remember if he'd ever heard the name. "*Non*, I don't think I do. Should I?"

Trooz shrugged. "Well, perhaps not. I've known him for a number of years. He owns several businesses that I'm familiar with, including one in the Ardennes, near Dochamps. I helped him finance it back in the thirties. He has a residence in Ghent and another in the Ardennes, not far from La Roche."

"La Roche? Does van Acker know him?" Boeynants asked.

"I don't know," Trooz said. "I haven't asked him about it."

Leffard nodded. Trooz's involvement in the Resistance was limited to the Comet Line organization. He would only contact van Acker to arrange an escort from the area.

"Apparently de Smet only uses the house near La Roche for occasional weekends," Trooz added. "It's not far from the factory in Dochamps. The name of the business is Precision Metals."

"Precision Metals?" Leffard asked. "What do they make?"

"Before the war they manufactured custom components for the railroads and the mining industry, all out of brass, primarily high-precision stampings."

"What about now?"

"Well, this is the important part," Trooz replied. "The Germans moved in and took control of the factory back in '41. They now manufacture shell casings."

Leffard was silent for a moment, thinking. "Wait a minute. This sounds familiar. I believe I have heard of this fellow. Wasn't there some type of lawsuit concerning this factory a few years ago?"

"*C'est correct.* I thought you would remember it," Trooz said with a smile. "In 1941, de Smet filed a lawsuit protesting the Germans' interference in his business. He alleged that he was being pressured into producing war materials for the Wehrmacht." Trooz sipped his cognac then set the glass down and leaned forward. "De Smet and I are not particularly close friends, but we've maintained an ongoing business relationship. He confided in me when this was all happening. He was quite upset about it."

"If I recall correctly, it was never really settled," Leffard said. "What happened?"

"He eventually dropped the whole thing. De Smet didn't talk about it for years . . . until just last week."

"So, what happened that made him bring it up last week?" Boeynants asked.

"There's more to the story," Trooz said. "But I think de Smet would prefer that you hear it from him. As I said, he was upset about the Germans commandeering his company. Perhaps he's decided he wants to do something about it."

Leffard was surprised. "What, pursue further legal action? That would be suicide. In 1941 they may have just threatened him and let it go at that. But if he tries something like that now, he'll wind up in Breendonck sleeping on straw and eating mush with his fingers."

Trooz shook his head. "I believe he may have other plans. That's why I'm suggesting that you meet with him."

"What have you told him?"

"Not a thing," Trooz said. "He doesn't even know your name. You know I'd never say anything without discussing it with you."

"I know, Rik. I just needed to ask—you understand."

"*Oui, oui, bien sûr.* No problem. Well, what do you think?"

Leffard looked at Boeynants who shrugged. "There's only one way to find out, Rene. Let's set up a meeting."

Before they left the study, Leffard hesitated for a moment. He said to Trooz, "Rik, I know Anna made a run last week."

"I'm not surprised that you do. I would've told you myself but you know that's not possible."

Leffard nodded. "I realize that, it's just . . . well, you know what I mean."

"I would never have considered it, Rene, but we had no choice. Since the de Jonghs—"

"*Oui, je sais!*" Leffard snapped. "I know! But, goddamn it, Justyn's . . . hell, you know the situation, Rik."

Trooz paused for a moment. "We're taking every precaution we can. But we're desperately short of qualified agents. I can't promise she won't be asked again, if she's willing."

Leffard stared at him, deeply conflicted. "I know, Rik. I know."

Chapter 38

THE LEOPOLD CAFÉ was situated at the end of the Cogels-Osylei, just down the street from Rene Leffard's home. It was nine o'clock on a cold, damp Sunday morning in January of 1944, and Leffard was sitting on a leather couch in the far corner of the empty café when Willy Boeynants entered.

In the two weeks since Leffard's Christmas party, Trooz had contacted de Smet and arranged this meeting. Trooz would not be attending, though. Both he and Leffard felt it would be safer for him, and his contacts within the Comet Line, if he backed out of the picture at this point.

The proprietor of the café nodded at Boeynants from behind the bar and prepared a cup of coffee for him. He stepped over to the table, set the cup down and returned to the bar. Boeynants took a sip and asked Leffard, "Did you get a report from London?"

Leffard nodded. "MI-6 has heard of him. He's in their files because of the lawsuit, but that's all. He's not on any of their lists of collaborators, and he's not known to any of the other Resistance groups here in Belgium. SOE is aware of the factory in Dochamps."

"Really? What do they know about it?"

"They know that it was taken over by the Germans and that it's producing war materiel for the Wehrmacht. It's on the RAF target list, but there's been no reconnaissance yet—other priorities and all that. If we learn anything, they're interested. Did you talk with van Acker?"

"*Oui.* He doesn't know de Smet, but he was aware of the factory. He didn't know what they produced, though, and I didn't tell him."

The door opened, and a bald man dressed in a fashionable gray suit entered the café. He was of medium height with the stocky build of an ex-athlete. Spotting Boeynants and Leffard, he stepped forward and held out his hand. *"Bonjour,* I'm Paul de Smet."

Leffard and Boeynants introduced themselves, and they sat around the table. A moment later the proprietor returned with another cup of coffee, then retired to the back room of the café. De Smet glanced around the empty room.

"The café doesn't open until noon," Leffard said. "We won't be disturbed."

De Smet took a sip of coffee and set his cup on the table. "So, I understand our mutual friend, Rik Trooz, has told you about my situation," he said to Leffard. His eyes darted around the room another time.

Leffard nodded but didn't respond.

De Smet continued. "My factory in Dochamps produces war materiel for the Wehrmacht—shell casings to be exact. It was not my choice, you understand. I objected. I even filed a lawsuit to stop it." He took another sip of his coffee and shook his head. "Now, it seems like a ridiculous gesture but at the time, none of us knew how ruthless these people would become. I was pressured into dropping the lawsuit, and for the last two years I have been afraid to act. I was afraid for my family." He glanced at Boeynants then back at Leffard. "But, that no longer matters."

"What do you mean?" Boeynants asked.

De Smet sighed and said, "Six months ago my wife died of cancer. She was very ill for several years. We had only one child, Karl, who ran the factory in Dochamps." He reached into his pocket and withdrew a handkerchief, wiping beads of perspiration from his forehead. "Unfortunately, my son was always rather bullheaded. He had more than a few run-ins with the Germans. I interceded and thought things had settled down, but last month the Gestapo showed up at the door of my son's home . . . and took him off to Germany."

Leffard stared at de Smet. The man was obviously having difficulty saying all this.

De Smet continued. "I tried every day for two weeks to find out where he had been taken . . . but I got nowhere. Finally, one of the agents I had been to see several times took me aside and told me to give it up. He said he had learned that my son . . . had been . . . *exécuté.*"

Leffard and Boeynants were silent for several moments. Finally, Leffard said, "I'm very sorry about your loss, M. de Smet, but why are you telling this to us?"

De Smet sighed. "I have nothing more to lose, M. Leffard. They took over my business, and now they've taken my son. My wife is gone . . . they can't hurt me any more."

Leffard looked at him in silence.

De Smet leaned over the table. "I want to help, M. Leffard. I have money—and I have information. I want to help."

Leffard stared at the bald man for a moment before responding. "I'm not sure I understand what you mean. What is it you want to help with?"

De Smet glanced around the empty room again. "With your patriotic activities, M. Leffard. In my heart, I am also *un partisan*." As he spoke, de Smet's voice became passionate. "For two years I have done nothing, while they forced my factory to produce war materials. I was afraid. I'm not proud of myself—but it's the truth. Now, it no longer matters. I can help you, M. Leffard, if you will allow me."

They sat in silence for several minutes. Leffard was intrigued. If the man was sincere, it could provide an opportunity to strike a significant blow against the German war effort. "What kind of information do you have?" he asked.

De Smet spoke softly as though he were still concerned about being overheard. "The factory is heavily guarded. All of the workers are closely watched by the local Gestapo. Shipments in and out occur on a very irregular basis, and the schedule is a closely held secret. I am no longer allowed to visit the factory—my own factory—can you believe it?" De Smet paused and shook his head. "Forgive me, this has been very difficult."

"I understand." Leffard said. "Please, take your time."

De Smet managed a thin smile and continued. "I still have a few contacts among the managers who are willing to provide me with certain information. One of them is in a position to know when shipments are leaving the factory."

Chapter 39

WRAPPED IN A COARSE WOOLEN BLANKET and shivering with cold, Jan scraped frost from the solitary window of his small room above the barn and looked out into Tadeusz Kaliski's farmyard. The sun was rising and cast a sparkling glow over the new snow that had fallen during the night. This was the harsh Polish winter Jan remembered so well. Pulling the blanket tighter, Jan wondered if Anna was warm.

Anna. Thinking about her brought up a myriad of emotions always churning just below the surface: frustration, anxiety, fear. After almost three months back in Poland, he still knew no more about her whereabouts than when he first arrived.

At first, Jan hoped that Slomak might be of some help, but the AK operative was closed-mouthed and secretive. Jan learned quickly that it was strict AK policy never to reveal true identities or have discussions about families, relatives or friends.

Only once, during a late-night conversation, had Slomak acknowledged their meeting in Krakow four years ago. But when Jan tried to push the discussion by mentioning the SS *special action*, Slomak became reticent, and the conversation ended. The longer he was here, the more Jan understood what living underground, in constant fear of exposure and death, did to a man. He knew he was on his own. When his mission was completed he would strike out, and one way or another, he would find Anna.

The mission. Another source of frustration. He had gained little useful information about the *wunderwaffen*. The launches continued, and the AK stepped up their surveillance of the area around Blizna and the SS training grounds.

Many hours spent in kitchens, barns and cellars discussing the possibility of infiltrating the test areas and launch sites led to nothing. They monitored the freight trains and trucks entering and leaving the area, searching for hijack opportunities. It all looked futile. German security was intense and organized to the point of appearing impenetrable.

Jan heard a noise outside and looked out the window again, wiping away the fog his breath created. A horse-drawn sleigh pulled into the yard, and a man bundled up in a brown woolen coat, a fur hat and heavy leather boots jumped down from the seat. The door of the house opened, and Tadeusz stepped onto the porch, shouting and waving to the early morning visitor.

Jan pulled on a pair of woolen pants just as Tadeusz yelled to him from the lower level of the barn. Jan wriggled his feet into his boots, buttoned up the heavy plaid shirt, grabbed his hat and coat, and climbed down the ladder.

Tadeusz awaited him by the open door. "Come quickly, there's been a discovery."

They stomped into the kitchen, kicking snow off their boots. Lidia stood at the old cast-iron stove, brewing coffee. Slomak sat at the table with the visitor Jan recognized as one of the AK operatives he had met a month ago but had never been introduced to. He and Tadeusz hung their coats on a hook by the door and joined the other two men at the table.

Slomak turned to the visitor. "Aaron, why don't you start at the beginning."

The man was excited and nervous. He wrapped his hands around the steaming mug that Lidia set before him and looked directly at Jan. "A rocket came down in a marsh along the Bug River."

Jan waited.

Slomak chimed in. "It didn't explode. It's intact, isn't that right, Aaron?"

The clearly flustered young man nodded vigorously. "Yes, yes, of course! It's completely intact. We covered it up."

"Covered it up?" Jan asked.

"With leaves and branches. Most of it's in the water—just the tail was sticking out. We covered it up so the SS wouldn't see it."

Jan glanced at Slomak. "Let's go."

The location of the crash on the Bug River was eighty kilometers east of Warsaw. Following an indirect route to avoid police checkpoints and obtain black market gasoline from AK partisans, it took Jan and Slomak two days to make the trip in the ancient Russian truck.

In the evening of the second day, they met a local AK operative in the rear of an abandoned blacksmith shop, just outside the village of Sarnaki. He explained to them that the Germans were desperate to find the unexploded rocket. SS troopers were combing the area, threatening local farmers and villagers with their lives.

Jan and Slomak waited with the AK operative in the cold, damp shop until after midnight before they headed out to the crash site. When they arrived they found twelve AK partisans and a team of draft horses attempting to extricate the fourteen meter, twelve thousand kilogram rocket from the icy mud in the marsh along the river. Jan couldn't see them, but he was certain another dozen or so men waited in the woods, heavily armed, keeping a lookout.

The effort continued all night until, near dawn, they succeeded in hoisting the huge device onto a wagon. They hauled it deep into the forest and concealed it with canvas tarps and cut pine boughs. At nightfall the following day they moved it to a nearby farm belonging to an AK partisan who served the cause by operating a long-range wireless.

For three days, the armed AK operatives kept a round-the-clock lookout in the area while the farmer sent to and received coded messages from a team of MI-6 scientists in London. He decoded instructions and passed them on to Jan and a Polish engineer who had arrived from Warsaw. Slowly, painstakingly, the two men dismantled the rocket, which the British code named "V-2."

Chapter 40

LEFFARD AND BOEYNANTS met Paul de Smet again in mid-February on the Schelde Kaai, near the Bonaparte Dock, the oldest in the port of Antwerp. It was just after noon, but the sky was slate gray and there was a stiff wind blowing from the north. Leffard spoke first as the three men walked along the busy avenue that fronted the River Schelde. "We've considered your proposition, M. de Smet, and we want to pursue it."

"*Très bien.* I was worried when I didn't hear from you," de Smet replied. "What's next?"

"We need more details about these shipments," Leffard said.

De Smet nodded. "The factory is producing 88mm shell casings. The railcars leave the factory after dark. They're hauled to a secluded rail siding near Salmchateau and get linked up with freight trains going to Germany." He glanced at Leffard then at Boeynants. Boeynants nodded and de Smet continued. "My source says the trains start in Luxembourg and end up in Cologne."

"How long do the cars sit on the siding?" Boeynants asked.

"Two to three hours."

"How do you know that the railcars will be hauled to that siding?" Leffard asked.

"That's the standard procedure," de Smet said. "All shipments leave after dark, and they're all hauled to that siding. The Germans never bring trains into Dochamps. They're very careful not to call undue attention to the activities at the factory."

"I assume the railcars are under guard at the siding." Boeynants said.

"*Oui, oui, bien sûr.* I have not been there myself, but my contact said six to eight guards ride with every shipment. There are also two permanent guards at the siding."

Leffard looked at Boeynants and nodded.

Boeynants removed a slip of paper from his pocket and handed it to de Smet. "Memorize this number before we depart. We'll need forty-eight-hours notice. When you know the date of the next shipment, call the number between ten and eleven o'clock in the morning. Identify yourself as 'M. Rodin' and ask if your order is ready to be picked up."

De Smet studied the number scribbled on the paper and handed it back.

Chapter 41

As FEBRUARY PASSED INTO MARCH, the winter of 1944 began to slide away and with it Germany's stranglehold on Europe. Since the first of the year the Wehrmacht had been moving backward. The Russians liberated Leningrad after a nine-hundred-day siege and marched into Poland for the second time in five years. American forces landed in Italy. The Allies neutralized the German Luftwaffe while British and American air forces conducted daylight bombing raids on German cities.

Belgium's underground newspapers speculated about the long-awaited Allied invasion, with rumors surfacing daily about where and when it would take place. The Resistance struck with increasing boldness, and German reprisals followed suit. The Gestapo worked overtime, trying to ferret out those financing and orchestrating the Resistance.

For Paul de Smet, the days were filled with tension and frustration. He waited for a message from his contact at the factory about the next shipment of shell casings but, for more than a month, none came.

When he finally received a message, it was not what he wanted to hear. Production at the factory was sharply curtailed due to supply disruptions. The Allied bombings were taking their toll. The German managers running the factory were under enormous pressure from Berlin to get back up to normal production levels, but the next shipment wouldn't occur for several weeks.

The next day Willy Boeynants met Paul de Smet in front of Antwerp's Cathedral. It was noon and the cobblestone pedestrian square was crowded with people carrying meager sacks of groceries obtained with ration coupons.

A few sat at the outdoor cafés sipping weak beer and lunching on herring and boiled potatoes and, for those who could afford it, perhaps an omelet.

"M. Leffard is not joining us?" de Smet asked.

"Let's walk," Boeynants said, ignoring the question. "What's the problem?"

"Production at the factory has been disrupted by the air raids, and the next shipment will be delayed."

"How long?"

"I don't know for sure. Perhaps until next month."

Boeynants didn't respond.

"Will that be a problem? We can still proceed I hope?" de Smet asked.

"I can't say for sure," Boeynants said. "Many things are happening now and—"

"But we *must* proceed! *C'est dangereux!* People are risking their lives."

Boeynants glanced at the stocky, bald man. He seemed edgy, nervous. "Keep your voice down. I'll pass along the information. Unless you hear otherwise, proceed according to the original plan."

"But, can you be sure that—"

Boeynants stopped and turned to de Smet with a hard look. "We'll wait to hear from you as planned."

De Smet nodded, and the two men walked off in separate directions.

Later that day, Boeynants visited Rene Leffard at his home. Mimi Leffard was out, and the two men sat together in the study. It was a damp, chilly day, and a fire blazed in the fireplace. Leffard handed his friend a cup of coffee before taking his seat in the big leather chair.

"I saw de Smet today," Boeynants began and related the news to Leffard.

"Do you believe him?" Leffard asked. "Or is he trying to back out?"

"I don't think he's trying to back out. My inclination is that he's telling the truth," Boeynants said. "We both know that factories all over Belgium are suffering from the bombings. If anything, he wanted to make sure that we were still committed to carrying out the action."

Leffard grunted and took a sip of coffee, the small ceramic cup all but invisible in the grasp of his thick hand. "I've been in contact with SOE," he said. "Destroying this quantity of 88mm shell casings is still very important to them, and they want us to proceed. But they warned me that things could change if it gets delayed too much longer. They've assigned several other missions to us to coincide with the invasion, and they would take priority."

Boeynants nodded.

"I've passed some of the target information on to van Acker," Leffard continued. "It's mostly telegraph and telephone lines that SOE will want taken out to disrupt communications, along with a few rail lines into France, that sort of thing." Leffard set his cup on the coffee table and leaned forward. "A network is being organized for the defense of the port."

Boeynants's eyes widened. "Defense of the port?"

Leffard continued. "If the invasion is successful and the Allies gain a foothold on the continent, they'll push through France and Belgium, heading as fast as possible for Germany. But they won't get too far without a major port for supply."

"Antwerp," Boeynants said.

"*Oui,* and the main concern is that the Germans will attempt to destroy the port if they determine they're going to lose it. SOE has been given the task of making sure this doesn't happen."

Boeynants whistled softly. "Who's going to be involved in this?"

Leffard shook his head. "I don't know all the details yet, but there is a contact in Merksem. He goes by the name of 'Auguste.'" Leffard paused. "For now, they have a task for us . . . for you actually."

Boeynants smiled at his burly dark-haired friend. "And what would that be, Rene? Let me guess. They want information from the Interior Department. Perhaps names of German officials involved in the operation of the port, and what they may be working on?"

Leffard sat back in the leather chair and laughed, the first time Boeynants had heard him laugh in a long time. "*Très bien,* Willy, *très bien.*" With a knowing glance forged through a long friendship he picked up the coffee pitcher. "Would you like some more coffee?"

"*Non,* I'd like some cognac."

Chapter 42

It was a warmer day than normal for the middle of April, and the air inside the railcar was stale and humid. Anna sat next to the window looking absently at the passing countryside. A light rain ran down the glass in grimy brown streaks. The trains these days were dirty, smelly and usually crowded with people of all ages lugging suitcases and boxes stuffed with black market goods. Despite the growing danger from air raids, people still rode the trains. Automobiles were next to useless because of the lack of gasoline and, for the same reason, few buses operated. Unless you really had to get somewhere, the best thing to do was stay home.

Anna knew that's where she should be—home, looking after Justyn, instead of going off on another mission. But how could she say no when people like Jules van Acker asked for her help? Jules, Leon Marchal, Paul Delacroix and the others were all risking their lives and putting their families in danger for the war effort. She couldn't stay curled up in her little cocoon in the woods.

This time when van Acker asked if she would take on the mission, the reluctance he had displayed on the previous occasions was gone. He was all business, and Anna sensed that he had no problem asking and was certain she would do it. She felt good about that. She had finally been accepted as a partner in the struggle rather than someone who had to be looked after and protected.

Anna felt more self-confident than she had been on her earlier missions. She understood the risk, but she also indulged in a small measure of exhilaration. Justyn had turned fifteen, and he was strong, well-behaved and had always shown a lot of common sense. It still bothered her to leave him, but she felt comfortable that he was in good hands with the Marchals. Besides, Leon could always use an extra hand on the farm, especially in spring, and Justyn was a hard worker.

The train arrived at the station in Brussels two hours late, which was not bad by current standards. Anna took the tram to the north side of the city and got off at the stop van Acker had suggested. It turned out his directions were rather vague, and it took another half hour in the falling rain to find the address she had been given.

The house was typical of the others in the neighborhood—narrow, three stories, built of brownish-red brick with a gray tile roof. There was a small plot of grass and a bush of some sort between the sidewalk and the front door. Anna pushed the buzzer and stood under her umbrella wondering what would unfold in the days ahead.

The woman who opened the door was about sixty years old, with gray-streaked hair pulled back into a bun. She wore a simple blue dress and, despite the warm, humid weather, a gray sweater.

"*Bonjour, madame,* I'm looking for Monsieur Coubertin," Anna said, reciting what she had been instructed to say.

"He is not at home at the moment; he has gone to the library," the woman replied with the answer Anna expected. "You're welcome to come in and wait, if you'd like."

The woman held the door open, and Anna closed her umbrella and stepped into the narrow entryway. The woman closed the door and extended her hand. "I am Claudia."

Anna shook her hand, surprised by the woman's firm grip. "And I am Jeanne," Anna said, using the name on her new passport, which identified her as "Jeanne Laurent" from Antwerp.

"Claudia" showed her into the neat, modestly furnished parlor. Standing in front of the fireplace was a tall, good-looking man. He appeared to be in his early twenties with jet black hair parted down the middle and a neatly-trimmed black mustache. He wore a white shirt and gray slacks that were clean and freshly pressed but obviously several years old.

The man stepped across the room and extended his hand. "So, you must be my escort—and quite an attractive one at that," the man said in English, giving Anna a quick look up and down.

Anna ignored his outstretched hand and glanced at Claudia. The woman just shook her head and left the room. Anna turned back to the young man. She was about to say something when he started in again.

"So, when do we leave? I've been cooped up in this blasted place for a week now. Hope the war's not over yet. I was just getting warmed up. Name's Ryan Sinclair, Captain, RAF."

Anna looked into the man's smiling face. "Well, Captain, that's the last time I want to hear *that* name."

The young man looked surprised.

He started to respond, but Anna interrupted him. "My name is Jeanne Laurent, and it's my job to help get you out of this country without you getting yourself killed. Now, it's my understanding you were given some documents that identify you as 'Henri Eyskens,' a Flemish engineer from the town of Mortsel, near Antwerp. Is that correct?"

He smiled again. "Right, Mum . . . or Miss . . . Laurent is it? They're here somewhere."

Anna took a step closer. "First of all, it's *Madame* Laurent, and you'd better get those documents right now. We've got work to do."

His smile faded.

"*Begrijpt u het?*" Anna said.

He looked at her with a blank stare.

"*Begrijpt u het?*" she repeated.

The young man's face turned red.

Anna could see he was flustered. "Henri!" she snapped. "I've just asked, 'do you understand?' in Flemish. Haven't you learned the Flemish phrases that you were told to commit to memory? Claudia has gone over that with you, hasn't she?" Anna was certain she had.

"Yes . . . yes," he stammered. "I'm sorry . . . I'm afraid you took me by surprise, just then."

Anna took another step closer. Her voice was a whisper. "Being sorry isn't good enough. Being sorry will get you killed! And worse yet, it will get *me* killed, and anyone else who's trying to help you. Where we're going, you're not going to get any second chances."

"Blimey, you're being bloody dramatic—"

"We're scheduled to leave in less than twenty-four hours. If you can't convince me by that time that you're Henri Eyskens from Mortsel, I'm not taking you anywhere."

His face was now very red.

"*Begrijpt u het?*" she asked, sharply.

He hesitated then nodded. "*Ja, ja. Ik begrijpt het.*"

Anna turned away from him and walked out of the room.

It turned out that Ryan Sinclair was actually very bright and a fast learner. The brash, cavalier attitude was still there, just under the surface, but Anna believed he had gotten the message. He had no difficulty mastering the Flemish that he was required to memorize and was able to communicate the pertinent facts about his new identity.

His problem was learning to keep quiet and, whenever Anna wasn't specifically drilling him on his Flemish and his new identity, he chatted away, telling stories and asking questions. Under normal circumstances, Anna would have considered him to be just another self-absorbed, but otherwise harmless, young man. She had some reservations, but he seemed to have a lot of self-confidence and that certainly counted for something. Among his other qualities, Ryan Sinclair could sound very sincere, even charming, when he tried. Anna guessed he was quite something with the ladies back in London.

They left on schedule, taking the tram to the Brussels Nord station to catch the train for Paris. A policeman stood behind the railway conductor, looking over the crowd of travelers, as Anna and Ryan waited in the queue on the platform. When they handed their tickets and passports to the conductor, the policeman glanced over the conductor's shoulder then looked away without comment. The conductor punched their tickets, and they boarded the train.

The car was practically full, but Anna found two seats facing each other next to a window. Ryan found a spot for their bags in the overhead rack, and they squeezed past the passengers sitting in the aisle seats and settled in.

Anna noticed Ryan studying the other passengers and, as she had done on her other missions, tried to imagine what it must be like for the young aviator. Everyone around him was speaking French, a language he couldn't understand. He was a combatant in enemy territory with no means to defend himself, and his survival was dependent on a person he had met just twenty-four hours ago. If he were asked any questions, he would have to respond in a convincing manner using another language that was foreign to him.

She glanced at Ryan again and was surprised to see a smile on his face. To her annoyance, he even winked at her. He appeared to be enjoying this.

The incident occurred halfway between Lille and Paris. It was the middle of the night, and a French conductor had replaced the Belgian at Lille. The stubby little man, wearing a dark blue uniform, entered the car from the front and made his way down the aisle, checking tickets and passports. Anna was relieved to see that he was working alone, and there were no German soldiers with him. Many of the passengers were asleep and had placed their tickets and passports in the little clip at the corner of their seats.

When the conductor got to their row, he examined the tickets and passports of the two persons sitting in the aisle seats who both appeared to be sleeping. He punched the tickets and replaced the documents in the clips. Ryan was also asleep, his head leaning against the window, and Anna held both sets of documents. She handed them to the conductor who took them and nodded.

As she leaned forward, her knee brushed against Ryan's, and he woke with a start.

"Huh . . . wha' . . ." he mumbled, dazedly looking.

Anna gripped his knee to caution him before he said anything else. He grunted, then followed her eyes to the conductor.

The conductor punched the tickets and handed the documents back.

"*Merci,*" Anna said.

"*Dank U,*" Ryan said.

The aviator's response caught Anna by surprise, but she didn't react.

The conductor nodded and moved on.

Ryan faced the rear of the car, and he continued to watch the conductor as the man moved on through the rows.

Several minutes later, Anna heard the rush of air as the door of the car opened and the conductor left. On these missions, every encounter with officials was stressful for her, and she had just relaxed a little when Ryan abruptly leaned forward and whispered in English, "How'd I do, Mum? Pass the test?"

Anna was so startled, she couldn't respond. She stared at him in disbelief. He had that arrogant smile again, as if he had just won a game of chess. Anna frowned and flicked her hand at him, hoping he'd get the message and shut up.

Ryan shrugged and leaned back against the window, closing his eyes.

Anna took a deep breath, dropping her eyes to the magazine on her lap. She waited a moment, then stole a glance at the heavyset man in the seat next to Ryan. The man was still in the same position he had been in before, turned slightly toward the window with his head resting on the back of the seat.

But his eyes were open.

Several minutes passed. Anna wanted to steal another glance at the man to see if he had fallen back to sleep but didn't dare.

The heavyset man grunted, then coughed, and a second later he lifted his bulk out of the seat and stood up. He coughed again and headed for the rear of the car.

Anna's heart was in her throat. Had he overheard Ryan's comment? She tried to keep calm. Most likely the man had heard something but, coming out of a sleep, he probably didn't recognize it as English. Even if he had, what would it matter to him? Unless he was a collaborator and wanted to cause trouble. But what were the chances of that? Don't imagine the worst, Anna thought. Most likely the man had just gone back to use the toilet.

By the time he returned Anna was worried. He had been gone a long time. She thumbed through the magazine as the man slumped heavily into the seat. Out of the corner of her eye she saw him reach under the seat and pull out a folded newspaper, which he opened and began to read.

A half hour later the door at the rear of the car opened and closed. Anna didn't turn around, but she could feel the footsteps of the conductor coming up the aisle behind her. It's nothing, she told herself, perfectly normal. Thankfully, Ryan was asleep, or doing a very good job of pretending.

The conductor paused at their row. His eyes met Anna's and he smiled, then moved on.

Anna watched him as moved up the aisle. He didn't stop at any of the other rows, just exited the front of the car. She leaned her head back and closed her eyes, wondering if she was paranoid.

The sun was up when they pulled into Paris's Gare du Nord. Ryan pulled their bags down from the rack and they made their way out of the car. When Anna stepped onto the platform she noticed the stubby little conductor standing next to their car. Was it a coincidence? The man had to be standing somewhere, she told herself as they followed the crowd into the terminal.

The plan was exactly the same as it had been on her other missions. Ryan went into the toilet while she walked to the newsstand and purchased a magazine. She headed for a bench to observe the crowd while pretending to read.

It was after seven o'clock and the station was busy. Anna didn't notice as many German tourists as she had on her last mission, but several groups of Wehrmacht soldiers trudged through the station heading to the platforms, all carrying large duffel bags. With the talk of an invasion coming soon, it didn't really surprise her. As expected, the Parisian civilians gave the soldiers a wide berth as they stomped through.

Anna was about to sit down when she spotted the conductor from their train again. He was on the far side of the terminal, talking with a policeman and two Feldgendarmes. She watched them for a few seconds then glanced toward the toilet just in time to see Ryan disappear inside. *Damn it all.* Maybe she and Ryan should have walked directly out of the terminal. But that wasn't the plan. That wasn't what she had been instructed to do.

She noticed the policeman nod his head and say something as the conductor looked at his watch and walked away, heading back to the platforms. The policeman and the two Feldgendarmes talked among themselves for another minute, then split up and moved off.

Anna stood next to the bench, holding her magazine but not even pretending to read it. Straining to see through the throng of people moving through the terminal, she tried to follow the movements of the three uniformed men. The Feldgendarmes had separated, each heading for one of the terminal's two exits. The policeman walked slowly through the cavernous building. She kept losing sight of him in the crowd.

Anna's heart beat so hard, she was sure it would burst. She spotted Ryan as he emerged from the toilet, looking as if he didn't have a care in the world. As she had instructed him, he paused and lit a cigarette, gazing in her direction.

Anna nervously checked out the exits. The Feldgendarmes had taken up positions next to each of the massive doorways and appeared to be watching the people leaving. She cursed under her breath. How could this have happened? Was it really all because of a few whispered words in English from a naive young man? She admonished herself for dwelling on it. This was no time for mind games. She had to make a decision, right now.

Hoping Ryan would remember the signal, Anna dropped the magazine on the bench, reached into her bag and pulled out a blue silk scarf. Trying to act nonchalant, but certain she wasn't succeeding, she put the scarf on her head, tied it under her chin and began moving through the crowd, toward the platforms.

Anna tried to spot the policeman so she could keep out of his way but she had lost him. Out of the corner of her eye she saw Ryan hesitate for a second then bend down and open his bag. He pulled out a gray felt hat, put it on his head and followed her. Donning the headgear wasn't much of a disguise, but the Comet Line operatives had told her that, in a crowded building, it was sometimes just enough to make a difference. It didn't do much to bolster her confidence.

As she pushed through the crowd, Anna went over the back-up plan. Her instructions were to use the alternate set of tickets and travel on to Le Havre. She stopped under the schedule display board and looked up at it. Ryan came alongside of her.

He leaned over as if to speak but Anna stepped on his foot, hard. She found the listing for the train to Le Havre. It was leaving in forty minutes. She glanced at Ryan and motioned for him to follow, hoping that he knew better than to ask questions.

Chapter 43

LEON MARCHAL WAS REPAIRING a wheel on his hay wagon when he heard the sound of an automobile coming down the road. So few people drove cars these days, it always caught his attention when he heard one. He looked up as Jules van Acker's battered Citroen pulled into the farmyard and stopped just behind the wagon.

Marchal knew it must be important for van Acker to use precious gasoline driving out here. He wiped his hands on a rag and walked over to the car. Marchal always marveled at how the rotund man managed to fit into such a small vehicle.

"I just received the call," van Acker said. "The action at the rail siding is on for tomorrow night."

Marchal nodded. "It's about time." He glanced at his watch. It was almost noon. "Would you like to stay and have lunch?"

"I've got to get back to the shop," van Acker replied. "Do you want to use the truck? I could get it for you again."

"*Non*, the wagons will be less conspicuous. We'll leave in the morning and have plenty of time."

"You'll contact me when it's over?"

"*Oui, oui, bien sûr.*"

Van Acker turned the car around and drove off.

The next morning Marchal drove the horse-drawn wagon out of the farmyard with Gaston next to him and Jean-Claude riding in the back. Paul Delacroix drove the second wagon, with Richard sitting beside him and Henri Delacroix riding in the back with Franc.

Buried beneath a load of hay in each wagon were canvas backpacks filled with weapons, packages of plastique, reels of wire and boxes of detonators. As he headed the wagon onto the dirt road, Marchal turned and waved at Luk and Justyn who were standing on the porch. He knew how badly they wanted to go along.

It was late afternoon before they arrived at the area of Salmchateau, hid the wagons in a barn owned by a friend of van Acker's and trekked off through the forest. It was warm and humid after the rains of the last couple of days, and the ground was soft, allowing them to proceed quickly yet quietly.

They arrived at the same creek Marchal and Delacroix had crossed when they conducted their first reconnaissance of the rail siding more than two months ago. It had been frozen then, but now they had to slosh through ankle-deep water. Across the creek they found the path leading to the top of the hill and the railroad tracks.

Marchal motioned to Franc that this was the spot and, in a flash, Franc slid down the hill, sprinted across the tracks and disappeared into the trees on the other side. Marchal led the rest of the group along the crest of the hill until they came to the point where the rail siding split off to the north side of the tracks.

Keeping out of sight, just below the crest of the hill, the group proceeded to the location where Marchal and Delacroix had observed the guards on their reconnaissance mission. It was a half hour before dusk. They were right on time.

Marchal crawled to the crest of the hill and spotted both guards, patrolling the siding as they had been before. He looked up and down the tracks, taking a long look at the hut. He knew that Franc was over there but well concealed.

Satisfied that there was no one around except for the guards, Marchal slid back down the hill. Gaston had removed the packets of PE-2 plastique from the backpacks and laid them on the grass. Richard had unpacked four rifles and loaded them with clips of ammunition. He handed one each to Paul Delacroix and Gaston and passed another to Marchal.

Marchal grabbed the weapon, looked at his watch and whispered, "Five minutes to go. Take up your positions."

Paul and Henri crawled off to the left and Richard and Jean-Claude to the right. Marchal and Gaston, each carrying a rifle, crept back to the crest of the hill. Marchal took one last look at his watch. In two minutes Franc would toss a hand grenade into the empty hut. He sighted in on one of the guards. If everything went according to the plan, he might not have to kill the man.

The blast came right on schedule, sending shattered pieces of wood and sheet metal in all directions. Both guards turned toward the explosion in stunned surprise. At that instant, Paul and Henri Delacroix burst from the woods on Marchal's left, and Richard and Jean-Claude raced out from the right. Both groups charged the guard closest to them screaming in German, "Drop your weapons! *Jetzt!* Drop your weapons!"

The guards spun around at the same time. The one on the left had dropped his submachine gun when the explosion went off, and now he bent down to retrieve it. Paul Delacroix pointed his rifle at him and screamed, "*Halt! Stoppen Sie,* or you're dead!"

The guard stared at the gun and straightened up, putting both hands in the air.

The guard on the right still clutched his submachine gun. He hesitated for a second then looked up at Richard as the big man pointed the rifle at his chest. He let go of the submachine gun, and it clattered on the tracks.

Ten minutes later both guards had been bound and gagged, and Jean-Claude and Henri, wearing their uniforms, took up positions on each end of the rail siding. The rest of the group emerged from the woods and began setting the charges of explosive and stringing wire.

They worked methodically in the growing darkness, and Marchal calculated they had at least an hour before the switch engine would arrive, towing the railcars loaded with shell casings. He felt good. So far, everything had worked according to plan.

Marchal was on his hands and knees, securing a detonator to a charge of explosive, when suddenly he was bathed in a piercing bright light.

Gunshots! Loud voices yelling in guttural German!

Marchal turned to his left, but the glaring searchlight forced him to look away.

A second later they were on top of him, shouting, "Down! Get down!" A heavy boot jammed into Marchal's back and ground his face into the gravel. Blood spurted from his nose.

More gunshots!

Marchal heard someone scream. The boot stomped on his back again and a searing pain shot through his ribcage.

Another gunshot! Another scream!

Marchal's face pressed into the gravel. Heavy boots ran down the tracks. More shouts: "Get down! Get down! *Schweinhund!*"

Marchal tried to look up, but the boot stomped on the back of his head and his face crunched deeper into the gravel, pain shooting through his broken nose and up into his forehead. He forced himself not to lose consciousness.

A minute passed. Marchal felt hands under his arms. The hands jerked him to his feet. Blood poured from his nose. A hand grabbed his hair and yanked his head up.

Through watery eyes Marchal spotted a large figure in a green uniform. He tried to focus. The man wore a metal chain around his neck and the heavy emblem of a Feldgendarme.

Marchal never saw the club, but when the Feldgendarme whacked his kneecap he almost fainted. The two sets of hands jerked him up again. His knee was on fire and his ears rang. He could barely hear as the Feldgendarme growled at him, "Your name! *Was ist Ihr Name!*"

Marchal sagged and the hands jerked him back up. The Feldgendarme cocked his arm for another blow. Then a different voice . . . from behind. "*Stoppen Sie!* I've got a better idea."

Another man moved into Marchal's blurry line of sight. This one was not in uniform. He wore a hat and a long trench coat. The man reached inside his coat and pulled out a revolver. "Bring one of the boys over here," he barked. "That one. *Jetzt!*"

It was Jean-Claude.

Blood oozed from a gash on the boy's forehead, and his left arm hung limp. The man in the trench coat shoved his face into Marchal's and said, "Tell me your name . . . or the boy dies."

Gasping for breath, Marchal stared at his wounded son, fighting the panic that wrenched in his gut. He had been in desperate situations before, and the code of silence in the White Brigade was absolute. They'd go after Antoinette . . . and Luk. They'd find out about Anna and Justyn. He struggled against the powerful hands holding him up, but he couldn't see anything beyond the man in front of him and the blurred vision of his son slumping in the arms of the Feldgendarmes. He hesitated, trying to clear his head, when a shot rang out.

Jean-Claude screamed.

Marchal jerked his head around and saw the smoking pistol still pointed at his son's leg. Blood spurted from Jean-Claude's thigh as the boy sagged to the ground. The Feldgendarme let him fall and stepped away.

The man holding the pistol pointed it at Jean-Claude's head. He looked at Marchal. "*Jetzt!* Tell me your fucking name! Right now!"

Chapter 44

IT WAS A LITTLE AFTER NINE O'CLOCK in the evening. Justyn lay on his bed, reading a book in the upstairs bedroom of the Marchal's house, when two automobiles roared into the farmyard. He jumped off the bed and looked out the window as the long black cars skidded to a halt on the gravel drive. The doors flew open. Four soldiers jumped out and ran toward the house.

Justyn heard a *wham* as the front door was kicked open. Men shouted in German. He heard Luk's mother scream—then a loud crashing noise. Luk, who had been studying at the kitchen table, shouted something that Justyn couldn't make out, and there was another loud crash.

Heavy boots stomped through the house. Another crash and glass shattered. More shouts and boots stomped up the steps.

In a panic, Justyn raced to the window on the other side of the room and threw it open. A large oak tree stood alongside the house and once, last year, Justyn had seen Jean-Claude jump from the window to the closest branch on a dare from Luk.

He didn't give it a second thought, and the next thing Justyn knew he was clinging to the branch, swinging his legs toward the trunk. Half sliding, half falling down the massive oak, he heard a shout from the window.

He hit the ground and rolled, scrambled to his feet and sprinted toward the barn.

A gunshot rang out! He veered off toward the garden.

Another gunshot!

Justyn stumbled over the low fence and sprawled into the plot of cabbages and tomatoes. He got to his feet, raced through the garden and charged into a wheat field, heading for the tree line a hundred meters away.

Men shouted!

Another gunshot!

Justyn didn't look back.

He ran through the wheat field, into the trees and made his way, stumbling and falling, down the steep hill toward the river. He followed the winding riverbank, pushing his way through dense foliage, until he came to a narrow, rickety footbridge. He stumbled across the footbridge and climbed the hill on the other side before collapsing on the ground, gasping for breath.

Justyn stayed there a long time. He didn't have a watch, but he guessed more than two hours had passed without a sound other than the rustling of the trees and the occasional hoot of an owl. He stopped shaking and gradually became aware of the pain from the cuts and scrapes on his hands, face and neck.

He tried to think. Something must have gone wrong with the mission that Luk's father and the others were involved in. He shuddered in a sudden chill, remembering Mdme. Marchal's scream . . . and Luk's. What would they do to them? His stomach tightened, and he wrapped his arms around his knees, fearing he might be sick.

After several minutes he forced himself to his feet and took a deep breath. He listened. It was quiet. He took another breath. He needed help.

Following the river, Justyn eventually made his way to La Roche. The sun was coming up as he climbed the bank and crept through the quiet town, sneaking behind buildings, heading for M. van Acker's butcher shop.

Justyn crawled on his knees alongside a building across the street and peered at the familiar little shop with the wooden sign above the door that read *Boucherie*.

He gasped out loud.

The windows were shattered and the door broken in. Shelves were overturned and the glass display case had collapsed. Sausages, steaks and other meat lay scattered across the stone floor. He closed his eyes and tried to control his breathing.

Then he opened his eyes and stood up, inching forward, trying to get a better look.

He spotted something . . . hanging above the broken display case . . . suspended a meter or two off the ground.

Justyn inched forward again, straining to see in the dim light of the dawn.
A little farther . . .

He recoiled and fell to his knees. His stomach heaved.

Hanging from the ceiling was the bloody, naked body of Jules van Acker.

Chapter 45

WILLY BOEYNANTS WALKED with a little extra spring in his step as he headed for the Antwerp Central Station to catch the tram to Merksem. A night with Hendrika always made him feel good, and last night was no exception. This morning, she had been up before him and had fixed a breakfast of boiled eggs with bacon and tomatoes from the black market. As he walked the short distance from her apartment to the station the thought occurred to him that perhaps married life wouldn't be so bad after all.

It was a little after ten o'clock when he got off the tram near St. Bartholomeus Church on Bredabaan. Ten minutes later he found the address on Beukenhof-straat that Leffard had given him.

The home was a simple but neatly maintained red brick row house with white trim and attractive stained glass transoms above the front door and the two front windows. He paused a moment to straighten his tie, lamenting the frays on the cuffs of the only decent suit he had left. Then he pushed the buzzer, glancing up and down the narrow cobblestone street. The row houses on the short block were all similar, modest three-story buildings of red, brown or gray brick. Some had bay windows projecting from the upper floors and others had arched entryways of intricate masonry.

The door opened and a short, slender man with an unruly shock of white hair stood in the doorway, eyeing him suspiciously.

"*Goedemorgen.* I have an appointment with 'Auguste,'" Boeynants said in less than perfect Flemish.

The man's eyes narrowed. "What is the nature of your business with him? Does it have to do with the new building?"

"I have information on the windows he was interested in," Boeynants replied.

The man nodded and beckoned for him to come inside. "*Ik ben* 'Auguste,'" the man said after closing the door. "I'm very relieved to see you after what's happened."

"What are you talking about?" Boeynants asked. "What's happened?"

Auguste looked surprised. "You haven't heard? You haven't heard about M. Leffard?"

Boeynants felt a rush of fear. "*What . . . ?*" He tried to speak but nothing came out.

Auguste led him into the parlor. "M. Leffard and his wife were arrested early this morning."

The words hit Boeynants like a hammer. He sat heavily in an upholstered chair in front of the windows. "Good God. What are you . . . this morning?"

Auguste sat across from him. "I found out just a few hours ago from a contact in Leffard's neighborhood. It was the SS—and another man, probably Gestapo. They broke down the front door." Auguste pulled a handkerchief from his pocket and wiped the perspiration from his brow. "The person who called me was awakened when they smashed the front windows of the Leffards' home. A short time later he saw Leffard and his wife taken out in handcuffs and put in a car."

Boeynants stared at him, scarcely able to breathe. Taken away in handcuffs? The Gestapo? The bastards would drag his friend into one of those rooms in the cellars of Breendonck and break his fingers then . . . and Mimi . . . God knew what they'd do to Mimi . . . and they'd make Leffard watch.

Auguste cleared his throat and wiped his brow again. "Before they left . . . they . . . set the house on fire."

"They set the house on fire?" Boeynants stood up and paced around the small parlor. His head throbbed. It had to be the action at the rail siding. When they met, Leffard had told him it was on for last night but that everything was under control. He put his hand over his mouth, swallowing hard.

"What's happening?" Auguste whispered. "Why would they have arrested him?"

Boeynants paused, allowing his stomach to settle. "I think I know why . . . but I need to contact someone. Do you have a telephone?"

"*Ja, ja, natuurlijk.*" Auguste said, getting to his feet. "It's in the hallway. Please, help yourself."

Boeynants gave the operator the number of Jules van Acker's shop in La Roche and waited, rubbing his eyes, trying not to think about Rene and Mimi or he'd lose his mind.

The operator came back on the line. "I'm sorry. I can't get through to that number. It must be out of service."

Boeynants hung up the telephone and slumped against the wall. God almighty, he thought, what had gone wrong? He pressed his fingers into his temples, forcing himself to think. Who knew?

Auguste touched his shoulder and motioned toward the kitchen. "Please, come. I'll make us some tea."

Boeynants blinked. "*Dank U*, I just need to make one more call." He picked up the telephone again and gave the operator the number of the elderly woman who lived in the apartment below his own.

The phone rang three times and a soft voice came on the line, speaking French. "*Bonjour?*"

"*Bonjour* Madame de Theux, this is Willy."

There was a gasp then a long silence. Finally the soft voice said, "Willy . . . *Mon dieu.* Where are you? Are you safe?"

His heart pounded. "Yes, I'm safe. What happened?"

"The Germans . . . they came early this morning. I woke up when I heard them on the stairs, yelling your name. I heard them break down your door. I was terrified . . . I didn't know . . . Willy, what's going on?"

"Are you all right? Did they come to your door?"

"I'm all right, just frightened. Two of them knocked on my door. One was wearing that awful black uniform. The other wore a suit and long coat. I almost fainted."

"Are you sure you're all right?" Boeynants asked.

"*Oui, Oui,* I'm all right. The man in the long coat, he wanted to know where you were. I said I had no idea. I told him the truth. He asked me if I was sure about that. I told him again that I didn't know. He gave me his card and a phone number to call if I saw you again."

"What was the man's name?"

"Wait, I have it right here. It's Reinhardt, Rolf Reinhardt."

Reinhardt . . . Boeynants made a mental note of the name. "Try not to worry, Madame de Theux. I'll get it cleared up. I'm sure you're in no danger."

"Will you be coming back?"

"*Non,* not for awhile. Take care of yourself."

Boeynants's hands trembled as he placed the receiver back on the hook. Had he not spent the night with Hendrika he'd be in a cell at Breendonck himself—*Hendrika!* He stood frozen. *Think! Think!* He looked at his watch. She might still be home.

He picked up the phone and gave the operator Hendrika's number. He held his breath.

"*Bonjour,*" said the velvety voice on the other end.

"Hendrika, it's Willy."

"Willy! What a nice surprise. I was just thinking—"

"Hendrika, listen. Something's happened."

"What? What's happened?"

"The Leffards . . . they were arrested this morning." He heard her gasp. "I don't have time right now . . . but you could be in danger."

Silence.

"Hendrika?"

"*Oui?*" Her voice was just a whisper.

"You have to leave. You can't stay in your house. You've got to leave now."

"Willy—"

"Hendrika, listen carefully. You don't have much time. Do you remember the name I gave you? The person to contact if there was trouble?"

"*Oui, oui,* I remember. I have the address. But—"

"Hendrika, there's no time. I'll find you. But please, leave now."

He hung up the telephone and stared at the ceiling. How did this happen? How could it possibly . . . He shook his head and stepped into the kitchen where Auguste was pouring tea.

The two men sat in silence for several minutes at the round, wooden table, Boeynants staring into the cup of tea trying to comprehend what had happened. The Gestapo found out about the plan to sabotage the shipment of shell casings. But how? The only ones who knew about it were he and Leffard . . . and van Acker. But van Acker's telephone was dead so they had gotten to him as well. There was Trooz, but he was out of the loop. And de Smet, of course but . . . de Smet? Was it possible? He was a friend of Trooz's, but not a close friend. What was it Leffard had found out about de Smet from the British? He wasn't on any of their lists of collaborators but . . .

He heard Auguste say something and looked up. "I'm sorry . . ."

"I couldn't help overhearing your telephone conversation," Auguste said. "My French isn't very good but it sounded as if you'll need a place to stay. We have two extra bedrooms, and it's just my wife and I. You can stay with us for now."

Boeynants looked up in surprise. He had just met the man. "No, I couldn't possibly impose."

"*Het geeft niet,* I insist." The older man paused, his brow furled. "They know your name, now. You'll need some new identification papers as well."

"*Ja* . . . I suppose . . ." Boeynants shook his head. I suppose? What the hell was wrong with him? He had to get under control. Now! He picked up the cup and took a drink of the sweet, hot tea. "Leffard always arranged those things."

Auguste smiled. "I know. But we have our own organization here in Merksem. We've been connected with the White Brigade since '41 and, just recently, we've been assigned to a special group operating in the port. M. Leffard knew all about it."

Boeynants stared at him. Rene Leffard was his best friend, but he realized he never really knew about all of his connections.

Auguste sat back in his chair and folded his hands in his lap. "Before we go much further, perhaps you should give me the information you came here to deliver."

It took a few seconds for Boeynants to comprehend. Then he sighed. "*Ja, natuurlijk.*" He recalled the information he had discovered and committed to memory. It seemed like a long time ago. "The German High Command is convinced that the Allied invasion is imminent. They expect that it will take place sometime in the next few weeks, probably at the port of Pas-de-Calais."

Auguste sipped his tea and nodded.

Boeynants continued. "The German's main effort, of course, will be to repel the invasion. But, in their tradition of planning for all contingencies, an entire group has been making plans for either defending or destroying other seaports in the event the invasion is successful. Antwerp is the key. They are determined not to let the port of Antwerp fall into the hands of the Allies."

Auguste was listening intently.

"A general by the name of Stolberg has been assigned to take command of the defense of Antwerp. He is to be transferred here shortly from Brittany. If he determines that the port cannot be defended he is under strict orders to destroy it."

Auguste let out a low whistle and shook his head. "We suspected that might be a possibility. Do you have any details?"

"Right now, just a few," Boeynants said. "According to our intelligence, General Stolberg is a capable army officer, but he is no expert on demolition operations, nor is anyone on his immediate staff. He will undoubtedly be requesting assistance from Berlin." He paused and picked up a spoon, stirring the tea even though he had added no sugar. A vision of Rene and Mimi Leffard in handcuffs flitted through his mind. He blinked and set the spoon on the table.

Auguste nodded patiently. It was obvious the man understood tragedy.

Boeynants continued. "One of my colleagues in the Department of the Interior is in a position to see the transfer documents relating to German officers and civilian personnel sent into or out of Belgium. The Germans, as you know, are fanatical about paperwork. They document everything."

"I know," Auguste said. "It's one of our best weapons. But with the Gestapo on your tail, you can't just go back to work."

"You're right, I can't. But my colleague is in a good position. The Germans think he's a collaborator." Boeynants noticed Auguste's raised eyebrows and shrugged. "We do what we have to do. I'll get the information."

Auguste considered him for a long moment then stood up and held out his hand. "Welcome to our organization. I must take you to meet 'Antoine.'"

Chapter 46

JUSTYN DIDN'T MOVE for almost an hour. The sun was fully up now, a bright round disc climbing above the rooftops. He could hear the sounds of the town coming awake and knew he would have to get out of there. The clacking of hooves and squeaking wagon wheels coming down the cobblestone street motivated him into action.

His stomach was still queasy and he sweated profusely. It made him shiver, but he forced himself to press on and soon he was out of sight of the main street. He sneaked through the backyards and side streets of La Roche until he reached the river again. Then he crawled down the bank. When he was certain he was out of sight, he sat down on a log and tried to think.

He couldn't go home. If the Germans knew about the Marchals and M. van Acker they probably knew about the chalet and who lived there. Besides, Anna was off on a mission . . . and that was another problem. He had to find a way to get a message to her before she returned. He had no idea where she had gone but she usually came back within a few days. There wasn't much time.

Justyn knew what he had to do: find a way to get to Antwerp and the Leffards. Although neither Anna, nor anyone else, had ever spoken about it directly, Justyn knew that M. Leffard was at the center of their activities. He would know how to get a message to Anna. He got to his feet and climbed up the embankment. When he reached the top he stood for a moment, looking around to get his bearings, then started walking in the direction of the railroad tracks.

He trekked through the fields, trying to work out a plan in his head. He had no money and carried no identification, so he couldn't allow himself to be seen. Teenagers and young men were prime targets for the Germans. If you couldn't prove you were in school or gainfully employed, they'd deport you to Germany for forced labor.

Also, Justyn was acutely aware of his other problem. He was a Jew. If he were picked up by the wrong type of policeman—or the Feldgendarmes—all it would take would be a simple physical exam . . .

He put it out of his mind. He had to stay focused or he'd lose his nerve. The trains bound for Brussels and Antwerp would be heading north, so he had to stay out of sight until he could hop onto a slow-moving freight train. He had never actually seen anyone do this, or known anyone who'd tried, but he'd read about it in the newspapers. He and the Marchal boys had talked about how easily it could be done. Jean-Claude once said he'd run into a boy in Bastogne who claimed he'd ridden the freight train from Louvain to escape the Germans. Justyn doubted that it was true, but it made a good story.

He thought about Jean-Claude . . . and Luk . . . the best friends he'd ever had. They had accepted him as one of their own. They knew Justyn's secret— he was certain of it, though they'd never said anything. He bit down on his lower lip and trudged on.

The sun was high in the sky, and it was getting warm by the time the path Justyn had been following intersected the railroad tracks. He was exhausted and settled down under a tree to wait.

He woke up when he felt the ground trembling. Then the chugging and wheezing of a laboring steam engine rousted him to his knees. The locomotive was less than a hundred meters away, moving slowly up a grade, black smoke belching from the stack.

He held his hands over his ears and stepped back as the locomotive thundered past. A long line of boxcars clattered along behind it, their steel wheels grinding and screeching on the tracks. He was immobilized, frozen to the ground. He couldn't do this.

Justyn stared at the huge cars. They were moving slowly, rocking back and forth. An empty boxcar with an open door passed him. He flinched but couldn't move. It disappeared.

He watched closely as the cars approached and passed by, sensing the rhythm. He began to move his body, mirroring the rocking motion of the cars. Then he was jogging along the gravel siding, almost keeping pace, but not quite.

He turned his head and saw it, three cars back. The door was open. The shabby boxcar approached slowly, two cars back, then one. Then it was alongside.

He reached out. His hand touched the rough wooden floor. He stumbled, regained his footing and jumped.

Justyn arrived in Brussels that night, the train lumbering into a massive rail yard and jerking to a halt in a blast of venting steam. Justyn peered out the door then jumped to the ground. There were dozens of tracks and, all around him was a beehive of activity as railcars were disconnected by switch engines and reconnected to other trains. He tried to guess at the direction to Antwerp, but he couldn't figure it out. He was terrified of being seen. Staying low, Justyn sprinted from the cover of one train to another and made his way to the periphery of the yard where he spotted a shed.

Glancing around, he approached the shed. The door was ajar. Justyn pulled it back, and it creaked on rusty hinges. He peered inside. It was pitch dark, and the damp air smelled like fuel oil. He hesitated, then stepped inside and stumbled on a tool of some sort. He kicked it aside and felt for the wall. He followed the wall to a corner, then sat down on the dirt floor.

At first it was deathly quiet. Then Justyn thought he heard something. He listened. It sounded like . . . breathing. He heard another sound, as if something were moving or shifting around. He thought about bolting out the open door again but he couldn't move.

A scratching sound.

Then a bright flash.

Justyn recoiled, his head banging against the wall, as the bright flare of a match illuminated a face.

Justyn scrunched against the wall.

The face was less than two meters away . . . rough, craggy, with shaggy gray whiskers and dark eyes.

A dirty hand held the match to a limp cigarette that protruded from the corner of the mouth. The mouth blew out a column of smoke, and the hand moved the burning match toward Justyn. Another hand removed the cigarette, and the mouth opened, revealing yellowed, broken teeth.

The match burned down and the hand shook it out. A raspy voice spoke French in the darkness. "You damn near stepped on me when you stumbled in here."

Justyn was rigid. He opened his mouth but nothing came out.

The raspy voice said, "You're kind of young to be out here alone, *mon ami.* Runnin' from the Krauts, are you?"

Justyn looked at the open door again. Could he make it? In the darkness he heard the man's heavy breathing as he took another drag on the cigarette. The smell of cheap tobacco overpowered the fuel oil.

"Tell me where you're headin' and maybe I can help you," the voice said. "I've been all over this country dodging the fuckin' Krauts."

"Ant . . . Antwerp," Justyn mumbled. "I'm trying to . . . get to Antwerp."

"Antwerp? Christ, that's the wrong way. If you want to get away from the Krauts you should go south . . . for the country."

Justyn told his story to the man behind the raspy voice. When he finished, the man lit another cigarette revealing his face a second time. His eyes were small and dark, almost black, and they glared at him through the flickering light of the match. They looked like eyes that had seen things they would rather not see again. The man held the match until it almost burned his fingers then shook it out. For several long minutes there was silence in the darkness.

Then the man spoke again, the raspy voice a whisper. "There's a freight train to Antwerp that leaves every morning at seven o'clock. I'll show you where to get on."

Leaning out the open door of the boxcar, Justyn recognized the neighborhood around Antwerp's Berchem station. The train slowed as it pulled into the station, and he hopped out. From here it was just a short walk to the Zurenborg district and the home of Rene and Mimi Leffard. He felt like running.

It had been over two years since Justyn last saw the Leffards but now, as he walked along the familiar streets, it seemed like yesterday. He recalled Rene Leffard's deep, commanding voice and thick, strong arms. He remembered being frightened of him when he and Anna first arrived from Poland, but the man soon became like a grandfather, the embodiment of security in a ten-year-old's fearful world. He breathed a little easier, certain that, once again, the larger-than-life man would take care of everything.

It was almost ten o'clock in the morning, and the sidewalks were busy as Justyn turned the corner onto the Cogels-Osylei. He became aware that people were giving him strange glances, and he suddenly realized how he must look. His clothes were dirty and torn, and he hadn't washed in two days. He guessed that he probably smelled pretty bad as well.

Justyn passed the Leopold Café, where he and Anna had often had Sunday evening suppers with the Leffards, and his pace quickened. Their home was just ahead, in the next block, and he knew he needed to get off the streets. He kept his head down, trying to avoid eye contact with the people he passed, and trotted across the familiar intersection with four magnificent white, stone homes on each corner. Just a few meters to go and he would be safe.

Justyn noticed the smell at the same time he saw the house and stopped dead in his tracks. He stopped so suddenly that a woman who had been walking behind him stumbled into him and almost fell. Justyn reached out to help her, but she jerked her hand away and hobbled off.

He looked back at the house and stared in disbelief, not comprehending. The acrid odor of burned wood wafted down from the charred remains of the once stately, elegant home that had filled Rene Leffard with such pride. It was the most beautiful house Justyn had ever been in, and it had been his home, his sanctuary, during the worst time of his life. Now the windows were smashed and the massive front door shattered, hanging precariously from its hinges.

Justyn backed away and glanced up and down the street. He considered the neighbor's house on his left. Should he knock on their door to find out what had happened? He remembered them as an older couple who had treated him politely but indifferently when he and Anna lived here. Would they remember him?

The door opened and a man stepped out. Justyn didn't recognize him. The man gave him a curious look, glanced at the Leffards' burned-out home, then closed the door behind him and stepped off the porch. "*Bonjour.* May I help you?" the man said. He spoke French with a German accent. "Are you looking for someone?"

Justyn felt his face flush. He fought to control his voice. "*Non*, I was just walking by. I . . . I'm not looking for anyone." He turned away and walked quickly, back in the direction he had come from. He fought the urge to run. Keep walking, don't look back, he told himself, expecting to feel a hand on his shoulder.

When he stopped he found himself at the door of the Leopold Café. Without thinking, Justyn pushed the door open and stepped inside.

Chapter 47

PAUL DE SMET ENTERED the Gestapo headquarters in Brussels and gave his name to the dour-looking SS officer sitting at the desk. Two SS troopers stood nearby, holding submachine guns. The officer picked up the phone and repeated de Smet's name, then hung up and glared at him. "Fourth floor, give your name to the officer on duty." He pointed at the elevator.

Rolf Reinhardt did not look up when de Smet was shown into his office. "Take a seat," he grunted and continued reading the document he held in his hands.

De Smet sat in a metal chair and glanced around the small office. The obligatory picture of Adolf Hitler hung on the wall behind Reinhardt's desk and a Nazi flag stood in the corner. A plaque of some sort hung on another wall but the only thing de Smet could make out from this distance was the eagle and swastika emblem and the name *Oberstleutnant Rolf Reinhardt*, written in bold script.

Reinhardt abruptly looked up and said, in perfect French, "*Bien fait*, well done, Monsieur de Smet. The little conspiracy you and I arranged has been executed to perfection, don't you agree?" The Gestapo agent leaned back in his swivel chair and propped his feet on the desk.

De Smet didn't respond.

Reinhardt smiled. "Come, come. As a friend of the Reich, surely you must be pleased that the terrorists were captured and are being appropriately dealt with?"

De Smet took a breath. "*Oui, oui, bien sûr* . . . I'm quite pleased." He felt beads of perspiration on his forehead and silently cursed himself for being nervous.

Reinhardt folded his hands in his lap and continued. "Unfortunately, we had to kill four of them at the rail siding, including both of the teenage boys. But the others were, shall we say, persuaded to cooperate."

De Smet stared at him, his stomach turning. *The bastard's enjoying this.*

Reinhardt locked eyes with him and smiled again. "As for that slovenly butcher, van Acker, he's swinging from the ceiling in his shop like a side of beef. And the master conspirator, the illustrious Rene Leffard, is scraping his meals off the floor of his cell in Breendonck. We have special plans for him."

De Smet forced himself to sit still. *Now was no time to get squeamish,* he told himself. *He knew it would be like this.*

Reinhardt suddenly sat upright and leaned across the desk. His glare hardened. "Your friend Rik Trooz was picked up last night as well. We know about his connection with the so-called 'Comet Line' and I'm confident he'll share what he knows. Right now only one of his legs has been broken—and a collar bone, I think—but we'll let him sit overnight then have another chat."

Reinhardt stood up and walked around the small office, circling behind de Smet's chair, brushing his hand across his shoulders.

De Smet could feel the sweat running down his forehead. He didn't move, terrified that he might piss in his pants.

The Gestapo agent continued on, as though he were giving a weather report. "Let's see, what else? Oh yes, Leon Marchal's farm was burned down, as well as the Delacroix's. Did you know them well?"

De Smet coughed and cleared his throat. "*Non* . . . I didn't. I didn't know them at all."

"Well, no matter. They're all dead now anyway, or will be soon." Reinhardt stepped back to the front of his desk with his back to de Smet. He seemed to be staring at the picture of Hitler. "The butcher I mentioned, and, oh yes, *le petit chalet* he owned in the woods near Warempage. That was burned down as well. Did you know anything about the people who were living there?" Reinhardt turned and stared at him. "Apparently, it was an attractive redheaded woman and her teenage son. We couldn't seem to locate them."

"*Non* . . . *non,* I didn't know them," de Smet said, "none of them."

"Are you certain of that? We think she was working with Trooz and the Comet Line."

"I'm telling you the truth. I only met Leffard and Boeynants." He shifted in the hard metal chair.

Reinhardt sat on the edge of the desk. "I see. Well, then that brings us to Monsieur Boeynants. I'm sure you can help us here. It seems that he was not at home when we dropped in on him. Have you been in contact with him?"

"*Non*, I haven't talked with any of them since I passed along the date of the shipment."

Reinhardt glanced at the desk and picked up a letter opener, rolling it over in his fingers. "You're certain of that. No contact at all?"

"I swear . . . I haven't spoken to anyone." The sweat dripped down his cheeks, and he had to fish out his handkerchief and wipe his face.

Reinhardt smiled, then stepped around to the other side of the desk and pushed a buzzer. A few seconds later, the door opened and two SS troopers entered the office.

De Smet's stomach tightened.

Reinhardt folded his arms across his chest, looked down at him again and spoke in German. "Well, Herr de Smet. We had a bargain. When we first met, I showed you a picture of your son, alive and well in Hamburg."

De Smet could barely breathe. He nodded.

Reinhardt continued. "You agreed to set up this little trap and help us round up the terrorists. In return, I would arrange for you and your son to be re-united. Wasn't that it?"

De Smet nodded again. "*Ja, ja*, that was it. My son is coming home, then?"

Reinhardt smiled. With a quick nod of his head he motioned to the two SS troopers. They grabbed de Smet under the arms and jerked him to his feet. The chair tipped over and clattered on the tile floor.

Reinhardt's smile faded into a sneer. "You're going to be reunited with your son. But there's been a slight change in plans. The reunion will take place in Germany."

De Smet's knees went weak. If the SS troopers weren't gripping his arms he would have fallen. "That's not what we agreed on," he cried. "I've been loyal to the Reich! I've performed other services." De Smet struggled in the iron grip of the troopers. "We had a deal. You said—"

Reinhardt lunged forward and slapped him in the face. "*Ruhe!* You rotten turd! How dare you raise your voice to me?" He grabbed de Smet's tie and jerked his head forward. "*Ja,* you performed other services—for which you were handsomely rewarded." He shoved de Smet backward and stepped away, wiping his hands. His voice dropped to a whisper. "Now, however, your services are no longer required." Reinhardt turned back to his desk, glancing over his shoulder at the SS troopers. "Get this *schweinhund* out of my office."

Chapter 48

THE TRAIN TO LE HAVRE pulled out of Paris's Gare du Nord more than an hour late. Anna had barely been able to contain herself while the train sat at the platform, expecting the Feldgendarmes to enter the car at any moment.

It didn't help that she wasn't able to properly communicate with Ryan. For the first time, she felt genuinely sorry for the impudent young man. She didn't dare speak to him in English so, for the moment, there wasn't much she could do to relieve his anxiety. Perhaps it was for the better. She just hoped he would keep quiet.

It was a slow train that stopped at every station along the way. Anna tried to keep track of their progress, but none of the small towns were familiar and she was just too tired. Ryan had fallen asleep and the gentle rocking of the car, warmed by the sun shining through the windows, lulled her into unconsciousness.

The train jerked to a halt and Anna woke with a start. She blinked a few times, trying to clear her head, and glanced at her watch. She was surprised to see that it was almost eleven o'clock. She had been asleep for almost two hours.

Anna looked out the window at the small railway station, but the train had already rolled past the sign identifying the town. It was apparently not a major stop since none of the other passengers made any attempt to get off. In the seat beside her Ryan stirred and woke up, rubbing his eyes.

Anna looked back out the window and spotted two policemen standing near the station house. Her stomach tightened. A few seconds later, a railway conductor joined the policemen, and the three of them walked toward the train. One of the policemen split off toward the rear of the car while the other entered the car from the front with the conductor.

Ryan nudged Anna's arm. She shot him a quick glance and touched her lips.

The conductor and the policeman stood in the front of the car studying some type of document. Anna heard the rear door open and close. She fought to keep her composure.

Out of the corner of her eye Anna saw the conductor and policeman start down the aisle. She kept her head turned away as the footsteps stopped at their seats.

"Monsieur, Madame, pardonnez moi, your tickets and passports please?" the conductor asked blandly.

Anna met his eyes and smiled. *"Oui, bien sûr."* She retrieved her purse from the floor, removed both sets of documents and handed them to the conductor.

He looked them over and showed them to the policeman, who glanced at them and nodded. The conductor opened the small leather case he was carrying and slipped the tickets and passports inside. "Come with us, please—both of you."

"Is there a problem?" Anna asked.

"Ce n'est pas grave, it's nothing. I'm sure we can straighten it out in a few minutes," the conductor replied in a bland, bureaucratic monotone.

"Je ne comprends pas," Anna persisited. "What sort of problem?" She knew she had to avoid getting off the train, although it was probably not going to be possible.

"It's nothing. I'm sure it will take only a few minutes. Now, please, come with us." The conductor stepped back and motioned with his hand for them to get up.

Anna noticed the policeman shift his weight and raise his right hand so that it was touching the handle of the revolver strapped around his waist.

At the same time the policeman standing behind their seats put his hand on Ryan's shoulder and gave him a shove. "Come on, get up," he commanded.

"Hey!" Ryan blurted and jerked around.

Anna grabbed his arm and said sharply, in Flemish, *"Het geeft niet, laten we gaan!* Never mind, let's go!"

Ryan turned toward her.

Anna slid her hand down his arm and squeezed his hand as they both stood up and followed the conductor and policeman out of the car. The other passengers stared out the windows or read their newspapers.

When they stepped down to the platform, two Feldgendarmes moved in around them. One of them pulled a revolver out of his holster and pointed it directly at Ryan. "*Halten!* Turn around and put your hands behind you!" he barked in German.

Suddenly Ryan lunged forward and grabbed the Feldgendarme's hand, forcing the gun toward the ground.

In a flash, the other Feldgendarme and one of the policemen pulled out their nightsticks and pounded Ryan on the back of the head and shoulders.

Ryan grunted and collapsed, blood oozing from the back of his head.

The Feldgendarme pulled out a pair of handcuffs while the policeman shoved his knee into the small of Ryan's back.

"What the hell are you doing?" Anna screamed. "You can't—" The slap almost knocked her down. A searing pain shot through her jaw.

"Shut up, bitch!" the other policeman yelled and stuck a revolver into Anna's ribs, shoving her against the side of the railcar.

Anna's head banged into the car and her knees buckled. She sagged to the ground. The policemen grabbed her under the shoulders and jerked her to her feet. He pulled her wrists behind her and snapped on a pair of handcuffs. His face was just a few centimeters from her own. His breath smelled of wine and garlic. "Not another word, bitch. Understand?"

Anna's head throbbed and her jaw hurt so badly she thought it was broken. She turned as the two Feldgendarmes pulled Ryan to his feet. The aviator's head hung down and he could barely stand as they dragged him toward the south end of the platform.

The policeman in front of Anna grabbed her shoulder and shoved her toward the north end of the platform. "Get moving," he snarled and shoved her again, almost knocking her off her feet.

When Anna awoke her first sensation was the pain in her jaw. She opened her mouth and moved it back and forth slowly. The pain brought tears to her eyes but just being able to move it was a good sign, she thought. She probed around with her hand, feeling along each side of her jaw. It was very sore but she doubted it was broken.

She winced when her fingers brushed across a deep scrape on her cheek.

She touched it tenderly, then pulled her hand away and looked at the traces of blood. The bastard who slapped her was probably wearing a ring. When she sat up her forehead throbbed. She swung her feet to the floor and lowered her head into her hands, closing her eyes.

After a few minutes the pain subsided a bit. Anna sat up and looked around. She was sitting on a cot at one end of a small concrete block room. In the corner of the room opposite the cot was a small hole in the concrete floor. The door looked stout, made of heavy wood with a small barred window. Sunlight shown into the room from behind her, and she turned to look up at another barred window. The effort made her head hurt again, and she turned away.

Anna stood up and stepped over to the door, trying to peer out of the barred window. It was high enough that she had to stand on her tiptoes, and she couldn't see much except another concrete wall. She looked down at her wrist to check the time and realized her watch was gone.

She sighed, stepped back to the cot and sat down again, rubbing her temples. Damn it all, she thought, how could this have happened? Part of her wanted to curse the brash young aviator for being stupid and another part of her felt remorse for having failed to get him to safety. She had no illusions about Ryan's ability to fake his false identity. Not under the kind of treatment he was sure to receive from the Feldgendarmes—or, even worse, the SS.

The sound of a key turning in the lock startled her, and Anna got to her feet as the door swung open. Standing in the doorway was a French policeman. He appeared to be no more than nineteen or twenty years old.

"Come with me," he said.

Anna stepped out of the cell into a concrete block hallway lined with ten or twelve identical wooden doors. The young policeman motioned for her to proceed ahead of him, and she walked down the hallway, stopping in front of another wooden door at the end. The policeman rapped on the door with his nightstick. A few seconds later a key turned in the lock and it swung open.

A much older policeman, fat and rumpled looking with a sweaty brow, motioned for her to step inside. The windowless room was about six meters square with concrete walls painted light blue. There was a metal table in the middle of the room and four metal chairs.

The young policeman pulled out a chair, motioned for her to sit and departed through a door at the other end of the room. Anna sat down at the table as the fat, older policeman closed the door she had come through, locked it again and retired to a grimy metal desk in the corner. There was a mug of what Anna guessed was coffee on the desk and a half-eaten sandwich on top of a haphazard pile of magazines and newspapers.

Perhaps twenty minutes later the door opened again and an SS officer stepped into the room. Anna squeezed the arms of the metal chair to keep her composure.

The fat policeman scrambled to his feet, knocking a pile of papers and the mug of coffee on the floor. The ceramic cup shattered, splattering coffee in all directions.

The SS officer glared at the slovenly man and jerked his head toward the door. The policeman squeezed past the crisply uniformed officer and exited the room, pulling the door closed behind him.

The officer laid a thin file folder on the table, then removed his black leather gloves. He removed his hat and laid it on the table with the gloves. He had neatly trimmed blond hair and icy blue eyes. He appeared to be about forty years old and looked like a man who took very good care of himself.

The officer pulled out one of the chairs and sat down. He smiled at Anna and spoke in German-accented French. "*Bonjour, madame.* I am Hauptsturmfuhrer Koenig. I apologize for the treatment you received at the railway station. It was unfortunate."

He looked at her as though expecting some type of response, but Anna couldn't think of anything to say.

Koenig shrugged and continued. "Well, what's done is done. Perhaps if your friend hadn't been so impulsive it wouldn't have happened."

Anna decided to take a chance. "Can you tell me where he is?" she asked.

Koenig smiled again but didn't respond. He opened the folder, revealing their passports and tickets. He picked up one of the passports and studied it for a few seconds. "Your friend would be this person . . . Henri Eyskens?" he asked.

"*Oui,* Henri. Can you tell me where he is?"

Koenig set the passport down and folded his hands on top of the file. "*Oui,* I can tell you where he is. But first, perhaps you should tell me *who* he is."

Anna struggled to control her emotions. She knew she had to stay calm if she had any chance of surviving this. "What do you mean? His name is Henri Eyskens. He's an engineer with our company, and I would like to know where he is."

Koenig's smile disappeared. He opened the file and removed the other passport. "Please, don't waste my time, Madame 'Laurent,' or whatever your real name is. Your friend is a very poor liar, and he doesn't know enough Flemish to buy a loaf of bread. We know that he's British and most likely an aviator. As such, he is responsible for the murder of thousands of German citizens. He will be dealt with accordingly."

Anna's throat was so tight she felt like she wouldn't be able to take another breath.

Koenig sat back and folded his arms across his chest. "But as for you, *madame*, that's quite another story, isn't it."

"*Je ne comprends pas*, what do you mean?" Anna replied. It was weak but it was all she could manage.

Koenig stood up and paced around the room with his hands clasped behind his back. He stared at her as he talked in a quiet monotone. "We know that you and the British murderer got on the train in Brussels. You were trying to pass him off as Flemish, but he was dumb enough to speak to you in English, which, unfortunately for you, was overheard by a patriot, a friend of the Reich. So, we ask ourselves, why is an attractive Belgian woman carrying a fake passport and traveling with a British soldier?"

Koenig had circled around behind her and stopped moving.

Anna stared down at the table, willing herself to stay calm.

He leaned close and whispered in her ear. "How long have you been an agent of the Comet Line, madame?"

Anna closed her eyes, squeezing the arm of the chair. She could feel his breath on the back of her neck. She counted to three then pushed the chair back.

Koenig straightened up as Anna stood and turned to face him. "I have no idea what you're talking about," she said. "And I resent the implication that my friend and colleague isn't who I've said he is. The whole idea is absurd."

Koenig stared at her then stepped back to the other side of the table. "*Très bien, madame, très bien.* Very good, indeed. I admire spirit in a woman. And *especially* a woman as attractive as you."

"*Monsieur,* I meant exactly—" Anna began but stopped as Koenig held up his hand.

He leaned forward with both hands on the table. "I have some information that may interest you, *madame.* So, please sit down and pay attention." He picked up the folder and removed a single sheet of paper. "During the last forty-eight hours, some arrests were made in Belgium. Perhaps you know these people." He looked at the list and said, "Gaston Rompaey."

Anna didn't recognize the name and didn't react.

"Richard Berghmans."

Again, Anna did not know the name. Perhaps he was off on the wrong track, she thought.

"Leon Marchal."

It was like a rifle shot to her heart. Anna shuddered. Suddenly she was overwhelmed with a feeling of dread about Justyn.

"Rik Trooz," Koenig hissed.

She gripped the chair so hard she thought her fingers would break. Goddamn him!

"Rene Leffard."

The name fell like a sword slicing through her soul. Anna whimpered and squirmed in her chair—then lost control.

She jumped to her feet, and the metal chair clattered to the floor. She ripped the folder out of the stunned officer's hand and swatted him in the face with it. "You goddamn sick bastard," Anna screamed. "Go to hell! Go to hell and be damned!" She flung the folder across the room and sank to her knees, sobbing.

Hauptsturmfuhrer Koenig stared at her for a minute, not saying a word. Then he picked up the folder, retrieved his hat and gloves and left the room.

Chapter 49

THE HARSH POLISH WINTER gave way to spring. The weather warmed and wildflowers bloomed in the soft, rolling terrain east of Krakow. The farmers were back in their fields, strapped to horse-drawn plows, beginning another season scratching out a living from the earth.

Jan and the AK operatives dismantling the V-2 rocket were busy. Working on the highly technical and sophisticated device under constant fear of discovery was nerve-wracking, and everyone was exhausted. But a plan had begun to unfold. They were informed by the MI-6 contact in London that Allied forces were rooting the Germans out of southern Italy. Very soon it would be possible for a plane to take off from Italy and reach the southwestern part of Poland to retrieve the rocket components and take them to London.

So, the dismantled components were transported, piece-by-piece, hidden in wagons loaded with sacks of flour, bushels of potatoes and hollowed-out bales of hay. Through circuitous routes, transferred from one partisan to another, the rocket parts made their way two hundred kilometers southwest, from the Bug River to another remote farm, a half kilometer from an abandoned airstrip near the confluence of the rivers Dunajec and Vistula.

By the end of the first week of June, the precious cache had been painstakingly concealed in cellars and sheds on the secluded farm. The AK operatives brought in a long-range wireless and established a communication link through London to coordinate the flight.

It was late on a Sunday afternoon, and Jan busied himself in a small room on the second floor of the farmhouse packing his few belongings. His work done, he was determined to leave for Krakow to begin his search for Anna.

He had no firm plan, but he knew he had to act now. News had just reached them that the long-awaited Allied invasion had begun at Normandy, and Jan was certain that this was the turning point in the war. The Russians had launched an offensive in the east, and the noose around Germany's neck was tightening. A desperate enemy in retreat would be certain to liquidate concentration camps. If Anna was in one of those camps . . .

He heard footsteps and turned to see Slomak standing in the doorway, holding a bottle of vodka and two small glasses. "Let's go have a drink," the AK operative said.

Jan followed the slender balding man out of the house and across the farmyard to a low, stone wall overlooking a freshly planted wheat field. The sun was low in the western sky, and a warm, gentle breeze drifted across the rolling plain.

Slomak filled the glasses, and they sat drinking in silence for several minutes.

"Tadeusz tells me that you're not planning to return to London with the rocket parts," Slomak said, peering at him through his thick glasses.

"No, Chmielewski will go," Jan replied.

"He doesn't speak English."

"They'll have interpreters."

"Where are you going?" Slomak asked after a pause.

"Krakow, at first. After that I'm not sure." Jan finished off the vodka and refilled his glass.

Slomak picked up the bottle and refilled his own glass. "A couple of months ago you asked me if I knew anything about the SS *special action* in Krakow back in '39. What is it you wanted to know?"

It took Jan a moment to comprehend the surprise question. Why now, after all this time? He hesitated; it had been a long time since he had talked about any of this. "My wife was an associate professor at Jagiellonian University. Her father was also a professor there, a law professor. I believe they both were arrested by the SS."

Slomak didn't respond.

Jan continued. "The day you and I met in Krakow, later that same day, I went to our home looking for my wife. The SS had been there. Our apartment was a wreck and she was gone. Then I went to my father-in-law's home. It was occupied by a German couple. I thought . . ." Jan poured another drink. This was harder than he imagined. "I thought you might know something—where they might have been taken, anything to help me get started."

Slomak's brow furrowed. "You said both your wife and your father-in-law were professors at Jagiellonian?"

"Yes, that's right. She taught—"

"What is your father-in law's name?" Slomak interrupted.

"Piekarski. Thaddeus Piekarski," Jan replied, his heart pounding.

"And your wife's name is . . ."

"Anna."

Slomak stared at him for what seemed to Jan like an eternity. "My God," he whispered. "You must be Jan Kopernik." Still staring at him, Slomak shook his head. "I don't think your wife was arrested."

Jan was so startled at hearing his real name for the first time in months that he barely comprehended what Slomak had said. "I . . . don't understand . . . she was . . ."

"I met your wife in Krakow," Slomak said, "right after the arrests at the university. She got my name from the wife of one of your father-in-law's colleagues."

Jan felt like he would explode.

"Excuse me, Major Kopernik. I'll get right to the point. I put your wife in contact with a man who was with the Italian diplomatic mission to Poland. He arranged for her to get a travel visa to Italy."

Jan shook his head, trying to process what he had heard. "Travel visa? To Italy . . . I don't . . . I . . . what the hell are you talking about?"

"The Italians were quite sympathetic to the plight of Poland for several months after the invasion. They secretly arranged travel visas for hundreds of Poles before the Germans shut down their mission." Slomak paused then continued. "From Italy she could have gone anywhere in Europe. It was just an expedient way to get out of Poland."

Jan ran a hand through his blond hair, glancing up at the sky. Was it possible? Then he recalled the mess at their apartment. "But our apartment, it had been ransacked. And I spoke with a neighbor who said she heard . . ." He paused. "Good God, could they have arrested her before she was able to leave?"

Slomak stood up and paced around in a circle rubbing his temples. "I'm trying to remember how . . . yes . . . that's it. I spoke with the contact at the Italian mission; Di Stefano was his name. He told me he had given your wife three travel visas, for her, her friend, and her friend's son. He said he had instructed them to leave immediately and not to tell anyone they were leaving. He was quite emphatic about that." Slomak stopped pacing and turned to Jan. "Major, as I recall, that was just a day or two before you came to see me. Did the SS ransack other apartments in your building? Was anyone else missing?"

"Yes, all three apartments. I checked Mrs. Koslofski's, the apartment just below ours. She was gone. The Grucas, their apartment is on the ground floor . . . ransacked . . . they were gone." Jan stood up and walked a few paces along the crumbling stone wall then abruptly turned back. "Why would the SS have come to our home? Were they after Anna? Or Irene, our friend, she's Jewish."

Slomak hesitated. "It could have been either, Major. It's true the Germans were arresting some Jews at that time, though not yet in large numbers. But the SS did make a concerted effort to track down the family members of those arrested at the university."

"For what purpose? Which ones?"

Slomak sat down again on the stone wall. "Major, there were two reasons for the *special action* at the university that night. One was that it was part of the overall plan by the Nazis to rid Poland of its intelligentsia—their plan to turn the entire country into a mindless slave state. The other reason was the SS had learned that several Jagiellonian faculty members were involved with the Resistance."

"Thaddeus?"

"We're not sure. But we do know that your father-in-law was a close associate of a man who was." Slomak hesitated again. "That's all I can tell you, I'm sorry."

"What happened to them, Thaddeus and the others they arrested?"

"They were taken to Germany, to a concentration camp called Sachsenhausen."

"What about Anna? Was she involved? Do you know if—"

"No, I have no reason to believe she would have been involved. It was very early in the Resistance movement. I don't even know if your father-in-law was involved." Slomak gripped Jan's arm. "Major, I met with your wife on two occasions. I sensed the kind of person she is. I could feel her strength, her determination. I believe she made it out of Poland."

Chapter 50

THE NEWS OF THE ALLIED INVASION at Normandy caused SS Hauptsturm-fuhrer Koenig a great deal of anxiety. Two weeks ago he had received word that his long-awaited transfer back to Berlin had been approved. At last, a chance to get out of the drudgery of the occupied countries. An assignment with some status, a chance for advancement.

But now this goddamn invasion was on and everything could change. There were certain to be complications with his transfer. Then . . . there was the issue of the woman.

Koenig knew it was crazy, but he couldn't help himself. He was completely captivated by the stunning redhead they had arrested. She despised him, of course, but he was confident he could overcome that with time. After all, it really wasn't him she despised—it was the persona of the SS officer, the enemy, that she detested. Once she really got to know Dieter Koenig, the person, things would be different. He was confident it would work out just like it had with the others before her.

The first time he met her, when she slapped him in the face with the file, Koenig knew he had to have her. Her outburst had sexually aroused him and ever since he had fantasized about what she might be like with that passion sufficiently harnessed as only he could.

What was really annoying was that he had worked out all the details. He had figured out how he would transport her to Germany and where he would keep her. Even under pressure from that lowly Gestapo agent in Brussels, the swine Rolf Reinhardt, he had been able to make the proper arrangements. Reinhardt had gotten wind of the arrest and had been calling every day, demanding that Koenig send her back to Brussels for interrogation. Ever since the smug bastard broke up that Resistance ring in Belgium, he thought he could have whatever he wanted.

Koenig knew what that meant. He knew about Gestapo interrogations. They'd rape her, many times. Then they'd break her fingers . . . and her ankles. Then, when they'd gotten what they wanted—and they always did—they'd put her out of her misery.

He wasn't going to let that happen, not to this intriguing woman. She was his, and he was going to take her to Germany. He had worked it all out.

But now everything was in turmoil. Koenig had never seen the chain of command as fouled up as it was at this moment. The Allied armies were swarming up the beaches at Normandy, and no one knew what to do. Rumors were flying all around. Rommel was in Germany visiting his wife. Hitler had been asleep, and no one had had the courage to wake him up. The panzer divisions were in position for a counterattack, but Jodl would not give the orders to release them because he didn't believe the invasion was the real thing.

Koenig was caught in a quandary, and he hated it. He hated being indecisive. Technically, he had his orders, and he could proceed to Germany. But he also knew that a crisis loomed and, at any moment, all transfer orders would be rescinded. With the invasion on, he would almost certainly be ordered to the front, in Normandy. For one of the few times in his life he really didn't know what to do.

He was still trying to decide, when there was a knock on the door. Koenig blinked and shook his head. "*Komm!*"

His aide, Oberscharfuhrer Strauss, stepped into the office holding a piece of paper in his hand. It was a copy of a teletype. "Your orders, *Hauptsturmfuhrer.*"

Goddamn it, Koenig thought. "Read them," he said.

The aide looked down at the paper. "You are ordered to close down the jail immediately and dispose of all prisoners in the most expedient manner. You are then to proceed without delay to Caen and report to SS Standartenfuhrer Hermann, Twenty-first Panzer Division."

Koenig slumped in his chair. One more day. One more goddamn day and he'd have been in Germany . . . with that gorgeous creature. Now it had all fallen apart. He closed his eyes and saw her face, once again imagining how it might have been.

Koenig heard Strauss shuffle his feet and clear his throat. Goddamn it, it was over. He shook his head and stood up. He had to put this out of his mind.

There would be others, another time. There always were. "All right, how many prisoners are there at the moment?"

"*Einundzwanzig*, sir. Twenty, plus the one woman."

"And what are our options for 'expedient disposal'?"

Oberscharfuhrer Strauss cleared his throat before answering. "Well, sir, I suppose we could arrange a firing squad."

"Oh shit, in a small town like this? Christ, there'd be an uproar, and we don't have time to transport them out to the woods and do it quietly. There's got to be a better way."

Strauss was silent for a moment then nodded. "Sir, I think there might be another way. I received a dispatch about an hour ago. There's a train coming through here bound for Paris."

"A train for Paris? So what? How does that help us? We can't—"

"Excuse me for interrupting, sir; this is one of the 'special trains.' It's heading for Drancy."

Koenig stared at him. Ordinarily he wouldn't give it a second thought. It was perfect. They could stop the train and throw the unlucky bastards on board, and that would be that. It would be fast and clean, and no one would know the difference. He knew all about the "special trains," boxcars loaded with Jews like so many cattle. He knew all about Drancy too, a "collection station," as his superiors called it, where they would stockpile Jews until they could be hauled off to "the east."

Koenig thought about it. Personally, he didn't care one way or the other about Jews. But the thought of pushing that beautiful redheaded woman into one of those vermin-filled boxcars almost made him sick. He turned away and stared out the window. Christ, what a mess. He had been so close . . . and she was so . . .

Strauss interrupted his thoughts. "Excuse me, sir. We have very little time. The train is due in here in less than half an hour and if we want to stop it I'll have to call the station chief."

Koenig whirled around. "*Ja, ja, natürlich.* I understand. Get to it. Put them on that train."

"All of them sir? Even the . . ."

"*Ja,* all of them. Now get going, I've got to get packed."

Chapter 51

WILLY BOEYNANTS WAS FRUSTRATED. He had contacted everyone he could think of, trying to find out what might have happened to Anna, but had precious little to go on. All he had discovered was that she was on another mission.

When he received the call from the proprietor of the Leopold Café, about a teenager asking for Rene Leffard, he had gone there at once. He recognized Justyn immediately, though the boy had grown considerably since he had last seen him. Justyn was frantic with worry about Anna, and for good reason, Boeynants thought. The Gestapo had to be looking for her, and when she returned to Warempage she'd certainly be arrested.

Boeynants had another problem. He was a fugitive himself, making it difficult to get information. He managed to make contact with his colleague at the Interior Department and learned that Rik Trooz had been arrested and had apparently given up some information that put the Gestapo on the trail of a woman agent leading a British aviator out of the country.

Some further digging led Boeynants to a woman in Brussels named "Claudia" who confirmed that a redheaded woman using the name "Jeanne Laurent" had picked up a British aviator at her home and left the next day. But she had no information about their destination.

At least Justyn was safe and in good health, Boeynants thought. That was something, considering what the lad had been through. Auguste and his wife, Elise, had immediately insisted that Justyn stay with them and fawned over him like grandparents, pledging to keep his secret until Anna returned. All that Boeynants could hope for now was that Anna's resourcefulness and strong will would keep her safe.

On this evening, however, those worries had to be set aside as Boeynants and Auguste attended a meeting of the special Resistance group operating in Antwerp's port. The meeting took place in the cellar of a four-story brick building on the street fronting the Kattendijkdok dock. The busy Café Brig on the building's ground floor provided sufficient cover for the comings and goings of the members of the clandestine group.

Boeynants took a seat next to Auguste and looked around. There were about twenty men in the musty, dimly lit cellar. The group's leaders sat at a wooden table at the front of the room. Boeynants recognized the short, slight man wearing a green beret. It was Antoine.

Boeynants thought back to when Auguste first introduced him to Antoine, almost two months ago, the day after the Leffards' arrest. The White Brigade leader had made an instant impression on him. He was a merchant naval officer who had been active in the Resistance since the outbreak of the war. Over the last two years he had quietly established an organization among workers in the port, all of them familiar with operations at the massive facility. It was this organization, Antoine had told him, that would defend the port when the time came.

Antoine stood up and conversation in the room ceased. *"Bonsoir,* Soldiers of the White Brigade. I appreciate all of you taking the risk to come here tonight on such short notice," he said. "We'll keep this brief." He paused and looked at each man in the room. His dark eyes were intense. "I'm sure all of you are aware that *l'invasion* is underway. According to the reports we've received, the fighting is intense, but in all of the landing areas, the Allies have established beachheads and are holding."

A murmur spread through the group, and several men clasped hands with the men next to them.

Antoine continued. "Breaking out of *côte de Normandie* will be a monumental struggle and, while it seems that the Germans were caught by surprise, we know they'll regroup and mount a powerful resistance. Now, here in Antwerp, our job begins in earnest."

Everyone was silent and all eyes were on him.

Antoine glanced at a paper he was holding. "In what was probably a coincidence of timing, a German general named Christoph Graf Stolberg arrived in Antwerp the day before *l'invasion*. General Stolberg is assuming command of the German forces defending Antwerp and will be followed shortly by members of his 136th Divisional Staff. We expect they will immediately begin shoring up their defenses around the city and the port."

Antoine set the paper on the table. "We have no idea how long it will take the Allied forces to break out and begin their drive across France and into Belgium, but our job is to be ready when they get here. We know that the Germans will do everything possible to prevent the port from falling into the hands of the Allies. If they can't defend it, they'll try to destroy it. It's our job to prevent that from happening."

Antoine stepped around to the front of the table and folded his arms across his chest. He looked over the group again, acknowledging each of the men with a nod or a thin smile.

This man is a leader, Boeynants thought.

Antoine continued, speaking quietly, forcing everyone to concentrate, his voice slowly rising in volume and intensity as he finished. "You have your assignments. You understand the chain of command. No breach of the rules of contact or the use of codes will be tolerated. We are now in the stage of the war that we have all been trained for, that we have all been waiting for. Watch every action of the enemy. Listen to every conversation. Commit every detail to memory and report it up the chain of command. *Restez vigilant,* and be ready for action."

When the meeting broke up, Antoine approached Auguste and Boeynants and led them to a quiet corner of the room. When they were alone, the Resistance leader gripped Boeynants's shoulder. He spoke just above a whisper. "I have news about the Leffards."

Boeynants stiffened.

Antoine continued to grip his shoulder, his dark eyes filled with pain. "We have a contact inside Breendonck prison. Last night Rene and Mimi were . . . *exécuté.*"

Boeynants sagged against the stone wall. He heard Auguste say something but it didn't register. His vision blurred, and he took several breaths, trying to focus his eyes on Antoine's green beret. For two months he had feared this would happen; they'd never release a man like Leffard—but hearing it, knowing it . . .

"I'm very sorry," Antoine said softly, his hand dropping to his side. "I know you were close to them. His loss is a heavy blow to our organization."

Boeynants nodded. He straightened up and glanced at Auguste then back at Antoine. "*Merci*. Thank you for telling me."

They stood in silence for a moment before Antoine spoke again. "You can be of service to us if you are willing."

"*Oui, oui, bien sûr,*" Boeynants replied, grateful for the distraction.

"Auguste tells me that you have a contact in the Interior Department."

"Yes, it's where I used to work."

Antoine took a step closer, keeping his voice down. "This may be dangerous, but your contact at the Department could be very important now that General Stolberg is here in Antwerp. Anything he can find out about their plans will be useful."

"*Je comprends,*" Boeynants said. "I'll do everything I can."

Antoine nodded. "Report directly to me." He put a finger up to his beret in a brief salute and stepped away.

Chapter 52

ANNA WAS NUMB, her mind a dark void as the sweltering, foul-smelling boxcar jerked to a halt. She huddled in a corner, wedged between two elderly women, one of whom had died during the night. The train had made at least a dozen stops along the way and, at each one, more people were jammed into the car until it seemed like death by suffocation was inevitable.

The lack of motion eased Anna's discomfort slightly, and a few thoughts trickled back into her mesmerized mind. She recalled how she had stared in disbelief at the waiting train when she and the other prisoners from the jail had been forced off the truck at gunpoint. It was dark, and the shabby boxcar was only partially illuminated by dim bulbs hanging under the eaves of the railway platform. Feldgendarmes stood on the platform, shouting orders. One of them struggled to control a snarling, barking dog wearing a spiked collar.

Then one of the Feldgendarmes pulled back the door of the boxcar, and Anna put her hand over her face, recoiling from the stench of sweat, urine and feces. Dozens of people—men, women and children—stared out from the dark interior. The Feldgendarmes jumped up on the edge of the car, shouting at the terrified passengers to make room, swatting those nearby with their nightsticks. The last thing Anna recalled as she was shoved up the wooden ramp, into the dark, stinking interior of the car, was a sign painted on the door: *Chevaux En Long 8.* Capacity, Eight Horses.

Anna's only consolation had been that Koenig was nowhere to be seen. Her initial hostility toward him had turned to loathing, then fear, as he sat in her cell night after night and rambled on about their life together in Germany. She was certain the man was demented and, even now, in the wretched confines of the boxcar, Anna felt her skin crawl as she thought about Koenig stroking her leg or her hair. She would jerk away in disgust, slap his hand and yell at him not to touch her, but he would just laugh and whisper what a "conquest" she would be.

Anna blinked, jerked back to the moment by people moving, shuffling about, trying to get away from the door as they did every time the train stopped. She braced herself against the side of the car and tried to fend off the crush of bodies with her arms. Pressed against the rough wooden planks, her back felt as if it would break.

The doors jerked open, and a burst of sunlight shot into the dark, steamy interior, causing everyone near the door to turn away. Men shouted in German, "Everyone out!"

Anna stumbled down the ramp from the boxcar, shielding her eyes from the glaring sunlight. As her eyes acclimated she looked around. They were standing at the far end of what appeared to be a large, open courtyard, surrounded on three sides by a complex of multistory buildings. Hundreds of people stood nearby, scrawny, stooped over, staring silently at the new arrivals but keeping their distance from the rail siding.

SS troopers and Feldgendarmes shouted instructions to keep moving, randomly swatting people with their nightsticks. Anna heard dogs barking and snarling but couldn't see them. As the group shuffled forward she heard a man behind her mumble to the woman next to him in French, "*Mon dieu*, this must be Drancy."

Anna turned and glanced at the man. He wore a felt hat and a soiled suit coat that looked like it had once been expensive. A yellow Star of David was sewn to his sleeve.

The man's eyes met Anna's. "We're doomed," he whispered.

Chapter 53

ANOTHER WEEK PASSED before the flight that would transport the rocket parts to London could be arranged, and Jan had become increasingly frustrated. As tempting as it was to believe that Anna had made it out of Poland, he couldn't bring himself to completely accept it. There was no doubt in his mind that Anna had the courage and resourcefulness to pull it off, but what about Irene and Justyn? Would Anna have been able to get two Jews through all the check-points? Possibly, but there was no way to know for sure, and that was the crux of his conflict.

The Russians had re-entered Poland, and war would soon be ravaging the country once again. If he left now Jan knew he would not be able to return, perhaps for many years to come. By then any chance of finding Anna would be long gone. On the other hand, if Anna *had* escaped to safety in Western Europe and he stayed in Poland, he could be trapped with no way out.

It was a quandary he couldn't solve. But the plane was arriving tonight and, of one thing he was certain: he was leaving here. He pulled the battered leather satchel from under the bed and, once again, started packing.

Jan glanced at the shelf above the bed and noticed the cut-glass model of the hand, Anna's favorite gift from the Leffards in Antwerp. He picked it up and turned it over, rubbing it with his fingers. He recalled how Anna would always do the same thing as she talked on the telephone. She kept it on the shelf in the hallway, with her Hummel collection, and she liked to pick it up and turn it over in her hand as she talked. He remembered finding it there, lying on the floor in the hallway among the shattered Hummel figures, the day he discovered their apartment ransacked.

He thought about it again.

No, that wasn't right.

That wasn't where he found it.

Jan sat on the bed and stared at the small glass hand. It hadn't been lying on the floor in the hallway. He had found it on the mantel above the fireplace . . . in the parlor.

He turned it over, again and again, feeling the smoothness, thinking, remembering the day he stood in the mess in the center of their parlor. He was sure that he'd found it there, in the parlor, on the mantel above the fireplace.

Jan had never paid a lot of attention to these things but he was certain that Anna always kept it on the shelf in the hallway, with the Hummels. He could see her, standing in the hallway talking on the telephone . . .

Jesus Christ! Anna had moved it. He was certain of it. She moved it. If it had been on the shelf in the hallway it would have been smashed with everything else. She intentionally put it on the mantel. She wanted him to notice it.

Jan stood up and paced around the small room, his heart pounding. It all made sense. Anna had no way to contact him, and she'd been instructed to leave immediately—that's what Slomak said. She couldn't leave him a note because she knew the Gestapo were looking for her and they'd come to the apartment.

So she put the small glass hand, the symbol of Antwerp, on the mantel, hoping he would return and notice it. Was it possible? Of course, that's what happened. He was certain. How could he have not realized it before this?

She left him a message, telling him where she was going.

Anna was in Antwerp.

It was after midnight when the Dakota appeared. It flew in from the west, using the conjunction of the two rivers as orientation and dropped in altitude attempting to locate the airstrip. Jan and Slomak stood just inside the tree line, alongside three horse-drawn wagons laden with rocket parts. Slomak lit a torch and waved it in the air giving the signal for the other torches to be lit, illuminating the four corners of the airstrip.

Then Slomak extinguished his torch and said, "Godspeed, my friend, you will find her."

Jan turned to him. He wanted to tell him how grateful he was; grateful that

Slomak helped Anna all those years before, grateful that they had met now . . . but nothing came out. He nodded and swallowed hard, waiting anxiously for the plane.

Two weeks later Jan sat in a small, sparsely furnished conference room in the basement of the SOE headquarters in London. He had been waiting about fifteen minutes when the door opened and Colonel Stanley Whitehall shuffled into the room along with a prim man of about sixty, carrying a steel briefcase.

"Good morning, Major . . . oh, excuse me, *Colonel* Kopernik," Whitehall said, noticing the new insignia on the collar of Jan's uniform. "Congratulations on your promotion. God knows you've earned it."

Jan nodded and shook Whitehall's pudgy hand.

"Colonel Kopernik, this is Martin Fletcher," Whitehall continued. "He's in charge of the team that's been examining the rocket parts. Let's all have a seat."

When they were seated, Whitehall leaned forward, folding his hands. "Colonel, we asked you to come here today because, given your extraordinary efforts, you deserve to know what we've learned."

Jan nodded again without replying.

"Well then," Whitehall said, settling back in his chair, "Martin, please brief the Colonel. It goes without saying, of course, that none of this must ever leave this room."

Martin Fletcher opened the briefcase and removed a single sheet of paper, which he placed on the table in front of him. Then he extracted a set of reading glasses from his breast pocket and set them on the edge of his long, thin nose. He glanced up at Jan, peering over the top of the glasses. "Colonel, first of all, let me congratulate you on your successful mission. Our team has been working around the clock, and the components you brought back have enabled us to reconstruct the critical portions of this device."

Fletcher paused for a moment and studied the paper in front of him.

Jan got the impression that the pause wasn't because the man needed to consult the notes as much as it was to determine exactly how much he was to reveal.

Fletcher continued. "This device, the V-2 as we call it, is a much more sophisticated weapon than the V-1s they've been firing at us. The V-2 is, in all respects, a guided missile. It is liquid fueled and we estimate that it will travel at least eight times faster than the V-1 with a range of more than three hundred kilometers. We also estimate that it is capable of achieving an altitude of approximately thirty kilometers before descending on its target."

Fletcher peered at Jan over the top of his glasses. "From that altitude, Colonel, it would be undetectable." He looked back at his notes. "Its guidance system is a form of three-axis gyropilot, which engages movable exhaust vanes and aerodynamic rudders. Quite ingenious, really. Rather crude, at this stage, but still, quite an achievement. We estimate the CEP at about 17 kilometers."

"Pardon me, the CEP?" Jan asked.

"The Circular Error Probable, the accuracy. That's the only good news, I'm afraid. The bloody thing's not very accurate. But I'm sure their people are working on that. They're quite good, you know."

"Well, there you have it," Whitehall said.

The three men sat in silence for a moment, before Jan spoke up. "Mr. Fletcher, I understand that British anti-aircraft batteries have been successful in shooting down a high percentage of the V-1s and that RAF fighter planes have been able to take them out as well. What is your defense against the V-2?"

Fletcher glanced at Whitehall then picked up the paper and placed it back in the briefcase. He folded his hands on his lap and stared down at the table.

Whitehall stood up, signaling the meeting was over. He looked at Jan. "Colonel, I understand that you've been re-assigned to the Polish First Armored Division and that you're shipping out for France in a few days."

"That's right," Jan replied.

Whitehall stepped around the table and extended his hand. "Kill the fucking Krauts, Colonel. Help us win this war as quickly as possible. There's no defense against this goddamn thing. If they improve its accuracy before we get to Germany, we're done for."

Chapter 54

By the first of August, fewer than a thousand prisoners remained in the rat-infested, disease-ridden camp at Drancy. Word had spread that the final train was due any day to collect the last of the survivors and haul them to the death camps in Poland.

Anna sat on the dirt floor, leaning against the clammy block wall in the cellar of her building listening to the sounds coming from the courtyard. In the nearly two months she had spent in this hellhole there had never been this much activity in the afternoon. At Drancy, things always seemed to happen in the morning—or the middle of the night.

Inbound trains loaded with Jews always arrived in the morning. The routine never varied. Feldgendarmes separated the men and women, clubbing to the ground anyone who resisted. Old people and any who appeared feeble were shoved off to the side and herded back to the boxcars for immediate transport.

Then the children were taken away, torn from their mothers' arms and hauled off to a separate building. The wailing of distraught mothers and the screaming of terrified children was more than Anna could bear. She had to keep her sanity. She had stopped watching.

The trains sat on the siding all day, a long string of empty boxcars, in plain view, as a sadistic reminder of what would happen to hundreds of unfortunate souls that night. It was almost impossible to sleep during the long, hot nights, not only because of the cramped and foul-smelling quarters into which they had been jammed like so many hogs, but mostly out of fear and anticipation that this might be the night they were chosen.

The sounds in the night were paralyzing: stomping boots, barking dogs, Feldgendarmes shouting in guttural German, women wailing. In an hour it was over, with only the sound of a chugging locomotive receding into the distance.

But this afternoon was different. The routine changed, and a flurry of activity broke out in the squalid camp. German army trucks and black motorcars roared into the courtyard. Wehrmacht soldiers jumped out of the trucks, shouting orders.

The remaining prisoners who could still walk were rounded up and forced into the cellar of the building where they sat, jammed elbow to elbow with scarcely enough air to breath. Anna assumed that the gunshots she heard had taken care of those who no longer had the strength to stand or walk.

An hour passed. The terrified huddled people in the basement with Anna were quiet, save for sporadic whispers of encouragement, occasional coughs or muted sobs.

Then stomping boots echoed on the floor above. A murmur rippled through the crowd. The boots descended the stone staircase.

A scraping noise, as heavy bars were lifted from the doors that sealed off the cellar. Anna got to her feet, a shiver running down her spine. Icy fingers.

The doors burst open.

Feldgendarmes shouted, "*Raus! Raus!* Everyone out! Move to the door!"

Those near the front of the dimly lit room struggled to their feet. The Feldgendarmes yelled louder, swung their nightsticks and herded the group up the stairs. The crowd moved as a single body, people clutching those nearby to keep from stumbling.

Anna felt someone lean against her and wrapped her arm around the skinny waist of an emaciated elderly woman. Keeping their heads down to avoid the swinging nightsticks, Anna and the woman moved with the crowd out of the cellar room and up the stairs.

In the courtyard, a voice barked from a megaphone, bellowing instructions in German and French.

"*Schnell! Vite!* Keep moving toward the train!"

"No talking allowed!"

"Do not step out of line or you will be shot!"

"*Schnell! Vite!*"

Squinting against the bright sunlight, Anna looked at the empty boxcars lined up on the rail siding, their doors open wide like gaping mouths of demonic monsters waiting to swallow their prey.

She struggled to force back the bile rising in her throat and concentrated on helping the woman who leaned against her. The group inched forward.

Soldiers cursed. Nightsticks crunched the skulls of those who stumbled and fell. The voice bellowed through the megaphone and the waiting boxcars loomed larger.

Anna thought about Jan and tears welled in her eyes. Could this be the end? Would she never see him again?

She heard another voice, off to her left, shouting in German. "That one, over there! That one, the redhead!"

Two Feldgendarmes shoved their way into the crowd. Before Anna could react, one of them, a large, thick man she had seen around the camp, grabbed her by the wrist and pulled her out of the throng. The elderly woman stumbled and fell to the ground.

The second Feldgendarme clubbed the old woman with his nightstick then shoved Anna from behind while the bigger man held her wrist in an iron grip, dragging her toward a building on the other side of the courtyard.

Up the stairs, down a hallway, pulled and prodded. It was all she could do to keep from falling. At the end of the hallway they stopped in front of a door. The big Feldgendarme opened it while the one in back shoved her into the room. Anna stumbled and fell on the tile floor. The door slammed behind her.

It took Anna a moment to get her bearings. As she got to her knees, she noticed the boots—shiny black boots. She lifted her head and looked into the ice blue eyes of SS Hauptsturmfuhrer Dieter Koenig.

She got to her feet and took a step backward.

Koenig moved closer and placed a gloved hand under her chin. "*Mon dieu,* look what's become of my pretty girl," he said in French. "Haven't these barbarians fed you?"

Anna turned away, swallowing, barely able to breathe.

Koenig touched her cheek.

She brushed his hand away.

He laughed. "Well, it's good to see you haven't lost your spirit, *ma chérie.* We'll get you cleaned up and give you a good meal before we leave; then you'll feel better."

Anna instinctively folded her arms across her chest and backed away, glancing around the stark room. It was obvious that it had been someone's office, but now all that remained was a metal desk and a single chair. Through the frosted glass in the top half of the door she could see the silhouette of the big Feldgendarme standing in the hallway.

Unconsciously, Anna rubbed her wrist where the Feldgendarme had gripped it with his enormous hand. She looked at Koenig. "What do you mean, 'before we leave'? Where are you taking me?"

Koenig smiled and stepped over to the single window overlooking the courtyard. He clasped his hands behind his back and glanced out, then turned toward her. "Why to Germany, of course, as we discussed before the unfortunate timing of the invasion." He paused. "That is, unless you'd prefer to join those wretched bastards outside."

Anna feared her legs wouldn't support her for another second. She had to blink to keep her eyes in focus. Her mouth was so dry she could barely get the words out. "That's where I belong. So, perhaps you should let me join them."

Koenig removed his hat and set it on the desk. He sat down in the chair, leaned back and put his hands behind his head. "I think you belong with me, *ma chérie*. Oh, I know you don't like me very much right now, but, in time, you'll come around. You'll see . . . it won't be as bad as you're imagining. After all, I'm no animal. I'm just a man who appreciates beautiful women." He stood up and moved around the desk.

Anna took another step backward.

He pretended not to notice and moved slowly, circling around her, brushing his hand on her shoulder.

He stepped away. "We certainly need to get you cleaned up and put a little meat back on your bones. But underneath all that grime lies a gorgeous creature who I—"

Anna bolted for the door.

Koenig lunged for her.

He grabbed her shoulder and whirled her around, slapping her hard across the mouth.

Anna stumbled backward against the wall.

Koenig grabbed her throat, pressing her head against the rough plaster. His eyes were wild, his face red with rage. He screamed at her in German.

"*Verdammt!* Don't ever turn away from me again, you fucking bitch, or I'll have you raped in the courtyard by every Feldgendarme in this camp!"

He squeezed her throat until she could hardly breathe and screamed again, louder. "You're mine! You're coming with me to Germany!"

Koenig leaned forward, his face close to hers and whispered. Anna could smell his breath . . . cigarettes, alcohol. "You'll give me what I want, whenever I want it and as often as I want it. If you refuse, even once, I'll have you raped until you wish you were dead. Then . . . *Ich werde Sie töten.* I'll kill you—slowly."

Koenig thrust her to the ground and stepped back. He glared at her then reached down and stroked her cheek, his fingers tracing the line of her neck. Then he abruptly picked his hat off the desk and jerked the door open. "*Kommen Sie!*" Koenig barked to the Feldgendarme. "Get this bitch cleaned up and get her some food. Then put her in my car. We leave tonight."

Chapter 55

Following the strict protocol of the White Brigade, Willy Boeynants had asked the bartender at the Café Brig to arrange a meeting with Antoine. Later that same day, the two men met near Antwerp's Kattendijkdok in the dwindling light of the humid August evening.

"I received some information from my colleague at the Interior Department," Boeynants said. "General Stolberg has requested the services of a demolition engineer. He has demanded that he be sent to Antwerp as soon as possible."

Antoine nodded. "*Oui*, we've been expecting he might do this."

"The engineer's name is Ernst Heinrich. He's a civilian. And, according to the cables my colleague intercepted, Stolberg only knows this man by reputation. He has never met him, and neither has any of his staff."

Antoine shrugged. "That's probably not all that unusual."

Boeynants continued. "In a stroke of luck, my colleague was on duty when Heinrich's personnel file arrived from Berlin. His department is responsible for processing these files. He managed to look at Heinrich's before passing it on to General Stolberg's office."

"*Oui*, but how does this—?"

Boeynants got to the point finally. "Ernst Heinrich is arriving in Antwerp on the train from Berlin on the 28th of this month."

Antoine's eyes widened. "*Mon dieu*, that's just five days from now."

"There's more. The file included Heinrich's resume—and his description."

"His description?"

Boeynants handed Antoine a piece of paper with the handwritten notes his colleague had given him. The two men stood in silence for several minutes as Antoine studied the notes.

Antoine dropped the cigarette he had been smoking and ground it out with his shoe. "We need the details on that train, the schedule at every stop along the way. Use our contact in Holland. The train will probably go through Amsterdam, and they can put someone on board."

Boeynants nodded.

Antoine extended his hand. "*Très bien,* very good work. Now I've got to contact SOE."

Chapter 56

IN ALL OF HIS YEARS as a military officer, Jan had never imagined a fighting force as formidable as the one that was now charging through France. When he arrived at Normandy the scope of the invading army had astounded him. Hundreds of ships moved in and out of the artificial harbors at Arromanches, disgorging tanks, armored cars, heavy-duty trucks and self-propelled guns by the thousands. Tens of thousands of troops slogged across the beaches: Americans, Brits, Canadians, Australians and Poles, all heading inland to assault Hitler's Germany.

A month later, the Polish First Armored Division reached the Falaise Gap, and the fighting was ferocious, as brutal as any of the battles Jan had fought in Poland, but this time it was the Germans who were crushed.

Jan was surprised at his emotions when the battle at Falaise ended. He hated the Nazis for the monstrous annihilation of his country, and he had been determined to have his vengeance. But when he looked out at the vast killing field from the top of Mont Ormel, he felt only sadness—and a great emptiness. He was so tired. After five years of war, he wanted his life back. He wanted Anna. But the end seemed nowhere in sight.

The Polish First Armored Division advanced rapidly eastward. With the First Canadian Corps on their left flank, the American Third Army on their right, and the skies overhead secured by Allied air forces, the contrast with the isolated, outgunned Polish forces of 1939 was dramatic. Jan looked around at the tanks and armored cars clanking along the dusty French roads. He watched the bomber squadrons flying overhead. The outcome of the war was no longer in doubt. Germany would be defeated. The unknown was how long it would take.

Having successfully landed an assault force of this magnitude, the Allies would settle for nothing less than a complete and total German surrender. But, in his gut, Jan feared that the Germany that existed under Hitler and his Nazi thugs would never surrender until their country had been destroyed and Allied tanks rolled through the Brandenburg Gate into Berlin.

How many hundreds of thousands of soldiers and civilians would die in the meantime, he wondered. He thought of the V-2 rockets he had seen in Poland and the destruction they had caused when they crash-landed in villages and towns. If Germany held on long enough to use this weapon, the hundreds of thousands could become millions.

Jan stood in the front seat of the scout car, gripping the frame above the windshield for support. His goggles kept out most of the dust as he surveyed the men riding in trucks and marching alongside the road. Like him, many of these men had been at war and away from their families for almost five years. They deserved to survive and go home. Stefan had deserved to survive, but he didn't. Irene and Justyn would never see him again—if *they* had survived. And Anna . . .

The sound of a motorcycle broke his train of thought. Jan glanced down at the rider who was waving and yelling at him. He leaned over to hear and the man yelled again, asking him to stop.

Jan motioned to his driver to pull over. The motorcycle pulled up behind them, and the rider stepped up, saluted and handed him a sealed envelope. Jan ripped it open and read the brief message inside.

RETURN IMMEDIATELY TO CHAMBOIS.
REPORT TO MR. ORTMUND AT THE HOTEL ELBE.

The message was signed by General Stanislaw Maczek, the commanding officer of the Polish First Armored Division.

"My instructions are to give you a ride wherever you need to go," the rider said, wiping dirt from his goggles.

When he entered the room on the third floor of the Hotel Elbe, a young man with short-cropped, sandy hair and wire-rimmed spectacles sat on a straight-back chair at an ornate desk. He wore a white shirt, bow tie and striped trousers. Jan thought he looked like a bank teller.

The young man stood up and extended his hand. "Good afternoon, Colonel Kopernik, I am Mr. Ortmund. Good of you to come so quickly."

Jan nodded without responding. He had been through enough meetings with British civilians that he was impatient with small talk.

The man cleared his throat, opened a small folder and withdrew an envelope, which he handed to Jan.

Inside the envelope was a single sheet of stationery bearing the letterhead of the SOE. Jan read the handwritten message.

To Colonel Jan Kopernik:

You have been transferred to the Special Operations Executive on the orders of General Stanislaw Maczek. Please follow the instructions given to you by Mr. Ortmund.

Sincerely,
Col. Stanley Whitehall

Goddamn it, Jan thought. Whitehall again. He dropped the paper on the desk, pulled out a pack of cigarettes and shook one out. "Well, 'Mr. Ortmund,' are you going to tell me what the hell this is all about?"

The man cleared his throat again and said, "There is an airstrip just a few kilometers out of town. My instructions are to drive you there this evening where you will board an RAF plane. We have some clothes for you. You may leave your uniform with me."

"That's nice," Jan said, blowing smoke in the air. "And where am I going?"

"I don't know. We all operate on a 'need-to-know' basis. I'm sure you understand."

"Yes, I understand." Jan answered, sensing that he'd seen the last of his military command for awhile. He only hoped it wasn't another trip back to Poland.

When they were airborne the copilot of the Halifax stepped back to where Jan sat and handed him a jumpsuit and a parachute pack. "It's a short flight, Colonel. You'd better get ready."

As Jan pulled the jumpsuit over the shirt and trousers that Ortmund had supplied, the copilot said, "We'll be dropping you just outside the town of

Kapellen, northeast of Antwerp, Belgium. The drop zone is a farm field—"

"Antwerp? You're dropping me near Antwerp?"

"Yes, that's right . . . something wrong, Colonel?"

Jan stood motionless while it sunk in. Antwerp? Could it possibly be . . . ?

He shook his head and said to the copilot. "No, nothing's wrong."

The copilot continued. "The drop zone is a farm field, owned by a member of the Belgian Resistance. We'll receive a signal . . ."

Jan tried to listen, but the words were coming through a fog. Anna's image flitted through his mind, waving at him. Her long, red hair . . .

". . . from the ground . . . torches outlining the field," the copilot was saying.

Jan blinked and stared at him. "Yeah, OK."

"Then we'll circle around, drop down and out you go."

Jan zipped up the jumpsuit. His hands were trembling.

"You'll be met by a man wearing a plaid shirt," the copilot said. "He will address you in French by saying, 'Do you wish to go to Antwerp?' You are to reply by saying, 'Yes, but I would like a warm meal first.' You got that?"

"Yes, I've got it," Jan said as he secured the clasps on the parachute.

"I'm told you've made these jumps before."

"Just once. I hoped it was my last."

The copilot smiled and slapped him on the shoulder. "Well then, good luck, Colonel. Maybe we can hoist a pint together when this thing's all over. You'd better sit down and get strapped in now. We'll be catching some flak when we hit the coast."

The man in the plaid shirt was the owner of the farm, and he led Jan into a cellar below the house. A tall silver-haired man was waiting for him.

When the farmer departed, leaving them alone, the man held out his hand and spoke French. "*Bonjour, monsieur.* Welcome to Belgium."

Jan shook his hand and peeled off the jumpsuit.

"I understand you're a military officer, a colonel?"

"*Oui, c'est correct,*" Jan replied.

The man motioned to a table in the center of the dimly lit, earthen floor room and poured two glasses of red wine that had been provided by the farmer. There was a plate of cheese, sliced sausage and fresh bread. Seeing the food made Jan realize he was hungry and, with a nod of encouragement from the silver-haired man, he helped himself.

"Perhaps I should give you some background on our mission," the man said.

Jan took a sip of the homemade wine and nodded. *"Oui,* I would appreciate that."

"I belong to an organization known as the White Brigade. From this point on, Colonel, you may refer to me as, 'Sam.'"

Jan nodded, acknowledging the code name.

Sam continued, "We are part of the Belgian Armed Resistance. One of our responsibilities is the protection of Antwerp's port."

"Protection of the port?"

"Oui. The Germans have sent a general by the name of Stolberg to Antwerp. His mission is to shore up their defenses and defend the port against the expected attack by the Allies. If they cannot defend the port, we believe they will try to destroy it."

Jan tried to listen but he was still stunned by the stroke of fortune that had dropped him into Belgium, just a few kilometers from Antwerp. Was it possible that Anna was here? He took another sip of wine, forcing himself to concentrate on what the silver-haired man was saying.

" . . . General Stolberg has received a dispatch from Berlin indicating that they are sending a demolition engineer from Berlin, a civilian by the name of Ernst Heinrich." Sam paused and picked up the wine bottle, topping off the glasses. "Do you have any questions so far, Colonel?"

"Non," Jan replied. "Just waiting to hear how I fit into all of this."

Sam took a sip of wine and continued. "Our intelligence was able to provide us with Herr Heinrich's travel itinerary and his description. You match his description quite well. I'm told that you speak fluent German and that you're trained in demolitions. You will become Ernst Heinrich, Colonel."

Jan could barely manage to set down his wineglass without spilling it. "What the hell are you talking about? That's the craziest notion I've—"

Sam interrupted him. "Please, let me continue."

Jan glared at him and sat back in the chair.

"I jumped ahead of myself," Sam said. "It's really not as crazy as it may sound. You see, General Stolberg has never met Ernst Heinrich and neither has any of his staff. Our orders are to take him off the train. You will replace him and report to General Stolberg at his headquarters in Antwerp. From that point forward, your instructions are to find out everything you can about the enemy's plans for destruction of the port and pass the information on to our organization. I will be your contact."

Jan stared at the silver-haired man, not knowing which of a dozen questions to ask first. His previous missions had been dangerous . . . but impersonating a German demolition engineer? Becoming part of a German General's staff in occupied territory? It was absurd. This was Whitehall's fault. He wished he could have the fat bastard alone for five minutes. This wasn't a mission—it was a death sentence.

Jan stood up and paced around the cellar. "How do you know that neither the general or any of his staff have ever met this Heinrich?"

"I have a source in the Department of the Interior," Sam replied. "He has seen all the messages and he—"

"Is he certain of it?" Jan demanded, cutting him off.

Sam was silent for a moment then folded his hands on the table. "*Non*, not certain. Nothing is certain, Colonel, you know that. We have what we believe is good information. It comes from a reliable source, a source that I know personally and would trust with my life."

"But it's not your life on the line here, is it?" As soon as he said it, Jan wished he hadn't. He sensed that this man was not a manipulator like Whitehall. He was like the AK operatives he had known in Poland. He was like Slomak, a patriot, whose country has been occupied by the enemy for years. Jan took a deep breath. "I'm sorry—"

Sam held up his hand. "It's all right, Colonel. This is all being dropped on you very quickly. *C'est correct*, it *is* your life on the line. We'll do our best to protect you, but beyond that I'm afraid . . ."

His voice trailed off and the two men fell silent.

Jan sat down and finished his wine. "Well, let's get on with it. What's the rest of the plan?"

Sam nodded. "We weren't given your name, Colonel, or any information about you—and we're not allowed to ask. From this moment, until your mission is completed, you are 'Ernst Heinrich.' Is that understood?"

"*Oui, oui, bien sûr.* I understand the routine pretty well by now," Jan replied.

Chapter 57

ERNST HEINRICH WAS NOT at all pleased with his orders. Though a civilian, he had frequent contact with officers in the Wehrmacht and was acutely aware of the situation. Contrary to the propaganda being fed its citizens, Heinrich knew that Germany's armies were in retreat and the Allies were pursuing them into Belgium.

He couldn't imagine a greater military target at this point in time than the port of Antwerp, and he'd be stuck in the middle of it. In reality, though, he knew it probably didn't matter. With the Russians bearing down on Germany from the east and the Americans and British from the west, his chances of surviving this madness appeared bleak.

In the fading light of dusk, Heinrich looked out the train window at the flat terrain, crisscrossed by narrow canals, and wondered if they were in Belgium yet. He had been to Belgium several times over the years—to Antwerp, in fact—and had always enjoyed himself. The food and wines were first rate, the service in the cafés was excellent, and the people had always been friendly and hospitable. That was before the war, of course. He guessed things would be different now.

The car he was in was only about half full, and most of the other passengers appeared to be businessmen, speaking primarily Dutch or French. Three Wehrmacht soldiers had boarded the train in Amsterdam and were sitting two rows behind him, but other than that Heinrich had seen few military personnel. He knew that practically all available men had been sent to the western front months ago. He yawned and leaned back in the seat. He had been on the train since the early hours of the morning, and he was tired.

Bang!

The car lurched, and Heinrich's head cracked into the window.

Another *Bang!*

The car lurched in the opposite direction, and Heinrich was thrown from his seat, landing face down in the aisle.

With its steel wheels screeching against the rails, the car jumped the track and pitched forward, bouncing hard to a halt.

A hand gripped the back of Heinrich's coat and jerked him up. He stumbled forward into a tangle of other passengers, but the hand pulled him backward, up the steep incline of the aisle, toward the rear door. A voice shouted, *"Raus! Jetzt!"*

Heinrich turned his head and saw that the hand belonged to one of the Wehrmacht soldiers. The other two soldiers were ahead, pushing people out of the way, clearing a path to the door, shouting, *"Raus! Raus!"*

The soldier gripping his coat yelled at him, "Which is your bag?" motioning at a jumbled pile of suitcases.

Heinrich stared at him, not comprehending.

"Your bag, *verdammt!* Your bag! Which one's yours?"

Heinrich pointed it out.

The soldier grabbed it and shoved him forward. When they got to the open door, two of the soldiers had already jumped to the ground. The one who had gripped Heinrich's coat yelled at him to jump and pushed him out the door.

He hit the ground, tumbled over on his side and started sliding down the steep embankment, but one of the soldiers grabbed his wrist and hauled him to his feet.

The soldier yelled at him, *"Gehen wir!* Let's go!"

"What?" Heinrich mumbled. "Where?"

"We've got to get out of here! *Schnell! Mach schnell!"* the soldier yelled and shoved him forward.

The three soldiers surrounded Heinrich as they scrambled up the other side of the embankment and trotted across a field.

Heinrich stumbled along, trying not to fall. "Where the hell are you taking me?"

The soldier behind him shoved him in the back, almost knocking him down. "Just shut up and keep running!"

They came to a canal and followed it until they came to a small bridge. They trotted across the bridge, crossed another field and came to a dirt road. A truck was parked at the side of the road.

Heinrich was gasping for breath as they slowed to a walk and approached the truck. The soldier in the lead pulled open the canvas covering the back of the truck, and Heinrich looked up at a silver-haired man standing inside.

The soldier turned to Heinrich and motioned for him to get in the truck.

Heinrich hesitated.

The soldier grabbed his jacket and jerked him forward while the other two grabbed his arms and hoisted him into the truck.

As Heinrich sprawled on the floor, the lead soldier climbed in behind him and pulled the canvas cover closed.

The silver-haired man switched on a flashlight and shined it into Heinrich's face, holding the light there for several seconds.

Then the light moved away and Heinrich blinked, trying to clear his eyes. He blinked again and glanced around. The flashlight was shining on another man, a tall, blond man.

The silver-haired man said something in French, and the tall, blond man nodded.

Heinrich didn't understand.

The silver-haired man shined the flashlight back into Heinrich's face and spoke again. Heinrich still didn't understand and shook his head.

The tall, blond man bent down and barked at him in German. "Take off your clothes, Herr Heinrich. *Verstehen Sie?* Your trip is over."

The rest of the operation went as planned. Jan changed into Heinrich's clothes, while White Brigade operatives bound and gagged Heinrich and put him into the trunk of Sam's car. The silver-haired man drove off, taking Heinrich to an unknown destination for a "debriefing."

One of the Wehrmacht "soldiers" drove the truck back to the scene of the train wreck while Jan rode in back with the other two. When they arrived at the site, two ambulances and a half-dozen Belgian policemen were on the scene, trying to restore order and assist the bewildered, stranded passengers. The "soldier" driving the truck called out to a policeman and offered to transport some passengers. Within a few minutes they were bound for a hospital in Antwerp with a dozen additional passengers all suffering from minor injuries.

Having complained of a stiff neck and a sore back, Jan was kept in the hospital overnight for observation. At five o'clock the next morning he slipped out of his room on the third floor, made his way past the single nurse doing paperwork at the nurse's station and found the staircase. He walked down to the lower level and into a long hallway.

Following his instructions, Jan proceeded to the end of the hallway and through a door to the loading dock. It was still dark, and it took a few seconds for his eyes to adjust before he spotted Sam standing in a corner on the other side of the dock.

"Did you get some sleep?" Sam asked when Jan joined him and they had moved back, out of sight from the street.

"Not much but I'll be OK. Did you learn anything?"

"*Oui, oui,* quite a bit, actually," Sam said. "It seems that Herr Heinrich is no fan of the Nazis, and he's not inclined to become a martyr for the Reich. Once we convinced him that his only chance of surviving was if *you* survived, he became quite cooperative."

"So, he's a pragmatist; that's encouraging," Jan said.

The silver-haired man smiled and continued. "His home is in a town called Langenfeld, just south of Dusseldorf, on the Rhine River. He was last there about two weeks ago before going to Berlin, then heading here. His wife's name is Frieda, and they have one daughter named Else, who is nine years old. He works for a company by the name of Kleigholst. He said they manufacture demolition devices: blasting caps, fuses, timing pencils, things like that."

Jan nodded and closed his eyes, concentrating. "Langenfeld ... near Dusseldorf ... wife's name Frieda ... daughter Else ... company is Kleigholst ... *oui, oui, je comprends.*"

Sam continued. "Heinrich was trained as a structural engineer and has been with this company his entire career. He spent most of last year in Normandy providing technical assistance on the installation of explosives at the landing beaches. Before Normandy, he spent some time in Russia working with combat engineers blowing up bridges and railways." He glanced at his watch. "That's all I have. You'd better get back before you're missed. Have you been contacted by anyone yet?"

"*Oui,* a nurse stopped in late last night with a message from someone on Stolberg's staff. Apparently I am to be picked up at noon today."

"*Très bien,*" Sam said, extending his hand. "Every night, at ten o'clock, I will be at Storage Building Fifteen on the Kattendijkdok. I will wait for thirty minutes. Good luck."

Chapter 58

ANNA SAT IN THE BACKSEAT of Koenig's motorcar, staring at the deserted courtyard. The train carrying the last survivors of Drancy had left while she was bathing and eating. The car was a Mercedes-Benz, like her father's. If she closed her eyes she could imagine Henryk sitting behind the wheel as they drove through the back roads of Poland during those first terrifying hours of the war. It seemed like it had all happened in some other lifetime.

The car was one of only a few vehicles left in the camp, and it was becoming obvious that there was some delay in their departure. Anna's wrists were secured in handcuffs and attached with a stout chain to shackles around her ankles. The big Feldgendarme sat in the front seat, behind the wheel, and periodically checked his watch. He had glanced at her in the rear view mirror a few times but hadn't spoken.

"*Wie ist Ihr Name?*" Anna asked in German.

"*Was?*" the big man replied.

"*Ihr Name. Wie ist Ihr Name.* Since we're obviously going to be traveling together, I'd like to know your name."

He turned his bulky frame toward her and said, in a deep, raspy voice, "*Mein Name ist Otto.*"

"Well, Otto, do you know where we're going?"

The man turned a little more until he could look at her, then abruptly turned back to the front and stiffened up.

The front door on the passenger side jerked open, and Dieter Koenig leaned in. Another SS officer stood behind him. Koenig glanced at Anna with a scowl on his face, then spoke sharply to Otto. "I won't be going with you. I have to report to Berlin immediately. Mueller will ride along with you. I'll be there next week. You know what to do."

Koenig turned and looked at Anna for several long minutes, his eyes moving down the neckline of the flimsy dress he had provided. He reached back with a gloved hand and brushed her cheek. "*Ja, ja,* already, such an improvement. Otto will take care of you until I return."

Anna's skin crawled. She remained silent, staring straight ahead.

Koenig backed out of the car and was gone. The second officer slipped into the front seat and pulled the door shut. He turned toward Anna and reached back, grasping her handcuffs and jerking on the chain that secured them to her ankles. Apparently satisfied that she was sufficiently restrained, he turned around again and motioned for Otto to get started.

Almost twelve hours later, they approached the German border near the city of Aachen, the flags of the Third Reich snapping in the wind at the checkpoint. Anna's heart sank, icy fingers of fear once again sliding down her back. She was entering the lion's den.

As they passed through the barricades the road descended into a tunnel, and Anna stared in awe at the hills on either side. The giant concrete bunkers of Germany's "West Wall" extended north and south as far as she could see. When they emerged on the other side of the tunnel, it was as if a giant door had slammed shut on her life.

They passed through a second set of barricades and headed in a southeasterly direction, driving slowly along an asphalt road lined with tanks, armored cars and thousands of Wehrmacht infantrymen. For the next hour and a half they made little progress as long convoys of soldiers and trucks clogged every road and every intersection. It appeared to Anna that every German male who could carry a gun had been pressed into action.

Eventually, they turned onto a dirt road and followed it for several kilometers through heavily wooded terrain, stopping at a wooden gate. Mueller got out and unlocked the gate, relocking it after Otto drove through. The trees gave way to a broad meadow and, at the far end of the meadow, a wooden barn and a sturdy-looking, two-story brick house.

Otto stopped the car in front of the barn, and Mueller jumped out, stretching and yawning loudly. Then he promptly unbuttoned his trousers and pissed onto the gravel drive. When he was finished he pulled the rear door open and motioned for Anna to get out. Otto opened the barn door and drove the car into it, while Mueller grabbed Anna's arm and led her hobbling up the steps and into the house.

It was surprisingly well furnished. In the parlor, two large, richly upholstered chairs stood on either side of a fieldstone fireplace. There was a long sofa in front of the windows and an artistic hand-carved coffee table.

Mueller maintained his grip on Anna's wrist and led her through the parlor and an adjoining, elegantly furnished dining room into a large kitchen. She struggled to keep from falling, forced by the leg irons into taking baby steps. He led her to the far end of the kitchen and stopped in front of a stout, wooden door. He fished some keys out of his pocket, opened the door and pushed her into a room. He followed her in, removed the handcuffs and leg irons then left, slamming the door behind her and turning the key in the lock.

At first it was dark. Then Anna heard a noise from outside that sounded like a muffled engine, and a few seconds later a soft glowing light emanated from a chandelier hanging from the ceiling. She looked around.

It was the most incredible, revolting room that Anna had ever seen: at least four meters on a side with three large windows behind heavy, braided drapes. The walls were covered with red wallpaper, textured in an intricate floral pattern, along with three gold-framed paintings of nudes in various provocative poses. The crystal chandelier hung above a massive, four-poster bed. On either side of the bed were night tables, handcrafted in rich veneers of walnut, maple and cherry.

She walked to one of the windows and pulled back the drapes, not surprised to see heavy steel bars. She wondered how many other women Koenig had brought to this private little bordello over the years . . . and what had become of them.

Anna looked into a smaller, adjoining room, lit only by a barred skylight in the ceiling. Inside was a wash stand with a hand pump and a chamber pot. Back in the main room, on the same wall as the door to the washroom was a closet in which Anna found a dozen dresses, all her size and all with the same slit skirt and plunging neckline as the horrid thing she was wearing. She slammed the door shut, her stomach churning with revulsion. There was also a bureau, on the wall opposite the bed, which she didn't need to open—she knew what would be inside. She slumped down on a wooden chair near one of the barred windows and buried her face in her hands.

Anna snapped awake at the loud knocking sound. She sat up, trying to figure out where she was. Her eyes scanned the red walls and the heavy curtains. When it came back to her she felt sick again. She was sitting on the bed, obviously having crawled up there at some point and fallen asleep. She pulled back the curtain and looked through the bars. It was dark outside.

Again the knocking, this time accompanied by a rough, gravelly voice. "*Kommen Sie.* Come to the door. Frau Laurent, come to the door."

At first, the name confused her. Then the cloud of sleep cleared and she remembered. Of course, he would know her as Jeanne Laurent, the name on the passport she had been carrying when she was arrested. In a fleeting thought she wondered if they still had her passport, though she couldn't imagine what good it would do her now.

Another knock, and this time she slid off the bed and opened the door.

Otto stood on the other side, his massive bulk filling the entire doorway.

"*Komm*, have your dinner," he grunted and motioned toward the table.

Anna thought it curious that he had unlocked the door but hadn't opened it. Was he a gentleman, respecting her privacy? She dismissed the thought as too much to hope for. It was probably some type of security measure to make sure she wasn't hiding behind the door ready to hit him over the head with the chamber pot.

Anna nodded at the big man and sat down at the table, wishing she had a sweater or shawl to cover the flimsy revealing dress. In front of her was a single setting of blue and white china, a platter filled with pork chops, boiled potatoes and cooked beets along with a plate of fresh bread. The aroma of the food was overwhelming, and Anna was starved. Her self-consciousness vanished and she eagerly filled her plate.

Otto brought a coffeepot to the table and filled her cup, then sat down across from her with his own mug of coffee.

"Aren't you going to eat?" she asked.

"I already ate," he replied and took a sip of coffee.

Too famished to talk, Anna finished all the food on her plate, then took a second pork chop and began cutting it. All the while Otto sat there, watching her but saying nothing.

"*Sehr gut, Otto.* Do you do the cooking?" Anna said, feeling uncomfortable by the silence.

"*Ja.*"

"Where is Mueller? Did he already eat, too?"

"Mueller left."

"He left? You mean he doesn't stay here?"

"*Nein.*" Otto picked up the coffeepot and poured more coffee into Anna's cup.

She finished the meal in silence, pondering the situation. A sharp knife was close at hand, but Anna dismissed the foolish thought in an instant. Even if she somehow managed to grab it before she was subdued, it would do little good against this mountain of a man. She glanced about the kitchen and realized that the windows were shuttered from the outside. The only other door was the one that led into the dining room, which was now closed and, she guessed, locked.

When she was done, Otto stood and motioned that she was to return to her room. The door closed behind her, and the key turned in the lock.

Chapter 59

AT PRECISELY NOON a black Citroen pulled up to where Jan stood outside the hospital in the center of Antwerp. A young Wehrmacht officer sprang from the vehicle and opened the right rear door. Jan handed the officer his suitcase and slid into the backseat where another officer sat.

The officer appeared to be about Jan's age but smaller and thinner. He extended his hand, speaking crisp, cultured German. "*Guten Morgen, Herr Heinrich. Ich bin Oberstleutnant Erich Bucher.* How are you feeling?"

Jan shook the officer's hand and forced a smile. "I'll be fine, thank you. Just some stiffness in my neck. I guess I was lucky."

Bucher nodded then turned to the front of the car and waved his hand to the driver, who pulled out into the busy street. "Well, at least you weren't injured," he said. "I'm not sure General Stolberg could handle any more setbacks."

"*Ist das so?*" Jan replied, looking out the window. Anna had described the city to him many times, but he didn't recognize anything. "What's the situation here?" he asked.

"We've had a devil of a time," Bucher said, removing a pack of cigarettes from his jacket pocket. He offered one to Jan, who accepted with the fleeting thought that he hadn't been told whether Ernst Heinrich smoked or not. Bucher lit both cigarettes and continued. "When we arrived in June, the state of the garrison was a mess. No proper defenses, the troops were just a bunch of fucking prison guards and invalids along with some Flemish renegades—*schwein*—you couldn't trust out of your sight. There was no artillery to speak of and nobody trained to use it anyway."

"I assume you've shored it up since then," Jan asked, shocked at what he heard and trying to look disappointed.

"*Ja, natürlich.* But there's a lot more to do. Fortunately, we still have time, at least a couple of weeks, before the British get here. We've built a ring of fortifications around the perimeter, but we'll get into all that soon enough. We've almost arrived."

Jan looked out the window again as the car turned into a large park ringed with barbed wire and concrete bunkers. They passed through a heavily guarded gate and stopped in front of a triangular grouping of three large bunkers surrounded by another barbed wire fence. They got out of the car, and Jan followed Bucher into one of the bunkers, down a flight of steps and into an underground tunnel.

The tunnel was about a hundred meters long, lit by bare electric bulbs hanging from wood rafters. When they exited the tunnel they were in an office building on the edge of the park.

"This is our headquarters building," Bucher explained as they climbed a staircase. "It's a former bank building, now inaccessible from the street. The only way in or out is through the tunnel. There are several other buildings around the park, all connected by tunnels to the main bunker, so none of the locals—and more important, none of the fucking Resistance groups—know exactly which building is the headquarters."

Jan kept silent, glancing out the windows, allowing Bucher to talk. He followed him into a large room that looked like a command center on the third floor.

The room had no windows and practically every available inch of wall space was covered with maps and aerial photographs of the city and the port. There was a bank of radio equipment along one wall, manned by two officers in shirtsleeves. One of them spoke into a microphone while the other tapped out a coded message.

Three other officers sat at a conference table, rummaging through a pile of documents and filling out a variety of forms. Bucher took Jan around the room and made quick introductions. Then he took off his coat, hung it on a hook and invited Jan to do the same.

"We'll be meeting with General Stolberg for dinner," Bucher said. "My instructions are to brief you in the meantime. Shall we get started?"

"*Ja,*" Jan said, ignoring the drops of sweat trickling down the back of his neck. He shoved his hands in his pockets to hide the tremors.

Bucher led him to a giant map of the city of Antwerp hanging on the wall opposite the radios and picked up a pointer. "I'm told you've been to Antwerp before, so you'll have to forgive me if I'm telling you some things you already know, but I don't want to overlook anything. The Americans and British are kicking our asses in France, and we don't have much time."

Jan nodded, thankful for German thoroughness.

Bucher tapped the pointer on the map, pointing to the River Schelde. "Antwerp, as you know, is one of the best natural harbors in Europe, its geography dominated by the river, which is more than a half kilometer wide. Here, on the river's east bank, is the center of the city and immediately to the north is the port, which extends along the east bank for more than nine kilometers. There are several vehicle and pedestrian tunnels that run under the river, connecting the central city to the west bank. They have all been prepared for demolition. We'll want you to inspect them, of course, but they're not the first priority. *Verstehen Sie?*"

Bucher glanced at Jan who nodded again.

The officer continued, tapping his pointer at a canal. "This is the Albert Canal, which enters Antwerp from the east and flows into the River Schelde. North of the canal is the suburb of Merksem. It's a workingman's town, and many of the dockworkers live there. The bridges across the canal, connecting Merksem to Antwerp, have also been prepared for demolition. The main road from the port into Merksem, the Groenendallaan, is heavily protected with machine guns and artillery. If worse comes to worst, our escape route out of the city is to Merksem . . . after we destroy the port."

Bucher looked at the floor for a few seconds as though the thought of this happening was more than he could fathom. Then he took a deep breath and returned to the map. "Now, as you can see, the Albert canal cuts through the center of the port. The older docks, Bonapartedok, Willemdok and Kattendijkdok lie to the south, and the newer, larger docks, Albertdok, Leopolddok and Hansadok lie to the north."

As he said this, Bucher painstakingly traced the outline of the various docks. "Right here, downstream from the Hansadok, is the crucial point: the Kruisschans Lock."

Jan took a step closer to the map.

Bucher continued. "This lock not only allows ships to pass into and out of the docks, but it also regulates the flow of water to and from the river, maintaining the proper level within the port."

Bucher glared at Jan. His eyes were intense. "Here, at the Kruisschans Lock, we have placed our most important demolition devices. Both the inner and outer gates have been rigged with carefully concealed explosives. We have kept this lock under tight security. None of the dockworkers are allowed anywhere near the area. The lock is manned and operated around the clock by Wehrmacht troops."

Bucher laid the pointer on the table and pulled out his pack of cigarettes. Jan accepted the offered cigarette, grateful for something to do with his hands. Bucher leaned against the wall, exhaling a precise ring of smoke as he spoke. "If we can't defend the city, the Kruisschans Lock is the first thing that gets blown. With the gates out of commission, the water level in the entire port will fall with the tide. The lack of water pressure will then cause the walls of the docks to collapse. The port will be out of commission for years."

Bucher took a drag on the cigarette and blew another smoke ring. "This, Herr Heinrich is your first assignment. I will show it to you today, and you will tell us if we've done our job properly. General Stolberg is counting on you." He smiled at Jan and slapped him on the shoulder. "*Jetzt*, some lunch? And a nice bottle of Bordeaux?"

Chapter 60

IT TURNED OUT THAT the luncheon included three bottles of Bordeaux, consumed primarily by Bucher and the two officers who joined them. Jan drank as little as possible using the excuse that he had been given pain medication the night before and warned not to drink. He needed to stay sharp for the afternoon and the dinner that evening with General Stolberg.

The other two officers were both leutnants who reported to Bucher. One was a big, affable fellow with thick glasses named Karl Rolfmann, who was in charge of the demolition detail. He talked in rapid, clipped sentences, going into great detail about the types of explosives they had used, the detonators and timers, and the clever tricks that had been employed to conceal the charges.

Jan concentrated so hard he was getting a headache. It had been years since he had had any real hands-on experience with demolition devices, and he struggled to absorb as much as possible without asking stupid questions.

The other officer was Leutnant Wernher Graf, short and stocky with intense, black eyes, a bald head and a dour disposition. It was unclear what his function was.

"It was a curious thing, the train wreck, *stimmt das*, Herr Heinrich?" Graf said during a lull in the conversation. "Obviously the work of one of the Resistance groups . . . but it was strange."

"Strange, in what way?" Jan asked.

"Normally these terrorists go after freight trains carrying munitions—or troop transports. This was just a passenger train, it doesn't make sense. Why would they waste the effort on a train with no strategic value?"

"I don't know," Jan said, "but it scared the hell out of me."

Graf glared at him with a strange look in his eyes. He appeared ready to pursue it further when Bucher summoned the waiter for dessert.

The security at the Kruisschans Lock was impressive. The land approach was heavily guarded at two checkpoints with barricades across the roadway and machine-gun emplacements on either side. Barbed wire fencing extended well into the scrubland, and flamethrowers were positioned in front of the outer and inner gates. Jan counted at least twenty heavily armed Wehrmacht soldiers in the immediate vicinity.

They spent almost two hours crawling around the massive structure with Rolfmann pointing out the placement of explosive charges and the well-hidden copper wires that ran back to the main guardhouse. As a competent and thorough German officer, he provided Jan with details about the size of each charge and the timing and sequence that had been set for the explosions.

Jan took notes and made a number of sketches for the presumed purpose of doing his own calculations. All the while, Graf hovered around while Bucher stood off at a distance, chatting with the guard detail.

Rolfmann knew a lot more about this than he did, but it was apparent to Jan that the explosive charges had been well placed for maximum damage and were cleverly concealed. Without his notes it would be impossible for anyone to locate them.

Knowing that he needed to make some intelligent-sounding contribution to the discussion, Jan asked several questions about steel I-beams and whether or not the concrete was reinforced.

Rolfmann thumbed through a notebook and produced the answers. Consulting his notes and sketches, Jan faked some mental calculations, asked another question about the time increment between explosions and nodded.

Graf wandered up and glanced at Jan's notes. "Will this do the job, Herr Heinrich?"

"I'll need to do some further calculations but, yes, I believe it will be quite sufficient, Leutnant," Jan replied. Then turning to Rolfmann and stuffing the notes in his pocket, he added, "*Sehr gut,* you've done your work well, Leutnant Rolfmann."

Rolfmann beamed at the compliment and, just as Graf started to ask another

question, Bucher stepped up, pointed at his watch and announced that the
general was expecting them for dinner.

It was an elaborate, protracted affair held at a small, out-of-the way restaurant
just two streets from the cathedral. It was a favorite of General Stolberg's, who
was obviously enjoying Antwerp's reputation for excellent cuisine.

The group of nine officers and Jan were the only patrons, and Jan had no
doubt that the occupying Germans had commandeered whatever fine food and
wine was left in Antwerp for the pleasure of the officers of the Wehrmacht.

Stolberg arrived late and when he was introduced to "Ernst Heinrich" he
extended his hand and smiled. "*Willkommen*, Herr Heinrich; we look forward
to your assistance."

"*Danke*, General. I'm pleased to help in any way I can," Jan said, aware that
all eyes in the room were upon him.

"I understand you were with the engineers in Normandy preparing for the
invasion," the general said affably. "Did you meet Field Marshal Rommel
while you were there?"

Jan blinked with an instant of hesitation. "*Nein*, I did not, general," he replied, praying it was the right answer.

The general shrugged and took his seat at the head of the table. As Jan returned to his chair, a portly officer who had come in with the general grabbed
his arm and said, "I hope you're going to do a better job for us than you did at
Normandy, Heinrich. All those fancy mines didn't do much good, did they?"

Jan hesitated before responding. "That was quite a different situation, sir.
From what I've seen today, your people have done an excellent job in the port."

The room became quiet as the officer glared at Jan.

General Stolberg interceded. "Gunter, Herr Heinrich is our guest. *Setzen
Sie, bitte.* Let him enjoy his dinner. I believe Marcel has prepared a nice trout
for our first course."

At that instant a proper-looking Belgian man wearing a dark blue suit appeared, followed by two waiters who began serving the group.

General Stolberg, Oberstleutnant Bucher and the portly officer Jan knew
only as Gunter excused themselves after desert. Jan attempted to leave a few
minutes later, hoping he would be able to slip away and meet Sam at the
Kattendijkdok, but Rolfmann grabbed his arm and pulled him back to the
table, refilling his glass with cognac.

"*Kommen Sie,* Ernst, enjoy yourself," Rolfmann said with an easy laugh. "There probably won't be many more meals like this. Isn't that right, Wernher?"

Graf propped his elbows on the table and fixed Jan with a piercing stare. "So, you think we've done an 'excellent job.' Is that right?"

"Lay off him, Graf," another officer said from farther down the table. "The poor bastard just got here."

Graf grunted and picked up his snifter of cognac. "*Ja,* I know he just got here. Just what we need . . . a fucking civilian expert looking over our shoulder."

It was almost midnight before the bleary-eyed officers finished off the cognac and cigars, and stumbled out of the restaurant singing loudly about the glory of the Fatherland. Faking the words of the song as best he could, Jan tried to keep away from Graf as the group crossed the cobblestone square under the towering cathedral.

"Don't know the words very well, do you?" Graf said as he sidled up to Jan. "Care to suggest another song?"

"I'm afraid I'm not much of a singer," Jan replied. "I've never paid much attention to music."

"This isn't 'music,' you dumb shit. This is patriotism. This is for the honor of the Reich!"

Suddenly Rolfmann stepped between them. His normal pleasantness had disappeared. "*Verdammt,* Wernher! What the hell's the matter with you? You're acting like some Gestapo shithead. We're all tired. Leave him alone."

Graf mumbled an expletive, then shoved his hands in his coat pocket and fell back to another group.

The next morning Rolfmann pulled up in front of Jan's hotel in a Volkswagen. As they drove out of town, heading south, Jan glanced around the interior of the innovative "people's car," whose development had been one of Hitler's brighter ideas to help revitalize the moribund German economy shortly after he came to power. He had seen pictures of the vehicle, but this was the first time he had ridden in one. It was smaller than he had imagined with simple round dials on the dashboard and stiff cloth-covered seats. Jan's knees were cramped and he was amazed that Rolfmann was able to squeeze his even larger frame into the tight quarters.

Jan knew he couldn't ask any questions, of course, because Ernst Heinrich would almost certainly have ridden in a Volkswagen, perhaps even owned one. He had a fleeting thought about how little he actually knew about the man he was impersonating. It scared the hell out of him.

They rode in silence for a few moments. Then Rolfmann glanced at him and asked, "So, what is there to do for fun in Langenfeld?"

Jan flinched. He had no idea. Had Rolfmann ever been there? Hopefully not, or he probably wouldn't have asked. "Well, we have a small concert hall in the center of town," Jan said, wondering if it was true. He coughed once to clear his throat, thinking as fast as he could. "I took my wife, Frieda, to a Brahms concert there last month. She enjoys Brahms. But I haven't been home very much the last few years."

"*Nein,*" Rolfmann grunted, "none of us have."

"What have I done to offend Graf?" Jan asked, eager to change the subject.

Rolfmann glanced at him, his eyes magnified behind the thick lenses of his glasses. "*Ach,* don't worry about it. Wernher's kind of a fanatic . . . naturally suspicious. He's a member of the party, you know."

"*Ist das richtig?* I'm surprised he's not in the SS."

Rolfmann gave him an intuitive smile and nodded. "*Ja,* it's been a sore spot with him for a long time."

"What happened?"

"As I understand it, he was a Brownshirt before the war and figured he'd step right into the SS after his officer training. But he's kind of a hothead, and he apparently mixed it up with the wrong person. He didn't get selected and found himself in the Wehrmacht. He's been pissed off about it ever since."

"What about the other one, the one they called Gunter?"

"That's Hauptmann Gunter Hermann, an old school friend of General Stolberg's. He's a sneaky bastard and tends to use Graf to dig up shit about people he doesn't like. Graf's ambitious, so he'll do whatever Hermann wants. They're two of a kind, and neither one of them have much use for civilians."

"Then I guess I'd better watch myself," Jan said. "Where are we going anyway?"

"To the town of Boom," Rolfmann said. He fished a map from under his seat and tossed it on Jan's lap. "We have substantial defense fortifications on the west bank of the River Schelde. Because of that, we expect the British will approach Antwerp from the south, and they'll have to go through Boom."

Rolfmann reached over and tapped the map that was unfolded on Jan's lap. "As you can see, the main road from Brussels to Antwerp crosses the Rupel River just south of Boom. There is a large highway bridge that spans the river at that location. We've placed demolition charges on the bridge. I'd like you to inspect them."

Jan studied the map, locating the bridge. "It looks like there's another bridge, a smaller one, east of the highway bridge."

Rolfmann nodded. "*Ja, der* Pont van Enschodt. Dates back to the nineteenth century. We doubt they'd try and cross it because it's out of the way and, from a distance, it doesn't look like it would support their tanks. But we've put a few charges on it anyway. I'll show it to you."

Jan looked out the window at the flat fields and the neat, brick farm buildings, hoping he'd be able to get away and meet Sam tonight. He had the feeling his cover wasn't going to last very long.

Chapter 61

On Beukenhofstraat, like many other streets in Merksem, the cellars of every house were connected by tunnels, dug during the long years of occupation, and it was possible to traverse the entire street without going outside. Auguste had led Justyn on a tour of the tunnel network shortly after they had taken him in.

It was after nine o'clock in the evening when Justyn, shaking with fear, pushed back the curtain and stepped through the tunnel into the neighbors' cellar. He wasn't surprised that the van Ginderens were waiting for him. He knew they would have seen the car arrive and the SS troopers enter Auguste and Elise's house, along with a Gestapo agent.

They looked frantic. "What's happened?" the elderly couple asked almost simultaneously as they led Justyn to a small seating area in a corner of the cellar. Fortunately, they spoke French.

"It was a Gestapo agent. He was looking for someone," Justyn said, careful to tell them only what Auguste had instructed him to. "Auguste's been hurt and he needs a doctor. I think his collarbone's broken."

"*Mon dieu!*" Dora van Ginderen cried, covering her face with her hands.

Her husband placed a hand on Justyn's shoulder. "*Oui, oui,* we'll take care of it. We can reach him at his home. And what about you?" he asked.

"I'm all right," Justyn said. "But I have an 'errand' to run."

Leo van Ginderen nodded. "Do you need help?"

"*Oui* . . . with some directions."

Leo van Ginderen led Justyn through the chain of tunnels and cellars to the end of the street where he exited through the back door of another understanding neighbor. Without asking for any more details than he needed to know, van Ginderen gave Justyn some advice on a safe route to and from the port.

Avoiding most of the main streets, it was almost an hour before Justyn spotted Storage Building 15 on the Kattendijkdok, the sign illuminated by one of the few streetlamps in the area of industrial buildings and warehouses. He saw a figure standing in the shadows, looking in the other direction. He moved closer, trying to get a better look.

Closer. The man was tall, his hair—

The figure suddenly turned toward him. "Who's there?"

"*Monsieur . . .* Monsieur Boeynants? It's Justyn."

"Justyn? What the hell!" The tall, silver-haired man stepped over and pulled him into the shadows. "What are you doing here? What's happened?"

Justyn took a deep breath. His hands were trembling. "A Gestapo agent came to the house, a man named Reinhardt, with two SS troopers, they were looking for you." He blurted it all out in one breath.

Boeynants stared at him. "What about Auguste and Elise?"

Justyn's eyes dropped to the ground. "Auguste has a broken collarbone. The neighbors called a doctor."

"They weren't arrested?"

"*Non.* But the man said they'd be watching the house. Auguste sent me to warn you."

Boeynants was silent for a moment, then he put a hand on Justyn's shoulder. "*Merci,* Justyn. You're a brave young man. Tell Auguste and Elise that I'll be all right, not to worry."

Justyn nodded.

"Can you find your way home safely? I'm expecting someone to meet me here." As he said this, Boeynants glanced around.

Justyn followed Boeynants's eyes and noticed the silhouette of a tall, broad-shouldered man about fifty meters away, walking toward them. "*Oui, oui, monsieur.* I'll be fine," he said, wondering who the man was but knowing he couldn't ask.

"You'd better be on your way," Boeynants said. He gripped Justyn's hand. "*Merci beaucoup,* and be careful."

Justyn nodded and walked back the way he came.

• • •

As Jan approached Storage Building Fifteen he slowed, peering into the shadows ahead. He saw two figures. One was that of a tall man that he guessed was Sam. The other was shorter and slender, like a boy, a teenager perhaps. Jan walked slowly, watching. The two figures were having a conversation. The taller figure turned and looked in his direction. A moment later, the shorter figure walked away, heading in the other direction.

"I'm sorry I wasn't here last night," Jan said, when he joined Sam. "It was a long dinner with Stolberg and several other officers. I couldn't get away."

"No problem. I'm relieved to see you. How is it going?"

Jan was curious about the person who had just left, but he knew that Sam would explain if it were necessary. "I think it has gone well so far," Jan said. "A couple of them are a little dubious about me, but the main demolition officer, Leutnant Rolfmann, has been very forthcoming."

"What about their headquarters? Do you know which building it is?"

"I'm not certain because you enter through a tunnel that originates in a bunker in the middle of the park. But when I first arrived, the officer in charge said that it's a former bank building. As we were climbing the stairs, I looked out the windows, and it appeared that we were on the western edge of the park. I could see the cathedral."

Sam smiled. "*Oui, merveilleux.* I know exactly which building you're talking about. Good work."

Jan was struck not for the first time by Sam's aura of steely self-confidence. The man looked tired though his silver hair was neatly trimmed and his suit freshly pressed, if a little tattered around the edges. He appeared thoughtful and deliberate, but there was a hard look in his eyes and an edge in his tone that suggested he was eager to get on with the action.

Jan continued the briefing, explaining everything he had learned about the Kruisschans Lock and the concealment of the explosive charges. He handed over his notes and diagrams and, in the dim light of the streetlamp, pointed out the locations of the charges.

"If they blow that lock, the water level will drop inside the port and the quay walls will collapse," Jan said.

Sam studied the diagram carefully for a long silent moment. Then his eyes met Jan's, the hard look intense and determined. "These bastards mean business."

"Yes, they do," Jan said. "There's no doubt in my mind they're serious about destroying the port. I also need to tell you about Boom."

Sam frowned. "Boom? What's going on there?"

"As I'm sure you know, the main road from Brussels to Antwerp crosses the Rupel River over a large highway bridge just south of Boom."

"*Oui, oui*, I'm quite familiar with the bridge," Sam said.

"The bridge has been set up for demolition. I examined the placement of the charges and the Germans have done their job well. Rolfmann also told me they have shored up their defenses west of Antwerp, and the tunnels under the Schelde have been set for demolition. Therefore, the Allied forces will have to approach from the south and cross the Rupel River using the highway bridge at Boom."

Sam nodded. "Yes, that certainly sounds logical. What do we do about it?"

"The problem is that the view from the lookout post on the highway bridge gives the Germans unobstructed observation for almost two kilometers down the main road. They will have plenty of time to spot an armored division moving up the road and to blow the bridge."

Sam scowled. He seemed about to say something, but Jan continued. "However, there's another bridge, a much older one farther to the east, which Rolfmann referred to as the Pont van Enschodt." Jan produced the map that Rolfmann had given him, which he had conveniently forgotten to return.

"I know the bridge," Sam said, examining the map closely in the dim light. "It's not used very much except for local traffic."

"Well, it turns out that the Germans have pretty much discounted this bridge. They don't think the Allies will use it because it's out of the way and they may doubt that it would support the weight of their tanks."

"Will it?"

"I took the opportunity to examine it quite closely. It's very well constructed. It'll support the tanks. Rolfmann agrees with me, but he still doesn't believe the Allies would attempt to use it. They've placed a few charges on it anyway, but they're quite obvious and would be easy to dismantle. They've posted a few guards, but the sight lines from this bridge are obscured by buildings."

"What are you suggesting?" Sam asked, examining the map.

"Someone must intercept the first Allied units coming up from the south before they reach this intersection and warn them," Jan said, pointing to a location three kilometers south of the highway bridge. "The Allies should be directed to follow this older road to the east then turn north. They'd be out of sight until they were practically on top of the Pont van Enschodt. They could attack by surprise, take out the guards and get across the river on the older bridge."

Sam was silent for a moment, staring at Jan. "If we have someone intercept them, will the Allied commanders listen? Will they take the person seriously?"

Jan nodded. "I'm an officer in an armored division. We're trained to be flexible and adapt to sudden changes in battle tactics. If whomever you send is credible and makes himself understood, they'll listen. They'll make their own decision, but they'll listen."

Sam folded the notes and diagrams, and slipped them into the breast pocket of his suit coat. "I've got to pass this information on right away. Time is short. We've been receiving coded messages over the BBC to begin our final preparations. The Allies could be here sooner than we thought, perhaps within the next few days."

"That'll catch the Germans off guard for sure," Jan said. "They're not expecting it so soon. I hope it's true. One of the officers seems suspicious of me. I'm not sure how much longer I can keep them fooled."

Sam shook his head. "You know we can't—"

Jan interrupted him. "*Oui, bien sûr.* I understand that."

"There is one other thing you must know," Sam said. "It just came up. As you arrived, I was talking with a young man. I'm sure you spotted him."

"*Oui.*"

"He came to warn me that the Gestapo is hunting for me. They came to the home of a White Brigade operative in Merksem."

"Was he arrested?"

"*Non*, and I'm sure that was intentional. They'll be watching his movements very closely, though he may not be going anywhere for awhile because the boy said they broke his collarbone."

Jan winced.

Sam continued. "We will not meet again until this is over. I'll have to remain off the streets until the action starts. If you discover anything else that you think we need to know, go to the Café Brig between eight and ten o'clock any night. It's just over there, on the street facing the dock. Go to the bar and ask for a Trappist Ale from Liege. They won't have it, so take any beer and have a seat. You'll be contacted. It's a last resort backup. Don't use it unless you think it's critical."

"*Je comprends,*" Jan said.

Sam paused and looked into Jan's eyes. "There's one more job you'll have to do. As soon as you hear that the Allies have crossed that bridge and are about to enter the city, you must find the telephone lines coming into their headquarters building and cut them. They're probably in a utility room of some sort in the lower level."

Jan nodded. "Then what?"

"White Brigade Resistance fighters will lead the first Allied units through the city. They will guide them to the park and the headquarters building. Stay in the building, or close by, and surrender to any Allied officer. Tell them you're with the White Brigade, and they are to take you to Antoine."

"Antoine?"

"That's all you need to know. Tell them to take you to Antoine. With any luck, they'll know what to do."

"I certainly hope so," Jan said with a thin smile. "At least I'm not wearing a German uniform so they may not shoot me on sight."

The two men shook hands and walked off in opposite directions.

Chapter 62

ON THE THIRD DAY of Anna's strange imprisonment, Otto finally consented to take her outside the house. It was early afternoon, and she had just finished another fine meal prepared by the massive man who was her jailer and private chef. She felt much better after three days of good food, soap and water, and fresh clothing, sleazy and garish as it was. Though the dread of Koenig's return was like a rock in her gut, the lethargy and mental dullness induced by the horror of Drancy had subsided and she was able to think more clearly.

They stepped onto the wooden porch, and Otto indicated that she should sit in one of the two wicker chairs. Then he placed a handcuff on her right wrist and clamped the other cuff around the arm of the chair.

Anna gave him a coy smile. "Is that really necessary, Otto? If I tried to run away you could shoot me before I'd taken ten steps." She gestured toward the pistol that was perpetually strapped around his waist.

He didn't respond.

"Ah, ja . . . natürlich," Anna said. "If Koenig returned and found that you'd shot his little concubine, that wouldn't be so good for you, would it?"

He stood, leaning against one of the pillars that supported the overhang, arms crossed over his mammoth chest and looked away.

The sun was warm and the tall grass in the meadow was waving in the soft breeze. Beyond the meadow was the dense forest that Anna remembered driving through when they arrived. She considered Otto and wondered what this man must think of the demented Koenig—or was he just as bad and she hadn't found out yet?

So far Anna had been unsuccessful in her attempts to engage him in any type of conversation, but she knew she had to keep trying. If she had any chance of escaping, it had to be before Koenig returned. "Where did you learn to cook?" she asked, hoping to get more than a one-word answer.

Otto appeared startled by the question. He hesitated then said, "From my mother . . . when I was a boy. We had a large family and my father died when I was young. I had to help out."

"Well, she taught you very well. The food *ist wunderbar*."

He nodded, uncertainly.

"So, where is your home?" Anna asked

"Munich."

Anna smiled at him. "I've been to Munich, once, with my father. It's a beautiful city."

He nodded again.

"What did you do before the war?" she asked, still probing, hoping to find some way to reach him.

"*Polizei.*"

"So, I suppose that's why they made you a Feldgendarme. Do you enjoy your work?"

His face darkened. He turned away again. It was obvious she had struck a nerve.

"I'm sorry, Otto. I didn't mean it that way."

"I enjoyed being a policeman," he said, staring out over the meadow. "This is different."

"Being at war you mean?"

He shrugged. "War is war. But the rest is different, not like being a policeman."

They remained in silence for several minutes. Clearly, something was eating at him, Anna thought. "How long were you at Drancy, Otto?"

He turned slowly, glaring at her, his eyes narrowed. Then he abruptly reached over, unlocked the handcuff and led her back to her room.

The next day rain spattered on the roof as Anna sat at the table finishing the breakfast Otto had prepared. As usual, he sat across from her sipping coffee but not eating. When she finished, Anna expected that he would order her back to her room, but he just sat there and stared at her for a long time.

Finally, he set down the coffee cup and folded his hands on the table. "Why were you at Drancy?" he asked. "You don't look like *ein Jude.*"

The thought of giving an honest answer to a German Feldgendarme was so foreign to everything that had been ingrained into Anna's soul over the last five years that she could scarcely bring herself to speak. Yet, there was something about this man. Something that suggested he wasn't just trying to pry information out of her. "No, I'm not Jewish," Anna said. "I was helping American and British aviators get back to Britain, and I got caught."

Otto raised his bushy eyebrows, and Anna thought she detected the slightest hint of a smile. "So, I don't suppose your name is really Jeanne Laurent, then, is it?"

"No, it's Anna Kopernik." As she said this Anna realized she hadn't spoken her last name out loud in five years.

"Kopernik?" Otto mumbled. "That doesn't sound—"

"It's Polish . . . I'm from Krakow."

Otto shifted in his chair, his dark eyes fixed on her, but it appeared as though he were seeing through her, back to another time and another place. He walked over to the sink, rinsed out his cup and leaned against the counter with his back to her, his broad shoulders twitching. He was silent for a minute then spoke in a low, gravelly whisper. "I was a guard at Auschwitz."

Anna closed her eyes and a tingling ran up her spine. She had heard the name whispered among the prisoners at Drancy. There were stories, rumors, about a Nazi death camp at a town near Krakow called Oswiecim. The Germans had renamed it *Auschwitz.*

"When were you there?" Anna whispered.

"1943. Then I was transferred to Drancy."

Anna took a deep breath. It's now or never, she thought. "Otto? Look at me."

The big man turned toward her. His eyes were glassy.

"Otto, it's not your fault. You were following orders, weren't you? If you didn't, they'd have killed you, wouldn't they?"

"Maybe they should have," he said.

Anna stood up and carried her plate and cup to the sink. She had never done this before. She looked up at him, not sure how far she could push this but knowing she might not have another opportunity.

"There's still time, Otto?"

"Time?"

"There's still time . . . for some good to come out of this."

He was silent. Anna could see he was trying to understand.

"You could help me, Otto."

Suddenly, he stood up straight, his giant frame towering over her. He took a step back.

"We could leave now, before Koenig returns. You're a Feldgendarme, you could get us to the border and we'd find a way—"

"*Nein!*" he growled, backing away another step. "I've said too much. Forget everything I told you. It's impossible."

"Otto, please, listen. I—"

"*Nein!*"

He grabbed her arm with a thick hand and pulled her to the door of the bedroom. He pushed her inside, slammed it shut and locked it.

Chapter 63

THE BRITISH ELEVENTH ARMORED DIVISION was moving so fast that Captain Steve Bradley, tank commander, Third Royal Tank Regiment, had difficulty keeping up with their position on his map.

Charging through the French countryside, they crossed the Seine on August 28, and two days later reached Amiens. They crossed the Somme the next day, and by September 2 they were at Lille, where they dipped slightly to the southeast, crossed into Belgium near Tournai and spent the next day heading north.

As they clanked along on the narrow, dusty roads, Bradley was amazed at the lack of serious opposition. The terrain was incredibly flat, and they constantly crossed small bridges over narrow canals where they should have been easy targets. Perhaps it was because they followed minor roads through small villages that they escaped detection but, whatever the reason, Bradley was thankful for the respite. He had been at Caen and at the Falaise Gap and had seen enough bloodshed for a lifetime.

On the night of September 3, in the flickering light of a kerosene lantern, Bradley examined the map another time. Word had just come down that tomorrow they would push into Antwerp.

At seven o'clock, on the evening of September 3, Willy Boeynants sat in the meeting room in the cellar of the Café Brig with Antoine and five other officers of the White Brigade. The group was silent as they listened to the French language broadcast on the BBC. The string of coded messages began. Most of the messages were meaningless, intended to confuse the German agents who were always listening. But others delivered instructions to agents of Resistance organizations who knew what to listen for.

The radio crackled a few times, and Boeynants strained to hear. Antoine held up his hand and leaned toward the radio as the announcer spoke in a dull monotone.

"Pour François la lune est clair."

The Resistance leader slapped his hand on the table and looked around at his compatriots, his dark eyes gleaming. "That's it! 'For Francois the moon is bright.' That's the final signal. They'll be here within twenty-four hours. You all know what to do. Let's get moving."

One by one the White Brigade officers slipped on their armbands and left the café, dispersing throughout the city to initiate the call to action. Plans developed over the past two years would be thrust into motion. Units of armed White Brigade fighters would move into positions along the River Schelde, prepared to harass the movement of German troops stationed in defensive fortifications on the west bank. Other White Brigade units would set up locations along the roads leading into the city, while still others would take strategic posts along the Albert Canal.

Armed with the drawings and diagrams Jan had provided, Antoine went immediately to the port to take command of the units he had organized to seize the Kruisschans Lock.

Willy Boeynants, driving a borrowed auto, set off in the opposite direction, to the south of Boom, where he intended to intercept the first Allied units and direct them over the Pont van Enschodt. As he sped along the nearly deserted roads, Boeynants gripped the steering wheel, concentrating, focusing all of his thoughts on the upcoming task. Everything was in place for the long-awaited uprising against the German oppressor. The hour was at hand . . . and everything depended on the Allies arriving in time.

The next morning Jan showed the badge identifying him as Ernst Heinrich to the Feldgendarmes and passed through the checkpoint into the park. He flashed the badge again at the main bunker and proceeded through the tunnel to the headquarters building.

As he climbed the stairs to the third floor he looked out the windows, wondering if today would be the day. It was the same thought that he'd had each of the last three days—the most stressful he'd ever experienced.

Commanding troops in battle had been dangerous, and the killing and maiming had been appalling. But that was a job he'd been trained to do. What he was doing now was something so completely foreign he didn't know what to expect from one hour to the next. He'd never felt so isolated, so vulnerable, in his life.

Jan entered the command center and gathered up the stack of reports that had been left for him by the night duty officers responsible for inspecting demolition emplacements. He glanced around the room. The usual officers were going about their usual tasks. The radio was quiet. Nothing seemed out of the ordinary. Either no attack was imminent, or, if it was, it would take them by surprise.

He put the papers in his briefcase, poured a cup of coffee and walked down the hall to the office that had been provided for him. He stepped into the office, set the briefcase on the desk and abruptly turned around, startled by the sound of footsteps behind him.

Leutnant Wernher Graf stood in the doorway. "You look a little jumpy this morning, Herr Heinrich," Graf said.

"Christ, Leutnant, I didn't see you in the hall. What'd you do, drop from the ceiling?"

"Well, I guess you *are* a little jumpy. Sorry if I frightened you."

"*Nein*, you surprised me, Graf. There's a difference." Jan took off his jacket and hung it on a hook next to the metal filing cabinet. "What can I do for you?"

"It's 'Leutnant' Graf to you," he said, glancing around the small room. "I've come for your notes."

"My notes?"

"*Ja*, your notes, Herr Heinrich. The notes you've been taking the last few days. And all the drawings you've been making."

"What the hell are you talking about, Leutnant? They were just scribbles; what would you want with them?"

"It's none of your goddamn business what I want with them," Graf snarled. He took a step closer to the desk. "Just hand them over, *Jetzt!*"

"I don't have them."

Graf glared at him, and a thin smile appeared on his face. Jan sensed that was exactly what the devious son of a bitch expected to hear.

"What did you do with them?"

"I destroyed them, every night in my hotel room. When I was done with my calculations, I burned them. Certainly you—"

"*Verdammt!* Who do you think you're fucking around with?" Graf shouted. "You've taken notes on a military installation and now you say you don't have them? I could arrest you for treason right here, you—"

"Graf!" another voice shouted. "What the hell is going on?" Leutnant Rolfmann stepped into the crowded office.

Graf whirled around. "I've asked Herr Heinrich for the notes he's been taking and the drawings he's made. Now he's tells me he doesn't have them."

Rolfmann seemed perplexed.

Jan looked at him and spoke slowly, trying to stay calm. "I've tried to explain to Leutnant Graf that it has been my practice each night to destroy the notes I've taken after I finish my calculations. I've been told that the Resistance is very active in Antwerp and there could be spies anywhere. This is certainly not information I wanted to carry around with me."

Rolfmann turned to Graf. "Well, Wernher, that certainly makes sense, don't you think?"

"Not to me it doesn't," Graf snapped as he pushed his way past Rolfmann and stalked off down the hall.

As they approached Boom, the Third Royal Tank Regiment came to a halt. Standing in the open turret of his Sherman tank, Captain Bradley peered ahead to see what had caused the delay. A tall, silver-haired man wearing an armband on his left sleeve stood in the middle of the road, gesturing to the lead tank commander. The tank commander leaned over the side of the turret.

A Jeep roared up the column and skidded to a stop next to the silver-haired man. A scout officer jumped out of the Jeep, and the strange man unrolled a map. A few minutes later they both climbed into the jeep and roared off to the east.

Bradley's headset crackled. The regiment was making a detour.

As the tank column passed behind several large factory buildings, Bradley stood in the turret, glancing around. He was nervous, this wasn't the plan. A few minutes later they turned north, and barreled at top speed along a gravel road with buildings close by on either side.

When Bradley first saw the bridge ahead of them, he was certain they had made a mistake. It looked too narrow and too old. But, with no hesitation, the Jeep and the lead tank roared onto the bridge, machine guns blazing. As his big Sherman tank bounced along the road, Bradley spotted a group of German soldiers running off the other end of the bridge. A battered wood sign at the base of the bridge read *Pont van Enschodt*.

The tank column roared over the bridge and followed the Jeep to the left, through a maze of narrow streets. Suddenly, dozens of men—civilians, armed with rifles and submachine guns, emerged from between the buildings and out of the ditches along the road. They ran alongside the clanking tanks, cheering and pumping their fists in the air, dressed in all manner of uniforms, berets and helmets. But they all wore the same armband as the silver-haired man, a white band with red, yellow and black diagonal strips. Bradley stared at them in amazement, wondering where in the hell they had come from.

They rounded a corner, and Bradley saw another bridge, a huge highway bridge spanning the same river they had just crossed. Suddenly, a burst of enemy machine-gun fire blasted at the tank column from two bunkers at the entrance to the highway bridge. The lead tanks returned fire and, in an instant, the German gunners bailed out and scrambled down the embankment toward the river.

The Jeep and two tanks roared onto the highway bridge as another unit of German soldiers fired at them from the middle of the span. Bradley's tank was still twenty meters from the bridge when a gang of the civilians wearing armbands ran past him. They charged onto the bridge, firing rifles and submachine guns, and tossing hand grenades. In less than a minute, the German guards broke ranks and retreated off the other side.

The Jeep stopped in the middle of the bridge, and the silver-haired man climbed out, holding some papers in his hand. A second Jeep barreled up from the rear of the column and three demolition engineers jumped out. They looked at the papers then climbed over the side of the bridge.

Bradley stopped his tank and watched. Twenty minutes later an officer waved the all-clear signal, and Bradley's headset crackled. He listened to the message then bent down and yelled to his tank driver. "Turn to the north, Eddie. We're heading into Antwerp."

· · ·

At ten o'clock that morning Leutnant Graf finally got in to see Hauptmann Gunter Hermann. He stood at attention in front of the desk, staring at the usual picture of Hitler on the wall until Hermann looked up and waved for him to take a seat.

"I'm concerned about the civilian, Heinrich," Graf said quickly, knowing that Hermann had no patience for small talk.

"Why is that?" Hermann asked, leaning back in his chair.

"He's been taking a lot of notes and making diagrams of all of the demolition emplacements that Rolfmann has shown him."

Hermann's eyes narrowed, but he didn't respond.

"Earlier this morning I asked him for his notes," Graf said. "He told me he had destroyed them."

"You obviously don't believe him."

"*Nein.* As you know, the train wreck was very unusual, and there's just something about him that bothers me. Now these notes—"

Hermann held up his hand as the signal that he'd heard enough. "I've been making some inquiries about that train wreck," he said, motioning for Graf to close the door. "Last night I received a very interesting phone call. It seems that one of the conductors recalls seeing three Wehrmacht soldiers running from the train right after the wreck. There was a fourth man with them. It appeared to the conductor as though the soldiers were leading the man away from the train."

"Was the conductor able to describe the fourth man?" Graf asked, sitting on the edge of his chair.

"He said the man was a civilian. He was tall and had blond hair."

Graf jumped to his feet. "Give me an order, sir."

Hermann was about to respond when there was a knock on the door. With a look of annoyance, Hermann barked for the person to enter.

His aide, a young Unteroffizier named Boettcher, stepped into the office and stood at rapt attention.

Hermann motioned for him to speak.

"Excuse me for interrupting, sir, but General Stolberg has called an emergency meeting in the command center."

"What the hell's happened?" Hermann snapped.

"The Kruisschans Lock has been attacked, sir."

"What? The Kruisschans Lock? Attacked by whom?"

"I'm not sure, sir," the young enlisted man said. "I heard something about Resistance forces . . . the White Brigade."

"Mein Gute!" Hermann burst from the office with Graf running behind him.

General Stolberg stood at the head of the table in the command center. The radios squawked and the telephones rang. The operators furiously jotted notes and passed them to the general's aides who read them and scribbled responses.

The rest of the garrison's officers were already in the room as Hermann and Graf burst in. The general began speaking immediately. "Fifteen minutes ago, we received a report that Resistance forces have seized the Kruisschans Lock."

"They've seized it? Already?" Hermann blurted out.

"They attacked from three directions and apparently overtook the guard unit within minutes. At least four of the guards were killed."

A murmuring broke out among the officers but stopped abruptly as the general continued. "We've also had reports of armed Resistance forces firing on Wehrmacht soldiers along the Schelde, the Albert Canal and in the central city."

Before any of the officers could respond one of the general's aides handed him a radio message.

The general read it and glanced at the aide.

The aide nodded.

General Stolberg cleared his throat and addressed the group of officers. "British armored units have crossed the Rupel River at Boom and are heading toward Antwerp."

"At Boom? That's . . . that's not possible," Hermann stammered. "That bridge was set for demolition. The guards . . . they had a clear sight line over two kilometers down the road. Graf, isn't that . . ."

The aide handed General Stolberg another message. He read it and glared at Hermann. His voice was acidic. "They apparently crossed the river on the Pont van Enschodt and circled through the town, taking the main highway bridge by surprise from the rear."

"The Pont van Enschodt?" Hermann turned toward Graf. "How could they have known?"

Graf pointed his finger at Rolfmann. "You took Heinrich to Boom, didn't you?"

"Yes, of course," the big man said. Beads of perspiration formed on his forehead. "I took him everywhere. I . . . Oh Christ . . . *nein* . . . he couldn't have."

"He took notes! He made drawings!" Graf screamed.

"What the hell are you talking about?" the general demanded.

"It's Heinrich, sir," Hermann said. "He's a traitor. Graf . . . go get that *schweinhund! Jetzt!*"

Chapter 64

JAN'S OFFICE WAS JUST AROUND THE CORNER from the command center, and when he noticed a group of officers racing down the hallway he knew the moment had arrived. He left the office and headed for the back staircase.

Taking the steps two at a time, he descended to the ground floor, where he walked down the hallway to a heavy, fireproof steel door that led to the lower level and the utility room.

A few meters past the fireproof door was the service entrance to the building and, as usual, two enlisted men stood guard. Jan made eye contact with one of them. The soldier was young, perhaps nineteen, and thin as a rail. He wore a handgun in a holster strapped around his waist.

"*Unteroffizier! Komm!*" Jan commanded, waving his badge. "I need your help with a crate in the utility room."

The young man looked perplexed but followed Jan down the stairs.

Jan opened the door to the utility room and stepped into the dark space.

The Unteroffizier followed him in.

Jan abruptly spun around and rammed his fist into the soldier's stomach, knocking the wind out of him.

As the young man crumpled to the ground, gasping for breath, Jan kicked the door closed and flicked on the lights. He grabbed the towel that he had placed on a shelf the night he found the room and tied it around the soldier's mouth. Then he took the roll of twine he had also placed on the shelf and bound the stunned boy's hands and feet.

Jan dragged the soldier into a corner and removed the handgun from his holster. He checked the clip and shoved the gun into his own belt. Jan paused for a second, looking into the boy's wide eyes. "Lie still and you won't get hurt," he said, then retrieved the wire cutters he had located the previous night and stepped over to the far corner where the telephone lines entered the building.

Leutnant Graf grabbed a rifle from the rack at the back of the room and burst from the command center. He sprinted down the hall and charged into Jan's office. When he found it empty, he grabbed the telephone on the desk, expecting to hear the voice of the main switchboard operator.

Nothing. Silence.

"*Verdammt!*" Graf roared, and raced from the office, bumping into Hermann's aide, Boettcher, in the hallway.

"The telephones have gone dead," the aide said.

"No shit!" Graf snarled. "Get the Feldgendarmes and meet me in the utility room. *Schnell! Mach schnell!*"

Graf ran down the back staircase to the ground floor and then down the hallway toward the fireproof door. As he pulled the door open he shouted at the single guard standing next to the service entrance. "Have you seen anyone go down these stairs in the last few minutes?"

"Yes, sir, a civilian. He showed his badge and—"

Before he could finish Graf bolted through the door and raced down the stairs to the lower level. When he saw the light coming from underneath the closed door to the utility room, Graf smiled and flicked off the safety on the rifle.

Down the hallway, Jan stepped out from around the corner and aimed his gun at Graf. He had reviewed his options when he heard Graf yelling at the guard upstairs and didn't hesitate.

He pulled the trigger.

Graf slumped to the concrete floor, a bullet hole just above his ear.

Jan rushed over, grabbed Graf's body by the shirt collar and dragged it into the utility room next to the terrified young soldier who pissed in his pants. Then he stuffed the handgun into his coat pocket, and retrieved Graf's rifle from the hallway.

The gunshot had been so loud in the confined area that Jan's ears rang, but he held out a slight hope that the report had been muted by the thick steel door at the top of the stairs. Jan backed into the utility room and closed the door. He quickly examined Graf's rifle. It was a Karabiner K43, semi-automatic. He checked the ten-round magazine. It was full. Then he switched off the light and stepped back into the dark room to wait.

It didn't take long.

He heard footsteps coming down the stairs.

Voices whispered in the hallway.

He raised the rifle and aimed at the door, his finger lightly caressing the trigger.

Suddenly the door burst open. The light from the hallway illuminated three figures, one waving a flashlight.

Jan fired three shots in quick succession hitting the first figure in the side of the head, the second in the throat and the last, and least visible, in the shoulder.

The first two collapsed without a sound, save for the flashlight bouncing off the concrete floor. But the third figure yelped and fell backward into the hallway. His gun clattered to the ground.

Jan bolted toward the door.

The third figure was a Feldgendarme. Blood spurted from his left shoulder as he retrieved his weapon and lurched across the hallway toward the staircase.

Jan stepped over the two bodies lying in the doorway and chased the wounded man into the stairwell.

Staggering up the stairs, the bleeding Feldgendarme turned to fire but stumbled. Jan shot him in the forehead.

Chapter 65

CAPTAIN BRADLEY COULDN'T BELIEVE what he was seeing. As the tank regiment rolled through the streets of Antwerp, thousands of people flooded out of their homes and offices, cheering, singing and waving banners. They climbed on the tanks, offering champagne, wine, flowers and candy. A young woman wrapped her arms around Bradley's neck and smothered him with kisses. Giant homemade flags, in the Belgian colors of red, yellow and black fluttered from the windows of apartments and office buildings, the first time in four and a half years that any flag except the Nazi swastika had flown in Antwerp.

In the midst of the mad, chaotic celebration, German snipers, crawling along the rooftops, fired at the tanks and into the crowd. British soldiers and White Brigade Resistance fighters returned fire, but dozens of civilians were killed and wounded. With bullets pinging off the steel sides of the tank, Bradley was terrified, amazed and exhilarated, all at the same time.

On and on it went, the wildly cheering crowds becoming more impenetrable the farther the tank column drove into the central city, to the point where it became difficult to maneuver the ponderous machines without running people over. Their progress slowed to a crawl.

Finally, two infantry platoons caught up to them and slowly pushed the throng back, clearing the streets. The tanks picked up a little speed. The firing from the rooftops continued, but the crowd of celebrating citizens seemed oblivious, undaunted in their jubilation. Crouched low in the open turret and yelling instructions down to his driver, Bradley was certain he would never see anything like this again.

A Jeep carrying two officers came up, weaving through the crowd with its siren blaring. A civilian, wearing a green beret and a leather jacket with the White Brigade armband, sat in the rear. The driver waved for Bradley to follow. They came to a roundabout and Bradley, followed by three other tanks and an infantry platoon, stayed with the Jeep as it veered off to the right. The remainder of the regiment headed toward the port.

Bradley's tank was first in line behind the Jeep, moving slowly along a wide boulevard. Ahead was an expanse of grass and stately trees. His headset crackled with instructions from one of the officers in the Jeep. "Dead ahead is a park where the German headquarters is located. We're going to let you pass. Take out the bunker at the entrance."

Ducking into the turret, Bradley yelled instructions to the firing crew, and the Sherman's big gun arced downward. The tank lurched as the gun fired.

The left half of the German bunker disappeared.

The turret swiveled a few degrees, and the big gun fired again, blasting away the rest of the bunker.

All civilians vanished, and the street ahead was empty as Bradley's tank accelerated toward the remains of the bunker, firing its machine guns at the fleeing German soldiers.

They turned left, crunching over chunks of concrete from the shattered bunker, and rambled down a broad street that traversed the western edge of the park. A hundred meters ahead Bradley spotted a large group of civilians in paramilitary dress and the now familiar armbands, firing into a three-story building with machine guns and grenade launchers.

Following the instructions coming over his headset, Bradley maneuvered his Sherman tank to the north end of the building while the other tank stopped at the south end. The turrets of both tanks swung toward the German headquarters.

One by one, Jan dragged the three corpses into the utility room then stepped over to the young German soldier who was twitching and sweating profusely. Jan pressed the rifle against the terrified boy's head. "Remember what I said before. Lie still. *Verstehen Sie?*"

The soldier nodded vigorously, his eyes wide with fear.

Jan stepped into the hallway and glanced up the staircase. The door was still closed.

It was the only way out of the lower level, which meant it was also the only way in. Provided they weren't going to come after him with flamethrowers, Jan calculated he had a momentary advantage. As he crouched at the bottom of the staircase, aiming the Karabiner K43 at the door, he heard muted sounds of gunfire and scattered explosions that he guessed were hand grenades.

Then a deafening blast shook the building.

A second blast and the steel door flew open, banging against the concrete wall, sagging on broken hinges.

Jan's ears rang and his pulse raced as he looked up the staircase. The ground floor hallway was filled with smoke and dust. Shadowy figures raced past the open doorway, heading for the service entrance, yelling and shouting.

Smoke and dust drifted down the staircase.

Jan waited.

Gunfire erupted and shadowy forms raced back the other direction.

The gunfire was constant, the yelling louder, but now different—it was in English! British soldiers yelled, "Get down! On the floor! Down, now!"

Heavy boots pounded down the hallway, machine guns rattled. British troopers screamed at the trapped Wehrmacht soldiers, "Lie down! Now! Lie down!"

Jan crouched at the bottom of the stairs, watching and listening, considering his next move. The British had taken the building. He needed to surrender. But how? He thought about the towel he had used to gag the young German, the white towel.

Jan stood up and turned back toward the utility room just as a voice bellowed out from the top of the stairs. "Halt! You there! Halt and drop the gun!"

Jan stopped and let go of the rifle. It clattered to the floor.

"Hands up! Hands up!" the voice yelled.

Jan raised his hands.

"Now turn around, slowly, and walk up the stairs."

Jan turned around and started up the stairs with his hands above his head.

A British soldier stood in the doorway, pointing a submachine gun at him, backing away as he reached the top of the stairs.

A second British soldier appeared. "Whatcha' got here, Tommy?"

The first soldier kept the submachine gun pointed at Jan. "I don't know. Looks like a Kraut in a suit. He understands English, though, and he was carrying a rifle." He jabbed Jan in the ribs with the gun barrel. "Lie down!"

Jan looked down the smoke-filled hallway, littered with massive chunks of broken concrete and shattered wood. Sunlight poured through a gaping hole in the outside wall. At least twenty German soldiers were lying on their stomachs with their hands behind their heads. British troopers moved among them, removing their weapons. Another dozen Germans lay sprawled in pools of their own blood.

Jan remained standing. "I'm with the White Brigade. You are to take me to Antoine."

The soldier jabbed him with the gun barrel again. "On the floor, asshole!"

Jan pushed the gun away and shouted at the startled soldier, hoping to attract the attention of an officer. "I said I'm with the White Brigade, you dumb shit! There are four dead Germans down in the lower level and another one bound and gagged! Go take a look!"

"What the hell's he talking about?" the second soldier asked.

"Damned if I know. Nip down and check it out."

"Are you daft? I'm not going—"

A British officer approached the group. "What's going on here, Private?"

"We found this man hiding at the bottom of the stairs, sir. He says he's with the White Brigade."

"Right, and I'm the bloody Prime Minister," the officer snapped. He stepped in front of Jan and glared at him. From his insignia, Jan could tell he was a lieutenant, which was unfortunate. He probably wasn't senior enough to make a decision.

"I'm with the White Brigade and—"

The officer cut him off. "Shut your mouth. Wilson, get over here and search him."

The second soldier stepped over to Jan and patted him down, instantly discovering the handgun. He removed it and handed it to the officer. Then he reached into the breast pocket of Jan's suit coat and removed the black identification folder.

Goddamn it, Jan cursed to himself. Everything had happened so fast, he had completely forgotten about the ID badge.

The soldier handed it to the lieutenant who opened it, then looked at Jan with contempt. "So, Ernst Heinrich, now the Belgians are letting Nazis join the Resistance?"

"You don't understand; that's just a cover. I'm—"

The lieutenant pointed the handgun at Jan's head. "You can bloody well get down on the floor right now—or I'll kill you with your own fucking gun!"

Jan stared into the lieutenant's eyes. The British officer was almost a foot shorter and much younger, no more than twenty-five. His cheek was twitching.

Jan stepped closer to him and shoved his face within a few centimeters of the young lieutenant's. He spoke just above a whisper. "Listen to me, Lieutenant, before you do something stupid. I'm an undercover agent with the White Brigade. There are four dead Germans down in that utility room, and they didn't die of heart attacks. Now, before you get yourself court-martialed, send someone down to check it out."

The lieutenant blinked. He took a step back and said, "Wilson, check it out."

Two minutes went by, and neither Jan nor the British lieutenant took their eyes off each other.

Wilson ran back up the stairs and blurted out, "There are four dead Krauts down there, sir. Three of 'em shot right through their bloody heads. There's another one all tied up, scared shitless."

Jan said, "Take me to Antoine. Now."

"Who the fuck is Antoine?" the lieutenant yelled. His face was red.

"He's leader of the White Brigade," Jan explained, painfully aware that he was talking very boldly about a man he had never met. "He's probably outside right now with the tanks that shot the hell out of this building."

The lieutenant glared at him, then stepped back and pointed toward the front of the building. "Get moving and keep your hands in the air."

With the British lieutenant and the two soldiers walking right behind him, Jan stepped out of the heavily damaged building into the bright midday sunshine.

"Over there," the lieutenant said and shoved Jan in the direction of two officers and a man in a leather jacket and green beret, standing in front of a Jeep and a Sherman tank. Several British soldiers and a group of civilians wearing odd uniforms, helmets and armbands milled about nearby.

As they approached the Jeep, one of the officers, a major, stepped forward. "Who is this, lieutenant?"

"He says he's with the White Brigade, sir. He says we're to take him to Antoine."

"Antoine?" The major glanced at Jan.

"We found this on him, sir." The lieutenant handed over the black ID folder.

The major examined the ID badge, then called over his shoulder, "Antoine, would you like to meet Ernst Heinrich?"

The man wearing the leather jacket and beret stepped forward. "So, you're 'Ernst Heinrich,'" he said in very good English as he shook Jan's hand. "I've been looking for you. Your intel has panned out so far. Care to join me to see what happens next?"

Chapter 66

THE BRITISH MAJOR OFFERED the use of his Jeep and driver, and a few minutes later Antoine and Jan wound their way through the narrow streets of the central city, heading toward the river, the driver constantly honking his horn trying to get through the crowds of celebrating citizens. Antoine leaned close to Jan to be heard over the noise from the crowd. "I'm sure you'd prefer not to use the name 'Ernst Heinrich' any longer, so perhaps we should just call you 'Colonel' for the time being. I believe Sam told me you're a colonel?"

Jan nodded. "That would be fine."

"I understand that all this secret identity business may seem a little silly to you regular army types, but it's vital to our success."

"I understand," Jan said, though he still hated the duty.

Antoine shouted some directions to the driver, then turned back to Jan. "This is only the beginning. With the Brits moving into Antwerp as fast as they have, the German forces have already begun to retreat across the Albert Canal into Merksem. It's crucial for the British to seize the bridges over the canal before the Germans blow them, or it'll be hell rooting them out. If the Germans gain control of Merksem they can attack the port by way of the Groenendallaan, the main east–west road north of the canal."

Following Antoine's instructions, the Jeep turned onto the Schelde Kaai and headed north. Antoine glanced at Jan. "Better hang on, now."

The wide boulevard that paralleled the river was essentially deserted, the crowd of civilians driven off by German machine guns, mortars and 88s firing at them from the west bank of the river. Craters pockmarked the cobblestone road, and hundreds of windows were broken in the apartment buildings that lined the picturesque riverfront street. The driver shoved the accelerator to the floor, and they sped forward, dodging exploding shells and bodies of Belgian civilians and British soldiers.

As the Jeep approached the docks, the driver weaved through the rear ranks of the British regiment returning fire across the river. They made their way to the head of the column where Antoine and Jan jumped out, keeping low and ducking behind tanks and machine gunners.

Antoine grabbed an artillery officer and asked for the regiment's commander. The officer led them to a location alongside the wharf, just beyond the range of the German guns, where a British colonel studied a map along with several other officers.

Across the street, Jan noticed a group of more than a hundred heavily armed men in paramilitary dress, wearing White Brigade armbands. He guessed they were waiting for instructions from Antoine.

When the British colonel saw Antoine and Jan approaching, he gave them an uncertain look and stepped forward. "Colonel Canfield, Third Royal Tank Regiment. Who are you?"

"My name is Antoine. We're with the armed forces of the White Brigade. I'm told you've been briefed on our activities."

"Well, yes . . . somewhat," the British colonel said.

Antoine stepped directly to the map spread out on the hood of the British officer's Jeep and pointed to their location. "We are right here, at the Bonapartedok," he said. "This dock, along with the next two, the Willemdok and the Kattendijkdok, were seized last night by White Brigade forces and are under our control. A few hours ago our forces also seized the Kruisschans Lock, located right here." As Antoine said this, he pointed to the location of the crucial lock, almost five kilometers to the north. "Our forces at the Kruisschans Lock are in desperate need of reinforcements."

Colonel Canfield studied the map but didn't respond.

Antoine glanced at Jan with a quizzical look then turned back to the British colonel. As Antoine spoke he traced a line with his finger from the Kattendijkdok to the Kruisschans Lock. "Colonel Canfield, I am requesting at least six tanks and a company of infantry to accompany my troops north, along the Kattendijkdok, across the Albert Canal and on through the remaining docks to the north. If we move quickly, we should be able to take control of them without much trouble. We will then have secured the entire port and be in position to support the men holding the Kruisschans Lock."

Canfield continued to stare at the map for what seemed to Jan like a very long time. Finally he looked up and rubbed his chin, shaking his head. "I'm sorry, but I don't have orders to penetrate that area. Besides, it appears to be very dangerous terrain to operate with an armored unit. All these canals and docks, lined with warehouses and cranes. It's over five kilometers, we've had no reconnaissance. We really don't know—"

"Excuse me, Colonel," Antoine interrupted. "Our reconnaissance of the entire port is very thorough. My men have been operating here for a long time. Most of them work in the port. We'll guide your troops all the way."

"Well, that may be true . . . but it's not the same as . . ." The colonel paused. "No disrespect, but I'm sure you understand. My orders are to proceed to the port as far as the Albert Canal. I have no authority to penetrate farther."

Antoine could not hide his annoyance. "Colonel Canfield, the Kruisschans Lock is vital to the safety of the port. The Germans rigged it for demolition, which we are now in the process of dismantling—"

"Well then, we have some time," Canfield chimed in.

"No, sir, we don't," Antoine snapped. "We were able to seize the lock with a surprise attack, but we won't be able to hold it without reinforcements. If the Germans retake that lock, they will blow it up. Do you know what will happen then?"

"Look old chap, really, I think we—"

Antoine interrupted him again. "Sir, the entire port could collapse. If they blow that lock, the water in the port will go out with the tide, and without the water pressure in the docks the sides of the quays will collapse. The port of Antwerp will be out of commission for years."

The two men stared at each other.

Jan knew that Colonel Canfield was clearly in a bind. He had incomplete orders and was suddenly being asked to risk an armored unit and a company of infantry in an unknown area on the word of a foreign civilian he had never before met. As a career military officer, Jan knew that was an untenable position. But he also knew that what Antoine was asking was absolutely necessary.

"Colonel Canfield, may I have a word with you in private?" Jan asked, stepping a few meters away from the group and gesturing for the colonel to join him.

The colonel stepped over to Jan, but he was clearly agitated. "And who the hell are you, again?"

Jan glanced around. Antoine and the other British officers had moved out of earshot. He looked at Canfield. "I am a regimental commander with the Polish First Armored Division, attached to the First Canadian Corps. Our unit was on Mont Ormel at the Falaise Gap. I also have advanced training in demolition devices. Two weeks ago I was assigned by General Maczek to special duty with the SOE. I have been operating undercover for the past week within the German garrison here in Antwerp. I am the one who routed you over the Pont van Enschodt. I've been to the Kruisschans Lock. I can assure you, Colonel Canfield, that what Antoine is asking for is absolutely necessary."

"Well, he may think it necessary, but—"

Jan held up his hand. "We also need support to seize the bridges over the Albert Canal."

"That may be, but my orders—"

"Quite frankly, Colonel, I don't give a shit what your orders are," Jan said, cutting him off. "We're both officers and we both know we have to make decisions in the field. Will it have made any sense to have fought your way into Antwerp and then let the Germans destroy the port?"

Canfield removed a handkerchief from his pocket and wiped his brow. He glanced around at the other officers who were all looking off in another direction. "You make a very persuasive argument, but I still do not have the authority—"

"If you don't have the authority, then get on the radio and contact whoever does," Jan exclaimed. "But let's stop fucking around! Those men out at the Kruisschans Lock need reinforcements, and they need them now!"

Canfield stared at him for a moment. Then he turned and stormed off, yelling to one of his officers, "Captain Anders! Get a radioman up here! On the double!"

Chapter 67

TWENTY-FOUR HOURS LATER, Jan wandered through the quiet battlefield surrounding the Kruisschans Lock. British medics tended to the wounded from both sides with the help of a Belgian doctor. Trucks were on their way for transport to the hospital.

Jan kicked at a small clump of dirt, staring at the wreckage. They hadn't gotten all they asked for from Canfield, but they'd gotten enough to save the lock and, as battles went, this one was minor. Compared with what Jan had experienced at the Bzura River and the Kampinos Forest, compared with Montbard, Chambois and the Falaise Gap, it was really nothing more than a blip on the chart.

But it had now been five years. Five years . . . and he was standing in yet another battlefield with bodies of young men sprawled in front of him. Dead Polish boys and French boys now replaced by British and Belgian boys. But they were still dead. And after five years, there were still dead German boys. Jan rubbed his eyes. By now, he thought, an entire generation of German youth had been wasted across the entire continent of Europe. From the vast expanses of Poland and Russia to the tidy hedgerows of Normandy and now, along the canals of Belgium and Holland, there had been one constant. Young men had died . . . millions of young men. For what?

A British officer named Wilson walked alongside him. "How long have you been at this?"

Jan shook his head and kicked at another clump of dirt. "It seems like forever."

• • •

A little before six o'clock in the evening, Antoine returned to the Kruisschans Lock with an additional British infantry platoon. The Resistance leader joined Jan and Wilson who were standing on the outer gate of the lock. "Another British regiment and two Canadian regiments have entered the city, and the Germans have been pretty well rooted out," Antoine said.

"What about the bridges to Merksem?" Jan asked.

Antoine shook his head. "They're all blown. The Germans have Merksem sealed off. Most of them got over the bridges before they were destroyed, but Canfield tells me they've taken more than two thousand prisoners."

"Two thousand?" Wilson exclaimed. "Where the hell are they going to put them?"

"Well, he asked me if I had any suggestions," Antoine said. "I told him to lock them up in the zoo. It's right near the Central Station."

"The zoo? What about the animals?" Wilson asked.

"They were all eaten long ago."

Wilson looked at Jan, an incredulous expression on his face.

Jan shrugged. After what he'd seen in Poland, he knew anything was possible.

Antoine continued. "We're clearing out the last of the Germans from the docks north of the canal. We should have complete control over the port by morning."

"But now we've got to hold it," Jan said.

The Resistance leader nodded. "Yes. And until Merksem is taken we can expect additional attacks. With the bridges gone, the only way into Merksem is over the Groenendallaan, which we've already tried and failed, or across the canal in boats—but that's for another day." He turned to Jan. "You've had a busy week. You're officially relieved from my command as of now. Get some rest and report to Sam at 1400 hours tomorrow at the Den Engle Café on the Grote Markt. Do you know where that is?"

"I'll find it," Jan said.

Chapter 68

It was after midnight and Anna was still awake, staring at the shadowy outline of the crystal chandelier. Frustrated, she turned onto her side, and her eyes fell on the garish flowered patterns of the wallpaper illuminated by moonlight shining through the window. Alone and isolated in this bizarre prison cell for almost a week, she felt herself slipping into a well of despair.

She had tried to fight it. She had tried to keep her mind occupied, devising a hundred different plans for escape, all of which seemed futile. Otto had shut her out, refusing any further communication, and the stark reality was that she was sealed in a room with a stout, locked door and barred windows in an isolated farmhouse at least fifteen kilometers inside Germany. The last thought she had before finally drifting off to sleep was that she may never see Jan again.

Anna snapped awake at the sound of footsteps outside the door. As the fog of sleep lifted she heard a key turning in the lock. She sat upright as the door opened, her eyes gradually focusing on a figure in the doorway.

For a few seconds the figure just stood there, then slowly stepped forward and flipped on the light switch.

Anna was momentarily blinded by the bright light and covered her eyes. Her heart pounded.

"I apologize for waking you," Dieter Koenig said. "But I've missed you terribly." He spoke French, his voice just a whisper.

Anna blinked to clear her eyes and tried to speak, but she felt as if she were choking.

Koenig turned away for a second, closed the heavy wooden door and locked it, slipping the key into his pocket. He took off his hat and placed it on the bureau, which stood against the wall opposite the bed. "I trust you are well? Otto has taken good care of you in my absence?"

His words made her stomach churn. She glanced quickly to her left, to the door of the washroom. Could she make it? She didn't think so. He stepped closer to the bed. Anna jumped off the other side, pulling a blanket around herself. "Get out of here," she snapped, backing into the corner.

"Now, now, *ma chérie*, that's no way to treat a soldier returning to his home."

Anna watched with loathing as he unbuckled his black belt with the holster and handgun and placed it on the top of the bureau.

He smiled, unbuttoning his black tunic. "We both know what's going to happen here," he said, as he hung the tunic on the bedpost. "If you're smart, you'll make the best of it. After all, you really have no choice." He moved around the foot of the bed, trapping her in the corner, and stepped closer.

"Get away! Don't touch me!" Anna spat out the words and grabbed the lamp from the night table, jerking the electrical cord from the socket, holding the heavy brass base like a club.

Koenig was on her in an instant. He ripped the lamp out of her hands and smashed it against the wall.

Anna pushed him away and crawled over the bed, but her feet became tangled in the blanket.

Koenig ripped the blanket away and lunged at her.

Anna rolled off the bed and landed heavily on the wooden floor. She got to her feet and started for the washroom, but Koenig was too fast. He scrambled over the bed and grabbed her by the hair.

He spun her around and slapped her across the face.

Anna screamed, clawing his cheek, frantically trying to grab the lamp from the other night stand.

"You fucking bitch! *Ich werde Sie Töten!* I'll kill you!" Koenig bellowed in guttural German as he grabbed her by the throat and shoved her backward against the wall.

She tried to knee him in the groin, but he slapped her again, harder, and pushed her to the floor. Anna scratched at his eyes but he was wild with rage and punched her in the stomach.

She heaved in a sudden spasm, gasping for breath.

Koenig pinned her to the floor with one hand around her neck, kneeling on top of her. With his other hand he grabbed the neckline of her nightgown and ripped it open, exposing her bare body to the waist. He stared at her breasts, then began to unbutton his fly. She squirmed beneath him and spat in his face.

"*Verdammt!*" he screamed, and grabbed her by the hair, banging her head against the floor.

Anna's sight shattered into a thousand bright lights as a paralyzing pain sliced through her skull. Then she slipped into a dull blackness.

Anna flinched as a coarse hand groped between her thighs. She blinked. Koenig was glaring down at her, forcing her legs apart with his knees. She struggled to hit him, but her hands were tied together above her head, secured to the heavy wooden leg at the head of the bed. She was naked, the rest of her nightgown lying in a shredded heap on the floor next to her. *Christ, had she passed out?*

Koenig's face came closer, his coarse hand now fondling her breasts. His forehead pressed against hers, intensifying the pain. "Now, you're mine," he whispered. His breath was hot. His saliva dripped on her face.

"Please," Anna begged. "Please! Don't!" She felt the prick of a sharp blade against her neck.

"If you resist, I'll slit your throat," he hissed, lowering himself into position, his weight pressing her against the hard wooden floor.

She squirmed again and cried, "*Non! Non! Attends! Halte—*"

The blade moved, cutting into her neck with a burning sting. "Be still!"

She threw her head back and bit her lower lip, convulsing with agony as he plunged into her.

He thrust again . . . and again, grunting each time, "You're mine! You're mine!"

When he finished, Koenig stood over her, pulling up his trousers. Anna lay on her back, pain coursing through her groin, her arms numb from the tight cord knotted around her wrists. Her stomach heaved and she swallowed, forcing down the bile in her throat. She wanted to curl into a ball, but she was terrified to move, praying he wouldn't touch her again.

Then, through the throbbing pain in her head, she heard a thumping sound.

She heard it again, a loud thump. The floor seemed to vibrate. She heard a voice, deep and raspy. At first it seemed far away, then it became louder, more distinct.

Koenig mumbled as he buckled his belt, "Fucking moron, I'll kill him."

Suddenly, a thunderous crash shook the room.

Koenig jerked his head toward the door. An instant later, two enormous hands grabbed him by the neck and flung him across the room.

Anna rolled on her side and pulled up her knees, the cord digging into her wrists.

Before Koenig could regain his feet, Otto jerked him upright and smashed a mammoth fist into the SS officer's face, knocking him backward against the bureau like a stuffed doll.

Koenig's face was a mass of blood. He clutched the top of the bureau to keep from falling.

Otto lunged forward and kicked him in the chest.

Anna heard the cracking sound of breaking ribs, as Otto kicked him again. Koenig crumpled to the floor.

The big man stepped back to the bed and knelt beside Anna. Instinctively, she turned away, but Otto picked up the knife and cut the cord binding her hands. He scooped her up as easily as if she were a small child and lay her on the bed. He glanced around, found the blanket, and gently covered her.

"I'll get some water," he said and turned toward the washroom.

The gunshot was so jarring that Anna couldn't comprehend what had happened until she saw Otto slumping against the washroom door, clutching his chest.

She sat up and stared in horror at Koenig, leaning against the bureau, holding his gun with both hands.

Blood streamed down Koenig's smashed face, and his hands shook as he pointed the gun at Anna. She rolled to her left just as he fired.

As Anna toppled off the bed, Otto stepped over her and staggered across the room.

Koenig swung around, trying to get off another shot, but the big man was on top of him.

Otto ripped the gun from the SS officer's hand and bashed it into his skull with a sickening thud. He hit Koenig a second time, then a third. Koenig sagged forward and collapsed.

Anna jumped to her feet and grabbed Otto as the big man stumbled backward. With every ounce of strength she could muster, she steered the wounded man to the bed.

Groaning in pain, Otto laid back while Anna lifted his feet onto the bed. She quickly wrapped herself in the blanket and stepped over to Koenig's body. She held her fingers to his throat to make certain the bastard was dead, then ran to the washroom and returned with a pan of water and towels.

Otto stared at the ceiling, his eyes glazed, his face wet with perspiration.

Anna picked up the knife and gently cut away his blood-soaked undershirt.

The wound was high on the left side of his massive chest, halfway between the collarbone and the shoulder. As Otto moaned in pain, Anna reached behind his back and felt around, her fingers finally touching an exit wound. The bullet had gone right through his body, and Anna knew enough to realize that was better than having it lodged inside.

But he was losing a lot of blood. Using the knife, she ripped the bed sheets and pillowcases into strips for bandages. When she finished, Anna leaned over and whispered in the big man's ear, "Otto?"

No response.

"Otto?"

He mumbled and opened his eyes.

Anna could see that he was struggling to focus. "Otto, listen to me. I've got to roll you on your side, but you've got to help me. Do you understand?"

He closed his eyes and she slapped him on the cheek. "Otto, stay with me. Do you understand? You've got to help me."

Otto opened his eyes and nodded. With a painful grunt he rolled onto his side.

Chapter 69

JAN WAS DUMBFOUNDED as he stood on the sidewalk, staring at the Leffards' burned-out house. Ever since that day in July when he climbed aboard the Dakota and flew out of Poland, his one hope of finding Anna had been here.

Jan was certain that it was to this house on the Cogels-Osylei, the home of her dearest friends and surrogate parents, that Anna would come if she had gotten out of Poland. He stared at the boarded-up windows and charred door, and felt nauseated.

An hour later, pushing his way through the raucous, celebrating crowd that filled the Grote Markt, Jan spotted Sam sitting at a small table outside the café Den Engle. As he approached the table, the tall silver-haired man stood up to greet him. He gripped Jan's hand in both of his own. "*Bonjour*, Colonel. It's good to see you again. Thank God you're safe."

Jan managed a smile and they sat down.

"Would you like a beer?" Sam asked, pointing to his own half-full glass. "It's still of very poor quality but, today, it tastes much better."

"*Oui*, that would be fine," Jan said.

When the waiter brought the beer, Sam raised his glass. "It's a great day for Belgium . . . and a great day for freedom."

Jan smiled at his new friend and raised his glass. Somehow, after everything he'd been through the last few years, it no longer seemed odd to feel a kinship with someone whose name he didn't even know. He wondered if Sam was married, if he had children, and what he had done for a living—before the war took all that away.

They sat in silence for several minutes.

Then Sam leaned across the table. "You look as though something's troubling you. Is anything wrong? I heard the mission went very well."

Jan studied the tall, urbane man sitting across the table.

"You can trust me, Colonel," Sam persisted.

Jan nodded slowly. It had been a long time since he'd had a friend he could trust, perhaps not since Stefan was killed. But he had already trusted Sam with his life. His only hope of finding Anna had been dashed, and he needed help. He had to take a chance. "I took some time this afternoon to visit a friend of my wife's family."

"Your wife has friends here in Antwerp?"

"*Oui*, they have a home on the Cogels-Osylei."

Sam set his glass down. "What is their name?"

"Leffard," Jan said, "Rene and Mimi Leffard. But when I went to their home, I found . . ."

Sam's face went pale. He leaned across the table, staring at Jan. "That it was burned out and vacant?"

Jan sat back, stunned. "*Oui* . . . but . . . do you know them?"

"*Oui, oui, bien sûr.* I know . . . knew . . . them." Sam rubbed his forehead, silent for a moment. Then his eyes widened. "*Mon dieu!* I should have guessed it from your accent—you're Polish. Is it possible? Are you Jan Kopernik?"

Jan stared at him, speechless.

"Rene and Mimi Leffard were my closest friends," Sam continued, his eyes moist. "And yes . . . your wife, Anna, and the boy, Justyn, were here in Antwerp, living with the Leffards. I met them both, many times."

Jan struggled to breathe. What were the chances . . . ? Then the image of the Leffards' burned-out house came back. He forced the words out. "What happened?"

Sam closed his eyes for a moment and took a breath. "The Leffards were arrested by the Gestapo."

Jan flinched; his throat tightened.

Sam reached across the table and gripped his arm. "*Non, non,* I'm sorry. Anna wasn't with them, neither was Justyn."

Jan shook his head. "I don't . . ."

Sam continued quickly, "Please, forgive me. Let me start at the beginning."

Jan sat spellbound as Sam told him of how Anna and Justyn came to

Belgium, of Irene's death, and of the chalet in the Ardennes, of van Acker and the Marchals. He told him about Leffard's connection with the White Brigade and Anna's involvement in the Comet Line. He paused several times to collect himself then finally stopped, took a deep breath and stared off into the distance. He was silent for a moment as if trying to summon the strength to continue. In a halting voice he told Jan about how they had been betrayed . . . how it had cost the lives of van Acker, the Marchals . . . and the Leffards.

"Thank God, Justyn escaped," Sam said, wiping away a tear. "He somehow managed to get to Antwerp. He's safe now, living with a trusted friend . . . a man named Auguste, in Merksem."

Jan's hands trembled and perspiration trickled down his neck. He whispered, "Anna?"

"She was gone . . . on a mission for the Comet Line."

The two men stared at each other for a long time.

Jan looked down at the table. "And, you haven't heard from her."

"*Non*. But that doesn't mean that—"

"I know what it means," Jan snapped. He stood abruptly, the metal chair falling over, clattering on the cobblestones. He turned and walked away.

Jan stood in the middle of the square, staring blankly at a large medieval statue of a warrior throwing a hand. He thought of the small cut-glass hand that had been Anna's. Was this it? he wondered . . . the symbol of Antwerp?

He ran his hand through his hair and looked around. People were drinking and dancing, laughing and waving flags. But he could barely hear them; it was as though he were deaf. This can't be happening, he thought. Not now . . . not when they were so close.

Think, he told himself. Think, be positive. Anna had made it this far. She was tough and resourceful. He had to have faith, to focus on one thing at a time. She hadn't been arrested with the Leffards, so she was out there . . . somewhere.

Sam joined him. After a moment he said, "Your wife meant a great deal to the Leffards. She and Justyn were like family to them." He paused and their eyes met, Sam's filled with the hard look of determination Jan had seen that night at the Kattendijkdok. "There was nothing I could do to help Rene and Mimi, but I promise you I will do everything in my power to help you find Anna."

Jan swallowed hard and gripped the silver-haired man's shoulder.

"I have to go to a briefing now," Sam said. "Will you meet me at the Café Brig for dinner . . . six o'clock?"

Jan nodded. "There's just one more thing I'd like to know. What's your name?"

Sam smiled and held out his hand. "It's Willy. Willy Boeynants."

The Café Brig was a noisy, rowdy place when Jan arrived. The celebrating crowd had spilled onto the street where dozens of hardy men hoisted beer glasses in the air, shouting and singing Flemish songs. Inside it was the same. A boisterous throng of tough-looking men that Jan guessed were mostly dock-workers, and a smattering of equally tough-looking women.

He pushed his way to the bar, managed to get a beer and found a small table in the back of the room. The beer was watery, but he hardly noticed as he sat there, staring vacantly at the jubilant patrons, still trying to process the mind-numbing news.

The tragic chronology of events marched through his mind again, and he became overwhelmed with frustration. He and Anna had come so far, they had been so close . . . and now this. The staggering revelation was like a heavy weight descending on him. Anna had actually made it here, to Antwerp, and now she was . . . missing? Had she been arrested? Injured? Was she in jail somewhere in France? Or had she been sent to . . . ?

Jan took a hard swallow of his beer and almost choked. He thought about Irene, dying in a train station in Prague and Justyn, now an orphan. He had been within fifty meters of Justyn just a few days ago and hadn't realized it. Even now, the boy was just a kilometer away but sealed off in Merksem, trapped under the heel of the same German bastards he'd been fighting for five years.

He needed air. He got to his feet and pushed through the crowd. His eyes were blurry and he was dizzy. A woman yelled something as he bumped into her, but he scarcely noticed.

Outside, he stood on the quay staring at the stagnant water in the ancient dock. A string of barges were tied up alongside, laden with coal. The sky had darkened and a light drizzle fell, causing some of the crowd to disperse.

Jan knew that staying in control would take every ounce of the self-discipline his military training had taught him. A rage burned within him, a rage that had been smoldering for five years and was about to boil over. He took a deep breath and looked up at the cloudy sky. The rain felt good.

"Jan!"

He heard his name and turned around. It was Willy Boeynants.

"You're not going to jump in, are you?"

"*Non,*" Jan replied grimly. "Not yet, anyway."

"Let's get some dinner." Boeynants put his hand on Jan's shoulder and led the way back inside.

It turned out there was another, quieter room tucked away in the back of the café. There were only a few tables, and Boeynants obviously had the right connections. A waiter appeared with a bottle of red wine and two glasses then quickly departed.

Boeynants filled both glasses, then glanced around the room making eye contact and subtle acknowledgements with the other patrons.

Jan guessed they were all with the White Brigade.

Boeynants took a sip of his wine, then leaned across the table. He spoke quietly. "About an hour ago, Antoine and I attended a briefing with Colonel Canfield and a few other British and Canadian officers." He paused, making sure he had Jan's full attention. "A brigade has been assembled to attempt a crossing of the Albert Canal into Merksem."

"When?" Jan asked, instantly focused.

"Tonight. They'll shove off at midnight in assault boats."

"Who do I report to?"

"Jan, listen to me . . ."

"Goddamn it, Willy," Jan hissed. "After what you told me this afternoon, you know I've got to go."

"*Oui, oui.* That's why I'm telling you." He took another sip of wine.

Jan sat back and folded his hands in his lap. "I'm sorry. It's just that . . . well, you know. Go ahead, I'm listening."

"You'll report to a Major Duncan. Antoine has advised him of your real identity and what your purpose is in joining the mission. You're to report to him at 2300 hours at the south end of what used to be the Yserbrug."

Jan nodded.

"The objective of the mission is to secure a bridgehead on the Merksem side of the canal and hold it long enough for the engineers to get a Bailey Bridge across."

Jan looked down at the table. The Albert Canal was over fifty meters wide. They'd be paddling across at night—in small boats—for a frontal assault on a secured position. Who the hell thought this one up?

Boeynants said, "Jan, you don't have to go. You could wait . . ."

"I'm going," Jan said. He understood what Boeynants was trying to tell him. This was a high-risk mission and he'd be of no use to Justyn if he got killed.

"I've drawn a map for you," Boeynants said, handing him a small, folded piece of paper. "Auguste's house is on Beukenhofstraat. It's marked on the map."

Chapter 70

IT WAS RAINING HARDER. Jan stood on the wharf along the Albert Canal watching British engineers lower the assault boats into the water. He had heard they could hold twenty men with two machine gunners in the prow. The wind had picked up, and there was a chop on the canal. The boats looked very small.

A White Brigade commander named Johann stood next to Jan, looking through the gloom across the canal. He shook his head and grunted in heavily accented English, "Fuckin' disaster this is going to be." He spat on the ground. "If the goddamn Brits would have listened to us, we could have saved these bridges. Now we're going to attack German machine guns in little boats."

Jan looked at the husky dockworker and nodded in agreement. The wreckage of the dynamited Yserbrug was just fifty meters away.

Johann and twelve other White Brigade soldiers familiar with Merksem were going along as guides for the British troops. Jan thought about the briefing they'd just had. It would be a tall order. The area of Merksem near the canal was heavily industrial, a snarl of narrow streets winding among massive brick buildings, factory yards, fences, and piles of steel and coal. They had no real maps, it was dark and raining, and the enemy was well dug in. If he had any hope of finding Justyn, his first task would be to avoid getting killed in the first hour.

Major Duncan gave the order. The British troopers and White Brigade guides lowered themselves down the quay into the boats and pushed off. There were twenty-six of them, strung out over a half-kilometer.

They were halfway across when a burst of machine-gun fire erupted from the Merksem side of the canal. A boat capsized. Men cursed and screamed, thrashing in the cold water.

Then all hell broke loose.

German machine gunners ripped the water up and down the canal. Boats sunk, men screamed, flailing the water, weighted down by heavy boots and packs.

From the Antwerp side, British artillery crews launched a barrage across the canal.

Jan hunkered down and paddled with every ounce of his strength.

The sergeant in command of the boat yelled, "Open Fire!" and the two submachine gunners in the prow blasted the shoreline.

A soldier on Jan's right grunted and slumped over the side, his head dragging in the water.

Another grunt, from the back of the boat, and a soldier fell forward. The tiny craft rocked wildly, and Jan was certain it would capsize.

"Goddamn it! Stay down!" the sergeant screamed. "Paddle! Harder! We're almost there!"

Clattering machine guns and thumping artillery shells echoed off the water in a deafening, paralyzing crescendo. The night sky blazed with fireworks.

Jan hunched lower and dug his paddle deep in the water, his head pounding.

They jarred to a stop.

"Grappling hooks!" the sergeant yelled.

Two men stood up and tossed heavy ropes with steel hooks onto the quay. The boat rocked and Jan bashed his head on the concrete wall. He felt a thick hand under his arm, and suddenly he was on dry land.

The sergeant screamed, "Get moving!" and they scrambled across the road.

German machine gunners fired up and down the line. Men toppled back into the canal. Jan tripped over a fallen soldier and fell on the cobblestones. He rolled, got to his feet and lurched toward a building.

Suddenly it was quiet. The British cut off the artillery barrage, and the German machine gunners ran out of targets.

Jan looked around. He was huddled with a group of about thirty men. He recognized only a few from his boat. Major Duncan squatted a few meters away, trying to raise someone on the radio.

They were alongside some type of factory. Across the street was a high, chain-link fence. Jan knew from the map Boeynants had drawn that the main road running along the canal was the Vaartkaai. Auguste's home on Beukenhofstraat would be less than a kilometer northeast.

Major Duncan was off the radio and moved to the center of the group. "All right, chaps, listen up. I've made contact with two other units. They're both to the east of us. We're going to move out, single file, hugging the buildings. Right, let's go."

It had been a long time since Jan was part of a battle group where someone else gave the orders. But he put his head down and followed.

Twenty-four hours later it was still raining, and they were pinned down among the maze of factory buildings along the Vaartkaai. The Germans had snipers on top of buildings and hidden in trenches. They had machine gunners positioned at strategic intersections, and panzer units clanked through the narrow streets, picking off British platoons trying to penetrate inland.

Jan looked around at the young British soldiers huddled nearby. They were no different from the Polish soldiers he had commanded at the Bzura River and in the Kampinos Forest. He knew exactly what they were thinking. It was obvious the mission was a failure, and the only thoughts going through the young troopers' minds were whether or not they'd get out alive.

"Colonel?" The voice came from behind him. It was a British corporal. "Major Duncan would like a word with you, sir."

Keeping low, Jan followed the corporal, sloshing through puddles of oily water, along the side of a brick building with shot-out windows. Ahead, Jan spotted a group of officers and the White Brigade commander, Johann, gathered around a radioman.

Major Duncan looked up as Jan approached and stepped over to meet him. He spoke quickly. "We'll be withdrawing back across the canal at 0300. The artillery barrage from the Antwerp side will begin at 0245."

Jan glanced at his watch. Less than an hour.

"We're still trying to round up all of our units," Duncan said, his eyes acknowledging the difficult tactical situation. "Do you know where you're headed, sir?"

"Yes. The street is called Beukenhofstraat. It's northeast of here, on the other side of the Bredabaan. I'm sure I can find my way. I'll stay here until your boats are launched, then—"

"Sir," Duncan interrupted, "if you don't mind, I have a plan to assist you."

"Major, I cannot allow any of your men to be put at risk on my behalf."

"I understand, sir. Please, hear me out."

Jan nodded. "Go ahead."

"One of our PIAT squads managed to cross the Bredabaan. They got tangled up with a panzer unit and disabled one of the bloody bastards. Then they ran out of ammo. In trying to withdraw they've apparently gotten lost. We've made radio contact and it sounds like they're off in the direction you want to go. I'm dispatching Johann to lead a patrol to find them. I suggest you go with them. At least you'll have some firepower for support between here and the Bredabaan."

The Bredabaan was Merksem's main business street, a wide boulevard, lined with retail stores, office buildings and churches. The tramline from Antwerp ran down the center, now littered with idle tramcars. A few autos and trucks, abandoned by their owners when the fighting erupted, were parked helter-skelter in the street. Except for patrolling German tanks and armored cars, the normally teeming thoroughfare was deserted.

Crouched in a dark alcove between two buildings, Jan peeked around the corner, looking left and right. The shelling over the last two days had shattered most of the windows along the street. In the middle of the boulevard was a crater at least ten meters in diameter and a wrecked tramcar lying on its side.

He spotted a large church that Boeynants had identified on his map as Snit Bartholomeus. It was a landmark for him. Beukenhofstraat was three streets to the east. But first he had to get across the Bredabaan.

Jan considered the church. The bell tower provided an ideal location for snipers or machine gunners who would have a clear line of fire up and down the entire length of the street. He checked his watch. It was 0230. The artillery barrage from Antwerp would begin in fifteen minutes. He retreated into the shadows and pulled a metal flask from his pocket that Johann had pressed into his hand as they parted. He unscrewed the lid and took a sip. The Irish whiskey burned all the way down with a welcome warmth.

At exactly 0245 it started. At first dull, thumping noises, like distant fireworks then, seconds later, thunderous explosions that shook the ground, shattering what few windows were left along the Bredabaan.

Jan knew the primary targets were the buildings along the canal and perhaps the first street or two inland. He should be out of range but he had been through enough artillery bombardments to know about stray shells. He crawled to the edge of the alcove, glanced left and right and bolted into the street.

He crossed the first cobblestone lanes and was almost across the tram tracks when machine-gun fire burst from the church tower. Jan veered to the left then to the right. The shells passed over his head. It was dark and raining. He was dressed in black trousers, a black wool sweater and a dark green beret. To the gunner in the tower he was just a fast moving shadow.

He darted behind a truck. The gunner blew out its windshield, and Jan bolted away, sprinting across the other cobblestone lanes. He dashed into a side street as the machine gun ripped up the sidewalk behind him.

Catching his breath, Jan spotted the metal plaque on the corner of the building bearing the street name. He could just barely make it out in the gloom: *Frans de l'Arbrelaan.* He had memorized Boeynants's map. Beukenhofstraat was two streets away.

Unteroffizier Karl Dietrich ground out his cigarette in the muddy trench and shuddered at the concussion of the shelling. He guessed the Brits were trying to retreat back across the canal. This salvo was landing to the south, along the canal, but it still shook the ground and broke windows along Beukenhofstraat.

Dietrich figured he was secure for the time being. He and Bucholz had dug the trench the night before and concealed it so well that a passerby on the street wouldn't even know it was there. Although he had a clear view for the entire length of Beukenhofstraat and Frans de l'Arbrelaan, he hadn't seen a soul since they arrived.

Until now.

The movement startled him. In front of the row houses, fifty meters up Beukenhofstraat, a shadowy figure was darting away from him. Dietrich couldn't imagine how the son-of-a bitch had gotten past him.

He nudged Bucholz, but the lazy bastard didn't move. How he could sleep through the shelling was a mystery. Dietrich peered over the top of the trench and stared into the gloom.

He spotted the figure again, crouched low, moving in spurts.

Dietrich wiped the raindrops off the telescopic sight of the Mauser K98 sniper rifle. It didn't help a lot in the dark—but he could see well enough.

The figure appeared to be dressed in black, wearing what looked like a beret. Dietrich wiped his eyes and peered through the sight again. A tree was in the way. He waited, breathing slowly, grinding his right foot into the mud.

The shelling was slacking off.

The figure moved again and disappeared into a shadow.

Dietrich cursed under his breath but kept watching. His finger caressed the trigger.

The figure emerged from the shadow and took a few steps then paused, looking around.

Dietrich had a clear view. He squeezed the trigger.

The gun recoiled, the shot reverberating like a thunderbolt off the brick walls of the homes lining the street.

The figure spun around and stumbled backward . . . then slumped to the ground.

Chapter 71

AUGUSTE, ELISE AND JUSTYN hunkered down in the cellar the night the shelling started as rumors spread through the connecting tunnels that British troops had crossed the canal. All the next day they heard sporadic gunfire then, late on the second night, the shelling started again. It lasted about an hour and, just as it was slacking off, they were jarred by the unmistakable *crack* of a high-powered rifle very nearby.

At noon the following day, Justyn was helping Auguste to the table for their daily portion of weak soup and stale bread when he heard a shuffling sound. The curtain covering the passageway to the adjoining house parted, and Leo van Ginderen stepped into the dimly lit cellar with a neighbor from down the street. His name was Jo Philips. He looked pale and unsteady.

Elise set the pot of soup on the table and went to him. "Jo, what is it. What's happened?"

"Last night . . . the gunshot . . . did you hear it?"

"*Ja, ja natuurlijk,*" she said. "Come and sit."

He went on as though he hadn't heard her. "The shot was so close, so loud. I looked out the window. I saw him lying there . . . right in front of our door."

"What?" Auguste exclaimed. "A man was shot in front of your door?"

Jo Philips nodded, his hands shook and he clasped them together.

Justyn's eyes darted around. He was concentrating hard to follow the conversation in Flemish.

Philips continued. "I opened the door and dragged him inside," he said. "I don't know why . . . I just did. He was bleeding . . . there was blood everywhere." He continued on, talking rapidly, hardly looking at them. "I sent my son to Leo and they fetched a doctor. The man was unconscious when the doctor arrived . . . he cleaned the wound . . . said the bullet passed right through . . . told us to watch him . . . to call if a fever . . ."

Philips stopped and stared at the floor. No one said anything for a moment then Philips said, "He had no identification card on him. He's a big man, broad shoulders, blond . . . my wife said he looks like a German and we should put him back in the street."

Elise gripped a chair and sat heavily. "*Mijn God*, a German?"

Philips shook his head. "No, I don't think so. He was awake this morning, for a short time but he's drifted off again." Philips took a breath. "The man was able to speak . . . only a few words in French. Fortunately, my daughter was there and she understood." Philips turned to Auguste. "He asked for you."

Auguste stared at him. "What?"

Philips swallowed hard then turned to Justyn. "He asked for you as well."

Elise gasped and covered her face with her hands. "The Gestapo."

They all started to talk at once, but van Ginderen held up his hand. "Wait, there's more. Tell them, Jo."

They fell silent.

"The man asked for his shoes," Philips said. "He was very weak; we could hardly hear him. My daughter bent down close. He told her to look in his shoe. There was something there, wrapped in a piece of brown paper."

"What was it?" Auguste blurted out.

"It was this." Philips removed a small item from his shirt pocket and held it out. It was wrapped in paper. "He said to give it to Justyn."

They watched in surprise as Justyn took the thin packet. He held it for a long time then slowly unwrapped it with trembling hands. The brown paper fell on the table, and Justyn stared at the item lying in his palm.

"Justyn, what is it?" Elise whispered. "Do you recognize it?"

Justyn's throat was dry. He tried to speak but couldn't. He laid the item on the table. It was a tattered red and white fabric patch.

Auguste put a hand on Justyn's shoulder. "What is this? Have you seen it before?"

Justyn's eyes filled with tears. He coughed and took a breath, trying to compose himself. "It's the . . . insignia . . . of the Wielkopolska Cavalry Brigade."

They all stared at him. He knew they didn't understand.

"You said he's a big man," Justyn said to Philips, "with broad shoulders . . . and blond hair."

"Yes, yes, that's what I said."

Justyn looked at Auguste and Elise through blurry eyes. "It's Jan. It's Anna's husband . . . Jan."

Chapter 72

A WEEK HAD PASSED since Anna buried Koenig's body in the woods, and she was desperate to leave. During the last few days she heard intermittent rumbles like distant thunder from an approaching storm. She knew it wasn't thunder; but a storm was approaching—a storm of Allied troops descending on Germany.

Every day she stayed in the isolated house Anna felt more vulnerable. German aircraft flew over the area several times a day, and the growl of heavy vehicles moving along the nearby roads drifted in when the wind was right. She was certain that a German patrol would show up at the house at any moment.

She stood on the front porch, clutching a cup of tea, and heard Otto shuffling through the parlor. She went inside to help him. He had been getting a little stronger each day and could walk from room to room for ten or fifteen minutes at a time before he would have to sit and rest. As she entered the house, he motioned for her to hold the door open.

"I'd like to go outside and get some fresh air," he said.

Anna thought his color was better today, and he wasn't wincing in pain quite so often.

Otto stepped out on the porch and leaned against the railing, breathing heavily. He cocked his head to one side and listened to the muted, thunder-like reports.

"How far away is it?" Anna asked.

"Quite a ways, still west of Aachen, for sure." He turned to face her, a twinge of pain in his eyes. "We should get going. We'll leave first thing in the morning."

Anna was surprised. "Are you sure you're up to it?"

"*Ja.* I'm sure that I'm strong enough to drive a car. Hopefully that's all I need to do. Have you found your passport?"

"*Nein.* That's a problem, isn't it?"

"Perhaps, perhaps not. I'm still a Feldgendarme, and until someone figures out what happened we should be able to bluff our way through."

The thought made her nauseated. "Bluff our way through where?"

"Aachen. If we can get to Aachen . . ."

"What? Go into a German city with no identification?"

Otto laid a big hand on her wrist. "Trust me, it's the safest way. It's a big city, and we'll be less conspicuous than if we try to approach the border out in the countryside." He glanced into the sky as they both heard another low rumbling. "But we can't delay any longer."

They were up early the next morning. Anna had hardly slept all night, but she was wide-awake with anticipation. She prepared a hearty breakfast, realizing there was no telling when they might see another meal. Afterward Anna carried a basket of fruit and bread out to Koenig's Mercedes. She helped Otto into his uniform, and he lumbered off to the car, squeezing behind the wheel.

Anna went back into the house for one last look around, making sure she had removed any traces of their presence. She walked through the kitchen and took one last look in the bedroom. It was fortunate that she did. Koenig's handgun was still on the bureau. She had wanted to bury it in the woods with the other things, but Otto insisted on taking it along. She put it in the small bag she was carrying then walked to the front of the house, desperate to leave the memory of Dieter Koenig behind.

She opened the front door and froze. A car was coming up the driveway. She backed away from the door and peered out the front window.

The car stopped and two SS officers got out. She recognized the one who had been driving. It was Mueller.

Anna pressed her back against the wall, closed her eyes for a few seconds to compose herself, then peeked out the window again.

Mueller approached Koenig's car. The front door of the house was still open, and she could hear what was being said.

"*Guten Morgen,* Otto. Are you going somewhere?"

"Hauptsturmfuhrer Koenig asked me to drive him to Aachen this morning."

"Aachen? He disappears for a week and now he's going to Aachen, when he's overdue to report back to Berlin?"

"I don't know, sir. I just do what I'm told," Otto said.

"*Ja,* I'm sure you do . . . like the good cretin that you are." Mueller turned to the other officer. "Koenig's been so busy fucking his brains out for the last week that he can't remember his own orders. Let's go see if he's left anything for us."

Otto opened the car door. "I'm not sure that's a good idea, sir." His voice was strained.

"Why not? He hasn't killed her yet, has he?"

"*Nein,* it's just that . . . he might be . . . you know . . . busy."

Mueller waved him off and headed for the house, motioning for his partner to follow. "All the better," he said, laughing. "She'll be all warmed up for us."

Otto struggled to get out of the car. With his right hand, he fumbled to extract his gun from the holster. The pain was wrenching, and he was only about halfway out when a thunderous gunshot roared from the house.

Ignoring the pain, Otto pulled himself out of the car.

Mueller was on the porch. He staggered backward and spun around, clutching a gaping hole in his chest. He collapsed into the other SS officer, and they both fell down the porch steps landing with a thud on the gravel.

The other officer pushed Mueller's body away and scrambled to his knees, reaching for his gun.

Otto looked up and saw Anna standing in the doorway, holding Koenig's gun in both hands, smoke wafting from the barrel.

She pointed the gun at the other officer and fired, striking him in the thigh.

The officer screamed and rolled on his side, still trying to jerk his gun from the holster.

Otto pulled out his gun and started toward the fallen SS officer, but Anna ran down the steps and fired again at point-blank range.

Chapter 73

As THE BATTLE for the port wore on, Justyn felt the noose tightening around the neck of Merksem. Every night he listened to the reports of neighbors on Beukenhofstraat as they snuck back and forth through the tunnels. Wehrmacht soldiers patrolled the streets enforcing marshal law. Residents were restricted to their homes. Schools and businesses were closed, bakeries and butcher shops shut down. People became desperate, and rumors spread about a flour mill and warehouse near the canal stocked with food for German troops. Night raids were attempted, and the streets were littered with corpses.

Through all of this, Justyn rarely left Jan's bedside. He changed his bandages and wiped perspiration from his face with damp cloths. But mostly he just sat by the bed and looked at him, thinking, recalling those days in Krakow, kicking a ball in the park. Jan didn't seem as big as Justyn remembered, and he looked older, his face pinched. Justyn twisted one of the cloths in his hands and thought about the last time he had seen Jan—and his father. They were in uniform, at the train station. His father had run a hand through Justyn's black curly hair and kissed him on the forehead, whipering to him to be brave, that he'd be back soon. Now Jan was here . . . but his father wasn't.

On the third day of their reunion, Jan's fever broke and he became more lucid. Justyn brought him tea and thin soup made from the few remaining vegetables. Jan was able to lift his head and talk, though his voice was hoarse and he was weak from loss of blood.

"Justyn, I want to tell you . . . about . . . your father," he whispered.

Justyn stiffened. He clenched his fists.

"He was very brave, Justyn."

The image at the train station came back, and Justyn felt his father's hand running through his hair. He remembered the feel of his father's hand on his shoulder on his first day of school. He slumped into a chair. "How did . . . ?" He swallowed and wiped his eyes. He didn't want to cry.

"An air raid . . . in the Kampinos Forest. Your father was leading a squadron. We never saw the planes."

Jan reached out.

Justyn took his hand. "My mother . . ."

"I know, Justyn." Jan's grip tightened. "Anna and I are your family now."

Justyn's eyes fell to the floor. "Anna's gone . . . she's . . ."

"We'll find her, Justyn. We'll never stop looking until we find her."

Justyn looked at the man lying in the bed, so familiar, yet it had been so long. So much had happened. Jan's eyes closed and he drifted off, but Justyn sat for a long time, holding his hand.

Chapter 74

CAPTAIN PETER DALEY was ready for a fight. Like everyone else in the Ninth Infantry Division of the American First Army, he wanted to get this mess over with and get back home.

They had been chasing the retreating Germans through Belgium since the beginning of September, crossing the Meuse River near Liege, and were now somewhere in the middle of an area where Belgium, Holland and Germany all came together. Their objective was the German border city of Aachen.

They had just passed through a Belgian town called Eupen and entered a densely forested area, when Daley received a message from Major Andersen. They were stopping to wait for artillery units.

Two hours later, Daley was summoned by Major Andersen.

The major and one of the scouts had a map spread out on the hood of a Jeep.

As Daley approached, Andersen called him over and pointed to their location on the map. "This is the road we're on now," he said. Then his finger traced a thin, barely legible line that intersected the road and headed northeast. "The scouts have just found another road, about a kilometer ahead. It could be a shortcut into Aachen." Major Andersen looked at Daley. "I want you to lead a patrol four or five kilometers up this road and make sure it's secure."

It was exactly the type of assignment Daley hated. Going off with a few Jeeps and a half-track in unknown territory wasn't his idea of excitement. Doing it just a few kilometers from the German border was nuts.

They set off a half hour later. The dirt road was narrow and bumpy with thick pine forests on either side. Four scouts were on foot a kilometer ahead to give them advance warning if anything came down the road. Sitting in the lead

Jeep, with the machine gunner standing behind him, bouncing along at less than ten kilometers per hour, Daley did not find that very comforting.

Anna's heart was in her throat as they approached the guardhouse at the German-Belgian border in Aachen. It was different from the checkpoint she had passed through going into Germany. There was no tunnel and the terrain on either side was flat. The concrete bunkers, anti-tank ditches and fencing came right up to the side of the road. Wehrmacht soldiers were everywhere. She was certain they were all looking for her.

She closed her eyes to shut it out, but then the vision of Mueller and the other SS officer lying in the gravel came back. They hadn't taken the time to bury the bodies, just dragged them into the barn, closed the door and drove off.

Anna had never fired a gun before, never even held one in her hand. But she felt nothing. Not regret, not sorrow, not elation. She didn't feel anything. She was numb.

The city of Aachen was busy, the streets clogged with soldiers, tanks and trucks. Windows were boarded up, and civilians carrying trunks and suitcases trudged out of the central city. It reminded her of Poland in 1939.

During the drive, she and Otto had discussed what name she should use in the event they were stopped or if she eventually met up with Allied soldiers. They finally agreed that sticking with "Jeanne Laurent" was best. If Anna made it to Belgium she would want to identify herself as a Belgian woman rather than Polish since she needed to stay in Belgium. If she was arrested in Germany, she was in trouble no matter what.

They sat behind a truck at the barricade. A Wehrmacht soldier talked with the driver and checked his papers. Off in the distance, Anna heard the thumping sounds of artillery fire.

They were the only other vehicle heading west, into Belgium. Heading east, into Germany, was a stream of military vehicles at least a kilometer long. Trucks laden with Wehrmacht troops, automobiles carrying officers, armored cars and flatbeds loaded with artillery pieces, all retreating behind the West Wall for the final struggle to save the Fatherland.

The truck moved off, and Otto pulled up to the barricade. Anna stared straight ahead, praying she wouldn't have to say anything. Just a few hours ago she had murdered two SS officers . . . and now she was sitting at a German checkpoint with no papers. How could she have been so stupid?

Otto rolled down the window and handed his identification to the Wehrmacht officer who peered into the car. He gave it a cursory glance and handed it back.

"And your companion's?" the officer asked.

"She would rather not show her identification," Otto replied.

The remark caught the officer by surprise, and it took him a few seconds to respond. *"Nein,* that's not possible. I must see her identification."

The noise from the artillery shelling and the trucks passing through the other side of the checkpoint made it difficult to hear. Otto motioned for the officer to lean toward the window so he could speak without shouting. "I am a special aide to SS Hauptsturmfuhrer Dieter Koenig, and this lady is his mistress."

The officer leaned in but didn't respond. Anna could feel his eyes looking her over.

"The hauptsturmfuhrer has entrusted me to escort her safely out of the country," Otto continued, his deep voice as calm as if he were ordering lunch. "He would prefer that she not have to produce her identification. *Verstehen Sie?"*

Anna glanced at the officer with a quick smile then stared straight ahead. She wore one of the slinky dresses, her hair was made up, her cheeks red with rouge and her lips glossy with lipstick. She felt like a whore . . . Koenig's whore. If they didn't move on quickly she was certain she'd vomit.

The officer cleared his throat. "This is highly irregular . . . I'm not sure . . ."

Otto leaned out the window. *"Was ist Ihr Name?* I will pass it along to the hauptsturmfuhrer. I'm certain he will be grateful for your discretion."

The young officer hesitated. He glanced around then leaned in and said, "Herzog . . . Leutnant Karl Herzog." He stared at Anna for a moment then stood erect and saluted. "Tell the hauptsturmfuhrer I am pleased to be of service." He waved to the gatekeeper to raise the barricade.

Otto rolled up the window and accelerated away from the checkpoint.

They drove for several kilometers before Otto pulled over to the side of the road and stopped. There were still German military vehicles heading in the opposite direction, but they were farther apart now. Otto stared straight ahead, breathing deeply, sweat dripping from his forehead.

Anna closed her eyes and pressed her hands to her forehead. Her temples were throbbing. "A brilliant performance," she whispered, "although I could hardly breathe."

"Fortunately he was young—and they were busy."

"Now what?"

Otto produced a map and unfolded it. "Koenig had this. I took some time to study it last night. We should come to a crossroad in another kilometer or so that heads to the southwest." He pointed it out to her. "It doesn't look like much on the map, probably a dirt road, but it cuts through a wooded area and leads to a town called Eupen. You should be able to find help there. I'll take you that far. Hopefully we won't encounter troops from either side."

Anna touched the big man's arm. "What will you do, Otto?"

"I'll return to Germany."

Anna expected that might be his answer. The prospect sickened her. "But you've been involved in the murders of three SS officers. You can't just go back."

"*Nein*, I can't go back as a Feldgendarme, or a soldier of any kind. I'd either be shot for desertion or tried for murder."

"Then what . . . ?"

"Once I get back across the border I'll continue on into the interior of the country. Germany is doomed, Anna. Russia is attacking from the east and the Americans and British from the west. *Der Führer* will demand a fight to the finish, but it can't last much longer. Germany will be in chaos. I'll just find a way to blend into the population. It's the best chance I have."

"Why not surrender to the Americans or the British, whomever we meet first? I'll vouch for you, Otto. I'll tell them how you've saved my life."

"I know you would, Anna. And I'm grateful, but it would never work."

"Yes, it could. Otto, please—"

"Anna, listen," he interrupted, shaking his head. "Sooner or later, the Allied armies will discover Auschwitz—and the other camps. The world will be outraged." He gripped the steering wheel and took a deep breath. "Believe me, Anna, I was there; I saw what happened. We Germans keep very good records, especially the SS. The Allies will find out I was there. My only chance is to melt back into Germany and hope for the best."

Anna stared at him through her tears. The man had saved her life. He was still putting himself at risk on her behalf. Yet, his own prospects were bleak. She knew he was right, and there was nothing she could do about it.

Otto put the map away and they continued on in silence. A kilometer farther on they came to the crossroads and, darting between two eastbound trucks, Otto turned down the narrow dirt road.

The radio operator sitting in the backseat of the Jeep tapped Daley on the shoulder and handed him the headset. Daley took it and put his hand up to halt the patrol.

It was one of the scouts. "A car is approaching from the east, sir."

"A car? Only one?" Daley questioned.

"Yes, sir. It appears to be alone. It just passed our position. We heard it coming and got off the road in time. I'm sure they didn't spot us. The driver is wearing a German uniform. It should be approaching you in just a few minutes."

"Understood. Two of you get on the road and head back this way to block them if they turn around. Leave the other two there to cover your backside."

"Roger, that. Out."

Daley waved for his lieutenant to come up alongside the Jeep. "A car is approaching. Get your men out of the half-track and into the ditch on each side of the road."

The soldiers scrambled out of the half-track and took up positions on either side of the narrow road. The machine gunner in the Jeep readied his weapon, and they waited.

Two minutes later the car appeared. The driver slammed on the brakes.

Daley heard the gears grind as the driver threw the gearshift into reverse and started backing up.

"Fire!" he yelled.

The machine gunner fired off a burst that ripped through the car's radiator and front tires.

The car careened to the left and skidded to a stop. The infantrymen charged forward with their weapons pointed and ordered the passengers out.

Daley was surprised to see a very attractive redheaded woman emerge from the passenger side of the car.

Major Andersen took Captain Daley by the arm, and they walked off by themselves to discuss the fate of their unusual prisoners. For the last half hour, they had been listening to the articulate, strong-willed woman as she pleaded her case for the German Feldgendarme.

Daley was convinced she was telling the truth. If it was up to him, he'd give the big guy a medal and let them both go. But he knew that wasn't going to happen. Andersen was a by-the-book career officer.

"It's all bullshit," Andersen said. "This guy is a German Feldgendarme. The woman has no identification, dressed like a streetwalker. What the hell were they doing out here all by themselves in a fuckin' car? For all we know, they're both German spies."

"She says she's Belgian," Daley said. He knew it was stupid the instant it came out of his mouth.

"Yeah, right. It's bullshit and we don't have time to fuck around with it." Andersen took out a pack of cigarettes and lit one up.

"So, what do we do with them?" Daley asked.

"The only thing we can do. You found 'em so you get to take the big hulk and his girlfriend back to Liege. Tell the MPs they're German spies and let them sort it out from there."

Chapter 75

IN THE FINAL ASSAULT on Merksem, the Second Canadian Division overpowered the German garrison holding the last remaining bridge over the Albert Canal and attacked from the east. The Royal Hamilton Light Infantry Division and the White Brigade attacked from the west, over the Groenendallaan. And from the south, under the cover of an intense artillery barrage, the Fourth Canadian Infantry Brigade managed to get a pontoon bridge across the canal.

By the second day of the battle, the Germans were in a panic and their officers lost control. Trucks overflowing with Wehrmacht troops roared through the streets, maneuvering around bomb craters and abandoned cars, retreating out of the city. German soldiers ran for their lives, stealing bicycles and ransacking homes for food as they fled.

By dawn on the third day it was over. Allied tanks rolled across the Albert Canal and down the Bredabaan, restoring order. The citizens of Merksem emerged from the cellars and poured onto the streets, cheering their liberators.

On the Antwerp side of the canal it was quieter. Having been liberated for more than a month, the euphoria had subsided and people had set to the task of rebuilding their lives. In the early afternoon, Willy Boeynants sat at a table in the Café Brig sipping a beer and reading the newspaper, which had just resumed publication.

On the front page was an article about a mysterious explosion, two days ago, destroying several houses in the community of Brasschaat, eight kilometers northeast of Antwerp. The article went on. Yesterday, another explosion, this one in Antwerp, on Schilderstraat. A dozen people were killed, and an eyewitness reported seeing something "just dropping out of the sky." Boeynants knew what was happening. Jan had told him about his mission to Poland.

The V-2 had arrived.

He tossed the paper aside and took another sip of beer. It was still the same watery, tasteless brew, but he didn't notice. Nor did he concern himself any further with the V-2 attacks. There was nothing that could be done except to end the war, and that was in the hands of others.

Boeynants had other things on his mind. He had spent nearly every hour of the last week trying to find a trace of Anna and had come up empty-handed. Frustrated and disheartened, he glanced at his watch. It was quarter to two. He tossed some coins on the table and left.

Fifteen minutes later, Boeynants sat in a conference room with a dozen other people at the Antwerp City Hall, waiting for a meeting to begin with the British SOE. The British had wanted Antoine to attend, but the White Brigade leader and his forces were with the Second Canadian Division, pursuing the Germans in the Schelde estuary, fifty kilometers north of Antwerp.

At precisely two o'clock a portly, disheveled man entered the room and introduced himself as Colonel Stanley Whitehall. Boeynants was curious. He had never met Whitehall, but he knew that he had been the one who had selected Jan to impersonate Ernst Heinrich. It had also been Whitehall who had selected Jan for the V-2 mission in Poland.

Toward the end of the meeting Whitehall informed the group that a German Gestapo agent had been captured by the British and was being held in Antwerp. The Gestapo agent had decided to cooperate and had given up a significant amount of information having to do with the arrests of Comet Line agents. When Whitehall mentioned the agent's name, Boeynants felt a knot in his stomach. It was Rolf Reinhardt.

After the meeting, Boeynants lingered behind and, when the others had left, he approached Whitehall who was stuffing papers into his briefcase.

"Colonel Whitehall, may I have a word with you?"

The heavyset man peered at Boeynants over the top of his glasses. "Of course," he said, glancing around the empty meeting room. "Please, take a seat, Mr. Boeynants."

"Colonel, do you know a Polish officer by the name of Jan Kopernik?"

Whitehall appeared startled. He didn't respond.

Boeynants went on. "I was the sole contact with Colonel Kopernik while he was impersonating Ernst Heinrich inside the German garrison in Antwerp."

"Yes, I know Colonel Kopernik." Whitehall paused. "Did he . . . ?"

"He survived the mission," Boeynants said.

Whitehall looked relieved.

"He was wounded in a subsequent action in Merksem, but he's recovering."

Whitehall pulled out a handkerchief and wiped his brow. "Pleased to hear that. Good man, he is."

Boeynants nodded. "Yes, he is. Colonel, did you know that his wife, Anna, escaped from Poland and was living here in Belgium?"

"Why no, I had no idea. He told me his wife had been arrested by the SS. That's quite remarkable. How is she?"

"Well, that's the problem. We don't know where she is. She was an agent of the Comet Line, and we believe she was arrested on a mission escorting a British aviator out of the country."

Whitehall's eyes widened. "Where? Do you know?"

"No, we don't," Boeynants said, shaking his head. "But we do know that she was using the code name, 'Jeanne Laurent.' We also know that Rik Trooz was aware of her mission."

"Rik Trooz?" Whitehall sat upright in his chair and leaned forward. "Rik Trooz was SOE's primary contact with the Comet Line. And we know that this animal, Rolf Reinhardt, was involved in his arrest. In fact, we're quite sure that Reinhardt was the one who had him tortured . . . and murdered."

"Yes, I know," Boeynants said. "Our own contacts confirmed that. In fact, Reinhardt has been hunting for me, but that's another story."

Whitehall stared at him.

Boeynants shrugged then asked, "But Reinhardt has said nothing about a redheaded woman using the name Jeanne Laurent?"

"No." Whitehall's eyes narrowed as he looked at Boeynants. "Apparently this chap hasn't told us quite everything he knows. Would you like to pay him a visit?"

When the guard brought Rolf Reinhardt into the interrogation room, Whitehall and Boeynants were seated at a metal table. Boeynants thought he spotted a flicker of recognition in Reinhardt's eyes.

Whitehall motioned for Reinhardt to be seated, and the guard shoved him into a chair, then stood back, in front of the door.

"This is Willy Boeynants," Whitehall said. "I believe you were looking for him a while back."

Reinhardt's face paled, but he didn't respond.

Whitehall stood up and walked around the small room.

Reinhardt stared straight ahead.

"When we last talked, Herr Reinhardt, you assured me that you had told us everything you knew about agents of the Comet Line."

Reinhardt remained silent.

"Tell us about 'Jeanne Laurent,'" Whitehall said, standing directly behind Reinhardt.

"I've told you everything I know," Reinhardt said, in heavily accented English.

Whitehall motioned to the guard, who removed a pistol from his holster and pressed it to the back of Reinhardt's head.

"You'd better move out of the way, Mr. Boeynants," Whitehall said. "I wouldn't want your suit to get stained when Sergeant Anders blows Herr Reinhardt's brains out."

The guard cocked the gun.

Reinhardt began to perspire. His hands twitched.

Whitehall leaned over and said. "Do you think for one moment I would hesitate?"

Reinhardt looked down at the table. "What did you say this person's name was?"

"Jeanne Laurent. An attractive, redheaded woman. Ring any bells?"

Reinhardt nodded. "Now I remember."

The guard removed the gun and backed away.

"Go ahead," Whitehall said, returning to his chair.

Reinhardt looked up. "There's not much to tell. She was arrested in France and held by the SS in a local jail for awhile. I tried to have her sent up to Brussels, but a certain SS officer blocked our attempts."

"Who was this SS officer?" Whitehall asked.

"Hauptsturmfuhrer Dieter Koenig," Reinhardt said. "After the retreat from the Falaise Gap, I tried again to have the woman sent to Brussels, but Koenig refused. I later learned that all of the prisoners in that jail were sent to Drancy."

"Drancy?" Boeynants asked. He felt sick. He had heard rumors about the camp.

Reinhardt looked at him with a smirk. "Yes, Drancy. And from there they were all sent to Auschwitz. She's probably ashes by now."

Boeynants jumped to his feet and smashed his fist into Reinhardt's face.

The next day, Whitehall attended yet another in an endless string of meetings. He looked around the room and sighed; he'd attended too many during his visit to Belgium.

This one was a briefing about German concentration camps. But it was all sketchy, mostly rumors and hearsay. Whitehall had no doubt that places like Auschwitz existed. He believed the Nazis were capable of anything. But until they had actually liberated some of these camps, what good was all this conjecture? He was about to excuse himself when something caught his attention.

A young American officer at the end of the table had just said something about the Comet Line.

"Excuse me, Captain, could you please repeat that," Whitehall asked.

The American looked up from his notes. "Uh, yes, certainly. I was saying that the Feldgendarme keeps telling us that the woman was an agent for the Comet Line."

Whitehall realized he hadn't been paying attention. "I'm dreadfully sorry, but I was thinking about something else. I'm afraid I haven't been following you. I've been involved with the Comet Line for a number of years. What is this about a Feldgendarme and some woman?"

The captain looked annoyed, but he deferred to Whitehall's rank. He read from his notes. "A German Feldgendarme was captured in Belgium a few weeks ago while traveling in a car near the German border. A woman with no identification was traveling with him. Both of them are now in custody in Liege on suspicion of espionage. The Feldgendarme confessed that he had been a guard at Auschwitz during 1943, and he has offered to reveal everything he knows, including the names of the SS officers in charge while he was there."

Whitehall was impressed. This was important information. But he still couldn't understand how the Comet Line fit in. "Has he given us any information yet?"

"That's what I had just started to say, sir. No, he hasn't. He insists that before he tells us anything, we must first release Miss Laurent, or whatever her name is."

Whitehall was stunned. Had he heard that correctly? "Excuse me,

Captain, did you say Laurent? Her name is Laurent?"

The captain shrugged. "Well, that's what she and the Feldgendarme say her name is. Undoubtedly, they're lying. But they both insist that she was an agent for the Comet Line and that she was arrested in France."

Whitehall stood up and leaned over the table. "Is it Jeanne Laurent? Is her first name Jeanne?"

The captain studied his notes. "Yes, that's correct. Jeanne Laurent. Do you know this person, Colonel?"

Chapter 76

THE TRAIN FROM ANTWERP to Liege slogged through one village after another on what seemed like a never-ending journey. Jan stared out the window but saw nothing, mustering every ounce of his strength to keep his emotions under control. Was it possible, after all this time? Had they really found her, or would it turn out to be a cruel mistake, another wrong turn? He doubted he would survive that.

Sitting next to him, Whitehall chattered on about the lack of cooperation from the Americans, the confusion in command between the Allied armies now closing in on Germany. The war, he pointed out, was far from over, a fact Jan was keenly aware of as he shifted in his seat, a jolt of pain shooting through his right arm, bound tightly in a sling.

"Hope she's still there," Whitehall said. "The American captain I talked to kept mumbling about moving prisoners somewhere or other. Bloody hell, it was like talking with a brick."

Jan glanced at the portly colonel then turned back to the window. A convoy of American army trucks, caked in dirt, headed east along the road that ran parallel with the tracks. Infantry troops slogged alongside. Jan sighed at the familiar sight, weary troops moving on to yet another battle. It was indeed far from over. He would be back in it, he knew, but first . . . there was Anna.

The cellar room was damp and cold. A thin shaft of sunlight drifted through the only window, which was too small for even her head to pass through. The glass was long gone, allowing free access to the rodents Anna heard scraping and rooting around in the night. She sat on a bench next to the cot and stared at the tiny window and the angle of the sunlight. It was close to noon, she guessed. Soon the American soldier would pull open the creaking door, exchange the bucket that served as her chamber pot, and place a bowl of soup and a plate of bread on the dirt floor.

Anna looked down at yesterday's soup bowl, overturned with a frustrated kick during her outburst at the soldier who never spoke. "I demand to see the officer in charge!" she had screamed at him. It hadn't been the first of her tirades, and it had produced the same result. Nothing. The taciturn soldier barely glanced at her, set the bowl on the ground and turned to leave. It was only when she kicked the bowl across the room and it clattered against the stone wall, splattering thick lentil soup in every direction, that he reacted. He stopped, looked at the mess, then turned to her and said, "I hope you're not hungry. That's all you get."

She *was* hungry. She was cold and dirty—and beside herself with frustration. They had made it out of Germany. Otto had saved her life. Why wouldn't they listen? What had they done with Otto? Was he in the barbed wire stockade across the road where they were stockpiling German prisoners?

She stood up, ran a hand through her sticky mat of hair and paced the small room to warm up. At least the silent soldier had found a sweater for her to wear over the flimsy dress from Koenig's obscene wardrobe. She tried to think. How long had she been here? She hadn't bothered to keep track. Everywhere else she had kept track: in the jail in the unknown town in France, in the hideous bedroom at Koenig's house, even at Drancy where she had scratched marks on the wall every morning. But here she hadn't kept track. These were Americans. Belgium was liberated. What was she doing in another prison?

The shelling started again, thumping claps of thunder that shook the ground beneath her. It seemed closer than yesterday. Or perhaps it was her imagination. Who was shelling whom, she wondered? What if the Americans had to pull back? Would they leave her?

The door creaked open, and a soldier stepped into the dank room. It was a different soldier, an officer with an armband emblazoned with the letters "MP."

He nodded and waved a hand at her. "Follow me. Someone here to see you."

Anna followed the officer up the stone steps into a room that appeared to be a kitchen. It was the only time she had been out of the cellar, and the light caused her to squint. The MP motioned for her to wait while he stepped into an adjoining room.

Shielding her eyes from the sun, Anna looked out the window at the stockade across the road, hoping to catch a glimpse of Otto. The stockade was nothing more than a farmyard enclosed by wood posts, wire fencing and rolls of barbed wire. American soldiers patrolled the perimeter while, behind the fencing, hundreds of German soldiers milled about, eyes downcast, uniforms filthy and torn. No sign of Otto.

The MP came back and led her into the adjoining room, which appeared to have been a parlor. Now there was just a single table and two or three wooden chairs. A heavyset man stood in front of the table. He nodded as she entered. "Miss Laurent, I am Colonel Stanley Whitehall of the British SOE."

Anna looked at him, wondering if she should know him. She glanced at the other man in the room standing at the far end of the table. He was tall and blond, his right arm bound in a sling. She looked at his face, and their eyes met.

She stared at him, her mind struggling to process what she was seeing.

He stepped forward. "Anna?"

She stumbled back, grasping for the wall.

"Anna . . . it's me."

The room seemed to move, closing in around her. She was still staring at him when her knees gave out and she slid to the floor.

They sat at the table in silence. Anna gripped the glass with both hands and took another sip of water. She set it down carefully, picked up the damp cloth and wiped her forehead. Clutching the borrowed sweater around her shoulders, she flinched as she felt his hand on her arm. His hand fell away, and she turned to look at him.

He was thinner. His blond hair was flecked with gray. There were lines around his eyes she didn't remember. She looked at his arm bound in the sling. "Is it . . ." her voice faltered, " . . . broken?"

He shook his head. "I was shot. It's healing."

She nodded and looked away. "How did you . . . I don't . . . ?" It wouldn't come. Her mind was submerged in a fog, as though she had been suddenly transported to another place, another time.

Whitehall cleared his throat. "Perhaps it would be best if I began. Would that be all right, Anna?"

Anna took a breath and looked back at Jan, their eyes meeting, searching. "Yes," she whispered.

"Very well," Whitehall said, "I have just a few questions. We understand you were on a mission for the Comet Line using the name 'Jeanne Laurent.' Is that correct?"

Anna nodded.

"And you were arrested in France?"

She had to think. It seemed like it had happened in another lifetime. "Yes . . . that's right."

"Where were you taken?"

"I was . . . put on a train and . . ." Anna closed her eyes and folded her hands on the table. Images flitted through the fog: black-clad soldiers, barking dogs, the woman leaning against her as they shuffled through the courtyard at Drancy, the wild look in Koenig's eyes as he squeezed her throat, *If you refuse me, even once . . .* Her heart pounded.

She flinched again when Jan placed his hand on top of hers, jolting her back to the moment. His skin was rough, the way she remembered. She glanced at him, then said to Whitehall, "We were taken to Drancy. I was there for two months. Then they sent everyone to . . ." Her voice trailed off.

Whitehall shifted in his chair, his voice dropped to a whisper. "How did you get to Germany?"

Anna looked down at the table, at Jan's hand on top of hers, and for a fleeting instant it seemed as though none of it really happened. Then it all came back in a rush. She slumped in the chair and covered her face, trying to hold back the tears, but it was no use. They streamed down her face. "His name was Dieter Koenig . . . an SS officer."

She felt Jan touch her shoulder and recoiled, shaking her head. "No, don't . . . I'll never get it out. He was a madman . . . he took me to Germany and . . . Oh God, I . . ." She sat forward and wiped her face, breathing deeply. "Otto killed him. He saved my life and brought me here." She stared at Whitehall. "Where is Otto? What have you done with him?"

Whitehall leaned forward, speaking softly. "Otto is the reason we found you, Anna. He's in our custody, and he's agreed to give us information about the concentration camps. But he first insisted that you be set free."

"Please help him. *Please!* He saved my life."

Jan stood up. "Do you have what you need, Colonel?"

Whitehall nodded. "Yes, for now I've got enough." He pushed his chair back from the table. "I'll get started on the paperwork."

• • •

They walked along the dirt road leading away from the farmhouse and the stockade. For mid-October it was warm and the sun felt good on her face, but she kept her arms wrapped around her chest. They followed the road, winding through recently harvested fields, and came to a narrow bridge over a stream. Anna leaned on the stone wall and stared down at the clear water trickling slowly over moss-covered rocks. So much time . . . so many things. She turned to Jan.

"I've seen Justyn," he said.

She stared at him, covering her mouth with her hands. She hadn't dared to ask. For months she hadn't been able to think about Justyn without breaking down over the guilt of leaving him. Tears welled up in her eyes. "Where?" she whispered.

"In Antwerp. He's safe, living with an older couple, Auguste and Elise, at their home in Merksem. Willy Boeynants helped me find him."

"Willy?" Anna leaned back against the wall, remembering the night in the jail when Koenig spit out the names of everyone they had arrested. He hadn't mentioned Willy Boeynants. She looked at Jan for a long time, struggling to understand. How could he be here?

Jan stepped closer. He reached into his pocket and removed the small glass hand.

Anna stared at it in disbelief. She reached out slowly and touched it, tears streaming down her cheeks. "You found it . . . God in heaven, you found it . . . and that's how . . ." She took a breath. "That's how you knew?"

Jan started to speak, but his voice caught. He stopped and looked away. Then, after a moment, he said, "Not at first. I didn't put it all together until later—when Slomak told me about the visas."

"Slomak? You met Slomak?"

"I was sent back to Poland last year . . . an undercover mission . . ."

Anna held up her hand and turned away. It was too much.

"He told me about your father, Anna."

It was like a sudden cold wind, taking her breath, seizing her heart. She felt his hand on her shoulder but didn't react, couldn't react. She remembered the last night she was with her father, and the phone call the next morning, the phone call that had ended one lifetime and thrust her into another. "They murdered him," she said quietly.

"Anna, Slomak didn't know anything for sure. He could still be alive."

She backed away and started walking, her mind burning with rage and frustration, blurred images of her father sitting next to her in church, of Henryk and Irene, the Leffards, the Marchals. Gone . . . all gone. They hadn't talked about Stefan but she knew, she could sense it. Gone . . . they were all gone.

She walked for several minutes then slowed and finally stopped. Jan had followed her but hung back, giving her space. She remembered: he had been like that. She turned and looked at him, searching his eyes, studying his face. He had always been so patient with her, so gentle.

He approached her, still holding the small glass hand. She reached out and took it from him clutching it tightly, then pressed it against her chest. "It's going to take some time, Jan."

"We have time, Anna. We have time."

Author's Note

IN HIS BOOK, *World Crisis,* Winston Churchill wrote, "Thus when all the trumpets sounded, every class and rank had something to give . . . but none gave more, or gave more readily, than the common man or woman." In these eloquent words lie the essence of the story I have endeavored to tell—a story of countless acts of nobility and courage performed by common people caught up in the catastrophe of humanity's darkest hour. I have tried to honor the bravery of these heroic people with this work of fiction.

Night of Flames is a historical novel set in Europe during World War II. The main characters, Jan and Anna Kopernik, are fictional as are all of the secondary characters. While some of these characters may be the outgrowth of persons I have known or read about (real and fictional), there was no attempt on my part to portray any particular real person. That being said, there are a number of actual historical figures who appear in the story. Among these are the following.

General Roman Abraham, commanding officer of the Wielkopolska Cavalry Brigade: wounded during the defense of Warsaw, he survived imprisonment by the Germans and returned to Warsaw where he lived until his death in 1976. Mario Di Stefano, First Secretary of the Italian Embassy in Poland in 1939: he was compelled by the Germans to leave the country in March, 1940, just a few months after he would have issued travel visas for Anna, Irene and Justyn. Andree de Jongh, founder of the Comet Line: She was arrested by the Germans in 1943 but survived the concentrations camps and, after the war, worked in a leper hospital in Africa. She was eventually made a Belgian Countess. Major General Christoph Graf Stolberg, commander of the German garrison in Antwerp: He was arrested by the White Brigade during the battle for the port and turned over to the British. In his book, *The Battle for Antwerp*, J. L. Moulton writes that Stolberg "was indignant that the British should have arrived before he was ready for them." General Stanislaw Maczek, commander of the Polish First Armored Division: he retired to Edinburgh, Scotland, and after the war he was decorated with the Belgian Order of the Crown, among other honors. Additionally, "Antoine," leader of the White Brigade Resistance forces in the port of Antwerp, was closely modeled after M. Eugene Colson, a merchant navy officer who established the actual Resistance organization in the port and whose code name was "Harry."

All of the locations in the story are real except for the Polish town of "Wiesko," near the Berkowicz farm. All of the battles, to the best of my knowledge, happened at or near the locations indicated and during the times indicated. The military units (armies, divisions, regiments, brigades, etc.) actually existed, except for the Twenty-ninth Uhlans Regiment, which is a composite of several of the actual regiments of the Wielkopolska Cavalry Brigade. I have attempted to describe the major battles of the story—the Battle of the Bzura and the Battle for Antwerp—as accurately as possible though I occasionally employed what the noted historian R.G. Collingwood described as "imaginative construction."

The Resistance organizations in the story—Armia Krajowa (AK) in Poland and White Brigade in Belgium—were real, though there were dozens of others operating in those countries and all over Europe during the war. These organizations were not part of any highly organized strategic scheme. Rather, they were the outgrowth of the will and determination of ordinary people who, against overwhelming odds, chose to fight back against their oppressors. The discovery and subsequent recovery of the V-2 rocket by the AK in Poland was one of the most remarkable achievements by any Resistance organization during the war. Similarly, the activities of the White Brigade during the Battle for Antwerp, including the seizure of the Kruisschans Lock and the re-routing of the British tank squadrons over the Pont van Enschodt, were crucial contributions in the liberation of this vital port.

Finally, Colonel Stanley Whitehall is a fictional character, but the British Special Operations Executive (SOE) was an actual World War II organization, established in 1940 by Winston Churchill to encourage and facilitate espionage and sabotage behind enemy lines. Sometimes referred to as "Churchill's secret army," the SOE was ordered by the British prime minister to "set Europe ablaze."

Chronology of World War II in Europe

September 1, 1939   Germany invades Poland, war in Europe begins

September 17, 1939   Russia invades Poland

September 29, 1939   Germany and Russia divide and occupy Poland

May 10, 1940   Germany invades Belgium, France, Netherlands

June 23, 1940   Hitler tours Paris, Germany occupies Western Europe

August 23, 1940   Germany begins bombing of London

June 22, 1941   Germany attacks Russia, driving Red Army out of Poland

September 3, 1941   First use of gas chambers at Auschwitz

October 2, 1941   German troops advance on Moscow

September 13, 1942   Battle of Stalingrad begins

February 2, 1943   Germans surrender at Stalingrad, begin retreat from Russia

July 9, 1943   Allies land in Sicily, offensive in Italy begins

January 6, 1944   Russians re-enter Poland as Germans retreat

June 6, 1944   Allies land in Normandy

August 25, 1944   Allies liberate Paris

September 4, 1944   Allies liberate Antwerp

January 17, 1945   Red Army enters Warsaw

January 26, 1945   Red Army liberates Auschwitz, Russia occupies Poland

April 30, 1945   Hitler commits suicide

May 8, 1945   V-E Day, war in Europe ends

Acknowledgments

The writing of this story would not have been possible without the help and encouragement of many people. Among those to whom I am eternally grateful are Dr. Slawomir Debski, Polish Historian, Warsaw, whose assistance with research of the war in Poland was invaluable; Dr. Filip Vermeylen, Assistant Professor in Cultural Economics at Erasmus University, Rotterdam, and also my son-in-law (though I'm certain he would have helped anyway), who led me through the history of Belgium and Antwerp during the war, as well as the Flemish and German translations; our dear friends, Antoine and Jet Vermeylen, who lived through the German occupation of Antwerp as children and shared their memories, including the still visible bullet holes in the wall at the end of their street; my daughter, Kerri Vermeylen, one of my toughest critics, who read every word of every draft and was instrumental in helping shape the vital character, Anna; my son, Kevin, and daughter-in-law, Mary, who were the first to read the initial draft and kept a straight face when they told me how much they liked it; Judy Bridges and the Tuesday Writer's Roundtable at Redbird Studio in Milwaukee, who helped this barely literate engineer write a story people might actually read; Jackie Swift at McBooks Press who took a chance on me and my story and, with great humor and wisdom, helped bring it to life; and finally, to my biggest fan and best friend for thirty-nine years, my wife, Janie, who would call me out of my cave each evening and listen patiently to every word.

green press
INITIATIVE

McBooks Press is committed to preserving ancient forests and natural resources. We elected to print this title on 30% post consumer recycled paper, processed chlorine free. As a result, for this printing, we have saved:

8 Trees (40' tall and 6-8" diameter)
3,849 Gallons of Wastewater
3 Million BTU's of Total Energy
234 Pounds of Solid Waste
799 Pounds of Greenhouse Gases

McBooks Press made this paper choice because our printer, Thomson-Shore, Inc., is a member of Green Press Initiative, a nonprofit program dedicated to supporting authors, publishers, and suppliers in their efforts to reduce their use of fiber obtained from endangered forests.

For more information, visit www.greenpressinitiative.org

Environmental impact estimates were made using the Environmental Defense Paper Calculator. For more information visit: www.papercalculator.org.